Victoria's Hope

Victoria's *Hope*

A Novel

Jessica Hallmark

Starfish Press
LLC

Book Design by Jessica Hallmark
www.jessicahallmark.com

Published by Starfish Press, LLC
59 Northrup Drive Franklin, NC 28734
www.starfish-press.com

Library of Congress Control Number: 2021931101

ISBN: 978-1-953129-00-0(Paperback)
ISBN: 978-1-953129-01-7(Kindle)
ISBN: 978-1-953129-02-4(EPUB)

To Janny Grein

The Lord is my light and my salvation; whom shall I fear? The Lord is
the strength of my life; of whom shall I be afraid?

– Psalm 27:1

Prologue

May 10, 1839
London, England

"I'm telling you, that Victoria Bolton is a prude."

"Victoria? Why, she's one of the biggest flirts in London."

"Yes, she flirts and plays with the best of them, but when the time comes, she doesn't pay up. This is her *third* season, yet not once has she allowed any of her escorts to take her for a turn in the gardens."

A loud gasp echoed throughout the lady's powder room. Victoria closed her eyes and cringed. The two gossips had no way of knowing that she sat on the other side of the room hidden from sight by a large column and a row of potted plants.

"You don't say." The woman made a disapproving clucking sound. "My, my. If this keeps up, she'll be ostracized by the *ton*."

"Of course she will."

Carefully pulling back a large waxy leaf, Victoria peeked out of her hiding spot. Miriam Williams fixed her hair in front of the floor length mirror as she spoke with Lady Roberta Perkins, a Patroness of Almack's and one of the biggest gossips among the *ton*.

Her heart sank. Miriam's coming out had been at the same Almack's ball as Victoria's. Consequently, she viewed Victoria as her chief rival and did everything in her power to disgrace her. A smug smile lifted Miriam's lips as she continued, "Eugene Lamond told me, and he ought to know. He escorted her to the last two balls."

"You don't say." Roberta clucked disapprovingly once again.

"Well," Miriam gave one final pat to her hair and started for the door. "I must return to the ball and not neglect Eugene."

"No, dear. You mustn't do that." Roberta followed Miriam, her nose positively quivering at the chance to spread the latest gossip. "I just don't know how Victoria expects to catch a husband with a reputation like that. Why, no decent man would…"

The door closing cut off the rest of their conversation.

Victoria let go of the leaf. It sprang back into place as she wilted back against the chair. By the end of the night, everyone in the *ton* would be talking. Roberta would see to that. It might even reach her father's ears.

She stiffened as a cold hard ball congealed in her stomach. Rolfe would surely thrash her for the breach in tradition. Remaining publicly pure yet still sneaking off for clandestine meetings with her escorts were expected. Both being caught or failing to follow convention's delicate balancing act would cause her to be ostracized. Her mouth tightened at the double-standard kept by the *le bon ton* despite the new Queen Victoria's frowning upon it.

A cascade of images filled her mind, causing her to shake. Her frail mother cowering from Rolfe's anger. The familiar sting of his hand when he thought she had overstepped her place. The stories her mother told of the arduous, but God-given, duties a woman had to endure to please her husband.

Icy needles prickled her skin.

Yes, she flirted outrageously in an effort to pacify Rolfe. But if her father thought anything had marred her chances of marriage, he would take measures to rectify the situation himself.

Victoria sat back up and straightened her shoulders. She would have to do something about it herself. This very night. While she still had control over the situation.

A small smile curved her lips. At least she had the appropriate escort. Paxton Burke, the most sought after bachelor in the *ton,* awaited her return to the ball. All of the young debutantes twittered over his ardent caresses. She might even find that kissing really wasn't such an arduous task after all. If anyone could make it bearable, Paxton could. Besides, her father hosted this party. Being in her own home would surely give her an advantage if the situation became untenable.

Rising from the chair, Victoria walked over to the mirror and checked her reflection. She absently straightened the bodice of her off-the shoulder, rose-colored ball gown. Why, she might even enjoy kissing Paxton. A few soft caresses that left a woman feeling special and cherished wouldn't be so bad. Every other girl seemed to find it pleasant.

"And I will, too," she promised her reflection in the mirror.

Lifting her chin, she swept out of the powder room. Standing not more than ten feet away, Paxton's blond hair and aristocratic features easily made him the most handsome man in the room. Her heart thudded as he caught sight of her. A smile lit his face, and he immediately moved to her side.

Lifting her hand to his lips, his eyes wantonly roved her figure. "Victoria, you are even more beautiful than you were ten minutes ago." He placed a lingering kiss on the back of her gloved hand before pulling it through his arm possessively. "Promise me that you will not leave my side again. I have found that a separation of even a few minutes is unbearable."

"Why, sir," Victoria giggled as she opened and shut her fan, indicating her desire to be kissed. "I must dance with others as well."

"Yes, to avoid the gossip caused by malicious tongues. Very well, beautiful lady, I will surrender your company, but just long enough to still the wagging tongues. Not a second more."

She giggled again. "You flatter me, sir."

"Nay, dear heart. I speak only the truth."

He swept her onto the dance floor. A most accomplished dancer, he expertly guided her through the intricate steps of the Quadrille, and she caught the jealous looks of more than one woman in the room. His broad shoulders and slender, tapered figure were the envy of the other men in the *ton*. Across the room, her father danced with his escort, the lovely Julia Hastings. Only a scant year older than Victoria's own seventeen, yet from Rolfe's enamored expression she may soon become the next Lady Bolton. At least he was thoroughly occupied for the moment which gave her more time.

She and Paxton danced three sets before he reluctantly relinquished her to Peter Clarkson, another would-be suitor. Ungainly and awkward as he danced, her toes throbbed from being stepped on within two minutes. Paxton rescued her after the set ended. The band struck up the new waltz, and she drifted along with his almost hypnotic movements. He pulled her closer than what some might deem acceptable, but she allowed it. His blue eyes burned hotly with desire as they bored into hers. Transfixed, she stared at that flame, unable to look away.

The dance ended, and Paxton led her off the floor. "It's such a lovely night, Victoria, let's take a turn in the garden."

Victoria's knees weakened, and she nearly stumbled. She hadn't expected the time to come so soon. Usually couples waited until later to slip away when there was less chance of being missed. Looking up into his shamelessly admiring eyes, she reached down deep inside for a few tattered remnants of courage. "Just let me get my wrap…"

Paxton stilled her by pulling her arm through his and walking towards the doors leading to the patio. "It is a most warm night. And I assure you, dear lady, that I will *not* allow you to become chilled." She trembled at the licentiousness blazing in his eyes as he gave her curvaceous form a leisurely once over from the top of her head to the toes of her dancing slippers. He pulled her a little closer as they stepped out onto the patio, and his eyes once again returned to hers. "Nay, Victoria. I definitely will *not* allow you to become chilled."

Keeping silent, she walked with him down the steps of the patio and into the rose garden. Only a few couples mingled there, but he steered clear of them all choosing instead a secluded, off-beaten path. He drew her deeper into the garden away from the light and the presence of others. Now that the time had come, her heart pounded, and her hands sweated inside her white gloves. The full skirt of her ball gown rustled, and the scent of early-blooming roses perfumed the evening air. Unusual this time of year, especially after an unexpected snowstorm at the beginning of the month, but a recent warming in the weather made it feel like spring.

Taking a deep breath, she tried to steady her nerves. Surely they had gone far enough not to be detected. But what did she know about clandestine meetings? Paxton continued down the deserted path so she trustingly followed him.

Soon, the sound of voices and the swelling of music faded into the distance. The path became even more dark and ominous. Still, Paxton maneuvered her on with even greater speed. Victoria frowned. They had gone far enough. Why, they were almost to the back gate! Yet, to say as much would offend him. What would be the best way to hint…

Without warning, he yanked her into the shadows of a large rose bush. She slammed up against his chest with a small "oomph". His strong arm slid around her small waist, pinning her against him. With his other hand, he reached up and lightly ran a smooth finger across her full bottom lip. "Ah, Victoria. How I have waited for this moment."

Despite the dim light, hunger visibly glittered in his eyes. Her stomach heaved at the possessive way he held her so closely against him, but perhaps it would become better. Still, she had to act the part so she forced a breathless smile. "As have I."

His arm tightened around her until she could scarcely breathe. Her body pressed fully against him so that not even a piece of parchment could be slid between them. She had never before been so close to a man. Heat flamed in her cheeks, and her insides writhed in agony at the way her soft body molded against his.

Paxton suddenly brought his mouth down on hers, swift and hard. So swift that she almost jumped though she had expected to be kissed. Pain exploded as her mouth smashed into her gums. Acid burned the back of her throat as his cruel, punishing lips hungrily explored her tender ones. His hand moved from her cheek to the nape of her neck as he pulled her even harder up against him.

A burning ache spread deep in her chest as her rib cage threatened to cave in from the ruthless pressure. If only she didn't have to do this! But if she refused to see this through, Rolfe would no doubt hire someone far worse to perform the exact same deed. No, it was better that she remain in control.

Finally raising his head, Paxton gave her a sardonic smile. "So, fair lady. Is mine the first kiss to touch your maiden lips?"

Run! her mind screamed. Instead, she called on all her years of practice and looked up at him coyly through her lashes. "Why, sir, surely you know a lady doesn't kiss and tell!"

He laughed before brutally claiming her once more. Long, interminable minutes passed as she withstood the assault. His hard mouth fell against hers again and again. Merciless. Bruising. The hot, demanding kisses intensified. Blood trickled onto her tongue as his teeth cut into her skin. The metallic taste made her gag, but she suppressed it.

So this is what it felt like to be kissed.

Tears pricked her eyes, but she forcibly held them back. Crying would do no good. Besides, she should have known that anything involving a man would repulse not please. It had been foolish of her to hope for anything different. If she could endure but a few minutes more, propriety would be an excuse to leave. The deed would be done, and she would have saved herself from an even worse fate.

His sweaty hand slid down her neck and across her bare shoulder. Another surge of acid burned her throat. She couldn't stand another moment! Lightly she struggled against his hold as a lady would do if she enjoyed herself but knew that she must leave. Several long moments passed before Paxton allowed her to break the painful kiss though he didn't let her go. His mouth hovered a mere fraction of an inch above hers. Hot, heavy air fanned across her cheeks as he panted slightly. The smell of the alcohol he had consumed burned her nose. "We really should return to the party before we are missed," she murmured.

"I'm in no hurry." He began trailing his hot, moist kisses across her face and down her neck, following the path his hand had taken.

She shuddered but allowed it for several seconds before struggling again, a bit harder than before, as a lady would do for propriety's sake. This time, he didn't stop but increased his intensity as he explored her neck and shoulders. Frantic, she pushed against his chest as hard as she could, but his arms were unbreakable steel bands imprisoning her in the crushing embrace.

Ice flooded her veins as her heart thundered in her chest. She could scream, but they were far enough into the gardens that it wouldn't be heard above the noise of the band. Her breath stalled. He had planned this! He had planned to get her alone and completely at his mercy so he could take liberties with her far beyond a few stolen kisses. She must get him in hand quickly before it went too far. But what could she do? How could she stop him? Nothing lay within her reach except the flowering bushes and hitting him in the head with a rose wouldn't have much effect.

God, help me!

A hysterical laugh bubbled in her throat, but she pressed her lips together, stifling it. Strange that a prayer rose unbidden now since she only ever prayed when Rector Pitt led the congregation on Sunday mornings. As if illusions of Divine help would do any good. No, she could rely only upon herself, and she only had one weapon at her disposal. Paxton's impatience had caused him to leave the dance early in the evening before the free-flowing liquor clouded everyone's minds, and the gossipmongers were sure to notice their absence. If they were gone much longer, both of their reputations would be in shreds.

Heart pounding, she opted for a playful tone this time. "As pleasurable as this is, we cannot forget that you are a gentleman and I am a lady. If we are gone overly long, we might well start the scandal of the century."

"Then let's start it," he murmured against the sensitive spot under her earlobe. His hand rubbed the exposed skin on her back and shoulders. Reaching the buttons on the back of her dress, his fingers expertly maneuvered the tiny pearls.

The first one slipped from its hole.

Victoria laughed, a slightly brittle sound as her stomach roiled and her knees quaked. He moved to the next button. She sucked in a breath as that one, too, slipped free. The heady, sweet smell of the roses filled her nostrils, adding to her nausea. Bile rose in her throat. If she did not get out of his arms soon, she would be physically ill! What could she say to convince him to rejoin the ball?

"As a gentleman, I know you would do nothing to ruin a lady's reputation…or your own." Her voice shook slightly at the blatant lie. He obviously cared nothing for her reputation, but surely he cared about his own!

Hand pausing with the third button only half undone, Paxton finally raised his head and loosened his hold on her slightly. She pulled back the scant inch he allowed. "We really must return."

Did that sound regretful enough to convince him?

"I suppose we must. On one condition."

Victoria arched an eyebrow at him. "Condition?" she asked in as flirtatious a tone as she could muster.

"Yes," he flashed her a smile that would have set her heart to racing ten minutes ago. Now it only caused her stomach to churn. "The night is still young. We must slip away again when we won't be missed, and…" his voice lowered suggestively as his hand trailed down her bare arm. "Take up where we left off."

She could barely hold his calculating gaze as she forced a giggle. Blood surged in her ears nearly drowning out the sound. He obviously fully intended to have her this night, either now or later, whether she desired it or not. She had only one recourse. Pretend she had enjoyed the embrace and would come back for more.

"Of course," she assured him with a dreamy smile. His gaze roved over her face though he didn't look entirely convinced. Victoria forced herself to reach up and run her finger tantalizingly around his mouth.

His eyes darkened in response.

"The minutes will stretch unbearably long until I can be in your arms again. My only consolation is that my patience will spare you from falling into disgrace with the *ton*."

Paxton finally smiled at her. He brought his hand back up to touch her face. "My sweet, I can hardly bear the wait, but you are right. We must return now before they miss us."

Relief turned her legs to jelly as she moved to step away from him.

A gasp escaped as he roughly pulled her back into his embrace and landed another punishing kiss on her raw lips. Long, tortuous minutes ticked by, but she held still. Something deep inside warned that if she struggled again she would not leave the garden with her innocence intact.

He eventually let up the painful pressure and let her go. Slipping his arm around her waist, he pulled her possessively against his side as he led her back up the pathway. His other hand reached up to stroke her neck as he bent and playfully nibbled on her ear. Her skin crawled as if a million ants had taken up residence, but she forced herself to giggle as though she enjoyed his attentions. Her buttons remained undone, but she would never tempt Paxton by mentioning it. Thankfully, the pearls were so close together that no one should notice the tiny gap until she had a chance to return to the powder room and do them up herself.

The walk back stretched interminably as Paxton continued to toy with her. Her shaking legs threatened to give out with each step. What if he changed his mind and pulled her back into the shadows for more? What could she do? How could she bear another moment of his touch? But she must. Each step brought her closer and closer to safety.

Finally, they reached the last turn in the path before the house came into view. Paxton stopped. Her pulse quickened. She could taste the safety on her tongue, sweet and heavy, like honey. She was so close! Maybe she should try to run…

Paxton's arm slid from around her waist, allowing her to step away slightly. Calmly, he pulled her arm through his and dropped a quick kiss onto her mouth. "Until later, dear heart," he whispered before walking her around the corner and back into the golden light spilling from the patio.

A few other couples stood nearby enjoying the night air. Paxton greeted them as they started up the five steps. Knees knocking, Victoria could only manage to nod and smile in reply. Her gaze remained fixed on the doors leading into the ballroom. Safety lay tantalizingly close.

Paxton stopped again. Jackson Bradshaw approached with her sister, Claudia, hanging on his arm. Her pale blue eyes impaled Victoria like ice picks before she smiled brilliantly at Paxton. "What a coincidence!"

"A delightful one." Paxton eyed her slender figure a moment before smirking at Jackson. "Going out to enjoy the…roses?"

"The Bolton gardens are supposed to be quite a sight."

"Well, take it from me. Tonight they live up to their famed sweetness."

Jackson and Paxton both chuckled as they looked at her and smirked knowingly. Claudia tittered behind her fan though her eyes remained cold as she glared at her. Victoria kept a pleasant smile on her face by sheer force of will.

After a few more pleasantries, Jackson and Claudia continued down the steps. Paxton led her back into the ballroom. Victoria sagged slightly at finally reaching the sanctuary of her home. Short of knocking her unconscious and bodily carrying her outside, Paxton could not force his attentions upon her again.

Rolfe and Julia stood next to the punch bowl with none other than Roberta Perkins. Anger darkened Rolfe's face as he caught sight of her. Eyes narrowed, he observed her and Paxton closely. He took in her puffy, swollen lips a moment before the anger slowly melted to be replaced by a satisfied smile. He spoke to Roberta who looked crest-fallen at having lost such a juicy piece of gossip. Rolfe winked at Victoria conspiratorially and turned away.

Victoria nearly fainted from the relief.

The rumors had been effectively squashed. All of the *ton* could tell just by looking at her that she had been well and thoroughly kissed by Paxton. She would not have to endure such agony again.

She managed to slip away a few minutes later to fix her buttons and then spent the rest of the evening playfully avoiding Paxton's increasingly insistent advances and trying not to think about what had transpired in the garden. Thankfully, Rolfe had hosted this particular party. If she had to ride inside a dark carriage with Paxton in order to return home, nothing could save her virtue.

By the time Paxton left the ball late in the evening, cold fury blazed in his blue eyes at the foiling of his plans.

Alone in her room that night once Betsy, her lady's maid, had helped her into bed, Victoria could not stop her mind from replaying the horrific scene in the garden over and over. She pulled her legs up and hugged them tightly to her aching chest as shudders racked her. Her bruised body and swollen lips throbbed painfully with every beat of her heart. She had scrubbed and scrubbed where Paxton had touched her, but she couldn't remove the feel of his mouth and hands so harsh and demanding on her soft skin.

Her trembling worsened until the whole bed shook with the force of it. Tears rolled down her cheeks. If only her mother were here to hold her close as she sobbed. It had been five years since her death, but at that moment she longed to feel her comforting touch more than she wanted her next breath.

How stupid she had been to even think that a kiss might be something pleasant instead of something to be endured! Her mother had warned her repeatedly about not falling for the romantic nonsense of moonlight and flowers. And Paxton…

Victoria could barely even think his name. From the way the other women spoke about him, his kisses were the best ones she would ever receive. His rough treatment, however, had not left her feeling caressed or cherished but manhandled and abused. He had taken what he had wanted from her and had given her nothing but disgust and revulsion in return.

Her first kiss had been a nightmare.

Unfortunately, it would not be her last.

Chapter 1

The next morning her door unceremoniously flew open. Fifteen-year-old Claudia walked in as regally and haughtily as a queen, eight-year-old Regina bouncing in behind her. Victoria barely resisted the urge to groan and pull the covers over her head. The last people in the world she wanted to deal with right now were her sisters.

Regina jumped onto the bed, her brown eyes sparkling. "Did you have fun with Paxton last night? You must have been the envy of all the debutantes being on the arm of a man so handsome."

Guilt pricked Victoria as she looked into her guileless face. She really did love her sister. Regina just had so many romantic notions not yet having learned the truth about the harsh realities of life. "It was fine," she finally answered as she carefully stood up and pulled on her robe. The throbbing pain had grown worse overnight. Most of the long, sleepless hours had been spent in the washroom trying to scrub Paxton's embrace off. Hard to do when faint mottled bruises colored her body.

Claudia seated herself at Victoria's dressing table and studied her reflection in the mirror. She patted her riot of blond curls. "I don't know why Paxton asked you to the ball instead of me," she pouted. She had been pouting ever since the invitation had arrived days earlier. "I am ever so much more beautiful."

She didn't comment. Claudia looked like an angel with her light blond hair, light blue eyes, and perfect, delicate features. But she was a late bloomer, her body barely showing her change from child to woman despite being nearly sixteen and well into her first season. Her own brown hair, dark blue eyes, slightly round face, and full lips were considered pretty enough but certainly not beautiful. Being amply endowed while still maintaining an hourglass figure had always been her main physical attribute.

With quick, jerky movements, she cinched the robe tight around her small waist. Why hadn't she been born fat and ugly? Maybe then she would be allowed to live her life as a spinster without being dominated and abused by a man.

She sighed. No, that wasn't true. Rolfe was not only the Marquess of Hartshorn, but one of the richest men in their elite social class. He would negotiate profitable marriages for each of his daughters, but, as the eldest, she stood in line to inherit. That alone would cause most men to desire to wed her even if she were fat and ugly.

Stomping over to the washbasin, she quickly cleaned her face. Men. She was so tired of dealing with them. They were all the same, arrogant and demanding. They expected complete obedience and if crossed grew angry and meted out harsh punishment. How many times had she been told that a woman should be meek and quiet, speaking only when spoken to, but never to voice an opinion? How many times had Rolfe beaten her for stepping out of a woman's place? A woman was only there to decorate a man's arm, fill his coffers with a large dowry, and bear him children.

She shuddered as memories of Paxton's embrace once again filled her mind. Grabbing the washcloth, she viciously scrubbed the places where he had touched her, but the disgusting feel of his hands and lips remained. Throwing the towel down with a huff, she turned around.

Regina stared at her with wide brown eyes. "What's the matter?"

"Bet Paxton didn't kiss her."

She ignored Claudia's smug comment and focused on Regina. "Nothing. I'm just overtired from last night."

"Yes. Being the belle of a ball would be tiring, but oh, how fun!" She smiled dreamily.

Victoria didn't say anything as she rang for Betsy.

Regina would learn the truth soon enough.

Two weeks, and many baths later, Victoria still hadn't washed the feel of Paxton's embrace off her skin. Would she ever rid herself of the vile sensation and feel normal again? At least the lingering bruises and soreness had finally disappeared. During that time, she had been hard pressed to keep him at bay. He had issued countless invitations, and she was quickly running out of excuses not to accept. She held the latest one in her hand; an invitation `

Picking up a quill, she started to pen him a note, regretfully declining his kind offer. A knock at the door brought her head up. "Yes?"

Betsy walked in and curtsied. "Miss Victoria, Lord Bolton wishes to see you in his study."

The words sent the dull throbbing into a full blown headache. Rolfe never sent for any of his daughters unless they were in trouble. "I'll be down in a minute. I have to finish composing a letter."

"Lord Bolton said you were to come immediately, Miss."

To disobey those summons would only invite trouble. He had beaten her severely the last time she had dallied when he said immediately. It had taken over a week for the puffiness and discoloration on her face to fade enough for powder to hide it. Sighing, she set the quill pen down. "Very well."

Her breathing quickened as she followed the young woman down the elaborate staircase. Why had Rolfe sent for her? She wracked her brain for some infraction she had committed but came up empty.

Unless he had discovered her continually declining Paxton's invitations…

Betsy knocked on the open study door then stood aside. Taking a deep breath and stiffening her spine, Victoria walked in. Rolfe, still an impressive looking man at fifty-five, sat behind his desk holding a cigar. The acrid smoke burned her nose. "You sent for me, sir?"

"Yes," he looked up and actually smiled at her as he waved her towards a chair across from him. "I have some important news."

The door closed behind Betsy as she sank down onto the leather cushion and faced her father. She could never remember seeing him cordial before. Her mouth went dry. At least his anger was familiar. And predictable. How should she respond to his pleasantness in a way that wouldn't offend him?

Rolfe leaned back in his chair and puffed on his cigar. Bluish smoke swirled around him while he observed her through narrowed eyes. She resisted the urge to squirm. Instead, she sat straight and still waiting for him to speak.

"I have great news, in fact." Pulling his cigar from his mouth, he tapped it against the silver ashtray with a soft *chink, chink, chink.* "I have just received word confirming your engagement."

Engagement?

Victoria went lightheaded as all of the air suddenly left her lungs. Nausea welled within her. Clenching her teeth, she fought it back lest she became sick right there on Rolfe's expensive, oriental rug. "M…My engagement?" she finally asked faintly.

"Yes, and what a profitable engagement it is! Your fiancé is the sole heir to one of the largest shipping companies in Europe. In fact, I have already entered into an agreement with his father for a lucrative three month contract which will go into effect on the day of your marriage. We'll make a fortune capturing and selling slaves abroad." His smug expression said she should be extremely proud of his latest accomplishment.

Quickly reviewing the people she knew, she couldn't recall anyone being heir to a shipping line. "Who is he?"

"Who?"

Victoria forced her voice to remain calm. "My fiancé."

"Oh, him. His name's Gregory Thornton."

"But…I don't know any Gregory Thornton!"

It would be bad enough marrying someone she knew, but a complete stranger? She started shaking and clasped her hands tightly together in her lap, hoping her father wouldn't notice.

"So?" He turned back to the ledgers on his desk in a dismissive gesture. "I imagine you'll get to know him quite well once you are wed."

Her nails bit into her palms as she held back a scream. How could he be so apathetic? After all, they were talking about the rest of her life!

Calm down. Deep breaths. Growing hysterical would serve no purpose except to see her punished. She had to remain calm and find out all she could. In control once again, she spoke. "Would you tell me more about him, please?"

Rolfe looked up at her, clearly annoyed. "Who?"

"Gregory Thornton," she managed to say lightly enough through her gritted teeth.

"There's not much I can tell you. I've never met him."

"Never met him?"

"No, he hasn't accompanied his parents to London in several years, not since he completely disgraced the Thornton name. Despite that, John's very anxious to see him wed."

John Thornton. He must be talking about the Earl of Holland. Born the second son of the reclusive Duke of Lincolnshire, he had left home as a young gentleman of a small inheritance and established the prosperous Thornton Shipping Line in 1812, marrying the youngest daughter of Baron Whiteworth in 1813. His older brother, Reginald Thornton, the previous Earl of Holland, had remained childless throughout his thirty-year marriage, until his wife's death in 1835. Consequently, John inherited the title Earl of Holland, and stood to inherit the Duchy of Lincolnshire, upon Reginald's death, two years previous. But why had she never before heard that he had a son? Especially one of marrying age in disgrace with the *ton*?

"John was even willing to buy you as a bride since that was the only way he could find a woman who would marry Gregory," Rolfe continued. "Everyone knows he's such an odd duck."

Black dots danced in front of her eyes. This nightmare kept going from bad to worse. She licked her dry lips, but her voice still came out raspy. "O…odd?"

"Yes. When he did come to London, he was always babbling about plants or some such nonsense."

"Plants," she repeated in a monotone.

Plants? What did *plants* have to do with anything?

"Yes. Are you alright, Victoria? You've been echoing me like a parrot, and it's quite annoying."

"I'm sorry." She tried to give him a pleased smile. "It just came as such a shock. I knew you were looking for a suitable husband, but I hadn't expected the arrangements to be finished quite so soon." She took a deep breath. "Do you know anything else about him?"

"No, just that he's twenty-three. We'll have to hurry, though, to have your trousseau ready in time for the wedding."

In time?

"When…when shall it be?"

"June eleventh."

"But…that's less than three weeks away!"

"Which is why we need to hurry. The Thornton's will arrive in London the week before. The official engagement party will be held then."

Victoria's mind raced, trying to find a way out. "Why all this rush, Father? Surely a longer engagement period would be more prudent, to avoid gossip and…"

Rolfe threw down his pen in exasperation. "You could drive a man insane with your senseless questions! Haven't you learned by now to just obey me?"

"I…I'm sorry." Her trembling increased. "I didn't mean to q…question your authority. I just w…wondered…"

"Not that it's any of your business," he interrupted her stuttering with a disgusted huff, "but it's the contract. John refuses to launch our joint venture until you are wed therefore you must be married as soon as possible." He shook his head as if he were explaining simple things to a five-year-old. She remained quiet. The angry glint in his eyes warned that she had pushed him as far as she dared. "I have already sent for my sister, Armelda. She will arrange everything for the wedding. Now, go! I want you to be ready when she arrives."

Demurely, Victoria left the study, but as soon as the door closed behind her, she took off running and didn't stop until she had reached her room and locked herself inside. Flinging herself onto the bed, she didn't even try to stem the sobs that welled up. How could her father have so little regard for her? Marrying her off to a man even *he* had never met, who was in disgrace and known to be odd, just for a lucrative business contract?

And the rushed wedding! She would be a ruined woman among the *ton*. The gossips would tear her reputation to shreds suggesting that she *had* to be married in a hurry. Even if children weren't immediately forthcoming, they would still look down their long noses in judgment on her.

She froze.

Children.

Her husband would expect her to bear his children.

She put a shaky hand over her mouth as her stomach suddenly heaved. Jumping up, she barely made it to the basin before ridding herself of her breakfast.

Chapter 2

Gregory Thornton slipped out of the house as his parents issued last minute commands to the servants. No way could he leave today without spending some time in his garden, not with the thousands of butterflies cavorting in his stomach. As he walked down the meandering paths, peace seeped into him. It was why he always had his prayer times here. God felt close enough to touch when he was outside in the beauty He had created.

Several chrysanthemums lay uprooted on the ground, their dirt-clogged roots swaying in the gentle breeze. Probably from the rain last night, poor things. Kneeling down, he carefully planted them back into the soggy soil. It had been unusually wet this year even for England. He finished patting the earth down around the flowers but stayed on his knees. After all, he had come to pray.

Until two weeks ago when his father had announced his betrothal, the idea of marrying had never entered his mind. His brief foray into London society had been a painful and embarrassing episode of his youth. Five years had passed since his parents required that he accompany them for the Season, but he vividly remembered every agonizing moment.

His first inclination at the engagement announcement had been to refuse to marry the girl despite any repercussions John might give. However, after he prayed about the matter, God had impressed upon him to honor his parents and go through with the marriage. He had been at peace about the decision, but as the time grew nearer, that peace became more and more threatened by the nervousness bent on attacking him. Especially since he knew nothing about his future bride except her name.

Victoria Bolton.

"Jesus," Gregory looked up at the blue sky above him. Gray clouds on the horizon promised more rain before the sun went down. "I need Your help badly. Tonight, I am to meet my future wife for the first time."

At their engagement party no less! His parents had planned to arrive in London a few days earlier for the introductions, but his mother had been terribly ill. Harriet didn't seem much improved today, but she insisted that they couldn't miss his engagement party for any reason. As things stood, they barely had time to make it. Even changing horses twice, they had at least a seven hour trip to London. Then they would have to dress for the occasion and be at the Bolton home by five.

It was already eight in the morning.

The coming night loomed before him. The first meeting with his future wife just moments before being thrust into a roomful of hostile strangers. His shy nature writhed in his gut just thinking about it.

But Victoria was probably just as nervous as he. Especially if she carried a child as the rumors said. John insisted the quick marriage was due solely to a business deal, but Gregory could think of no man heartless enough to rush his daughter into marriage to a complete stranger just for business. Either way, he had no wish to embarrass her. He had already resolved to love his wife, and if she was carrying a child, to love the babe as well.

"Help me, Father. Help me to love my wife as You have commanded. To be sensitive to her needs and to place them above my own. To be a wise spiritual leader. To know how to reach out to her with friendship and compassion as we work to build a marriage glorifying to You…" He continued to pray for several minutes, pouring out his heart, until he heard his father calling him.

"Gregory! Gregory, we have to leave. Now!"

"Coming!" He pushed himself to his feet and hurried through the house to the front door. The time must have gotten away from him.

He finally reached the waiting carriage. Harriet took one look at him and sighed. "Just look at you."

Gregory glanced down and cringed. Why hadn't he thought about the mud before kneeling in it? He could have brought a blanket from the toolshed to protect his clothes.

"You are a mess! Dirt all over your hands and trousers. You would think that just *once* you could manage to stay out of the garden and stay clean. Well, we have no time to fix it now. You have to change in London, anyway, and we'll just have to make sure that no one sees you until then. The embarrassment would be simply intolerable."

His heart gave a slight pang. "Yes, ma'am."

James discreetly pulled a clean towel out of his pocket. Gregory accepted it from his valet with a grateful smile. Having experienced the same situation countless times, the faithful servant always stayed prepared. He only wished they had the room to bring James to London with them to help make the coming days more bearable. "Thank you."

James gave him a small smile and a nod before stepping back.

Climbing into the carriage after his parents, Gregory obligingly took the rear-facing seat, allowing them the more comfortable forward-facing seat. Their butler, Martin, closed the door, and they took off with a small lurch. Settling back more comfortably, he wiped off his hands and trousers as best he could. His fingers fumbled with the towel almost dropping it as the heavy, tense atmosphere pressed down around him. The disapproval radiating from his parents was so strong he could almost smell it. They had never understood him or his fascination with botany, considering him weak and mindless to spend so much time with his plants.

The seven-hour ride passed in spurts of polite, stilted conversation followed by long bouts of heavy silence. But it had always been thus between them. When they reached the outskirts of London, Gregory's stomach clenched up even tighter. The city had grown in the five years he had been away. There were so many buildings. The press and crush of the crowd outside the carriage… The confusion of hundreds of voices speaking at once… The miasma of thick dark smog hanging like a shroud over the land…

Nausea churned. How could anyone stand the chaos of so much humanity pressed into such a small space? How could they live without fresh air, green grass and trees?

It only became marginally better when they reached the exclusive Mayfair district. Though the throngs fell behind them and the streets grew quieter the buildings continued to close in on him.

They finally reached their townhouse. Harriet sailed out of the carriage, a woman clearly on a mission. "Come John, Gregory. We have less than an hour to be ready. It's a good thing I sent our clothes on ahead yesterday so the servants could have them cleaned and pressed…" Her voice faded as she entered the house with John close behind. Gregory followed more slowly, stretching out the last few seconds before the whirlwind of activity descended. He liked peace and quiet and order.

The coming days promised to be anything but.

Once inside the house, an older valet with a stern frown whisked him away to his room where a steaming bath awaited, and his life was no longer his own. The valet had him washed, dried, dressed, and styled in an amazingly short amount of time. As he fashioned a tall, stiff trone d'Amour tie, the material tightened like a vise around Gregory's throat. Who came up with these uncomfortable fashions anyway? "Can't we just do a simple Napoleon?"

"No, sir. Lady Thornton gave specific instructions about your attire."

Gregory sighed but said no more. He always disappointed his mother. The least he could do was wear some fancy French cravat for her if she so desired. Even if it did strangle him.

The first one ready, he had ample time to pace the hallway as thousands more butterflies attacked his stomach. He ran a hand through his hair as panic threatened to overwhelm him. What would Victoria be like? Would she be haughty and austere? Or demure and bashful? Would she, like most of the *ton,* ridicule him for his botanical interests?

By the time John and Harriet appeared, Gregory's stomach had tied itself into a hopeless knot. "Oh, Gregory, must you always insist on looking like a wild man?" Harriet pulled a comb from her handbag and fixed his hair before straightening his tie. He suddenly felt five years old again being sent off to his first birthday party at the Stuart-Hornsworth Manor.

It wasn't a comforting feeling for that party had been a complete disaster. The children had cruelly teased him about his thick spectacles and for his fascination with their flower garden.

It seemed every time he ventured out into society it proved to be a mistake.

Harriet gave his cravat one final pat before standing back and giving him a critical once over. "Must you wear those horrid spectacles? You are homely enough already, but those spectacles make you positively repugnant."

He silently sighed at the familiar mantra. "Perhaps, Mother, but I have to wear them to see clearly."

"Victoria might prefer you to be blind rather than repugnant," Harriet muttered before heading down the hall. "Hurry up. We are already fashionably late. If we delay any longer, it would appear inexcusably rude."

Frowning, Gregory followed his parents. Victoria probably *would* prefer that he didn't wear his eyeglasses, but anything beyond a foot away became a hopeless blur without them. He had to rely on coloring to distinguish people instead of facial features. In the safety of his home, among the friends and neighbors he had known his whole life, he always took off his eyeglasses when Harriet held a party. Surely he could do it now to appease both his mother and his fiancée.

Climbing into the carriage, his stomach tightened even more. The short ride to the Bolton home seemed to pass in the blink of an eye. He ran his hand through his hair trying to think with a brain that had suddenly gone completely blank. Should he remove his eyeglasses for the engagement party?

Harriet leaned forward and slapped his arm. "Gregory, stop that!"

"Sorry," he muttered. He clenched his hands in his lap to keep them from straying to his hair again. The carriage jerked to a stop. His breath stopped as well as he stared out at the imposing Baroque styled mansion. The racing of his heart seemed unnaturally loud in the silence as time hung suspended.

Searing pain in his lungs caused him to release the breath he had been unconsciously holding and gasp in another one. He couldn't do it. Not for his mother nor for his bride-to-be. Going into a strange house to meet strange people, one of whom would be his wife in less than a week, was bad enough.

But doing it nearly blind would be impossible.

Victoria stood at the base of the stairs in the entryway, her toe tapping quickly against the mahogany parquet floor. Her gloved hands smoothed her dress before she clasped them tightly in front of her waist. On any other occasion, she would have loved her beautiful gown. Made of midnight blue satin and overlaid with a blue and silver gossamer fabric, it shimmered in the light every time she moved. Small, puffed sleeves encircled her upper arms, showcasing her white, sloping shoulders. The bodice nipped into a point at the front to accentuate her tiny waist and full bosom before falling into a rounded skirt that brushed the floor. She had argued against the off-the-shoulder bodice having a sudden aversion to the style after her encounter with Paxton, but Aunt Armelda had a formidable will that would not be swayed. Victoria's brown hair had been elegantly looped, braided, curled and styled around her head with a few pearls peeking through to match her necklace and earrings. A glance in the mirror earlier had proven that she had never looked more beautiful. But then, tonight was her engagement party. Unfortunately, her fiancé was overdue.

Days overdue, in fact.

They had received word that Lady Thornton had been too ill to travel, but that hadn't made the situation any easier. She had wanted to be able to meet her fiancé and take his measure before they were thrust into the limelight where they would both have to pretend to be a happy, loving couple. Now, social events filled every single moment of their time, starting tonight and ending with the wedding ceremony, four days hence. There would be no time for her to learn what to expect from him before their wedding night was thrust upon her.

Not that it mattered. During the past two weeks, Victoria had resolved herself to this marriage. Her mother had taught her how a lady should act both in public and in the privacy of her bedchamber. She knew what was expected of her and would endure it without complaint. To show any of the fear and trepidation she felt would dishonor the memory of the mother she had loved so dearly. Which she refused to do. No, she would make a go of this marriage.

She had no choice.

Claudia stood beside her looking bored while Rolfe paced the entryway. As time passed, Victoria's muscles grew more and more taut. The muted rise and fall of the guests' voices in the ballroom scraped at her already fragile composure. She gritted her teeth. Why didn't he come?

Rolfe muttered something about a cigar before disappearing down the hall in the direction of his study.

"Victoria!"

She jumped slightly before looking up. Regina popped up above the second-story balustrade and leaned over it. "Has he come?"

"Not yet."

"I hope he arrives soon. Do you think he'll be handsome?"

She barely bit back a derisive snort. "We'll have to wait and see."

"Don't worry. He will be handsome. I just know he will."

A distant door slammed. Regina dove back behind the banister just before Rolfe came into the foyer and paced again. The smoke from his cigar swirled over his head, filling the hall with a pungent aroma.

Poor Regina; hiding out and hoping not to be caught just to catch a glimpse of her fiancé. The fanciful child had probably spun dreams of a handsome prince coming to sweep Victoria off her feet.

Sadly, she would be disappointed.

The *ton* had been enjoying a gossiping heyday for the past two weeks. Not only speculating about Victoria and the supposed child she carried but also about Gregory Thornton. It seemed he had been introduced to London society, very briefly, five years before. From their stories, he was gangly and awkward with an overly long, scrawny neck and a thin, pointy face. His clothing hung on his bony frame in a most displeasing manner, and he wore hideous eyeglasses. He was also weak, obsessed with plant life, and an extreme disappointment to his parents. The final straw had come when he had cowardly refused to defend his honor. He had been openly insulted yet refused to partake in a duel even when Silas Newton had grabbed him by his cravat! Afterwards, his parents had sent him home in disgrace never to be seen in London again.

Until now.

The ringing of the doorbell abruptly brought Victoria back to the present. Her heart lurched then raced like a fox being chased by a pack of hounds. She stiffened her already ramrod straight posture and waited as their butler, Claude, opened the door. John and Harriet Thornton swept over the threshold and exchanged warm greetings with Rolfe. She studied Harriet's gown in an effort to avoid looking at the man who followed them into the entryway. A giggle bubbled up at the lavish nightmare made of purple taffeta edged in maroon velvet piping and roses. She pressed her lips together to repress it. The door closed behind the Thornton's as she counted the ruffles on the skirt. Twenty-five. A bit ostentatious for her taste, but still…

Stop this! Just look at him and get it over with.

"Rolfe, may I present my son, Gregory," John said.

Clasping her fingers tighter together, she lifted her attention from Harriet's outlandish skirt and glanced at her fiancé.

Her breath caught in her throat.

Surely this couldn't be Gregory Thornton! Not this slightly tall, boyishly handsome young man whose tailored clothing clung to his well-muscled frame.

"Good to meet you, boy! No need to stand on formalities, just call me Rolfe. Let me introduce you to my family," Rolfe greeted him heartily, shaking his hand vigorously and leading him over to Claudia before he could respond.

Victoria took the moments respite to study him more closely. Black hair carefully styled. Wearing the latest fashions made from the finest of cloth. But not slender as the men in the *ton* strived to be. In fact, the strength apparent in his physique seemed more in keeping with a common laborer than an idle member of society. All in all, he presented a pleasing appearance. Quite handsome, actually.

Her heart fluttered.

The only thing the *ton* had right was that he wore eyeglasses though the simple, gold-framed spectacles were hardly hideous even with the extra thick lenses. But they prevented her from really seeing his eyes. Her knees wobbled, threatening to send her sideways. She had always been able to tell by a man's eyes what he was thinking. Gregory's spectacles made it impossible for her to read him. She couldn't even tell whether he found her appearance pleasing or repulsive.

"And this is Victoria." At Rolfe's words, she tore her gaze away as Gregory turned to her.

She extended her gloved hand and curtsied, demurely keeping her attention on the floor. "I'm pleased to meet you, sir."

"And I, you," he replied as he bowed over her hand and kissed it. A shiver of pleasure coursed up her arm at the light touch of his lips, even through her mid-length gloves. She nearly frowned at her strange reaction.

Odd.

Rolfe clapped his hands together. "Well, now that the formalities are over, we shouldn't keep our guests waiting any longer." He extended his arm to Claudia and led the way into the ballroom. John and Harriet followed leaving her alone with Gregory. He offered her his arm, and she slipped her hand through it to rest lightly on his rock-hard forearm.

A forearm that trembled slightly.

She glanced sideways at him. Face set and looking straight ahead, he followed the others down the hall. They arrived in the doorway of the ballroom a second later.

Taking a deep breath, she pasted on her happiest smile and waited as the band finished the set then blew the fanfare to signal their arrival. Everyone immediately quieted and turned towards them. "Friends," Rolfe boomed. "May I present my daughter, Lady Victoria Bolton, and her fiancé, Lord Gregory Thornton!"

A smattering of applause trickled through the crowd as they entered the room. Not the usual boisterous congratulations that greeted an engaged couple. But with the rumors floating around and Gregory's reputation, they were here to gawk not celebrate her engagement.

The guests cleared the floor as the band broke into the prearranged waltz. Rather stiffly, Gregory led her onto the deserted floor and pulled her into his arms. He didn't try to hold her inappropriately close as she had become accustomed to men doing. Instead, he kept a respectful distance between them. His hands were not heavy upon her but light as they waltzed. An adequate dancer despite his stiff posture, they moved gracefully across the floor.

The waltz seemed interminably long with all the guests watching and whispering; the men smirked while the ladies tittered behind their fans. Her cheeks burned as she gazed fixedly up at Gregory. He remained silent, his face still straight ahead. Was he looking at her or over her shoulder? Impossible to tell with his spectacles. Her breathing quickened slightly as the not knowing ate at her composure.

Finally, the band played the last notes of the waltz. They glided to a stop, and Gregory let her go. Victoria curtsied as he gave her a formal bow. The band moved on to a Quadrille, and the guests once again started to mingle with many couples joining them on the dance floor. Without asking, Gregory led her into the new set. Usually, she would have been furious, but given the awkward situation, she barely noticed his faux pas. After all, as the guests of honor they would be dancing most of the night with each other.

At the end of another long, silent dance, Paxton suddenly appeared and tapped Gregory on the shoulder. "I say, you don't mind my cutting in, do you?"

Victoria's stomach plunged.

Gregory hesitated a moment before giving her another bow and handing her over to Paxton. As the band struck up another waltz, he gave Gregory a mocking smile. "Watch me, old man, and I'll show you how it's done."

He swept Victoria up in his arms and twirled her away. She soon lost sight of Gregory as Paxton took her all over the dance floor in an obvious show of his superior skill. She hadn't seen him since the incident in the garden, and the feel of his possessive hands on her sickened her, especially after Gregory's light touch.

She clenched her teeth in an effort to keep the roiling nausea at bay. *It's only for one dance.*

Paxton suddenly bent his head until his lips nearly touched her ear. "Victoria, I believe we have some unfinished business," he whispered. His hot breath swept across her bare neck and shoulders, causing her to shudder. "Why have you declined every invitation I have sent you in the last month?"

She forced herself to laugh lightly. "Sir, surely you know that a lady who is affianced cannot accept invitations from a man other than her intended."

"You were not formally engaged until now."

"Both myself and my betrothed knew of the engagement long before it was announced." Long was a loose term in this case. Hopefully, Paxton would accept it and say no more.

Her eye caught on Gregory dancing with Claudia at the edge of the dance floor. Tilting her head back, her sister smiled brilliantly, showing off her perfect, delicate features to their best advantage. Heat surged through Victoria's veins. How could her sister flirt with her intended? Claudia had become quite accomplished at capturing a man's attention. Could Gregory prefer her over Victoria?

"Are you really going through with this ridiculous engagement?"

"Of course." She twisted her head slightly to keep Gregory and Claudia in sight, but Paxton swirled her so her back faced them. Victoria fixed her gaze over his shoulder. If only this interminable dance would end!

"You'll regret it. A woman like you needs a man who knows how to appreciate your charms. That cold fish will never be able to stir your blood the way I could." The lewdness in his voice caused her face to grow hot. He suddenly bit out a mocking laugh. "Cold fish. It suits him. Right down to the bulging eyeglasses."

Right now, "that cold fish" was looking better and better to Victoria. *Anything* would be an improvement over this churl whose mere look made her skin crawl.

The dance suddenly ended, saving her from having to reply. For a long moment, Paxton held her against him even after the other dancers broke apart. His eyes blazed into hers speaking his licentious thoughts without words.

"Sir, the set has ended."

Slowly, Paxton let go of her waist, but he kept her hand imprisoned in a painful grip. She tried to tug it away, but he only smiled and tightened his hold, forcibly causing her to stay beside him. Bile rose in her throat. How could she endure another dance with him? Yet she could not gracefully extricate herself from his hold. And Rolfe would be livid if she caused a scene.

Just as the band struck up the next set, someone gently lifted her hand out of Paxton's harsh grip. She gasped and looked up. Gregory gave Paxton a nod, then, without a word, pulled her in his arms and slowly danced her away.

Victoria's knees turned weak. "Thank you for rescuing me."

This time, Gregory's head bent. Her cheeks heated feeling his gaze even through the spectacles. "I take it you don't wish to dance with him?" His low, smooth voice fell on her like a gentle, cleansing rain, soothing away the effects of Paxton's harshness.

Weariness filled her. Finding an appropriately coy answer took too much energy so, for once, she answered honestly. "No, I don't."

He nodded and looked back up. "Then you won't."

And it was as simple as that. When Paxton came back to claim her for the next set, Gregory politely informed him that he intended to dance with her for the rest of the evening. Red-faced, he glared at Gregory for several long moments before abruptly spinning on his heel and stalking away, obviously unwilling to create a scene over another man's fiancée with half of the *ton* watching.

Victoria didn't see him again.

Once the last party guests had left, the Thorntons with them, she trudged slowly up the stairs, completely exhausted. Her legs felt as heavy as if they had been molded from cast iron making each step a monumental effort. She had been on edge all evening. Unable to see Gregory's eyes properly, she hadn't known what to expect or when to expect it. But he had remained politely distant the whole evening and left without once asking her outside for a few stolen kisses. Relief and frustration battled for prominence. Which was worse, the nervous waiting for when he would try to claim her? Or the wondering if he found something lacking in her that made him desire not to? If she could only make it through the first time he kissed her, the next time would be easier. At least, then, she would know exactly what to expect from him.

Tonight, several people had gossiped loudly about the rumors of her carrying a child within earshot of Gregory. Victoria's face had burned even though he had acted as if he hadn't heard. He had, though, and if he believed them…

She shuddered. He would surely unleash the full force of his anger on her once they were wed. After all, no man wanted a soiled wife or to raise another man's child. Especially since he had no more say in the marriage than she did. It had been arranged entirely by their fathers.

Victoria reached her room and kicked off her slippers as she rang for Betsy. Yawning, she walked to the bed, intending to rest her weary legs.

The covers moved.

She jumped back with a shriek.

Regina popped up.

Staggering a few steps, she steadied herself on the bedpost. Her pounding heart slowed. "Regina! Don't ever scare me like that again!"

"I didn't mean to." Regina brushed her tousled brown curls from her face. "I was waiting for you and must have fallen asleep."

Victoria sank down on the edge of her bed and pulled off her gloves. "You should have been in bed hours ago."

"Maybe, but I couldn't sleep thinking about you and Gregory. He was so handsome, even handsomer than Paxton! But somehow, I just knew he would be. I snuck down and watched you dance. Isn't he just so exciting?"

"I wouldn't know. He hardly said a word all evening."

"Oooh. The silent, mysterious type. How romantic!"

Victoria nearly laughed. Where on earth did she pick up such starry-eyed notions?

"Ha! More like a complete bore," Claudia's haughty voice suddenly spoke up from the doorway. "I found him to be tedious and dull. And those hideous eyeglasses! They make him look like a frog."

"He wasn't *that* bad."

The spectacles weren't nearly as ugly as everyone made out and did nothing to detract from his handsome features.

"He was worse."

"I don't care what you say. I liked him!" Regina huffed and turned back to Victoria. "When will I be able to meet him?"

"Whenever Father deems it appropriate, but with the way our schedule is filled up, I doubt it will be before the wedding."

"Sometimes it's horrible being the youngest. You miss out on all the fun."

Fun?

Victoria shook her head. If she had her druthers, she would be Regina's age again and never grow up.

Betsy knocked softly on the door before slipping into the room. Victoria stood and smiled at Regina. "I know you're excited, but you best go to your room now. I'm exhausted and would like some sleep."

"Alright." Regina climbed out of the rumpled bed and wrapped her arms around her in a tight hug. "Goodnight, Victoria."

"Goodnight."

She stuck her tongue out at Claudia as she passed. Claudia returned the rude gesture before sitting down at Victoria's dressing table. She sighed as Betsy started unbuttoning the long row of minuscule buttons on the back of her dress. "Aren't you retiring as well?"

"In a minute," Claudia primped in the mirror. "I just wanted you to know that you're going to have competition. I've decided to pursue Paxton myself."

Victoria sucked in a startled breath. She had never dreamt that Claudia would want a man twice her age. And Paxton! What if Claudia actually succeeded in capturing his attention? Icy fingers crept around her spine.

She needed to warn her, but how? Her sister usually listened to no one but herself.

"Claudia…Paxton is much older and more experienced than you. He can be very…insistent in his demands. If you pursue him, you might end up over your head."

Her sister sighed and shook her head. "I should have known you would take that attitude. You've always been jealous of my beauty and tried to keep me away from eligible men because of it."

"That's not true! I've only wanted to protect you!"

"Poor Victoria. You never could stand being the plain one. You tried to capture Paxton for yourself but failed. Now, you're going to have a cold, lifeless marriage with frog face while I'm going to have Paxton, the most sought after bachelor in the *ton*."

Hot anger surged through her veins. Of all the lying, scheming… She clenched her hands into fists, digging her nails into her palm. "I never wanted Paxton! He's a despicable scoundrel who preys on innocent girls and then casts them aside. And he'll prey on you, too. Please Claudia, listen to me! I don't want to see you hurt, and Paxton…"

"I won't listen to another word!" Claudia stormed towards the door but turned back around just before leaving. "I really do pity you, Victoria. You never could accept defeat gracefully nor could you stand the fact that I was born more beautiful than you. But I'll try to forgive you for your resentment of me. After all, you are getting stuck with frog face for the rest of your life!" With that parting dart, Claudia left, slamming the door behind her.

"Ooohhh!" Picking up her brush, she hurled it across the room. Betsy jumped when it thudded against the wall. "Sometimes she makes me so mad!"

Calming down a bit, she let Betsy resume unbuttoning her dress. Claudia just didn't know what she was talking about. Her heart ached at what her sister would endure if she succeeded in capturing Paxton's attention. But maybe she was wrong to try to warn her away. After all, everyone agreed Paxton was the best catch in the *ton*. He was the best man Claudia was likely to find.

Yet, even that truth couldn't stop Victoria's nausea at the picture of her delicate sister caught in his ruthless embrace.

Gregory crossed his arms behind his head as he lay back against the bed. The party had lasted into the wee hours of the morning, completely exhausting him, but still, sleep wouldn't come. The events of the night flipped endlessly through his mind. Victoria had caught his eye from the moment he stepped into the house, but he had been shocked to discover that the beautiful vision in blue was actually his fiancée. Somehow, he had retained the false impression that Victoria was a plain woman. It had made him even more tongue-tied and awkward than usual; so, like an idiot, he had said nothing as they danced.

Neither had she.

Right away, he had noticed the handsome, blond man brazenly watching her. When he came over to claim her on only the third set, he'd had the surprising urge to tell him a curt no. The man had been overtly possessive and overly familiar with his fiancée making it obvious they knew each other well. Still, he had gone back to Victoria once the dance had finished not entirely sure she would welcome his interruption. The relief in her voice as she thanked him, however, had lifted his spirits.

For just a moment when she had first looked up at him there had been a hint of hurt and vulnerability on her face only to disappear a mere second later, leaving him unsure if he had only imagined it. They had been together the rest of the evening but hadn't spoken beyond polite formalities. He still knew nothing about his intended except that she had an almost unflappable poise.

He desperately needed to speak to her before the wedding. To become acquainted with the woman underneath her cool, confident demeanor, yet he had seen the list of social events they were expected to attend. They hardly had time to take a breath much less have a heart-to-heart talk.

Groaning, Gregory rolled over and punched his pillow. Who was he trying to kid? Even if they had had nothing to do, he would still have to break through his natural shyness to initiate such a conversation.

Jesus, I need Your help. We must talk privately sometime before the wedding. Please give me the words to say, and the courage to initiate such a conversation.

Hard though it would be, he would find a way.

Somehow.

35

Chapter 3

Victoria discreetly stifled a yawn as the servers took the last of the dishes away. Hard to believe only forty-eight hours had passed since Gregory's arrival. The time had both flown yet seemed to crawl by. As tired as she felt right now, it could have been two years instead of two days.

As the people at the table began to stir, Gregory stood up and politely pulled out her chair. She glanced at him as she accepted his help. He remained an enigma she had yet to figure out. Stiffly formal, he rarely spoke. The spectacles he wore effectively hid all of his thoughts from her, and she had yet to see him without them.

Taking his arm, she allowed him to lead her into the ballroom. They danced several sets together in the silence she had come to expect from him. Paxton watched them angrily from across the room. She suppressed a shiver. One point in Gregory's favor, he had been good to his word. Paxton had been at every social gathering and had tried on more than one occasion to claim her, yet Gregory had not allowed him to dance with her or to touch her again. Even the time Paxton insisted on talking with her alone, he had remained by her side the sheer strength of his presence being an effective deterrent to whatever Paxton had planned to say. He had finally left them alone, more furious than ever.

Later on in the evening, throat parched and weary beyond belief, she suggested that they sit out the next dance and drink some refreshments.

Gregory agreed and led her off the floor. He poured them both a glass of punch and handed one to her. She took it with a murmured "thank you." Something else odd about Gregory, he never imbibed in the alcohol available at the parties. He always chose the non-alcoholic punch that she preferred.

A burst of laughter pierced the quiet between them. She inwardly cringed when Claudia's voice rose above the others. "I tell you, frog face is the perfect name for Gregory Thornton. Not only do the spectacles give him bulging, glassy eyes, but he has a frog-shaped nose, thin frog lips, and a cold, slimy nature to match!"

More laughter followed her comment. Gregory continued to sip his punch, a slight tightening of his mouth the only indication that he had heard.

Since their argument about Paxton, Claudia had been insufferable. Not only did she openly insult Gregory to his face, she took every opportunity to ridicule him behind his back...but always within earshot. Gregory had endured her behavior without attempting any sort of retaliation. In fact, he never even acknowledged her unkind remarks. Many times Victoria had felt like apologizing for Claudia's behavior, but she had refrained since he seemed bent on ignoring it.

"Poor Victoria. She kissed a prince but ended up marrying a toad!" Laughter swallowed up anything else Claudia said, and a few seconds later, the small crowd broke up as another set started. Her tense shoulders relaxed a fraction.

She finished her glass and allowed Gregory to take her cup. "Miss Bolton, would you care to take a turn with me in the garden?"

For a moment her heart stopped before it began thundering in her chest. So, they had come to it at last. A tiny quiver of disappointment ran through her. Had some small part of her actually hoped that he would be different?

As much as she longed to refuse, she couldn't. Not only was Gregory her fiancé, but Rolfe stood with Julia at the wine table. Within earshot of the entire conversation. She forced her voice to be light. "I would be delighted to, Mr. Thornton."

She took Gregory's arm and followed him out into the garden. The sweet scent of roses filled her nostrils. Bile rose, but she pushed the feeling aside. She had to be alert now to make sure that Gregory didn't gain the upper hand.

As they walked along in silence disgust curled in her stomach. Gregory really was a lot like Paxton after all. Oh, he feigned great interest in the roses, even stopping now and then to touch one, but he chose a dark path away from any of the other couples, and their meandering walk led them well away from the house.

But she had learned her lesson the first time. She would not be caught unawares the second. Besides, with her vast experience with flirting she could surely keep Gregory in hand, especially since he didn't appear to be an expert. Just in case, though, she planned to keep within screaming distance of the house.

They entered an alcove a few moments later. The perfect spot. Small, only five feet across, but it had a stone bench on the right side for sitting. A torch standing next to it gave the area sufficient lighting. She had no intention of being caught in the darkness again. A glance back at the house showed they were still close enough to receive help should she need it.

Victoria stopped walking naturally forcing Gregory to stop as well. She looked flirtatiously up at him through her lashes. "Mr. Thornton, didn't you have something in mind besides just strolling along in silence?"

He cleared his throat. "Well, ah, actually, Miss Bolton, I did."

"I thought so." She turned to him with a breathless smile. He froze as she pushed closer and trailed her fingers up his arm to tease his ear.

She didn't know quite what happened next. One second she pressed close up against his side, playing with his ear, the next second he stood five feet away from her, as far as he could be on the opposite side of the alcove. What on earth…

He cleared his throat again. "Miss Bolton. That…that wasn't…exactly what I…I meant. I just thought we should…talk."

She tilted her head coquettishly and gave him a disappointed pout. "Talk?"

I just bet you did.

She didn't know what his scheme was, but she hardly thought it was to "talk". Moving over to the stone bench, she settled herself down and primly folded her hands in her lap. "Alright, Mr. Thornton. Let's talk."

"Could we…walk…and talk?" he asked rather lamely as he glanced back towards the pathway.

So that was his game. The proposed talk was just a trick to move her further away from the house. "Really, Mr. Thornton, I'd be much more comfortable sitting right here." She tilted her head and smiled flirtatiously at him. "What did you want to talk about?"

He cleared his throat again. "Well, about…about us."

"What about us?"

"Well…we're, uh, we're getting married the day after tomorrow."

"I know! Isn't it wonderful? I can hardly wait."

Gregory seemed rather taken aback at her sudden enthusiasm, feigned though it was. "Well, uh, yes, it's wonderful." He nervously rubbed his hands down his coat and cleared his throat again. Annoying habit. Hopefully not a normal one, but one brought on by the awkward situation. Having him clear his throat after every sentence would become very old very fast. "But I was thinking that we should become better acquainted before then."

"Just what would you like to know, Mr. Thornton?"

As if she didn't know. Why were all men alike?

"Well," he cleared his throat. She inwardly winced. "Things like…like…what pastimes do you enjoy?"

"Oh," she pretended to give it some thought while waiting for him to make his move. "Embroidery. Reading." She waved her hand airily. "Nothing you would be interested in."

After a small silence, Victoria suddenly grew serious. She was tired of staring at his eyeglasses and guessing at exactly what he intended. It was time to find out, here and now. "As long as we're getting to know each other, Mr. Thornton, there *is* one thing…"

She stood up and walked towards him. Gregory actually backed up into the rose bush behind him at the movement. However, she didn't stop until she stood a mere inch in front of him. "I want to see your eyes."

"My…my eyes?"

"Yes. I've never been able to see them because of your eyeglasses."

"Oh." He seemed to relax. "Of course. I should have realized."

He started to raise his hand, but she stopped him. "Let me," she whispered. Reaching up, she slowly pulled the spectacles off his face to reveal the most strikingly beautiful eyes she had ever seen. A rich hazel color surrounded by long, thick lashes. He blinked a little when the spectacles were gone, and his eyes held a glazed look for several seconds before finally focusing on her face.

She studied them intently as they stared down at her. They seemed like kind, gentle eyes, but she also detected a hint of wariness as well. They almost puzzled her even more than when she couldn't see them for they held none of the things she had come to expect from a man.

Still, however beautiful his eyes, Gregory had brought her out here for only one reason.

And she'd rather get it over with.

She slowly folded his spectacles up and placed them in his breast coat pocket behind his pristine white handkerchief. His eyes widened when she slid her hands underneath his coat, around his waist and pressed closer until their bodies touched. She raised her mouth to receive his kiss.

"I…" He cleared his throat. "I think we should return to the party."

Before she could even blink, he had spun her around and propelled her up the walk at a fast clip while fishing his spectacles back out of his pocket. Once inside the ballroom, he deposited her in a chair and took up a position beside her.

Well out of arm's reach.

Victoria surreptitiously eyed him, but he kept his attention on the activity of the dance floor. What could have gone wrong? Why had he not followed through on his intentions? Had she done something wrong? Something that displeased him? Was that why he had…rejected her?

Quickly reviewing the events in the garden, she could not find any action on her part that should have caused such a reaction.

Gregory didn't say another word all evening; not until they had reached her home and he bade her a hurried goodnight. Standing in the doorway as he strode back down the sidewalk to his carriage she felt more confused than she had ever felt before in her life.

Once his carriage turned the corner out of sight, she softly shut the door and turned to go to her room.

Rolfe stood by the foot of the stairs glaring at her. She stiffened as icy dread crawled up her spine and pooled in the back of her throat.

He took a few menacing steps forward. "What did you do?"

"I...I didn't do anything."

"Don't lie to me!" He grabbed her arms and shook her until her teeth rattled. "I saw Gregory take you into the garden and come back out again angry. You denied him! You denied your own fiancé a few harmless liberties. Now he's so angry he might decide not to marry you. Then John won't honor our business arrangements!"

He lifted his right arm. Heart pounding, she automatically ducked away. "No! No, you don't understand. He...he didn't even try to kiss me."

Rolfe paused with his fist in midair. "What?"

"He just wanted to talk. That's all!"

Her knees weakened as he slowly lowered his hand and chuckled. "Just talk? I always heard he was an odd duck. But what did you say to him to make him so angry he wouldn't even dance with you?"

"Nothing." Rolfe's eyes narrowed as she rushed her words out, her tongue tripping over itself. "We hardly said anything, just walked. When we came back in, he didn't want to dance. I don't know why."

"Hmmm." He studied her face for a moment. Slowly, deliberately, he tightened his fingers into the tender flesh of her arms. They dug in like talons as he yanked her forward and shook her as hard as he could as if she were a rag doll. Her hair flew out of it's coif as her head cracked back and forth like a whip. Pain shot through her neck. The foyer dimmed as stars danced across her vision.

Suddenly, he pushed her away. Unable to find her footing, she stumbled and fell back against the door. Rolfe put his dark, menacing face within an inch of hers. The alcohol on his hot breath burned her nose and caused her eyes to water. Trembling uncontrollably, she pressed back against the door, trying to escape, but he only moved closer. "That's just a warning.

Whatever is wrong, fix it! I don't care what you have to do to please him. If he calls this marriage off, I promise you, daughter, I'll make you rue the day you were born. Understand?"

She quickly nodded without looking up from the parquet floor at her feet.

He straightened and gave her a pleasant smile. "Now, go to your room and decide how you'll patch things up with Gregory."

"Y…yes, sir." She fled up the stairs, her unbound hair billowing behind her. Reaching her room, she fell through the opening and locked the door behind her with trembling fingers. Her thoughts raced as she paced back and forth in front of her dressing table. Unconsciously, she rubbed her sore arms. Knives of shooting pain stabbed her head and neck as she tried to think.

How could she fix things when she didn't even know what was wrong?

The next morning, Gregory arrived at the Bolton house at eight. An indecent hour for a social visit, but he didn't care about the rules laid out by the *ton*.

He had to speak to Victoria.

The butler seemed surprised to see him, but he took his hat and card and showed him to a small receiving parlour before going to inform her of his arrival. Unable to sit still, Gregory paced the room. His entire insides seemed to have taken up acrobatics in his gut. The incident last night had kept him from sleeping, and he had spent hours on his knees in prayer. Even now, pain speared through his chest at the knowledge that Victoria actually thought he had asked her into the gardens in order to dally with her affections. She obviously believed he expected her to allow him certain liberties that should only happen after marriage, and yet, he had sensed a hint of disappointment when he had first asked her to take a walk. He had only wanted to talk, to find out more about her. He had planned a mental list of questions, the first one being about her beliefs in God. Her sudden boldness had surprised and confused him, sending all sensible thought flying right out of his head. Instead, he had stuttered and stammered like an idiot and asked her the first question that popped into his mind. He didn't even remember what it had been, exactly, just some nonsense about pastimes.

Jesus, please give me the words to straighten this out. Help me to remember what to say.

He had been praying the same prayer all night long.

Victoria suddenly appeared in the doorway causing Gregory to freeze midstep. Wearing a simple dress with her hair pinned into a haphazard bun, she obviously hadn't been prepared to receive visitors. Face pale and with dark circles under her eyes, she didn't appear to have rested any better than he had.

Yet her beauty still took his breath away.

Giving him a shy smile, she extended her hand. "Mr. Thornton."

Gregory automatically walked over to grasp it. "Miss Bolton. Please forgive the untimely hour, but I thought it imperative that we talk."

"Of course."

He led her to the settee and seated her at one end before taking his own seat a respectful distance away. Taking a deep breath, he plunged into his memorized recitation. "I need to apologize for last night. I had just thought to spend some time alone so that we could talk." Victoria nodded though he could still see she doubted the validity of his statement. Nonetheless, he had prepared his speech thoroughly last night, and he intended to finish it. "However, knowing the customs of the *ton,* it was thoughtless of me to invite you into the gardens. It gave you the wrong impression of my intentions, and for that, I offer my deepest apologies. I also want you to know that I am a Christian man, and as such, I…What are you doing?"

Victoria slipped the spectacles off his nose.

He blinked for a moment at the complete fuzziness of the room. After a few seconds, his eyes cleared slightly, and her face swam into view.

She lowered his spectacles to her lap. "I'm sorry, Mr. Thornton, but I just…" She paused for a moment, and her shoulders lifted as she took a deep breath. "I just wished to see your eyes as we talk."

"Oh. Of course. Where…where was I?"

"You were saying that you are a Christian man."

"That's right." He took another deep breath. "Thank you, Miss Bolton. I am a Christian man, and as such, I do not believe in dallying with a woman, any woman, even if she is my fiancée." His cheeks warmed at the delicate topic. "And I…I would like to assure you that I do not expect you to permit me liberties that do not belong to me."

"But they will belong to you after the wedding tomorrow."

He nearly fell off the settee at her matter-of-fact statement. She stared at him completely calm, as if she had not just made such a startling proclamation. But she was correct. They would be married in the morning, and tomorrow night…

Flames scorched his face, all the way to the roots of his hair. Victoria tilted her head slightly, still waiting for an answer. He licked his suddenly dry lips with an equally dry tongue and cleared his throat. "I…I hadn't thought about it that way, but I suppose…I suppose you could say that. Yes."

She looked down and toyed with the spectacles in her lap for a moment before glancing back up and offering him a warm smile. "Now that we understand each other, what is it that you wished to speak about last night?"

Understand each other?

She might understand him, but he found her completely baffling.

Victoria nearly giggled at Gregory's visible befuddlement as he stared at her. The poor man had been completely embarrassed by the topic of conversation, and she found the blush that still tinged his cheeks rather… endearing. She hadn't known, until that moment, that a man was even capable of blushing.

Once again, she studied his beautiful hazel eyes. During the course of their talk they had changed color, going from a honey brown to a stormy green. And his eyelashes! Lashes that long and thick had no business belonging to a man. She absently fingered the spectacles in her lap. What a shame that he had to wear them and hide those magnificent eyes.

Gregory took another deep, audible breath. "The first question, Miss Bolton, is rather or not you are a Christian."

A Christian? Of all the things she might have imagined he'd ask, this would have never been one of them. "Of course I am, Mr. Thornton. I have attended church my entire life."

"Attending church doesn't make one a Christian, Miss Bolton. I'm speaking of giving your heart to Jesus. Acknowledging that you are a sinner and accepting Jesus as your Savior."

A vague memory stirred inside her mind. Years ago, she'd had a governess who had spoken similarly. She frowned and tried to pull the fuzzy recollections into focus. There was a day when she was but five years old that she had knelt with her governess and, with tears streaming down her cheeks, asked Jesus to be her Savior. Rolfe had found out, however, and had fired that governess the next day. She had been forbidden to speak of the incident again. Strange, but she hadn't thought about that in years.

"Actually, yes, Mr. Thornton. It was so long ago, I had almost forgotten about it, but I have."

A full-blown smile crossed Gregory's face and lit up his eyes, causing her breath to catch. This was the first time she had seen him actually smile. Why, he was positively...devastating.

Reaching out, he gently clasped one of her hands in his. Neither wore gloves this morning, and to Victoria's surprise, his skin felt work-roughened not smooth and polished like the men of the *ton*. A different but strangely pleasant sensation. "I am so glad. My faith and relationship with Jesus are most important to me. I would like for us to set aside a time each day to read the Bible and pray together. It will give us a strong foundation upon which to build our marriage."

What an odd thing to say. Stranger than anything else he had said to date, but she nodded in agreement. "Of course; if that is your wish."

"I pray that soon it will be your wish as well, Miss Bolton."

Victoria didn't know how to respond to that so she remained silent. As they sat on the settee and stared at each other an awareness suddenly shot through her causing her whole body to tingle. She let her eyes roam over his handsome features before settling on his firm lips. What would it be like to kiss him?

For the first time, anticipation zinged through her instead of fear.

A loud gasp brought her back to earth with a jarring thud. "You're here!"

At Regina's childish cry, Gregory dropped Victoria's hand and stood up. Blinking to bring the room back into focus, she slowly followed suit. What had just happened?

Gregory squinted towards the door. Oh my goodness, she still had his spectacles! "Mr. Thornton, your eyeglasses." She brought her hand up just as he turned and reached for them.

Their hands collided knocking the spectacles to the ground. They spun around on the floor before sliding halfway under the settee. He knelt down to retrieve them and began groping around the floor nowhere near the eyeglasses. Her heart softened. Why, he couldn't even see them! "Here, Mr. Thornton, allow me."

Reaching down, she picked them up. Thank goodness they were still intact. He stood back up and accepted them from her, looking embarrassed. "Thank you, Miss Bolton."

He put the spectacles on, once again hiding his lovely eyes from her view. She turned, taking a quick half-step-back to avoid colliding with Regina who had moved less than an inch away while they had been occupied. Her sister stood right in front of Gregory, staring up at him with a dreamy expression. She shook her head in mock exasperation. "Mr. Thornton, may I present my youngest sister, Regina."

Gregory smiled down at the girl. "How do you do, Miss Regina?" By the even tone of his voice, he didn't seem the least bit put out by her sudden appearance.

"Oh, I'm fine, sir." Regina suddenly straightened to her full three-foot four-inch height and held out her hand regally. Her face grew hot at her little sister's attempts to act like an adult. Grown men did not spend their time pacifying eight-year-old girls who wanted to pretend to be ladies.

Gregory, however, took it all in stride as he politely took her hand and bowed over it. "Pleased to meet you, Lady Bolton."

Regina giggled and curtsied. "Likewise, Mr. Thornton."

"Regina!" Rolfe's sharp voice caused Regina to pale as she spun around to face the doorway where he stood. Victoria tensed. Rolfe visibly struggled to control his anger for a moment before addressing Gregory. "Mr. Thornton, I am so sorry for the inconvenience. She won't bother you again."

He strode towards Regina, but Gregory spoke, stopping his angry approach. "She was no bother, sir. On the contrary, I had wanted to meet the rest of your family for some time."

Rolfe relaxed causing Victoria to relax as well. Gregory had effectively headed off any harsh punishment that Rolfe might have given her sister, and at that moment, she would have gladly done anything for him.

"Come, Regina," Rolfe held out his hand. Regina reluctantly crossed the room to take it. "We must leave the two lovebirds alone. I'm sure they have many things to…discuss." Heavy innuendo colored his voice, and the conspiratorial wink he sent Gregory only confirmed it. Her stomach writhed as heat crept up her neck.

An awkward silence followed their departure. She struggled to break it. "I…it was very kind of you to play along with Regina."

"She seems like a delightful child."

"Mr. Thornton, may I…may I ask you a personal question?"

"You may ask me anything, Miss Bolton."

"I noticed you squinting towards the door when Regina first came in and then feeling around on the floor for your spectacles…I wondered…" Her voice trailed off. *How bad your eyesight is* sounded so tactless, but how else could she phrase it?

"You are wondering how well I can see," he easily finished for her. She nodded glad that he didn't appear to be upset by her curiosity. "Everything that is within about a foot, I can see clearly. Beyond that, it is a complete blur."

Her brows furrowed as she tried to envision it.

"If Regina were standing beside you now I would know it was her by the size and coloring. However, if there was another girl standing next to her, the same size and with the same color hair, I wouldn't be able to tell them apart. Details, such as facial features, are completely blurred beyond a foot away."

How sad. "I'm sorry, Mr. Thornton."

He smiled at her. "You needn't be. With spectacles, I can see quite well."

"How…how did your eyesight become so blurred?"

"Apparently, I was born with weak vision. My nurse first noticed when I was a toddler since I always brought things close to see them. As long as I can remember, I've worn heavy spectacles."

The mantel clock chimed the hour. She automatically counted the gongs. Nine o'clock! How had the time gone by so quickly? They were due for a luncheon at the Bentinck house in an hour and a half. There would scarcely be enough time to get ready!

Gregory seemed to realize it as well. "Well, Miss Bolton, I had better be off. It has been a pleasure even though I hadn't intended to detain you so long."

"The pleasure is all mine, Mr. Thornton," she murmured as she saw him out to the entryway. Claude handed him his hat.

He placed it on his head and gave her a polite nod. "I will be by to pick you up at ten-fifteen."

"I shall be ready."

After Claude closed the door behind him, she walked upstairs replaying the conversation again in her mind. She found Betsy already in her room waiting to help her dress, and Regina sitting glumly on her bed. She sat at her dressing table and studied the downcast girl in the mirror as Betsy loosened her hair and brushed it. "Are you alright?"

"Yes."

"He didn't punish you, did he?"

Regina sighed and picked at her skirt. "No, he just gave me a long lecture about staying in my proper place." She looked up. "But Mr. Thornton didn't mind my coming in, did he?"

"No, he didn't mind."

"Mr. Thornton's nice, isn't he?"

She paused for a moment. "He seems to be." But then, she had already proven not to be the best judge of character. She had thought Paxton nice as well until the incident in the garden. Actually, she was glad for Regina's timely interruption of her and Gregory's discussion, especially since she had escaped unscathed. On that settee her thinking had been going in a dangerous direction. She knew better than to raise her hopes up about a man.

Yet, she had to admit that Gregory did act in a different manner than Paxton. When Gregory escorted her, his touch always remained light and respectful not heavy-handed and possessive as Paxton's had been. Gregory had never mastered the flowery words that fell so easily from Paxton's lips nor had he ever studied her figure licentiously. At least, not that she was aware of though with his eyeglasses on she couldn't be entirely sure. The main difference, however, was Gregory's claim that he didn't believe in taking liberties with a woman other than his wife. To be fair, he more than claimed it. Despite her natural inclination to doubt such a statement, he had proven the truth of his words the night before. But Gregory was still a man.

His kisses will probably be no better than Paxton's.

Yet the tiny ember of hope in her heart refused to be squashed no matter how hard she tried.

Chapter 4

$\mathcal{E}$arly the next afternoon, Victoria stood in the vestibule of the cathedral wearing her simple yet elegant wedding gown of pale lavender silk. Hordes of butterflies attacked her stomach and wreaked havoc with her composure. In just a few minutes she would become Mrs. Gregory Thornton.

At the thought, all the oxygen siphoned from the room. The overwhelming urge to run filled her mind.

Trying to calm herself, she studied the stained glass windows near the ceiling.

Rolfe stood next to her staring off into space. Probably counting the money he expected to make from her marriage. Beside her, Regina fairly hopped from excitement. She thought it the most romantic thing she had ever seen and had been ecstatic to be an actual part of the wedding party. Claudia stood on her other side. She pulled a tiny mirror from the secret pocket in her dress and rearranged the curls around her face. She noticed Victoria watching her and lifted her chin a bit higher, still put out at Victoria's supposed jealousy over Paxton while being stuck with frog face.

If Victoria had her way, she wouldn't marry anyone, but if she had to choose between the two men, she would pick Gregory. Despite his quietness she found him to be a more pleasant escort.

Her heart ached for Claudia. As spoiled as she was, she was still her sister, and Victoria loved her. If she succeeded in capturing Paxton's attention, she knew exactly what kind of harsh treatment she would receive. But, was there really any man who was any different?

Gregory.

The soft answer came straight from her heart and startled her so much she nearly dropped her bouquet. Her hands grew damp as her breathing quickened. She had no way of knowing that. She didn't know anything about Gregory. Not really. Yes, he had been kind so far, but anyone could put on a front for a few days. Once they married, he could turn into a monster. She knew of several men who had done that after marrying her friends.

Deacon Paley scurried into the vestibule. "It's time."

The room tilted and spun around her. Not yet! She wasn't ready!

Rolfe grabbed her arm, his fingers digging into her flesh as he propelled her towards the sanctuary door. Regina gave her a radiant smile and giggled before she stepped sedately out into the church proper. After a few moments, Claudia followed her, head held high and positively preening at all the attention.

Suddenly, she stood in the doorway of the church. The crush of people inside seemed to close in and press against her. She had to escape. To find a place with enough space and oxygen for her burning lungs.

As if sensing her desire to flee Rolfe tightened his fingers, sending pain streaking up her arm. No way could she break his vise-like grip. The music swelled as Claudia neared the altar. She gasped for air. She couldn't go through with this. She just couldn't! Black dots danced in front of her vision. The church swirled around her in a dizzying kaleidoscope of colors. Her eyes frantically searched for something to hold on to, anything to keep her from swooning where she stood.

Suddenly, her eyes latched onto Gregory...

And held.

Standing tall and strong at the front of the sanctuary, he became the anchor in the midst of the storm brewing inside of her. Slowly, breath returned to her lungs, and her mind cleared. She could do this.

She had no choice.

When the organist launched into the prearranged music, everyone stood up and turned towards the back of the church. Rolfe led her out of the doorway and slowly started down the aisle for the longest walk of her life. Legs wobbling, she kept her eyes fixed on Gregory, the only thing that seemed to keep her fear from consuming her entirely.

When they were still a few feet away, Gregory reached up and unobtrusively pulled his eyeglasses off, slipping them into his coat pocket. His eyes squinted slightly as he struggled to focus on her face. What on earth was he doing?

She sucked in a startled gasp, and her heart nearly melted.

He had done this for her!

He knew she preferred to see his eyes when they talked, and during their vows on this most important day of her life, he had chosen to accommodate her. But at what a sacrifice! She could only imagine how horrible it must feel to stand in front of a roomful of strangers unable to see anything but a dizzying blur of color.

Unexpectedly, the butterflies in her stomach vanished. Strength infused her, and she walked the last two steps on steady feet.

Rolfe stopped when they reached Gregory. "Who gives this woman away?" Rector Pitt boomed.

"I do."

He nodded, and Rolfe handed her over to Gregory. His warmth seeped through her glove as he gently gripped her hand. Together they knelt in front of the rector as he intoned a blessing over them. From that point on, the ceremony passed in a haze. She kept her gaze fixed on Gregory. His eyes and face were solemn as he slid his ring onto her finger through the slit in her glove and gave the vows that would bind him to her for life.

Her whole body trembled as she did the same.

Then suddenly Rector Pitt announced them man and wife. "You may kiss your bride!"

Mouth dry, she took a deep breath and held it. Gregory turned to face her. His right hand came up to rest lightly on her waist as he slowly leaned forward and gave her a feather soft kiss on her upturned mouth.

The kiss ended almost before it began, but the impact shook her to her toes. The soft sensation of his lips on hers had been…pleasant.

Decidedly so.

If only it could last.

"May I present, Lord and Lady Gregory Thornton," Rector Pitt announced happily as her husband led her back up the aisle.

Her husband.

She could barely grasp the fact that she was actually married.

Once in the vestibule, Gregory fished the spectacles back out of his pocket. She stopped him just before he put them back on. "Thank you, Mr. Thornton."

He studied her a moment before giving her a gentle smile. "You're welcome, Mrs. Thornton."

Mrs. Thornton.

She turned the name over and over in her mind.

Mrs. Thornton.

A small smile tipped her lips. She actually liked the title.

The guests began streaming into the foyer. Gregory barely had time to slip his spectacles back on before they were swept through a shower of rice and into their waiting carriage. The driver shut the door, effectively shutting out the noise of the crowd.

Suddenly, she was quite alone with, and sitting quite closely to, her new husband. Somehow they had both ended up on the same bench in the carriage whereas before Gregory had always sat opposite her. She tried to ignore the awkwardness as she attempted to remove the rice from her hair and clothes. Beside her, Gregory did the same, brushing at his clothes and hair with a strong hand. A small flood of rice tumbled to the floor.

The carriage lurched as it moved away from the church, throwing her against his shoulder. Her face burned as she quickly straightened. "Well, we're off," she announced brightly.

Gregory turned slightly in the seat, studying her. She stiffened when his hand suddenly reached for her. "You still have a few grains of rice in your hair."

Victoria sat still as he gently picked out the last pieces of rice. Her pulse picked up it's tempo at his ministrations. His fingers in her hair felt far different than Betsy's.

Pleasantly so.

A strange, empty feeling hollowed her stomach when he moved away. "Thank you."

Her voice sounded husky even to her own ears. Gregory didn't say anything. He just took her hand and held it tenderly during the ride to his parent's house where the wedding party would be held.

For the rest of the afternoon and on into the evening, they had no time alone. Bride and groom stood in line to receive unending congratulations, ate the fashionable dinner and danced at least twenty-five sets. Nearing midnight, Harriet Thornton, acting the part of Victoria's mother, approached them where they stood by the dance floor. "It's time for the bride to prepare herself," she announced loudly and with a wide smile. Several people around them tittered, and one of the men drunkenly called out a lewd comment.

Fire scorching her face, she couldn't even look at Gregory as Harriet led her away. The sound of the party faded behind them as they climbed the stairs and walked down the hall to the last door on the right. Pushing it open, Harriet ushered her inside. Betsy already waited there with the valise she had packed for the coming night.

Elegantly appointed, the main motif of the room consisted of dark blue birds on creamy white wallpaper. Matching mahogany furniture filled the large space. Renewed heat filled her cheeks at the large canopied bed with an embroidered blue coverlet and white throw pillows. She quickly turned away and finished her perusal of the room. Very tastefully done but stark and sterile without any personal touches. In fact, it looked more like a guest room than a private bedchamber.

Her nerves jumped, and she nearly stumbled. It probably *was* a guest room. After all, Gregory hadn't been in London for five years.

Betsy helped her out of her wedding gown and into her nightshift and house coat. Sitting down at the dressing table, she tried to look anywhere but at the bed as Betsy brushed out her hair. However, her eyes seemed drawn to it like a magnet. In just a few minutes, Gregory would come and...

Fire and ice surged through her body in alternating intervals as images of the coming night flooded her mind despite her best effort to suppress them.

Harriet silently watched with an eagle eye from her perch on the divan. Finally, once Victoria's waist-length brown hair lay soft and smooth around her shoulders and shone in the muted candlelight, Harriet stood up with a smile. "I'll tell Gregory his bride is ready."

Ready?

Trembling from head to toe, she hardly felt ready, but she said nothing as Harriet motioned Betsy to follow her, and they both left the room.

The waiting seemed interminable as long minutes stretched past.

Taking deep, measured breaths, she forced herself into a practiced calm. A glance in the mirror showed a pale but composed face. She bit her lips and gave her cheeks a couple hard pinches until color bloomed before giving her reflection a slight nod. Gregory would never know of her inward turmoil. She would willingly, and seemingly eagerly, submit to whatever he required of her.

It was the only way. If he ever guessed how terrified she felt, he would surely grow angry and hurt her worse.

A quiet knock suddenly shot through the room like a bullet.

She jumped then braced herself and stood up on quavering legs. "Come in, Mr. Thornton."

The door slowly swung open. Gregory entered and silently latched the door behind him before turning to face her. She threw him a coquettish smile. "Welcome, Mr. Thornton."

A long beat of silence followed. "Gregory," he finally said a bit abruptly. "My name is Gregory."

Keeping the mood playful, she ducked her head slightly and looked at him from the corners of her eyes. "Gregory."

Taking off his spectacles, he set them carefully on top of the chest of drawers before slowly walking towards her. When he stopped less than a foot away, she suddenly didn't have to feign anticipation. It washed over her in waves, stealing her breath. His beautiful eyes searched her face. She kept her expression open and inviting though inside her heart pounded so hard it was a wonder he didn't hear it.

Finally, he reached out and pulled her into a loose embrace. "Are you nervous?"

Her legs went weak. How had he known? How had he seen inside her to the deepest parts of her heart? To the fear that she kept so carefully hidden?

But she couldn't let him see her fear. It would only stoke his anger, feeding it to new heights until he became drunk with it. Reveling in it and enjoying the pain he inflicted. Just as it always did with Rolfe. She had to do something to take his mind off it. Quickly.

She pasted on another coy smile. Slowly, deliberately, she reached out and let her hands roam up his muscular chest to rest on his shoulders before pressing close against him. This time, Gregory stood completely still and allowed it. Standing on tiptoe, she nuzzled his neck and trailed a few kisses along his jaw. He closed his eyes, and his chest lifted in a deep breath.

"Whatever would make you think that, Gregory?" she murmured before placing another kiss on his chin.

Several seconds of silence ticked by.

Reaching up, she ran her finger tantalizingly along his lips. Then, she let it roam up to his cheek as she pressed a kiss to the corner of his mouth. Sliding her fingers into his hair, she prepared to fully pull his lips down to hers.

"Because I am."

His quiet admission froze her just an inch shy of his mouth. Never had she heard such a thing. *He* was nervous? What did that mean? Men were never nervous. They were always the instigators, lording their power over their hapless wives. Wives who were, legally, nothing more than another possession subject to their every whim and fancy.

And they never let them forget it.

Gregory opened his eyes again. Closing the short space between them, he placed a soft, tentative kiss on her lips. He lingered there for several long moments before lifting his head slightly.

"Victoria."

Her name, murmured in a throaty whisper against her mouth, sent shivers of longing running through her. Gregory pulled her closer as he gently claimed her lips again. His hands wove their way into the thick hair cascading down her back.

Nothing in her life had ever prepared her for the feel of his mouth claiming hers. Pleasurable sensations shot through her like miniature starbursts. His fingertips, lightly grazing her spine, left a trail of fire in their wake. Desire, strong and heady, threatened to sweep her away, and her hands, resting on his shoulders, nearly began exploring his firm muscles of their own volition. It took all her willpower to not give into the emotions and lean into him. Instead, she forced herself to stand still, waiting for the tender caress to become harsh and punishing.

But, even when Gregory's arms tightened around her, pressing her close against him, he remained gentle. The strong arms around her were not imprisoning her against him as Paxton had done, but cradling her, sheltering her as if she were the greatest, fragilest treasure he would ever own. He gave the impression that at the slightest resistance from her, he would immediately let her go. Only, she found that she didn't *want* him to let her go. The haven of his arms beckoned her closer. Closer to the safety and protection they offered. Never had she experienced such sensations!

Almost shyly, his lips began to explore hers as he deepened the kiss. Still, he didn't demand or take anything from her. He gave. He gave her the feeling of being special and cherished.

Cherished.

Just as she had secretly yearned for.

She unconsciously sighed as she finally let go of her iron self-control and relaxed into his tender embrace. Her arms entwined around his neck, and her fingers curled into his oh-so-soft hair. She finally kissed him back, matching his ever-increasing fervency. Weak-kneed from the desire coursing through her, she clung to him, pressing as close as she could, but it still wasn't close enough. Never would she get enough of such gentleness in the midst of such overwhelming passion!

How could he be so gentle yet ravish her so thoroughly?

Her breath caught when he suddenly swung her up into his strong arms. Gasping from the effects of his ardent caresses, her eyes locked onto his smoldering ones. Tingling excitement surged through her veins as he carried her to the bed. Somehow, it didn't even occur to her that she should be afraid. Instead, it felt like the most natural thing in the world.

In the carriage the next day, Victoria bounced when they hit another jarring pothole. Gregory, who had once again seated himself beside her, steadied her. "I'm sorry the streets are so rough."

"It's not your fault." She straightened her hat that had been knocked askew. Their normal route through London had been cordoned off by the police, and they were taking a detour through a seedier side of town. They had the carriage to themselves since John and Harriet had chosen to remain in London. Harriet claimed the newlyweds should be alone, but she secretly thought the older woman just wanted to do some more shopping. Whatever the reason, she was glad that they would finally have some time to themselves.

She smoothed the skirt of her traveling outfit. The narrow red skirt had cream colored accents and a creamy, high-collared blouse topped by a fitted red jacket with gigot sleeves. A matching red hat perched on her upswept hair, the small round brim framing her face. The stylish outfit showed off her full bosom and hour-glass figure to the best advantage.

Did Gregory notice?

Her eyes once again drifted to her husband who stared out the carriage window. Her heart gave a little flutter just looking at his strong profile. All morning, she had been having trouble keeping her eyes off of him, even during all the hectic last minute emergencies that always cropped up before embarking on a long trip. She had always considered him to be handsome, but after the wondrous night he had given her, his face had suddenly become something more to her, something precious.

Her entire body thrilled as she once again recalled how infinitely patient and tender he had been. His had been the first gentle touch she'd felt since her mother had died five years previous, and she hadn't realized how much she had craved that gentleness until last night. She had responded like a weary traveler who had suddenly found an oasis in the desert. This morning, she had wanted to remain in his arms instead of facing the long trip out to the country, but he had been so excited to be going home, more excited and animated than she had ever seen him, so she held her tongue. As it turned out, they had been unable to leave London until early in the afternoon.

Despite her best intentions, Victoria's eyes grew heavy. She blinked them open fighting back yawns as they drove down one twisted street after another. Finally, they reached the edge of London, and the driver picked up the pace. As the city fell behind them, the stiffness she had always associated with Gregory slowly drained out of him as his body relaxed back into the seat. His shoulders lifted as he took a deep breath and held it for a moment. A contented smile crossed his face as he released it. His smile became embarrassed, however, when he turned to find her watching him. He shrugged a bit self-consciously. "I feel like I can breathe again."

"Pardon?"

"I feel so stifled when I'm in the city, but this…" he waved his hand to indicate the gently rolling hills outside the window. "Being out in the beauty of God's creation is liberating."

What an odd statement. An icy tendril of foreboding worked it's way around her spine. She really knew very little about this man. Her husband. Hard to believe that it had only been five days since they had met.

Five short days.

Having spent nearly every waking moment together, it felt much longer, yet, she still knew practically nothing about him.

She hadn't really cared, before. All she had wanted to know had been what he expected of her so she could plan accordingly. But today at odd times as they had worked together to leave London, she had found herself wondering about *him*. Wondering about his likes and dislikes. Wondering what his childhood had been like. She smiled as she envisioned a tousle-headed, black-haired boy with eyeglasses. He had probably been adorable.

She had even been wondering about the little things like whether or not he liked broccoli. Or about his thoughts on the political situation with Russia in Afghan. Did he believe the British troops had been right to cross into Bolan Pass? Not that she was supposed to be knowledgeable about such matters, but she overheard people talking. Still, knowing a man didn't like a woman who asked too many questions, she only pondered these things in her heart.

Looking up, Victoria found Gregory now watching her. He gave her a slow, heart-stopping smile that sent delicious shivers coursing through her. "Well, Mrs. Thornton. We have quite a long drive ahead of us. We might as well be comfortable."

"I suppose we should, Mr. Thornton."

Sliding an arm around her shoulders, Gregory settled her against his chest. Removing her hat, she placed it in her lap before laying her head against his shoulder. "Is that better?" he asked quietly.

She sighed as she snuggled a little closer. "Much better."

Closing her eyes, she relished the strength of him. Strange because she had always related strength to fear and abuse. Gregory was physically stronger than any other man in her acquaintance. She had suspected it from the beginning because of his rock-hard muscles. It had been confirmed this morning when he had easily lifted a full steamer trunk all by himself. Yet she found his strength gentle and comforting.

Very comforting.

She sighed again. If only it could stay this way, but it wouldn't. It was impossible for a man to always be so kind.

Stifling another yawn, she settled in, intending to enjoy the comfort of Gregory's arms while she could. But the rhythmic sway of the carriage lulled her, and she drifted off to sleep.

Gregory smiled as Victoria finally lost the battle to sleep. Her breath puffed soft and even against his neck. Closing his eyes, he once again thanked God for her. Already he couldn't imagine his life without her in it. His former existence seemed dull and lifeless compared to the way he felt right now.

But he probably shouldn't have pushed for them to return home so soon. It might have been best to rest up for a few days after the grueling week leading up to their wedding. The thought of going home had energized him, and Victoria had pitched in without complaint. Only after they were out of London had he noticed that she stifled yawns. She had looked so weary that he knew she would sleep if he could help her to relax. He should have realized earlier how exhausted she must be.

He wanted nothing more than to take care of her but already he had failed.

Going back to London now, though, made little sense. The worst part, the effort of getting everything ready, was behind them. They could sleep the rest of the way home if need be.

Victoria shifted in her sleep, snuggling closer to him. Several strands of hair fell across her face, and he gently pushed them back behind her ear.

She was so breathtakingly beautiful. Gregory still found it hard to comprehend that she was his wife! He once again prayed for wisdom in how to be the husband she needed. Despite the calm, confident exterior she presented to the world, something about her sometimes seemed so hurt and fragile.

Jesus, please don't let me do anything to accidentally hurt her!

With her face relaxed in sleep, Victoria looked extremely young though she had already passed her seventeenth birthday. What could have happened to wound her? At first, he thought it might have been the child the gossips claimed she carried, but after a couple of days, he dismissed the rumors as untrue. It had become apparent that Rolfe had his eye on the lucrative business contract that went with the marriage, and he would do anything to get it. Even force his daughter to marry a complete stranger. And last night, once Victoria had stopped trying to hide her nervousness behind a bold facade, she had displayed a shyness and innocence that could not have been feigned.

If she had been with child, he would have never held it against her, but a thrill shot through him knowing she had saved herself entirely for him.

But that still didn't tell him what might be wrong.

Instead of spending his time fruitlessly wondering about it, he closed his eyes and took it to God in prayer.

Victoria only napped for about an hour. Once awake, she sat back up and started straightening her hair making his arms feel suddenly bereft. He crossed them to hide the feeling and glanced out the window. Nothing interesting to converse about out there. Not yet, anyway.

The silence in the carriage pressed down on him as they continued to drive.

Occasionally, an interesting landmark appeared, and he pointed it out. Victoria would look out, smile and make the appropriate comments before the silence stretched between them again.

Vast.

Empty.

It pervaded even when they stopped to change horses.

They were rattling through the small town of Cuckfield when the driver suddenly pulled off the road and stopped. He frowned. They weren't scheduled to change horses again. Opening the door, he stepped out. "What's the matter, Brad?"

"Horse threw a shoe, sir. We're going to have to get it replaced. There's a blacksmith on the edge of town, but I'm not sure how long it'll take. Ye Olde White Harte Inn is just ahead if you and Mrs. Thornton would prefer to wait there."

Gregory sighed as weariness filled him. They had such a late start today only to be delayed even further by the detour through London. And now this. "That will be fine."

Helping Victoria out of the carriage, he tried to smile. "Well, we should at least be able to have some dinner while we wait."

"I am a little hungry."

He took her arm, and they walked the short distance to the inn as Brad drove the carriage off. Once inside the White Harte, they were seated at a rough-hewn table and served steaming bowls of thick, savory stew and a plate of fresh bread. At breakfast that morning, when he had first explained to Victoria that he liked to pray before meals and had asked her to join him, she had been surprised but readily agreed. Now, she sat with her hands folded primly in her lap, waiting for him to bless the food.

He would have preferred to hold hands.

Bowing his head, Gregory gave a brief blessing. Despite the rustic setting the food tasted quite good. He waited until the edge of his hunger abated before speaking again. "Victoria, we're still over two hours away from Thornton Hall. If you're tired, we can take a room here and continue on in the morning."

"What would you like to do?"

"It really doesn't matter to me. We'll do whatever is best for you."

Her blue eyes widened before she turned back to her food. He waited while she took several bites of stew. Firelight from the hearth danced over her face, highlighting the sweet curve of her cheek. His fingers itched to reach out and stroke that smooth skin. In his lap, he curled his hand into a fist to resist the urge. She finally glanced back at him. "I think I would like to continue on. I am tired, but I would rather arrive late tonight than have to wake up to another day of traveling."

"Then we shall press on as soon as the horse is shod."

They lingered at their table for over an hour before Brad came to retrieve them. Back in the dark carriage, he once again held Victoria close as she fell asleep. This time, he joined her.

Chapter 5

ictoria drifted towards consciousness. Glue seemed to hold her eyelids shut. After several seconds of struggling, she pried them open. Bright sunlight momentarily blinded her, causing her to blink rapidly. Shapes slowly took form. Pushing her wildly tangled hair out of her face, she glanced around at the strange room and the strange bed she lay on.

Where was she?

Her heartbeat quickened a moment before she relaxed. They must have reached Thornton Hall. By the amount of sunlight streaming in, the day was already far spent. But how had she gotten here? And why did she still wear her traveling clothes? The last thing she remembered was snuggling against Gregory in the dark carriage as she fell asleep.

Her face grew hot when she realized that he must have carried her up here from the coach. She had always been a sound sleeper; a fact she abhorred. Sitting up, she glanced over her outfit. Gregory had removed her shoes and jacket and undone the first two buttons on her blouse to loosen the tight collar. He had also removed the pins from her hair and placed them in a neat pile on the nightstand. Nothing untowards, but her cheeks still blazed as she climbed out of the lusciously soft bed.

Feeling tight and a little achy, she stretched as she took in her surroundings more closely. A large, airy room decorated mainly in a dark green color. Situated on a corner of the manor, enormous windows practically made up two of the walls. The huge four-poster bed stood opposite the door and seemed to divide the room into three sections with the middle part as the bedroom. Carefully arranged on a conspicuously new dressing table were Victoria's toiletries confirming that her valise had been unpacked.

A sitting area took up the right side of the room with a small ladies writing desk for correspondence tucked into a corner. A peek in the large doors on either side of the fireplace revealed a washroom on the left and an enormous changing room on the right. Gregory's clothes hung on the left half of the changing room, leaving the other side empty and waiting for her clothes to be unpacked from her steamer trunks.

He had obviously prepared for her arrival before he had left for London.

Closing the door, Victoria crossed to the other side of the bedroom. A study of some sort with a heavy roll-top desk and a large drawing table clustered together on the right side next to two of the huge windows. Arranged across the top were several dried leaves and flowers, a cup full of pencils, and a few scattered papers containing drawings interspersed with hand written notes. She picked them up, gasping at the life-like pencil drawing of a tiger lily. She could almost feel the petals and smell the scent. Amazing.

Had Gregory drawn this?

She read the short paragraph underneath the picture.

Lilium bulbiferum commonly called Tiger Lily, Orange Lily or Fire Lily. A herbaceous perennial plant with underground bulbs. Belongs to the genus Liliums of the Liliaceae family. 3 year perennial. 60 cm. height. 7 cm. long. Bright yellow-orange with reddish-brown dots. April 10, 1839. Catalogue: 04101839-35-4512.

The notes were carefully written in a neat, masculine hand.

Flipping through several more papers, she found drawings of a horse, a butterfly, a violet, a snapdragon, a Oriental Poppy, a passion flower and a Lily of the Valley. All were rendered in that same artistic hand, each appearing so realistic that it astounded her, and underneath were written notes about the subject.

Replacing the papers as she had found them, she moved on to the large bookcase. *Flora Londinensis, A Specimen of the Botany of New Holland, English Botany, Flora Graeca...*

A quick glance at the rest of the shelves showed they were all botanical books so she moved on to a large, handcrafted filing cabinet. On top were bottles of…herbs, she thought. Opening a drawer, she found more dried plants carefully labeled and preserved in glass. Closing the drawer, she glanced around the room again noting that all the paintings on the walls were either of wildlife or of nature.

Apparently, Gregory's rumored obsession with plants had been accurate.

A soft knock sounded on the door. She jumped slightly before composing her features. "Come in."

The door opened to reveal a housemaid who looked to be in her early thirties. She gave a small curtsy. "Good morning, mum. Me name's Gladys, and housekeeper has asked me to attend you."

"Have you ever worked as a lady's maid before?"

"Yes, mum."

"Good." She gave her a friendly smile as she moved to the dressing table and sat down, gesturing to her hair as she did. "Maybe you'll be able to do something with this wild mess."

Gladys smiled back. "Yes, mum." She picked up Victoria's silver brush and slowly worked the tangles out of her hair. "Is there any particular style you would like, mum?"

"No, just something simple."

"Yes, mum." Gladys retrieved Victoria's hairpins from the nightstand and expertly twisted her hair up into a soft knot at the nape of her neck. After putting in the last pin, Gladys set the brush down. "I unpacked your valise, mum, but didn't find a gown."

"No gown?" Her mind raced. She had planned to pack her apricot day dress in the valise but with the rush to leave London…

She nearly groaned. She had accidentally packed the dress in one of her steamer trunks. Now, until the gown had been pressed, she had nothing to wear but the wrinkled traveling suit she had slept in. "In my green trunk, you'll find an apricot dress."

"I'll have it pressed in a jiffy, mum."

The door suddenly burst open, and Gregory rushed into the room carrying a large bird-of-paradise flower.

Her mouth dropped open in a decidedly unladylike manner.

Who was this disheveled stranger with the wild black hair? What had happened to the fashionably put together gentleman that she had married? There was no denying it was Gregory, but he looked nothing like he had in London. His loose white shirt remained unbuttoned at the top revealing a hint of his masculine chest and a few dark, springy hairs. The sleeves were rolled up to his elbows showing off his corded forearms. Simple brown pants were tucked into sturdy black boots, and he was liberally coated with mud from head to foot. He even had several smudges of mud on his face and streaked in his hair!

He stopped mid-step when he noticed her seated at the dressing table. "Victoria," he said in some surprise. "I didn't realize you were awake, or I would have knocked."

"That's quite alright."

Gladys unobtrusively slipped out the door as Gregory walked towards her holding out the flower excitedly. "Look, a strelitzia reginae. It's the best specimen I've ever seen around here."

"It's lovely."

She had to admit the flower *was* beautiful but certainly not anything to be *that* excited over.

"Yes, I must preserve it." He went over to the drawing table and placed the flower in a small jar of water. Sitting on the stool, he pulled out a sheet of paper.

She stood up and went to stand next to him, wanting to see what on earth he was doing. Gregory didn't seem to notice her as he leaned close to the flower and studied it intently, absently adjusting his spectacles as he did. Then he picked up a sharpened pencil and with a few sure strokes the flower seemed to come to life on the page. Astounded, her mouth gaped again as he quickly added on leaves and a stem. The entire process took less than three minutes, yet he'd produced the most lifelike drawing she had ever seen.

Finished with the flower, he began writing notes beneath it. With his attention occupied, she took the time to study him closer. The mud on his cheek, tousled hair and forehead scrunched in concentration made him look like a little boy.

A very appealing little boy.

She wanted to touch him, to establish some sort of connection and without any conscious thought reached out to smooth his windblown hair, enjoying the feel of the soft strands slipping through her fingers.

She froze when Gregory stopped writing and looked up at her. Dropping her hand, she took a step back. "I…I'm sorry. I didn't mean to interrupt your work."

He carefully set down his pencil and turned to face her. "Please don't apologize, Victoria. I'm the one who should be asking your forgiveness. In my excitement over the strelitzia reginae, I didn't even greet you properly."

He gently tugged her onto his lap and gave her a long, slow kiss. He remained gentle, just like he had on their wedding night, proving it hadn't been an aberration. Nor had she made him angry.

Relaxing, she curled her arms around his neck and kissed him back with all the ardor in her heart. Finally pulling away, breathless, he shot her a roguish grin. "Good morning, Mrs. Thornton…or should I say afternoon?"

She blushed. "I'm sorry. I don't usually sleep so late."

"There's no need to apologize. You were exhausted, and I have only myself to blame. I should have realized you would need to rest and arranged to stay in London, but it didn't even occur to me until after we had left."

"It is probably better this way. With all of the invitations, I doubt we would have any rest in London."

"You're probably right about that."

Gregory continued to hold her in his lap with apparently no thought of letting her go, causing a smile to rise. As comfortable as she felt right now, she could very happily stay there the rest of the day. She took a deep breath inhaling his masculine scent. He smelled so nice. Not perfumed like the men in London but fresh, like soap and earth and something uniquely Gregory. The mud still streaked across his face so she pulled her handkerchief out of her sleeve and started to rub it off. "You have a bit of dirt on your face."

When she finished, Gregory surprised her by bending down and claiming another kiss. "Thank you, Victoria." He stayed quiet a moment. "I suppose I should warn you of my interest in botany."

"I had heard you liked plants." Gregory didn't say anything, but a slight crease appeared on his brow. Finally, unable to stand not being able to tell what he thought, she reached up and slipped off his eyeglasses. At first, he looked surprised but as he studied her his face softened. "I can't tell what you're thinking when you have your spectacles on," she whispered suddenly breathless. She had forgotten just how beautiful he looked without his spectacles. Right now, however, his eyes looked troubled. "Is something wrong, Gregory?"

The silence stretched so long she didn't think he would answer.

"I can just imagine what the *ton* had to say about me," he finally said. Though he attempted a light tone, the slight darkening of his eyes revealed how much it bothered him.

Absently smoothing his collar, she tried to think of some way to put his mind at ease. "The *ton* is always gossiping about someone in order to make themselves feel more important. I've already realized that most of what they said is untrue, and as far as your interest in plants…there's nothing wrong with it if that's what makes you happy."

"And you don't think less of me for it?"

"Not at all."

He finally smiled and gave her another light kiss. "Thank you."

She rested her head against his shoulder. Think less of him? How could she think less of the most wonderful man she had ever met just because he happened to like flowers? An undeniably better hobby than what appealed to most of the men in her acquaintance. And to think of how the gossips had cut his reputation to shreds because of it. All the belittling stories they had told about Gregory…

And about her.

Her breath caught in her throat. The past two days she had completely forgotten about the rumors declaring her to be with child. Gregory had without a doubt heard the stories though he'd never asked her about it. But after his kindness and gentleness on their wedding night, she couldn't bear the thought that he might think she carried another man's child. She had to tell him the truth, but how could she explain without raising his ire?

"Speaking of gossip," she began casually rubbing her thumb against his hand where another streak of dirt had dried. It began to flake off. "I know the hastiness of our marriage started many unfounded rumors, and I wanted to assure you that...that the rumors about me..." Her face grew hot. "The rumors about my being with..."

"I know the rumors about you carrying a child are not true."

"You do?"

"Yes, I do. I must admit that I wondered about it at first. I couldn't imagine a man marrying his daughter off to a stranger so quickly just because of business. After meeting Rolfe, however, I realized he was doing just that. And after meeting you," his eyes softened as he looked at her. "I knew you were too innocent to have been with a man. I want you to know, though, that it wouldn't have mattered to me even if you had been with child."

Pain speared her heart like a lance. Wouldn't have mattered to him? Did he deem her of so little consequence that he wouldn't have cared if she'd been with another man? She ducked her head down against his shoulder to hide the hot tears that suddenly pricked her eyes.

"You were going to be my wife, and I knew I couldn't care for you properly if I held any past mistakes against you. So I dealt with the issue before coming to London." As his words sunk into her heart, she cautiously glanced back up at him. "I had already resolved to love you the way God commands a husband to love his wife, and if you were with child, to love the babe as well. I have to admit, though..." Gregory reached up and gently touched her face with work-roughened, dirt-smudged fingers. His voice came out slightly husky. "I am so glad that you saved yourself entirely for me."

His words, and the tenderness in his eyes, washed away the pain she had felt moments ago and left her feeling treasured beyond her wildest dreams. He would have cared, but he had already forgiven her before they had even met! She had never heard of anything like it before and didn't know quite how to respond so she grasped onto the first thought that came to her. "I didn't know God commanded a husband to love his wife."

"It's mentioned several times in the Bible, but perhaps the most explicit is in Ephesians. Why don't we start our devotions together by reading it?"

"If that is what you wish."

"I think it would be a most appropriate start to our marriage." Setting her back on her feet, he stood up and went over to his nightstand. He pulled a well-worn Bible out of the drawer before leading her over to the settee.

He sat next to her and started flipping through the pages, holding it only a few inches away from his nose. His eyeglasses! She still held them in her hand. "Gregory, do you need your spectacles?"

Looking up from the Bible, he smiled at her. "In a minute. I really don't need them for close reading." After a few more seconds, he found the place he looked for. "This is it. Ephesians 5:22–33. 'Wives, submit yourselves unto your own husbands, as unto the Lord…'"

At the familiar verse, Victoria settled back against the settee and concentrated on the cadence of Gregory's smooth voice. Back home Rector Pitt had often expounded on a wife's duty to her husband. As the head of the household the husband must rule his wife, the weaker vessel, with an iron hand; as such, a wife owed her husband fear, reverence and unquestioning obedience. And she would do it. She would submit to Gregory's authority in every aspect of their life.

"Husbands, love your wives, even as Christ also loved the church, and gave Himself for it…"

Amazement filled her as Gregory continued reading. She had never heard any of this before! The commands God laid out for husbands seemed so much harder than the ones He had given to wives and was completely opposite of everything she had ever been taught. How could this be?

He finished the passage then closed the Bible and set it on the table. Getting up, he knelt in front of her and gently took her hands in his. The earnestness in his eyes took her breath away.

"Victoria. I'm far from perfect. I can't promise that I won't ever be frustrated or angry, but I want you to know that I will do my utmost to live up to these verses. I will do my best to love you as Christ loved the church, to cherish and nourish you as I would my own body, and to always treat you with the respect and honor you deserve. With God's help, I will try to be a wise, spiritual leader, and when we have children, I will endeavor to be a kind and loving father, raising them up to fear and love God."

By the time he finished, tears streamed down her cheeks, and this time she did nothing to hide them. She had never, ever heard anything so wonderful.

"Ah, Victoria." He reached up and gently wiped the wetness from her cheeks. "Will you pray with me?"

Nodding, she slid from the settee and knelt

down beside him. Still holding her hands, Gregory bowed his head and closed his eyes. She followed suit. "Jesus, Victoria and I come to You right now to commit our marriage into Your Hands."

She jerked slightly. How could he speak so familiarly with God? Even Rector Pitt always used the Book of Common Prayer during church.

"We know that to make this marriage work we must put You first and foremost in our lives. Show us how to build a marriage that glorifies You and that lasts forever. Thank You, Father, for Victoria. For the gift You have given me in her. Help me to care for her and to love her as You would have me to do. Teach me how to be a Godly husband."

Just then, her stomach let out a loud, long, growling rumble. Mortification burned her face. She couldn't even look at Gregory. She wanted nothing more than to melt through the floor and disappear.

After a second, he chuckled. "Alright, Lord, I'll take the hint and feed my wife! We ask these things in the Name of Jesus, Amen."

"I am so sorry," she said quickly to the floor still too embarrassed to look at him.

Gregory gently lifted her chin and forced her to meet his gaze. His eyes sparkled with amusement. "Don't be," he told her before giving her a quick kiss. "Come on, we'd better procure you something to eat." Standing up, he helped her to her feet. "Do you see my spectacles anywhere?"

"Oh!" She looked around frantically. They had been in her hand when they sat down on the settee...

She nearly wilted with relief when she spied them nestled between two cushions. Picking them up, she handed them to Gregory. "Here they are."

"Thank you." He slipped them back on just as a knock sounded on the door. "Come in."

The door opened, and Gladys slipped into the room carrying Victoria's apricot dress. "Your gown is ready, mum."

"Thank you." She hesitated before glancing shyly up at Gregory.

He quickly understood her unspoken request. "I'll wait for you out in the hall."

After the door closed behind him, she allowed Gladys to help her dress. Over and over, her mind kept replaying Gregory's words and the prayer that followed as she stored them away in her heart. He might not have mastered the charming flattery and flowery phrases used by most of the *ton,* but the words that fell from his lips were infinitely more beautiful and precious.

Yet, he had confirmed what she had always known.

No man could always be so kind.

Once finished dressing, she opened the door and stepped out into the hall. Turning from the window, Gregory gave her a smile that made her heart pound.

By his own admission there would be times that he would grow angry with her, but as he gently pulled her arm through his and led her to the kitchen, pointing out the various rooms along the way, she knew she would gladly endure any punishment he meted out during his fits of rage if he could but remain this thoughtful and tender in-between times.

Something she didn't even dare to hope for.

After a light but filling repast, Gregory gave her a tour of the central wing of Thornton Hall. The sheer size of the manor house astounded Victoria who had never been outside of London. Rolfe always turned down the occasional invitation for a weekend getaway to a country estate so she didn't know if the palatial home was common for the landed gentry or not.

Afterwards, he showed her the grounds. The vast panorama nearly overwhelmed her senses as she feasted her eyes. Gently rolling hills spread as far as she could see, and every acre belonged to the Thornton family. On the east side of the estate, he pointed out where a forest began explaining that John had left it intact for his own private hunting preserve. The ocean lay only a couple of miles to the south causing a slightly salty smell to linger in the air. Invigorating.

Eventually, Gregory led her to the large stables. "Do you enjoy riding?"

"Very much. In fact, riding is one of my favorite activities."

"Mine, too."

Gregory opened one of the stable doors and ushered Victoria inside. Her eyes slowly adjusted to the dimness as the scent of horseflesh and hay assaulted her nose. The cavernous room echoed with the sound of horses. They could easily have housed up to two hundred, but only a few dozen stalls were occupied. The largest man she had ever seen pushed a full wheelbarrow down one of the long aisles towards them. He stood nearly seven feet tall with bulging muscles rippling underneath a simple white shirt stained gray and streaked with grime. Probably in his forties as a sprinkling of gray dusted his shaggy brown hair.

She instinctively took a step nearer to Gregory as the imposing man drew closer.

He stopped in front of them and tilted his head respectfully. "Afternoon, Mr. Gregory."

"Good afternoon, Horace. May I present my wife, Victoria?"

Horace gave her another nod of his huge head and smiled broadly, revealing a couple missing teeth. "Miss Victoria."

She gave him what she hoped passed for a smile trying to hide the way her knees knocked against each other.

"Horace is our stablemaster and blacksmith," Gregory explained. Turning back to Horace, he asked a question about one of the stallions that had been limping. They discussed it for several minutes while she tried not to let the giant intimidate her or smell too deeply of the sweaty odor wafting from him. It mixed with the smell of the manure filling the wheelbarrow making her lightheaded. Discreetly, she pulled a perfumed lace-edged handkerchief out of her sleeve and dabbed at her nose. The pleasing scent of violets filled her nostrils. Much more enjoyable.

Horace finally picked the wheelbarrow back up and strode through the door. Giving Victoria a smile, Gregory led her past rows of stalls before stopping in front of a beautiful chestnut stallion. "This is Liberty," he said with an unmistakable note of pride in his voice. "I raised him from a colt."

"He's beautiful." She reached out a cautious hand. Liberty shook his head and nickered before settling down and allowing her to stroke his soft nose. A small brass plate with *Liberty* engraved in swirling script had been mounted on the stall door.

A white head suddenly poked over the dividing wall of the stall and soft brown eyes regarded her.

She gasped and walked over to the beautiful solid white mare. "Oh, how exquisite!" Gently, she stroked her soft forehead. The mare extended her head over the stall door inviting her to rub her neck. With a laugh, she complied. The mare nuzzled her, looking for a treat. "Sorry, girl. I didn't bring any sugar with me."

"Here," Gregory dug around in his pockets before pulling out a lump of sugar and handing it to her. She fed it to the mare. "Do you like her?"

"Oh, yes."

"I hoped you would." She glanced at him. He suddenly looked shy and actually scuffed the toe of his boot against the wooden floor like a schoolboy. "When Father told me about our engagement, I picked her out of our herd and taught her to accept a sidesaddle in hopes you would enjoy riding with me. She's yours, Victoria."

"Mine?"

He nodded.

"Oh, Gregory. Thank you. Thank you!" Unable to contain her excitement, she lunged into his arms and wrapped her own tight around him. "No one has ever given me such a wonderful gift before!"

He laughed and hugged her back. "You're welcome. I'm just glad you like her."

For a moment, she just enjoyed the embrace, but sudden embarrassment caused her to pull back. Had she really just flung herself into his arms? Thankfully, Gregory didn't seem to notice anything amiss as he turned his attention back to the mare. "What are you going to name her?"

"Doesn't she have a name?"

"No." He slipped his arm around her waist and gently pulled her back against his side, making it difficult for her to concentrate on his words. "I thought I would let you do the honors."

"Well, let's see…she's such a pure white…do you think we could call her Daisy?"

"If that is your wish."

She considered it a moment before nodding. "Yes. Her color reminds me of the snowy petals on a daisy."

"Then Daisy it shall be. I'll have Horace make her a nameplate."

"Thank you, Gregory."

He bent and brushed a kiss on her temple. "You're welcome. Now, would you like to see my garden?"

"Of course." She once again slipped her arm through his as he led her to the rear of the house. At the massive, sweeping vista her mouth fell open. "Oh, Gregory, it's beautiful!"

A pleased look crossed his face. "Thank you," he said modestly as he led her in. She marveled over the profusion of flowers, so many different kinds and colors and sizes, arranged in a pleasing array.

"I've never seen anything like it!" With the limited space in London, the *le bon ton* only focused on rose gardens, but this…this was absolutely magnificent!

They spent over an hour meandering through the artistically laid out walkways, yet they hardly saw even half of the garden. She enjoyed every moment until a sudden whiff of roses wafted her way. Her feet stopped walking as dread writhed through her.

Directly ahead of them lay the large rose section, and suddenly, she was back in her own garden trapped in Paxton's ruthless embrace. She could feel his harsh hands and lips on her.

Mercilessly taking. Hurting. Bruising.

Closing her eyes, she shuddered.

Gregory stopped walking and looked at her. "Are you alright, Victoria?"

"I…I'm sorry, Gregory, but I suddenly feel faint," she whispered truthfully. With her stomach heaving, black dots dancing in front of her eyes and trembling from head to toe, she felt she could swoon on the spot.

He immediately put his arm around her and began helping her back to the house. "Your face is as white as a sheet. I should not have kept you out here so long. You must still be exhausted."

The minute they were out of sight of the roses, Victoria could breathe again. Strength returned to her shaking limbs, and her stomach settled down to normal as they neared the house. "I was enjoying it immensely. The heat must have overcome me for a moment, but I feel much better now."

He studied her intently. "Your color is better, but it still might be prudent for you to rest until dinner."

Feeling suddenly weary, she acquiesced. "Alright."

Gregory helped her to their room and onto the bed. Wetting a washcloth in cold water, he knelt down beside her and gently wiped her face. Unaccustomed to such concern, she nevertheless found his tender ministrations quite welcome.

"Are you feeling better?"

"I'm fine now. Truly."

Setting the washcloth aside, Gregory picked up her hand and placed a gentle kiss on her palm causing tiny shivers to radiate up her arm. "You scared me, Victoria. I don't think I've ever seen anyone turn so white."

"I'm sorry. I really do feel much better now. You go on back to your work and don't worry about me. I'll just rest here for a few minutes until dinner."

"If you're sure. I'll be at my desk if you need anything."

She nodded dumbly. Interrupt him while he worked? Never!

Gregory placed another kiss on her palm before standing up and going to his drawing table. Curling on her side, she watched him as he finished his notes on the flower he had sketched earlier and carefully pressed the beautiful blossom between two pieces of glass. She took pleasure in just watching him work…and in the frequent looks of concern he sent her way.

If she wasn't careful, she could become very accustomed to his tender care.

Chapter 6

A month later, Victoria gazed out the window of the blue salon. Her favorite room because of the sweeping vista it had of the gardens. Below her, Gregory rolled a wheelbarrow of dirt down one of the pathways. He stopped in front of a new flower bed and emptied it. Probably for the new Japanese fuchsia cuttings he had received from Veitch Nurseries early that morning. He had been so excited when the messenger interrupted their breakfast that he hadn't even finished eating but rushed upstairs to examine them. An hour later, he had come back carrying the small fragile sticks like a trophy and took the time to show them to her before going outside to prepare a spot in the garden. She rested her fingertips on the cool glass, longing to be outside with him.

Sighing, she turned back to the elegantly appointed salon.

Her prison.

She sat on the blue divan and picked up her needle to continue working on her embroidery. The move to the country had turned her life completely upside down but most of the changes had been nice ones. So far, her married life had proven to be quite pleasant. She had been very careful not to anger Gregory, and in return, he had remained gentle and tender with her. The long, quiet days of country living suited her. She didn't miss London's parties or the backstabbing friendships and had quickly grown used to going to bed early and getting up even earlier. Yet, one thing kept her from being happy.

The insidious loneliness.

John and Harriet had arrived at Thornton Hall a week after she and Gregory had, yet she rarely saw them. With such a massive dwelling, it became easy to miss someone, even the myriad of servants, unless one rang for them. And Gregory spent most of the day outside puttering around with his plants. Then he would return to their bedchamber and catalogue his findings a few hours before bedtime. For the last few days, she had taken to joining him there, either sewing or reading quietly so as to not disrupt his work. To her relief, he had accepted her intrusion without complaint, and she just enjoyed the time in his presence.

The loneliness wouldn't be so invasive if she had something to occupy her time with besides embroidery, but the hours her governess had spent training her how to manage a household had come to naught. Harriet ran Thornton Hall with a tighter hand than a sea captain did his ship, and she had informed her quite bluntly that she did not like any interference.

Victoria changed her thread to a light blue and started a flower petal. The few times Gregory sought her out were the only breaks in the monotonous routine, and they had become the highlights of her days.

Just then, the clock on the mantle chimed the noon hour. She immediately put her embroidery aside and stood up. Gregory would be washing up outside, and she wanted to be at the table to greet him when he came in. Making her way to the dining room, she only had to wait a few seconds before she saw him striding down the hall his hair still damp from the washbasin.

And still wild from running his hands through it all morning. She hid a smile, having grown used to his nearly constant state of dishevelment something the *ton* would never tolerate. Yet, it somehow suited Gregory.

He looked up, and a smile instantly lit his face as if he were actually glad to see her. As had become his custom, he dropped a quick kiss on her lips before pulling out her chair. Heart pounding and lips tingling, she demurely took her seat, carefully hiding the fact that she waited all day for those smiles and brief kisses. She sat still while Gregory took his own seat then bowed her head as he offered a blessing for the food. Another tradition she had grown to enjoy.

When he said "amen" and raised his head, a maid carried in the first course, a creamy celery soup. "Thank you," he said when she set the bowl in front of him.

"You're welcome, sir." Smiling, she served Victoria before unobtrusively slipping back into the butler's pantry.

Gregory never took the servant's for granted or thought himself above them as everyone else in her acquaintance did. In return, they fairly doted on him often going out of their way to make sure he had everything he needed.

She had never seen anything like it.

Gregory looked at her as she dipped her spoon into the soup. "How was your morning?"

I was lonely and missed you.

She pushed aside the longing in her heart and pasted on a bright smile. "Wonderful. I actually accomplished quite a bit on my tapestry."

"I'm glad you're enjoying it so much."

Not as much as I would enjoy being with you.

Once again, Victoria pushed aside her true feelings. "Yes, it is quite exciting to see the project coming together. How has your day been?"

"Actually, I'm making better progress than I had hoped." Excitement shone on his face as he launched into an explanation of his attempts to create a hybrid between the common cowslip and the silver-edged primrose. She listened attentively having learned that her husband, usually a quiet man, could talk for hours about his work in the garden.

At first, she had encouraged him to talk about his hobby because she liked to hear the low, soothing timbre of his voice as he spoke to her. After her father's severity, she couldn't seem to get enough of the comfort it brought. As she listened, however, she discovered a liking for the subject of botany and wished she could study it more in depth. The little she learned from Gregory's conversations merely whetted her appetite.

One day last week she had even started going through his large portfolio, enjoying reading his notes and amazed at how much he knew. Later that same afternoon, though, he had been unable to find one of his specimens because she had accidentally placed it in the wrong drawer.

He had hunted for over thirty minutes muttering to himself the whole time and then wondering how it had gotten in the wrong place. Thankfully, he hadn't suspected her of tampering with it, but she hadn't dared to go through the portfolio again.

"We should have a new flower by the end of the week. Then I'll know for sure whether I was able to create the lavender cowslips I wanted or just a yellow primrose."

She laughed with him. "I'm sure whichever one it turns out to be, it will be beautiful."

Gregory stayed silent a moment before giving a self-deprecating chuckle. "Here I am, going on and on about my flowers during the entire meal. You must find me a most uninteresting conversationalist."

"Not at all. In fact, I find your work quite fascinating."

"Really? Then perhaps one day you might want to join me in the garden, and I can show you exactly what I'm doing."

"We'll see," she replied lightly and noncommittally. He often invited her to join him in the garden, but she always declined, knowing that a man didn't really want a woman around disturbing him as he worked. If she began inserting herself into his business, he would quickly grow frustrated and annoyed at her. She just felt blessed to be able to unobtrusively join him when he worked in their room.

Gregory nodded as he stood and then pulled out her chair. The meals always passed by too quickly. Now, several hours of loneliness stretched out before her until they left for their afternoon ride.

"I'd like to take our ride a bit early today," he said as if reading her mind. "The weather is cool now, but it looks like it will become quite hot by mid-afternoon. Would you care to go now instead of waiting until later?"

Would she care to prolong their time together? Did he even have to ask? "That sounds lovely. Just let me change into my riding habit."

"I'll have the horses saddled and meet you at the front of the house."

"Alright." She walked sedately towards the stairs, but the minute Gregory disappeared down the hall, she raced up them to their room. Ringing for Gladys, she didn't wait but rushed into the changing room to hunt for her royal blue riding habit. Gregory had mentioned one day that he liked that color blue. It was the closest he had ever come to complimenting her looks so she tried to wear it as often as possible.

Where could it be? She found her black and red riding habit. Several day dresses. The rose-colored ball gown…

A flash of blue caught her eye. She practically dove into the back of the closet tossing shirtwaists and cloaks aside in her haste. Finally, her hand fell on the material, and she followed it up to the hanger.

Success!

Gladys walked into the room just as she emerged triumphantly from the changing room carrying the gown. "You rang, mum?"

"Yes. Please help me change."

Victoria fidgeted and kept an eye on the clock as Gladys tediously unhooked the long row of tiny buttons on the back of her dress. A fashionable style, but it hardly lent itself to hurrying. Once in her riding habit, she barely gave Gladys enough time to straighten her hair before pinning on her tall black top hat with the matching veil and flying back down the stairs. Her shoes slapped against the marble and echoed through the foyer until she skidded to a halt by the front door. Stopping with her hand on the knob, she took a deep breath to compose herself and walked calmly outside.

Gregory already waited for her with Liberty and Daisy. She gave him a demure smile. "I hope I didn't keep you waiting long."

"Not at all."

His hands wrapped around her waist causing delicious tingles to quiver in her stomach as he gently lifted her up into the saddle. Inordinately pleased that he always helped her in and out of the saddle that way instead of the more traditional way of lifting her up by lacing his fingers together and allowing her to step on his hands, she tried to suppress her smile as she modestly arranged her skirts around her ankles.

Gregory swung up onto Liberty as she picked up the reins. "Where are we riding today?"

He smiled at her. "It's a surprise."

Victoria smiled back as they cantered out of the yard. Everyday he managed to show her some new part of the vast estate though he almost always ended their rides by swinging down to the beach for their return to the house. She didn't mind because she found the endless expanse of water awe-inspiring. It never looked the same, and the roar of the waves pounding towards the shore made her realize just how small and insignificant she really was. Yet, as Gregory had read in the Bible a few days ago, the God Who had created such magnificence cared enough about her to know even the number of hairs on her head.

The thought filled her with wonder.

Today, Gregory took a path that led them through the forest. The trail quickly narrowed, and they were forced to ride single file, preventing any conversation. Nearly an hour into their ride, he stopped in a small copse of trees and dismounted. "We'll have walk the rest of the way on foot."

"Oh." She glanced around but only saw rocks and dense trees. Where was the "surprise"?

Gregory tied the horses to a small sapling before lifting her down. For a moment after setting her on her feet, he continued to hold her, his large hands easily spanning her waist. She glanced up at him, her heart pounding at the soft look on his face.

A look she was beginning to recognize.

She loved it when Gregory got that look.

"I think…" his voice came out a husky whisper as he reached up and smoothed a piece of windblown hair from her cheek. "I think you'll really like this spot."

"I…I think so, too."

Even if it ended up being nothing more than a shallow cave.

Smiling, he released her waist but clasped her hand as he led her up a barely discernible trail. Parts of it were steep, and she panted for breath after only a few minutes. Her legs burned even though Gregory looked as fresh as ever.

The way grew even more rocky and treacherous. Putting his arm around her, he helped her over a downed tree limb. "We're almost there. Just around that bend."

She looked up at the ever vertical rocky trail. No wonder he said the horses couldn't make it. She didn't even know if *she* could make it, but they were only a few yards from the bend. Surely she could last that long. Gregory continued to help her at one point even picking her up and swinging her over the pebbles of a particularly loose, slippery section.

By the time they reached the top and level ground, sweat trickled down her face causing the loose wispy strands of her hair to plaster against her cheeks and neck. Her chest heaved as she gulped in air. By the amount of heat in her face, she probably looked like an overripe tomato.

Thankfully, Gregory kept his arm around her waist helping to support her as he led her through the trees. She leaned heavily on him as she slowly caught her breath. Reaching up, she pushed the annoying strings of hair off her face leaving a slimy, wet trail in their wake. The trees started thinning, and suddenly, they stepped into a small clearing dappled in sunlight.

She gasped.

Directly ahead, a waterfall fell nearly fifty feet into a small, foaming pool. An iridescent rainbow arced through the glittering water. "It's beautiful," she breathed the hard climb already forgotten.

Gregory smiled and helped her up onto a large rock that over-looked the pool. Sitting down, they watched the rushing water as a fine mist rose up around them. She sighed again and scooted a little closer to Gregory. He took the hint and wrapped his arm around her letting her lean back against his chest. Closing her eyes, she focused on the feel of the cool mist on her face and on Gregory's warmth behind her. She could be happy staying here, just like this, forever. *Thank You, Jesus.*

A small smile crossed her face. Praying had slowly become more natural to her. Near the beginning of their marriage, Gregory had invited her to pray during their devotions whenever she wanted. He always paused a moment before saying amen giving her a chance to speak even though she had yet gathered the courage to pray out loud. But, as Gregory taught her more about God, she had found herself praying silently more and more often.

Opening her eyes, she turned to Gregory, but he wasn't watching the waterfall. Instead, he watched her with a soft smile on his face. Mist had collected on his spectacles. She reached up and pulled them off intending to clean them. He responded by leaning forward and kissing her. Eyeglasses forgotten in her lap, Victoria clung to him as she kissed him back.

It still amazed her how this man could make her feel so special and cherished…and alive. When Gregory kissed her, she forgot all the reasons why she should be wary and careful around him.

His arms tightened pulling her close against him, and time vanished as she lost herself in the wonder of his embrace.

Sometime later, he pulled slightly away though he rested his forehead against hers. His breathlessness matched her own. His heart pounded beneath her palm causing hers to speed up in response. "We had better return," he murmured, but he made no move to leave.

Feeling safe and languid resting in his strong arms, she reached up and traced her fingers along his strong jaw. He captured her hand with his, pressing it fully against his face. With a soft groan, he turned his head and kissed her palm.

Gregory had never told Victoria what he thought about her looks, whether he found her beautiful or plain, leaving her wondering about it most of the time. Wondering what he thought about her; wondering if she pleased him. But then there were a few times, like right now, when the smoldering look in his eyes made her feel like the most beautiful, desirable woman that had ever lived.

Moving her other hand to the back of his head, she urged him closer. Delight filled her at how little urging it took before he once again captured her mouth with his.

Several minutes later, he pulled away again, for real this time. "We really do have to leave," he said as he set her slightly away from him. "If we wait any longer, the sun will be beaming mercilessly, and the ride home will be miserable."

"We could wait until the sun sets to ride home," she said with unaccustomed boldness.

For a moment, Gregory's eyes darkened with molten desire, and he seemed to be seriously contemplating doing just that. Delicious shivers coursed through her. She had only seen that look a handful of times since their wedding, but oh, how wonderful it made her feel! Then, he sighed and shook his head, his eyes going back to their normal hue. "I didn't bring my pistol with me, and too many animals come out at night for it to be safe."

Her heart fell. One thing she had learned about Gregory in the past month, he was practical to a fault. He would never do anything that he thought might endanger them.

Gregory placed a finger on her chin, urging her to look at him. When she did, he gave her a mischievous grin, his eyes sparkling. "But I'll be sure to bring my pistol from now on." He landed a quick kiss on her surprised mouth before scooting off the rock.

A silly grin spread across her face. He had actually wanted to stay with her! Picking up his spectacles, she accepted his help down from the rock.

"Do you have my spectacles?"

Playful, she smiled impishly up at him. "Yes, but you'll have to catch me to get them!"

She darted off before he could respond. With a surprised laugh, he came after her. As she ran through the trees, the thud of Gregory's boots grew closer and closer until he seemed to be right on top of her. Giggling, she looked over her shoulder and saw him a mere step behind.

The toe of her boot hit a tree root.

She flew towards the rocky ground.

"Victoria!"

Gregory lunged, catching her in midair and twisting so that he took the brunt of the fall.

The thud as they landed still jarred her bones even cushioned against Gregory's chest as she was. For a moment she lay there stunned and shaky. Her heart pounded erratically in her chest as she gulped in a breath. "A...are you alright?"

When he didn't respond, she looked up. Gregory's eyes were closed, and he seemed to be having trouble breathing.

"Gregory!" She started to clamber towards his face.

His arms tightened around her, holding her still. "I...I'm fine," he finally said softly. After a few more seconds, he opened his eyes and gave her a ghost of a smile. "Really. It just...knocked the wind from me."

She slumped against him muscles weak. For a moment, she had thought he had been seriously injured. Opening her eyes again, she gasped. Gregory's eyeglasses had smashed on a rock a few feet away. The mangled wire frame twisted among the glittering shards of glass from the shattered lenses.

"Oh, no." She reached over and picked up the uselessly bent wire. "Your spectacles are broken. I'm so sorry, Gregory. I shouldn't have been playing like that. I'm so, so sorry." She could scarcely breathe as panic squeezed her insides. Her hands started trembling.

What had she done?

"Victoria, it's okay."

She didn't even hear him. "I'm sorry. It's all my fault."

"Victoria…"

"It won't happen again. I promise."

"It's okay."

"I'm so sorry. I'll never touch your eyeglasses again. I promise."

"Don't you dare promise such a thing!"

The sudden sternness in Gregory's voice startled her into silence. "Don't you dare promise that," he said again in a softer tone. He tilted her face towards his and smiled at her. "I've grown rather fond of having you pull my spectacles off."

For a moment, she stared at him, speechless. It had become her habit at night once Gregory finished his work and turned his attention to her. She had come to think of it as their special thing, but she hadn't been sure if he liked it or not. "I broke them," she finally said in a small voice.

"It's alright. I have an extra pair at home. But, even if I didn't, it would be alright."

"You aren't mad at me?"

"Of course not."

"But I broke your eyeglasses," she repeated, unable to believe that such a travesty could go unpunished.

"Victoria," Gregory pulled her closer. "You can break my eyeglasses anytime you want. We can even buy a hundred pair of spectacles and line them all up so you can break them all one at a time."

She giggled despite the fear still twisting her insides into knots.

"In fact, I'll just buy a new pair for everyday of the year, and at the end of each day, we'll hold an eyeglasses breaking ceremony with you doing the honors. I think it would be a great addition to our evening devotions. I'll even supply you with a hammer."

By this time, she laughed outright. "Gregory, that's ridiculous," she finally managed to gasp out.

"Maybe," he smiled at her again. "But I want you to realize what a small thing it really is. I've broken more spectacles through the years than I can count. That's why I always keep an extra pair on hand."

Victoria instantly sobered. "I really am sorry."

"There's no need to be. It was an accident, and accidents happen."

She stared at him in wonder at his calm acceptance. Finally remembering that she still laid on top of him, pinning him to the ground, she rolled off sitting up as she did so. Gregory sat up more slowly wincing slightly and rubbing his back. He pulled himself to his feet before reaching down and helping her to stand. She couldn't bear the careful way he moved obviously hurting worse than he let on. "Are you sure you're alright?"

"I'm fine. Just a little bruised." He looked around them, squinting at the trees as he turned a slow circle. She felt even more terrible watching him try to see. "Do you remember the way to the trail?

"Yes."

He smiled at her. "Then lead on because all the trees are looking the same to me."

Feeling worse than ever, she started walking towards the trail, looking back frequently to make sure Gregory stayed with her. He followed her, completely at ease, confident that she would lead them to the horses.

That confidence boosted her. He actually trusted her!

Reaching the top of the rocky ascent, she looked down the steep, slippery slope. A wave of dizziness hit, leaving her lightheaded. She pushed it aside and took a deep breath. "We're about to start down the steep, rocky part. Be careful."

"I will be."

Taking another deep breath, she started down. She stepped carefully, but without Gregory to lean on, she had to use her hands to hold onto the rocks and bushes to steady herself. Reaching the place that he had swung her over earlier, she walked even slower, concentrating on where she placed each foot. Tiny pebbles and rocks shifted under her shoes with each step, threatening to send her flying. She sighed in relief when she reached more sturdy ground and turned to watch Gregory. He, too, walked slowly and carefully, his forehead scrunched up as his eyes squinted towards the ground, but he obviously couldn't see the path.

He stepped on a loose rock slightly larger than the rest. It went sliding out from under him. She gasped as he started skidding, unable to stop, heading straight for her!

Gregory slammed into her his arms going around her waist in a bear hug as they tilted dangerously towards the slope. Victoria's heart pounded, sure they were going to fall over and tumble down the trail, but somehow, after a few seconds, he managed to right them.

"Gregory! Are you…"

"I'm fine," he told her softly before she could even ask. "Are you alright?"

"Y…yes. I just feel terrible about your spectacles."

"Hey, I thought we settled that. Besides, how do you know I didn't slip just to have an excuse to hold you?" He waggled his eyebrows.

Once again, his silliness made her giggle. This was a side of her husband she had never seen before. "Well, then, hold on tight, sir, and we just might make it down this hill."

"Gladly."

He kept his arm around her, and they steadied each other as they finished making their way to the horses. Gently, he lifted her onto Daisy before swinging up onto Liberty. "Do you think you can find the way home?"

Victoria straightened in the saddle hoping to appear confident. "Yes."

He smiled. "Lead the way, then."

Taking another deep breath, she clucked to Daisy and set off at a walk down the trail praying the entire way that her memory would not fail her.

Chapter 7

Three days later, Victoria once again stood by the window in the blue salon watching Gregory work in the garden below. The temptation to rush out there and join him in the rare morning sunshine filled her so strongly she could taste it. He had repeated his invitation at breakfast. He had also asked, as he had several times since they were married, if she had thought of anything else that she wanted them to do together. She declined as always, sending him out to the garden where he really wanted to be.

But maybe…maybe she *could* join him this once especially if she found a way not to intrude on his work. After all, he had asked her to.

Repeatedly.

Excitement thrummed through her veins. Harriet always had fresh flowers about. If she went out to pick some, and just *happened* to wander into the same area as Gregory, surely he couldn't object.

But could she really execute such a daring plan?

Glancing outside once again, she worried her lower lip. Gregory worked in the farthest corner away from the roses, clinching her decision. Running to their room, she dug around in the changing room until she found a basket and a pair of scissors. Taking a deep breath for courage, she headed out the back door.

On his knees, Gregory absently cut the fading blossoms off the peonies. As had been happening more and more often over the last month, his mind did not stay on his work but strayed to Victoria…

And their relationship.

He honestly didn't know quite what to think about it. She always responded eagerly to his kisses, yet she rarely touched him first, just a light hand on his shoulder or perhaps smoothing his wild hair. At night, she snuggled close to him, and a couple of times she had even murmured his name in her sleep. She seemed to enjoy the time they spent together, but despite all of that she still did not want to spend any more time with him during the day than she had to. The only time she had even hinted at a desire to prolong their ride was at the waterfall a few days ago.

Gregory had been carrying his pistol ever since, but she had reverted back to being eager to return home.

He moved on to the next plant. For the past week, she *had* been joining him in their room when he worked on his catalogue though she didn't ever speak. She could read or sew in any room of the house, yet she chose the room where he worked. He tried to find encouragement in that, but in truth, he felt discouraged.

Very discouraged.

Victoria seemed interested in horticulture, asking him intelligent questions which showed she really listened when he talked, yet she had refused to step foot in the garden since the first day they had arrived. Countless times he had asked her what else she might want to do together, but she always sent him on his way to the garden.

Alone.

Just like this morning.

Sometimes he thought she was relieved to have him gone. But what else could he expect? Victoria was young and vibrant and beautiful. He often felt old and ugly and boring.

Just like everyone always said.

Botany was the only subject on which he could converse at any length, and most people could only talk about that for a few minutes until their eyes started to glaze over. Besides which, she must find country life quiet and dull after the excitement and glamour of living in London where daily activities and nightly parties abounded.

She also didn't seem to be any closer to the Lord than when he had first met her. Not once had she prayed during their devotions although he consistently gave her the opportunity to do so.

The thought humbled him. His discouragement was so petty when compared to her walk with the Lord. *I'm sorry, Jesus. You know I'm confused and a little hurt, but that's not really what's important here. You know Victoria's heart. She needs You desperately. I think she is seeking because she seems so interested during our devotions. I know it doesn't really matter if she ever comes to care for me or even want to spend time with me, but it does matter that she comes to care for You. Let her want to spend time with You. Soften her heart, God. Woo her to Yourself with Your love...*

He continued to pray as he worked his way down the line of bushes, but eventually his mind drifted again. Back to the day at the waterfall. When she had broken his spectacles, she had been so abject in her apology, staring at him with her blue eyes so big they seemed to swallow her face. He didn't know what, exactly, she had expected him to do. Rant and rave, maybe. He didn't know why. It had just been an accident, and he had already ordered a backup pair, which had arrived in the post that morning.

Scrubbing a hand through his hair, he sighed before bending back over the flowers. Most of the time, Victoria appeared completely calm and confident, yet hints of her vulnerability sometimes peeked through her armor, like at the waterfall. He still didn't know what had happened to hurt her so deeply. She was so good at hiding her true feelings; could he really trust the emotions she let him see?

A soft rustling broke into his thoughts. He glanced up and nearly fell into the bush. Victoria stood shyly a few feet away, carrying a basket. Just the sight of his wife lifted his heart, and a silly grin slid across his face. It happened every time he saw her. It probably made him look like a buffoon, but he couldn't help it. Brushing the dirt off of his hands, he walked towards her. She held up the basket. "I...I thought I would pick some flowers for our room...If that's alright?"

Gregory frowned. Why did she ask that so timidly? As if he would deny her a few flowers?

Her eyes widened, and the uncertainty in their blue depths nearly broke his heart. Wrapping his arms around her, he pulled her the last couple of steps to him and kissed her, trying to pour all of his caring into her. Raising her arms, she wrapped them around his neck as she stood on tiptoe and kissed him back. The basket bumped against his shoulder awkwardly, but he didn't care.

He finally pulled away before he lost his head completely. Her eyes were closed, and a contented smile graced her face. As she slowly blinked her eyes opened, the dreamy look in them caused his heart to flip. When she looked at him like that, he knew she had to care for him a little bit even if she hadn't admitted it yet. He cleared his throat, but his voice still came out slightly husky. "You can pick every flower in the garden if you want to."

She smiled at him before stepping out of his arms. "Thank you, Gregory."

Walking a few feet away, she stopped in front of the carnations and bent to snip off a red bloom. He went back to pruning his peonies. The soft sound of her humming distracted him, and he had to force himself to concentrate before he hacked off the entire plant.

They worked like that for nearly an hour. Near each other, but not speaking. Gregory kept casting about in his mind, trying to find something intelligent to say, but he couldn't think of anything. Why did he have to be so shy? He didn't want to always be so quiet, but how could you talk when nothing came into your mind to say?

Finished with the peonies, he walked over to check on his hybrid. Several small buds had just begun to form and would probably open up within a day or two.

Victoria lingered a few feet away. He turned to her, noticing that she had filled her basket to overflowing. She would probably disappear into the house to work on her tapestry.

Leaving him alone once again.

"Is that your hybrid?"

"Yes. It should bloom in a couple of days. Would you like to see it?" He held out his hand, hoping against hope that she would say yes.

She hesitated for a moment, causing his spirit to sag. Finally, she set her basket down, walked over and took his hand. He couldn't stop his smile as she knelt down next to him, and he eagerly showed her the small plant.

She reached out and touched one of the hard, tiny green buds. "I can't tell what color it's going to be, yet."

"No, but we should be able to by tomorrow. Maybe even tonight."

"That will be wonderful. I don't know how you do it."

"I could teach you."

Victoria glanced at him, and for a split second, what looked like fear flashed across her eyes. "I wouldn't want to impose."

"You wouldn't be. I would love to have someone to teach. I've just never found anyone who seemed interested before."

Did he sound as pathetically eager to her as he did to himself?

She worried her lower lip and cast a longing look at the flower before glancing back up at him. "Are you sure I wouldn't be in the way?"

"You could never be in the way."

"I...I would like to learn."

Gregory fought to keep from dancing a jig across the garden. "Alright. I planned to prune the blue bugle next. Let me grab another pruning shear from the shed for you." He jumped up and started down the pathway before suddenly turning back around. "Don't go away while I'm gone."

Victoria gave him a soft smile. "I won't."

Suddenly feeling more encouraged than he had in weeks, he started for the toolshed, whistling. He stopped just before entering and looked up at the cloud studded sky. "Thank You, Jesus."

That afternoon, Victoria sat at Gregory's drawing table staring at her pathetic picture of a hollyhock, hoping she could glare it into transforming into a more artistic rendering. Alas, the wobbly lines didn't move. Gregory leaned over her shoulder. "That's excellent."

She switched her glare to him. "Excellent? How can you say that? It's awful! You can't even tell it's a hollyhock unless you read the title. It certainly looks nothing like yours," she added with an envious glance at his life-like drawing on the other side of the table. Gregory's had only taken less than three minutes as usual. She had been working on hers for half-an-hour, and it still looked like a child's scribbling mess.

He laughed, a deep, rich laugh that caused her entire body to tingle. Picking her up, he sat down in her chair and placed her on his lap. "Don't feel bad, honey."

She nearly gasped at the endearment coming from his mouth. He had never called her anything but Victoria. "It's taken me nearly twenty years of practice to become adept at drawing them. Your flower looks great for a beginner."

She recognized the truth in his words, but it didn't make her feel any better about her picture. "I'll just throw it away."

"No you won't. We'll start your own portfolio."

Finally, she smiled at him. How could she not after the wonderful day he'd given her? He had spent hours patiently, and seemingly eagerly, teaching her in the garden how to care for the flowers, and then in their room, how to catalogue. Never once did he seem to mind her presence or grow frustrated at her bumbling attempts. Who really cared if her drawing had turned out right or not? She had been able to spend the entire, glorious afternoon with her husband.

"What do I need to do next?"

"Hmm?" Gregory muttered distractedly.

How odd. He usually seemed so focused on his work. "What do I need to do next?"

"Next?…Oh! Next." He set her on her feet and jumped up. "Well, you can either write your notes on the bottom or press the flower. It doesn't matter which one comes first."

"Will you show me how to press the flower?"

"Of course." Gregory pulled out two thin pieces of glass. He showed her first with his own flower how to arrange it and press it so the blossom showed from the best angle then slid the glass into a premade frame. A small hinge held the top of the frame on. Gregory swung it closed after sliding the glass in and latched it shut.

He handed her two more pieces of the paper thin glass and pulled out another frame. "Where did you find these supplies?"

"I have them special made. The frames come from a woodworker in Brighton. The glass is shipped in from London."

"Oh." She carefully set the expensive glass on the desk and arranged her flower. Not as easy a feat as Gregory made it appear for her blossom kept trying to smash down the wrong way, but she finally deemed it acceptable. She carefully slid the plates into the frame he held for her. Swinging the top closed and latching it, she smiled triumphantly. "There."

He returned her smile. "It looks perfect. Now I'll have to clean out a drawer for you to keep your own specimens in."

"You don't have to do that."

After all, a whole drawer would be terribly large for her one flower. She didn't dare to venture into the garden again, at least not anytime soon; she had imposed on Gregory enough already.

"It's no trouble." Gregory pulled an empty crate out from under the drawing table and began carefully emptying the top left drawer of his cabinet. He pulled out flower after flower, many of them of the same species. "I have to clean these out when they become full, anyway. I have more filing cabinets in the next room. I use those as my permanent storage area."

"What are you planning to do with all the flowers you catalogue?"

He hesitated a moment before reaching into the drawer again. "Actually, I...I'm in the process of creating a book," he said casually. So casually, she instinctively knew how very important it was to him.

"I think that's wonderful."

Gregory stopped and glanced up at her. "You do?"

"Of course! You have so much knowledge, it will be wonderful to share it with other people. And you're such a good teacher. Just look at everything you taught me today."

"You were a good student. Would...would you like to see what I've done so far?"

"I would love to."

He closed the top drawer he had started emptying and opened the bottom one on the left. Reaching all the way into the back, he pulled out a leather portfolio before closing the drawer again. He turned around and sat down, leaning back against the cabinet. She sat beside him so close their shoulders touched. He silently handed her the portfolio.

Feeling as if he had just handed her a precious part of himself, she carefully reached inside and pulled out the sheaf of papers. *The Flowers of England: An Anthology by Gregory Thornton.* She lifted away the title page...

...And could not stop her gasp of delight.

The two line title read: *Campanula rotundifolia. Common name: Harebell.* The pages were laid out differently than the ones he composed for himself. The notes were in the middle of the two page spread with six small drawings of the plant from a seed to a full flower in the left and right-hand margins, three on each side. Not only were they the life-like drawings she had come to expect, but he had carefully colored them, transforming the drawings from magnificent to...beyond magnificent. She could hardly believe they weren't real. The colors were so exact, and the shading of light and shadow done so perfectly, she nearly expected to see the images jump off the page and start growing in the garden.

She looked back up at Gregory amazed at his sheer artistic talent. He watched her uncertainly. "Do you like it?"

Unexpectedly, tears sprang to her eyes. "Like it? Gregory, this is beautiful. You are so talented. I'm just...in awe."

He somehow managed to look pleased and bashful at the same time. "I've never shown this to anyone before. Having a book published has been a dream of mine for years, but I'm not sure if it's good enough."

"Good enough? It couldn't be any better." She flipped to the next page. *Centranthus ruber. Common Name: Red Valerian.* "Is it finished?"

"No, I only have about half of it done. I've thought about it for a long time, but I only started working on it the month before I found out about our engagement. I haven't really worked on it since then because I've been so busy. And a little distracted."

She couldn't look at him. "I'm sorry I've disrupted your life so much."

Gregory gently turned her head to face him. "I'm not," he whispered just before kissing her. Conscious of the valuable work in her lap, she held still so it wouldn't be wrinkled.

Just then, a knock sounded on the door. He pulled away, seeming reluctant. "Yes?"

"Mr. Gregory, sir." His valet's voice came through the door. "Your parents sent me to fetch you and Miss Victoria. They said dinner was served five minutes ago, and it is becoming cold while they wait for you."

"Thank you, James. We'll be right down."

"Very good, sir."

Gregory sighed before standing up and offering Victoria his hand. She carefully placed the papers back inside the portfolio before accepting his help off the floor. He looked at her then down at himself and started laughing. "We're a sight. If we arrive to dinner looking like this, I think Mother would swoon."

She tilted her head as she studied him. Gregory looked normal to her. Glancing down, she examined her muddy skirt, wondering what he could be talking about.

It suddenly came to her.

Mud!

With a gasp, she rushed to the mirror. She looked *awful!* Mud caked her dress and smeared across her face. Her hair, so carefully arranged that morning, now looked like a rat's nest with almost half falling in straggles out of her hairpins. She'd been having so much fun in the garden, she hadn't even realized how dirty and disheveled she'd become. "I can't go to dinner with your parents like this!"

Gregory crossed the room and rang for Gladys, grinning at her. "I think you look cute."

Her mouth gaped open like a fish. Ever since they had been married, she had carefully dressed in her most flattering outfits and made sure her hair stayed perfectly coiffed, all in an effort to hear one teensy, weensy, little compliment from him. Instead, he waited until she looked like she had wallowed in a mud hole like a pig.

A knock sounded on the door before she could come up with a suitable response. "Come in." She nearly fainted with relief when she saw Gladys. All thoughts about Gregory fled as the urgency of the situation hit her once again. The elder Thorntons were expecting them at any moment! "Oh, Gladys, I need help!"

Gladys smiled, seemingly pleased, as she began unbuttoning the back of her dress. "I'll have you ready in a jiffy, mum."

"Do you think the mud will come out?"

"Yes, mum. I'll make sure it's soaked and washed real good. We've had a lot of practice scrubbing out mud because of Mr. Gregory."

"Oh, thank you!" she breathed as she stepped out of the dress. Gladys threw it over her arm.

"Now, you better wash your face and neck, mum, while I get a clean gown out of the changing room."

"Right."

She headed for the washroom and had nearly reached the open door when Gregory suddenly walked out. She stopped stock-still and so did he.

How could she have forgotten that he was there? He always left the room when she dressed, understanding that her delicate sensibilities found it too embarrassing to do so in front of him. Acutely aware that she now stood before him in nothing more than her corset and chemise, her cheeks flamed. Dropping her gaze, she became suddenly intent on studying the oriental rug under her bare feet.

She felt more than saw Gregory moving towards her. He stopped only a couple of inches away, the toes of his boots landing in her sight. After several long seconds when he didn't move or speak, she finally gathered up the courage to peek up at him. Gregory was smiling broadly. "Yes, Mrs. Thornton, I think you look very cute."

Reaching out, he gently tugged her the rest of the way to him and gave her a slow, ardent kiss. Victoria melted against him as her embarrassment remarkably disappeared. Finally pulling back, he smiled at her again. "Very cute, indeed." He planted another kiss on the tip of her nose before letting her go and heading for the changing room.

She stared after him long after he disappeared.

Suddenly becoming aware that Gladys stood next to the dressing table holding a fresh dress, she jerked back to the present. She quickly hurried into the washroom and cleaned the mud off herself. By the time she came back out, Gregory had already changed and seemed ready for dinner. He hadn't left the room, however. Instead, he had settled into one of the chairs to wait for her.

He had stayed.

Bubbles of happiness rose and fizzed around in her chest as she went back over to Gladys, who looked even more pleased than she had earlier. She helped her into the gown and quickly re-did her hair.

A fraction of her happiness evaporated as they walked into the dining room to the sour disapproval of his parents. Harriet began lambasting him before they had even sat down. "You would think, Gregory, that you would have enough respect for your parents to at least arrive for dinner on time."

He pulled out Victoria's chair, the one to the left of John who sat at the head of the table. "I'm sorry, Mother. I lost track of the time."

He didn't mention the fact that his parents were usually absent from dinner altogether.

She didn't think she could have been as forbearing.

Harriet barely waited until Gregory had taken his seat beside Victoria before ringing the tiny bell sitting next to her plate.

Immediately, servers came out with dishes of steaming food. Gregory bowed his head and murmured a quick blessing in a barely audible voice.

Both his parents looked put out by the gesture, having made it abundantly clear that they wanted nothing to do with Gregory's "fanatical religion", but they didn't say anything. Picking up her fork, Victoria stared at the succulent roast. Her hunger had vanished, making it look as appetizing as a piece of shoe leather. Even the servants felt the dark, disapproving atmosphere pervading the room, going about their duties as somber as if they were at a funeral instead of the cheerful, smiling faces she had come to expect.

Taking a deep breath, she forced herself to take a bite of the roasted potatoes. Just as she placed the fork in her mouth, Harriet spoke again. "I've decided you've had long enough to get settled. It's high time to introduce Victoria to Lewes society."

She nearly choked on her bite. Carefully, she swallowed but had to take great gulps of water to help it down. Gregory looked at her in concern, but Harriet kept talking. "Victoria and I will spend the day with the modiste tomorrow. I'll also send out the invitations, and her introduction party will be held here at Thornton Hall on Friday."

"That's only three days away, Mother. Victoria might prefer to have a little more time to prepare."

"Nevertheless, the party *will* be held on Friday. I have given you both a month to initiate it yourselves. We are inexcusably late as it is. If Victoria needed more time to prepare then she should have done her duty as your wife and held the ball two weeks ago."

Her face flamed. In London, she would have known to hold a party, but here in the country she had just assumed that there wasn't a society to impress. After all, she hadn't seen anyone else. "I…I'm sorry, Mrs. Thornton. I didn't realize…"

Gregory's hand suddenly clasped hers where it nervously picked on the napkin in her lap, stopping her in mid-sentence. "Mother, Victoria isn't at fault here. She has had to settle into a new house filled with complete strangers and to learn a whole new way of life. Country life is different from London society, and she doesn't yet know all of our customs. Personally, I think she has done a wonderful job adjusting, and if anyone is at fault in this, it is you and I. I honestly did not think about the introduction ball, but if you did, you should have mentioned it to her weeks ago. After all, you are now her mother, and as such, should be giving her advice and guidance in these matters."

Gregory had just made the longest, firmest speech she had ever heard him make to his parents. He always accepted their criticism of him with a mild apology and then went on about his business.

But he had stood up for her.

A thrill shot through her, making her feel giddy.

"Gregory!" John slapped his fist onto the table hard enough the dishes rattled. Victoria automatically winced away, leaning closer to Gregory. "Don't you dare speak to your mother in such a disrespectful way! Apologize this instant!"

The hand on hers tightened as Gregory took a deep breath. For the first time, he seemed to be struggling to control his temper. Strangely enough, she didn't feel afraid. But then, his anger wasn't directed at *her*.

He suddenly blew out a breath as his shoulders relaxed. "I'm sorry if I was disrespectful, Mother," he finally said in his usual soft voice. "However, I will not stand by while you malign Victoria."

"I wasn't trying to malign the girl. I was merely pointing out to you her breach in etiquette. But maybe you're right. Victoria is young and has been without a mother for several years. She probably doesn't know what's expected of her. I'll have to take her in hand and teach her myself."

It took all Victoria's efforts to keep a calm face. The *last* thing in the world she wanted was to be *taken in hand* by this domineering, forceful woman.

"I don't think she has much to learn. But the country is a little different from London society, and we need to help her over the rough spots as she adjusts. I'll try to remember from now on, as well."

Gregory gave her hand a final squeeze and went back to his dinner. She forced herself to follow his example though the rest of the meal passed in frozen silence. Harriet didn't speak again until she rose to leave the dining room. "Victoria, I expect you to join me in the gold salon at eight sharp tomorrow morning."

"Yes, ma'am." She heaved a silent sigh of relief when they were gone. Gregory politely helped her out of her chair, and she gladly followed him back to their bedchamber.

Later that night, wrapped safe and snug in her husband's arms, she couldn't sleep for thinking about her new family. How had Gregory turned out so wonderful with parents like that? How did he stand it? He always accepted their unkind words without retaliating. Yet, he had stood up for her.

Once again, the thrill of that knowledge shot through her.

Nestling her head closer against his chest, she listened to the reassuring thud of his heart. She had never, ever had anyone stand up for her before, and she just lay quietly, relishing in the feeling.

Gregory moved slightly. "Victoria, are you asleep?" he whispered.

"No."

His sighed, his breath stirring her hair. "I'm sorry about dinner. My parents have strong opinions and aren't afraid to express them. I don't think they realize how hurtful it can be."

"It's not your fault."

He stayed silent for a moment as he absently rubbed her back. The movement of his warm, calloused hand was hypnotic. Languidness seeped into her limbs as she practically purred in contentment. The unpleasantness with his parents, and her need to constantly be on guard around him, seemed so far away at times like these. "Did you enjoy working in the garden today?"

"MmmHmm."

"Would you like to join me again sometime?"

"I'd love to."

"Really?" The surprise in his voice and the way his hand suddenly stopped woke her out of her trance-like state. Her stomach knotted.

How could she undo the damage she had just done?

"Y…yes. As long as I'm not interrupting. I understand if you're too busy."

"I'm never too busy for you, Victoria, and you could never be an interruption." Gregory started rubbing her back again. "Is that why you've never come before? Because you thought it would be imposing?"

"I…I don't want to be a bother."

"Oh, honey," he pulled her closer. That was the second time today he had used an endearment when addressing her.

The second time in their marriage.

She relaxed again.

"You could never, ever be that. I loved having you with me today, and I would be happy to have you everyday, anytime you want to join me. I had begun to think…"

He fell silent. She tilted her face up even though she couldn't see him in the darkness. "Begun to think what?"

He didn't speak.

"Gregory?"

He sighed. "Well, just that…that you didn't want to spend any more time with me than you had to."

Her mouth fell open as she stared in the direction of his face. After a few seconds, Gregory's hand moved away from her back, and he lifted his arm from around her, leaving her suddenly bereft.

"I understand though. I know I'm not the most interesting fellow around, and I certainly don't want to bore you with endless talk about my hobby. I've tried to think of something else we might do together that you would enjoy besides just our rides, but…"

She placed her fingers over his mouth, stopping him in the middle of a sentence. He had sounded so unsure that, after a moment, she gathered up enough boldness to replace her hand with her lips, giving him a long kiss. Pulling back breathless, she traced the contours of his dear face. He went very still. "Gregory, don't ever think that again. I find you extremely interesting, and everything you've shared about botany is fascinating. I would love to learn more about it."

She ran her fingers through his hair. He made a soft noise in the back of his throat, almost like a moan, as he wrapped his arm back around her and pulled her close. She laid her cheek against his, her fingers still entwined in his thick hair. "I've wanted to spend more time with you, but Father always said a man didn't want a woman around being a nuisance while he worked. 'A wife shouldn't demand too much of her husband's time because he has more important things to do'," she quoted one of Rolfe's oft stated phrases.

"That's not true. Having you around is a joy not a nuisance. I am happy to share my love of flowers with you, but you are much more important than any work I might have. I want you to know that."

Tears pricked Victoria's eyes. No one had ever told her that she was important before. "Oh, Gregory…" Unable to say anything else, she just gave him another kiss, trying to share the feelings roiling inside her without words. Her heart soared when he rolled over slightly and deepened the kiss.

The next afternoon, Victoria wanted to scream! A woman clearly on a mission, Harriet had ignored every suggestion she had given, not even allowing her input into the style and color of her dress. Besides that, she hadn't seen Gregory since their morning devotions, and she missed him terribly. Harriet had insisted that they eat breakfast and lunch in the salon while they worked.

Even now, Harriet and the modiste, Madame Blanchet, were bent over patterns. Madame Blanchet had shot her several commiserating glances but dutifully listened to the older woman. Harriet pointed to an off-the-shoulder design that plunged daringly low. "I like this bodice the best. With the skirt we decided on earlier."

She shuddered, looking at the revealing neckline. A few times, Rolfe and Aunt Armelda had forced her to wear similarly low bodices to parties. All the men leering at her exposed skin had made her skin crawl. It had taken weeks for the dirty feeling to finally disappear. "Mrs. Thornton, I really don't like wearing that style. This would suit me much better." She again held up the picture in her lap. A simple, rounded, modest neckline with small puffed sleeves on the shoulders.

"Nonsense." Harriet dismissed her and turned back to the modiste. "And I want it in that green fabric I picked out before. The one with orange accents. We need a light, cheery color for spring."

She shuddered again. A lime green dress with bright orange accents? "Mrs. Thornton, perhaps the yellow with the white accents would be better. It would be a very cheerful, spring color."

"Yellow is too common a color. The green will stand out in a crowd."

Victoria rubbed her aching temple as Harriet and Madame Blanchett continued planning her hideous dress. Sighing, she glanced up.

Her heart jumped in happiness. Gregory stood in the doorway, his shoulder propped against the doorframe and wearing a slight frown. "Gregory!"

He smiled at her and straightened.

How long had he been there?

"What are you doing here?" Harriet's tone bordered on rude.

"I've come to steal Victoria away for a couple of hours."

"You'll do no such thing! I have all I can do now trying to have her ready in time. It will be impossible if she goes gallivanting off with you every time you take a notion."

"You've had her all day, Mother. And we always go for an afternoon ride." Walking over, he picked up the pattern Victoria held in her hand. "Madame Blanchet, Victoria will be taking the yellow and white dress in this style."

"She will not!"

Gregory faced off against his mother. His soft voice held an edge of steel. "Either Victoria wears the dress of her choosing, or we shan't attend the ball. It's that simple."

"You wouldn't do that." Harriet's protest lacked conviction.

"Actually, Mother, I would because I'm very serious about this. Victoria is a grown woman fully capable of making decisions for herself, and she will be allowed to decide what she wears."

"It was you who said I should advise Victoria in these matters."

"I was speaking of the social activities expected by the *ton* that she may not be aware of not her wardrobe. Besides, I like her modest taste."

Victoria gasped at Gregory's admission. Every man she had ever known before had always wanted their wives to flaunt themselves, seeing it as a way to show their wealth, power and position. Her muscles tensed as he and Harriet stared at each other for a long moment. Both wore determined expressions, and it looked as if neither would back down. Finally, though, Harriet huffed. "Oh, alright. I don't know what's come over you, Gregory, but if Victoria would prefer to wear such a drab, unbecoming dress, so be it."

Giving her a smile, Gregory bent down and kissed her cheek.

She didn't look pleased at the gesture.

"Thank you. Now, we are going for a ride. I'll have her back in two hours."

Harriet pinched her lips tightly together but didn't say anything else. Victoria accepted Gregory's hand as he helped her out of the chair completely amazed that the woman had given in.

They were outside and on the way to the stables before she spoke. "You don't usually stand up to your mother, do you?"

"Not in small things, no. I've always been such a disappointment to them it seems the least I can do is to wear the clothes Mother picks out for our social engagements. In certain issues, though, I've had to. When I came to know Jesus, they didn't understand it and wanted me to stop 'my silly nonsense'. I could no longer attend their church because it was so spiritually dry. Now, I go to a smaller congregation."

"You go to church?"

"Yes. I haven't been since we were married because I wanted to give you some time to adjust, and I wanted to keep you to myself for a little while before having to share you with everyone," he added teasingly. She didn't know quite what to say to that so she kept quiet. After a few seconds, Gregory spoke again. "We should probably attend this Sunday, though."

He suddenly veered from the path and led her into the garden.

"I thought we were going riding."

"We are, but I wanted to show you something first." He stopped in front of his hybrid. She looked down and smiled. The small buds had grown, and the tips showed tiny lavender petals. "It's going to be gorgeous! That lavender is so light and rich."

"It should be in full bloom soon."

They stayed for a few moments admiring the flower before continuing on to the stable. Victoria stood by while he saddled Liberty and Daisy and spoke with Horace, who mucked out a stall a few feet down. She tuned out their conversation about the need to hire a new stablehand, having grown more used to the gentle giant of a man who ran the stables and always called her "Miss Victoria". Instead, she watched Gregory. The muscles in his arms and back rippled as he hefted the saddles on. Her fingers itched to run over those well-defined muscles despite the heat that flared in her cheeks at the thought. She loved his fine, well-muscled physique so different from the men she'd known in London. But unlike the indolent men of the *ton*, Gregory thrived on physical activity of all kinds. She didn't mind. Especially since she got to enjoy the benefits.

He lifted her into the saddle. She quickly arranged her skirt.

A printed cotton skirt.

She had forgotten to change into a riding habit! Oh, well. It's not like they ever saw anybody else, anyway, and she was determined to wring every ounce of enjoyment she could out of the next two hours.

Maybe it would give her the courage she needed to go back into the fray with Harriet Thornton.

Chapter 8

$\mathcal{F}$riday night, Victoria nervously clasped and unclasped her white gloved hands as she stood in the enormous ballroom. Still an hour until the guests would start arriving, but per Harriet's instructions, everyone had already assembled downstairs completely dressed and coiffed. Harriet bustled about attending to last minute details with a gimlet eye.

Looking down, she smoothed the soft, buttery yellow skirt of her dress. Adorned with white ribbon and lace and with the modest, rounded neckline she had picked out, she thought it gorgeous, but Harriet sniffed with disapproval every time she saw her.

Warm hands cupped her bare shoulders. She instantly recognized Gregory's touch. He must have come up behind her without her knowing. For a moment, she closed her eyes and breathed in the clean scent that characterized him. The aroma helped to steady her frazzled nerves and ease some of the tension in her muscles.

"That gown is perfect, Victoria," he murmured before placing a soft kiss on the nape of her neck. Delight shivered down her spine. "And I like the pearls. It reminds me of the first time I saw you."

He remembered?

Twisting around, she looked up at him. She was wearing the same pearl set she had worn at their engagement party, but she had never expected Gregory to notice. "They were Mother's."

"I'm glad you have something of hers to remember her by." He slid his hand from her shoulder and down her bare arm to settle around her waist as he moved to stand by her side.

His light touch left a trail of fire in it's wake. Desire filled her, so intense it nearly took her breath away. If only they were alone! An image of Gregory swinging her up into his arms and whisking her up the stairs caused her cheeks to flush and a giggle to build in her chest. Closing her eyes, she tried to find her equilibrium.

Gregory's voice broke into her thoughts. "Don't let Mother's attitude affect you. This is your night, and I want you to enjoy it."

He had obviously mistaken the reason for her silence. She opened her eyes and turned to him not bothering to hide the stark longing that surely shone on her face. "It's our night," she corrected boldly. Gregory rewarded her by claiming her mouth in a searing kiss that nearly rocked her off her feet. Her arms slid up around his neck, and she clung helplessly as he pulled her tight against him.

"Stop that, Gregory. You'll wrinkle her dress."

Harriet's shrill voice was like a bucket of ice water thrown on them. Victoria jumped back in shocked embarrassment, but Gregory didn't let her go very far. He kept his arm around her waist firmly anchoring her beside him. Before anyone could respond, the distant sound of the doorbell echoed throughout the house. Harriet sighed in exasperation. "That has to be that scallywag, Broderick Holmes. He's the only one who would dare show up so early. I don't know why you put up with him, Gregory." She suddenly gasped. "Sally! What are you doing with that platter?" Harriet marched away, her attention now focused on the newest serving girl.

Victoria winced as Harriet berated her soundly.

A young man wearing evening clothes appeared in the doorway. His dark blond hair liberally streaked with gold indicated his time spent outdoors. Cool blue eyes scanned the chaos in the room before lighting on them. Tall and slender, but he moved towards them with the litheness and grace of a cougar. Goose bumps rose on her arms. He reminded her so much of Paxton it was eerie.

"Gregory," he greeted warmly as he drew closer.

Gregory smiled and reached out to clasp the man's hand while keeping his other arm around her. "Broderick. It's been too long."

"I know. I had just about decided that a month was long enough for you newlyweds to be alone. If the invitation hadn't come when it did, I would have saddled up and invited myself to dinner anyway."

Gregory laughed. "Well, thank you for being as patient as you were. I'm sure it was hard since you're so out of practice."

"Hey!"

Ignoring his cry of outrage, Gregory turned to her. "Victoria, may I present Broderick Holmes. Broderick, this is my wife, Victoria."

"He forgot to mention that I'm also his long-standing best friend," he added before accepting the hand she reluctantly held out and kissing the back. "It's a pleasure to meet you."

"And you," she forced herself to murmur.

Straightening, Broderick scanned her from the top of her head to her feet before grinning mischievously. "I must say, you did alright for yourself, old chap. For sure, Victoria is the reigning flower in your garden. In that gown, she looks like a cheerful buttercup."

She gasped at his audacity.

"And if you could ever get over your ham-handed, backwards compliments, you might find yourself a wife just as sweet."

Gasping again, she stared at Gregory. She had never heard him say anything so insulting! Looking at her dismayed face, they both burst into laughter. "You'll have to excuse us," Broderick finally said, once he had his mirth under control. "We tend to be a bit much until you get to know us."

Gregory smiled at her before turning back to Broderick. "I have a new hybrid in the garden if you would like to see it."

"In just a minute. First, I have to see if I can finagle myself some food. I'm starving."

"You're always starving."

Before Broderick could retort, Maggie, the gray-haired housekeeper, entered carrying a large tray of hors d'oeuvres. His face lit up. "Ah! Perfect."

He made a bee-line towards the housekeeper. "Maggie, me darlin'," he called in a surprisingly good imitation of her Irish brogue. "Could you be sparin' a wee morsel for your favorite laddie?"

Apparently sensing how stunned she felt, Gregory smiled again. "He's a tease, and his humor takes a bit of getting used to, but I would trust him with my life."

"O…of course."

Gregory brushed a kiss across her temple before walking towards Broderick, who busily filled both hands with food. Maggie finally slapped him away, and they went out into the garden. Victoria tried not to shiver as she rubbed her arms, bereft and suddenly cold without Gregory's warm support. It didn't help that Broderick looked just like Paxton. Blond-haired, blue-eyed, good-looking and too charming by half.

Gregory might trust him, but her guard went up.

Out in the garden, Gregory and Broderick walked slowly down the wide pathways as Broderick ate the pastries he had finagled from Maggie, devouring them as if he hadn't had a bite of food all week. Gregory smiled at the familiar sight. He had missed his friend, only seeing the Holmes family briefly at his wedding before entering the seclusion of his honeymoon.

Broderick finished off the last bite and wiped his fingers on a hand-kerchief before turning to him. "How is it going?"

"Actually, I think it's going pretty well. It would be better if I could overcome my blasted shyness, but so many times when I'm with her, I don't know what to say."

Broderick grinned. "You looked pretty chummy when I came in."

"It's not that. It's just…I think something's deeply hurt her. She's learned to show calmness and confidence, but sometimes I feel that inside she's really scared. And I don't know how to help her."

"Could it have anything to do with the rumors?"

"Rumors?" It took him a moment to realize what Broderick meant. He had already forgotten the gossip about her being with child. "No. The rumors aren't true so it isn't that. I'm beginning to think it might have something to do with her father."

"Really? Why?"

"Well, for one thing, rushing her into marriage with a complete stranger."

"John did the same thing to you. It's actually a common practice among the *ton*. Not the rushed wedding, but marrying a stranger."

"Yes, it is, but when we were in London, he seemed almost indifferent to her." Broderick raised his eyebrows and gave him a pointed look. Gregory laughed. "I know, Father and Mother could be accused of the same thing. But, a couple of days ago, she said that Rolfe told her that a woman was a nuisance if she hung around her husband while he worked. He also said a wife couldn't expect too much of her husband's time because he had more important things to do. She claimed that's why she would never join me in the garden. She didn't want to be a bother. I assured her she wouldn't be."

"And has she joined you since then?"

"Mother's been keeping her completely occupied since then. I've barely been able to snatch her away long enough to go riding. She did say she was interested in botany, but I'm not sure if she just wanted to please me or if she really meant it. If I knew for sure that she enjoyed it, I would pester her until she joined me, but I just don't know."

"Hmm. Why don't we pray about it?"

Gregory nodded and bowed his head right there on the walkway between the London Pride and the Welsh Poppy flower beds. Broderick followed suit. "Jesus, we come to You right now for Gregory and Victoria. You know their lives and their situation, Father. Give Gregory the wisdom he needs to be a loving husband, to learn how to reach out to Victoria and for her to reach out to him. Whatever is keeping her afraid, God, please give her peace. Help her to conquer her fears and anything else that would come between her and Gregory. Lord, we thank You for both of them, and we ask that Your Love be shed abroad in this situation. In Jesus' Name."

Gregory had prayed about their marriage every day, yet there was something powerful about agreeing in prayer with another believer. At that moment, he felt more at peace than he had since arriving home from London.

Four hours later, after standing in line and greeting what seemed to be every living soul in Sussex county, Victoria danced a waltz with a buck-toothed young man about her age who wouldn't stop talking about horse racing as he bounced her vigorously around the room. If only Gregory could rescue her from this overly eager, energetic, horse-fanatic! Yet for her introduction ball etiquette dictated that she would dance only the first and last dances with her husband. The others were reserved for everyone else.

Glancing around surreptitiously, she located Gregory dancing with a gorgeous, young woman with flaming auburn hair. White, hot heat flared across her middle at the sight. Who was she? She wracked her mind but couldn't remember being introduced.

Tuning out her partner's monologue about the racing speed of a current favorite, she studied Gregory closely. Could he be interested in a dalliance with her? The woman openly flirted as they spoke in low tones. Gregory laughed at something she said. Her echoing laughter tinkled musically across the room.

Victoria's stomach tightened as hot tears pricked her eyes. The red-head had a willowy, statuesque figure that left her feeling short and dowdy. The top of the woman's elaborate red silk gown left little to the imagination. Her own simple, yellow dress suddenly seemed childish in comparison.

How could she compete with a woman like that?

Don't think about it.

Blinking back the stinging in her eyes, she focused on enjoying the unobstructed view she had of Gregory. He didn't dance nearly as gracefully as he had in London. In fact, his movements were almost clumsy as he accidentally bumped into the corner of a table.

Fury coursed through her veins. Right before the guests arrived, Harriet had marched over to Gregory and demanded he take off his spectacles. Victoria had sputtered when Gregory had complied, but he had explained to her that he knew everyone here well enough that he didn't have to see them to distinguish them from each other. Still, she could see how hard it was for him. How could Harriet be so uncaring towards her own son? No wonder Gregory had the reputation for being awkward. His mother insisted that he go around practically blind!

Still, since Gregory knew everyone here well that had to include his mysterious dancing partner. How close, exactly, were they?

Deliberately, she turned her mind away from it. She could do nothing to prevent him from being unfaithful nor was she naive enough to believe it wouldn't happen. After having watched Rolfe openly flaunt his indiscretions in her mother's face from her earliest memories, she had resigned herself to the inevitable long ago.

She just hadn't expected it to hurt so much.

Her own partner suddenly released her. She stumbled about for a second before realizing that the set had finished. A blush crawled up her face as she automatically clapped politely. She had been so engrossed in watching Gregory that she hadn't even noticed.

The band broke into a lively reel. Giving her a wide-toothed grin, her partner, whose name Victoria had completely forgotten, reached for her again. She pulled back and gave him what she hoped looked like an apologetic smile. "I'm sorry, but I've promised this dance."

"To me."

The voice made her jump as she turned around. A moan rose, but she clamped her lips together to stifle it. She had been keeping an eye out for Broderick and deliberately avoided him all evening. But in her distraction over Gregory and the red-head he had managed to sneak up on her.

She would rather dance with bucktooth.

Broderick gave the crestfallen youth a sympathetic smile before pulling Victoria into the dance. Tense, she took her place in line. She wanted to see if Gregory still danced with that woman, but she couldn't look around for him.

She would need all her wits to deal with Broderick.

"Henry is a nice enough boy, but he dances as if he were racing a horse." His eyes twinkled as he performed the intricate steps effortlessly.

She lifted her chin haughtily. "I found him to be a fine partner."

Broderick didn't seem to be put off in the least at her cold tone, and his easy smile clearly said he knew she lied. "Still, I'll try to go slower so you can catch your breath. How have you found married life?"

His abrupt question caused her to miss a step. Quickly catching up, she glared at him. An intimate friend might ask such a question, not a stranger she had only met a few hours before. "It's fine."

Again, her short answer didn't faze him in the least. "You know, I wasn't very happy when I heard that John had arranged a marriage for Gregory with one of the *ton's* debutantes."

"I don't see how it was any of *your* business."

"Of course it was. Gregory's been my best friend since I was five. I knew he would throw his whole heart into his marriage, and I didn't want to see him hurt. Most debutantes are shallow, selfish creatures who wouldn't take the time to look past outward appearances and realize what a special man he really is."

Indignation rose. Had he just called her a shallow, selfish creature?

Narrowing her eyes, she really studied him. His blue eyes blazed as he returned her scrutiny. Intense and challenging, yes, but no lewdness or meanness lingered there. He honestly seemed to be concerned for her husband.

Unexpectedly, her ire disappeared as she softened towards him. "I know Gregory is a special man."

Broderick continued to study her a moment before smiling. "Glad to hear it. I also want you to know that I and my parents are praying for both of you."

"Your parents?"

"Yes. Let's see, they're…" Broderick scanned the room before finally nodding towards a middle-aged couple standing in a small group, chatting. "There they are. Clarence and Margaret Holmes."

"Oh, I didn't know they were your parents." Victoria had met so many people names and faces had blurred together. However, she did remember the Baron of Glynd and his wife. She had given her a long embrace saying how happy they were to meet her. And they had both hugged Gregory as if he were their own son.

With Broderick occupied, she took the opportunity to scan the room. The redhead was easy to spot, dancing with a handsome man in his thirties. Relief filled her that she no longer danced with Gregory. She gave the room another quick scan but didn't spot him.

"What do your parents do?" she asked politely after realizing that several moments of silence had passed as she searched for Gregory.

"Holmes Apples. That's us."

"Really?" In London, every family sought Holmes Apples because they were the best.

"Yes." He rolled his eyes and chuckled. "I know more about apples than anyone has a right to."

"Do you enjoy growing apples?"

"It's a good business. But I'm not completely wrapped up in it like Father is. I also enjoy sports like fencing and hunting. There's nothing like the taste of fresh venison on the dinner table."

Aghast, she stared at him. "You eat it?"

Broderick laughed. "I forgot. You're a *city* girl."

Once again, she studied him sharply, but his blue eyes only held friendly teasing. No innuendo or lewd undertones colored his comment.

The set ended. As they were clapping, Broderick laughed again. "Oh, no. Gregory's been cornered by Mrs. Culpepper." Turning around, she finally spotted Gregory talking to a short, portly, gray-haired lady who held a fancy black hearing horn in one ear. "Come, we must save him." Pulling her arm through his, Broderick walked her across the room. "Mrs. Culpepper is a sweet old lady who attends our church. But she's mostly deaf and likes to repeat the same stories of when she was young every time you see her. By the time you're finished talking to her, your ears will ring."

They were getting closer, and she could already hear Mrs. Culpepper's voice screaming as she reminisced about a ball she had attended as a new debutante. Gregory patiently nodded as she described her dress in excruciating detail. Broderick lowered his voice to a whisper. "When Gregory leaves, watch. Mrs. Culpepper will pinch his cheek and tap it a couple of times like he was five years old."

Bewildered, she nodded as they pulled up to the couple. Mrs. Culpepper quit yelling and turned to them. "Broderick!" she roared right in his face before hooking a pudgy arm around his neck and pulling him down for a kiss on the cheek.

"Hello, Mrs. Culpepper!" he yelled into the horn she held in her ear with one hand. Victoria nearly winced but managed to keep a smile on her face. "Victoria wants to dance with Gregory!" he continued in a booming voice. Every head in the vicinity turned towards them.

People tittered. Her cheeks heated up in embarrassment especially when she noticed the redhead watching with a derisive lift of her well-sculpted eyebrow.

"Victoria?" Mrs. Culpepper shouted back. She glanced around before noticing her. "Oh, his new bride! Come here, dear, and let me give you a hug!" Her voice shrieked into her ear as she was enveloped in a well-perfumed embrace. Mrs. Culpepper pulled back and gave her a smile so big her dentures nearly fell out of her mouth. "Of course Gregory should dance with his bride!" she bellowed right into Victoria's face. She barely withstood the blast without stepping back. "Such a pretty little thing, too!"

Mrs. Culpepper turned to Gregory. Grabbing a hunk of skin on his right cheek, she pinched it good before giving him a couple of soft slaps in the same spot just as Broderick had said. "You did right well for yourself, boy!" she screamed. "Now, go dance with her!"

Gregory smiled at her before placing a kiss on her wrinkled cheek. "Yes, ma'am!" he yelled into the horn before leading her away.

Broderick had been right. Her ears rang, and everything seemed strangely muted even after Gregory led her to the dance floor and pulled her into his arms for a waltz. She shook her head slightly to clear her ears.

"Did you really want to dance with me, or was that some of Broderick's maneuvering?" Gregory whispered. At least, it sounded like a whisper, but she had a feeling he spoke in a normal voice.

"A little of both." When he raised his eyebrows, she explained, silently praying that her voice didn't shriek across the ballroom simply because she couldn't hear. "I wanted to dance with you, but since I didn't mention it to Broderick, he was trying to do some maneuvering."

"I wanted to dance with you, too." The simple words filled her heart with joy. Just then, he bumped into a chair, jarring them for a second. "I'm sorry," he said as he straightened them out and moved nearer the middle of the dance floor.

"It's not your fault."

Gregory smiled at her. "Are you enjoying the party so far?"

"I am now."

His smile grew wider. "So am I."

They fell silent, but she was content. She had been embarrassed when Broderick yelled that out in front of everyone, but, right now, she could have hugged him for it. They managed to dance two wonderful sets together before an older gentleman, some sort of distant relative of Gregory's, came to claim her.

That night, thoughts of Broderick and his family consumed her mind as she carefully removed her mother's pearls and placed them in their velvet lined box. Broderick had danced with her again, spending the time alternately teasing her in a friendly way, almost like she imagined an older brother would do, and making hilarious comments about the other guests that had her giggling helplessly the entire time. Then he had led her over to where Gregory spoke with Broderick's parents. She had found them to be warm and friendly and completely accepting of her.

And of Gregory.

If they were that way, why couldn't his own parents be?

Sighing, Victoria stowed the box in the bottom drawer of her dressing table and spun around on the stool. Gregory sat on the settee, flipping through his Bible. He still wore his evening clothes though he had pulled off the cravat and loosened the top buttons on his shirt. He'd thrown his coat over the back of the settee. "Broderick and his parents are nice, aren't they?"

He glanced up at her. "Yes, they're very nice."

Getting up, she walked over and settled down on the settee beside him in a pouf of yellow material. She still wore her ball gown since she hadn't yet rung for Gladys. Gregory turned to face her more fully, stretching his arm out along the back of the settee. "They seem to be very genuine and caring."

"They took me under their wing from the first time I met them at Broderick's fifth birthday party. In fact, they're the ones that led me to Jesus when I was twelve."

"Really? I had a governess when I was about five who led me to Jesus. But when Father found out the next day, he fired her and forbade me to speak of it again."

"That must have been hard."

"I barely remember it, but I do recall crying at the time so it probably was." Leaning her head against his shoulder, she studied the worn Bible in his lap. "I've attended church my entire life, but lately I've come to realize that I know nothing about the faith I profess."

"Do you have any questions about what we've been reading? I might not know the answer, but we could search for it together."

"That's just it, I can't really think of any questions to ask, but I've found myself wanting to know more."

Gregory stayed silent a moment. "Do you have a Bible of your own?"

"No."

"We'll have to buy you one the next time we go to town, but in the meantime, you know you're welcome to use mine anytime you want."

"Oh, I wouldn't do that." She sat back up, alarmed at the very thought. "I might hurt it."

Gregory gently tugged her back down against his shoulder. "You won't hurt it, but even if you ruined it, it wouldn't matter. I can buy a new one."

"But I couldn't use your Bible, Gregory. It wouldn't be right."

"Why not?" He sounded completely mystified.

"Because it's yours, and you're my husband. 'A wife should never touch her husband's personal belongings'," she said, once again quoting Rolfe. "And I won't, Gregory, I promise."

"But, Victoria," he tilted her face up until she looked at him. "Don't you know that what's mine belongs to you as well? Once we were married, it was no longer my things and your things. Everything became *ours*. I want you to feel free to use anything you want even if you think it's mine because everything should be completely shared between a husband and his wife."

Wide-eyed, she stared at him. His radical proposal made her tremble. "But, Gregory…"

He placed a finger on her lips, silencing her. "There are no buts Victoria. I want to share everything with you." He gave her a gentle smile as he brushed his finger down her cheek. "Does that scare you?"

"Y…yes." She worried her lower lip before asking in a small voice. "What if I accidentally ruin something and make you mad at me?"

Gregory turned until he sat sideways on the settee and could look her directly in the face. He put both hands on her shoulders. "You're my wife. I would never grow angry at you over something like that. Anytime you're afraid, just remember the eyeglasses. I have my extra pair in the desk if you want to find a hammer. Here," he pulled the spectacles off his face and handed them to her. "Whale away."

Once again, the serious way he made that ridiculous statement made her giggle. He finally smiled when she did. "That's better. I don't like it when you look at me with those big blue eyes like you're Little Red Riding Hood and I'm the big bad wolf about to pounce."

Feeling suddenly, dreadfully alone, she threw herself into his arms, wrapping her own around his waist and holding on for dear life. She wanted to beg him to never let her go. To never turn into the big bad wolf like he'd said, but it was too much to ask. Eventually, she would make him angry, and he would punish her. It would happen many, many times over the years. There was no way to avoid it.

Uncontrollable tremors wracked her body. Her mind filled with images of Gregory, red-faced and furious, towering over her as he landed blow after punishing blow. And it would be an agonizingly harsh punishment just because of the simple fact that, physically, he was so much stronger than Rolfe had ever been.

But it wouldn't matter. None of it would matter just so long as he offered her the comforting haven of his arms once he was done.

After his first few moments of utter shock, Gregory wrapped his arms around Victoria and pulled her onto his lap. He cast about desperately in his mind, trying to find something comforting to say, but once again, he drew a complete blank. *Jesus, help her,* he prayed silently as he ironed his hand up and down her shuddering back in a way he hoped imparted comfort. *I don't know what's wrong, but You do. She looked so...so frightened.*

And she had. Just before she had launched herself into his arms, she had looked like a terrified child. He finally found his voice. "Victoria? Victoria, honey, what's wrong?"

She whimpered and buried her face deeper against his chest. Deciding it might be best just to hold her and pray, he did just that. He prayed straight from the anguish in his heart as he held his trembling wife close.

After awhile, her shaking slowed then ceased all together. She lay still against him though he could feel her taking deep, measured breaths. When she finally let him go and sat up, she had her calm facade firmly in place.

Gregory didn't fall for it for a second.

He brushed some of the loose hair that had fallen out of her coif behind her shoulder. "Sweetheart, what's wrong?"

She gave him a brazen smile like the ones she had worn in London when they first met. "Nothing. I just...grew frightened for a moment. I don't really know why." She laughed. "It was probably your reference to Little Red Riding Hood. That story always gave me nightmares as a child. Silly, isn't it?"

"No," he contradicted her softly. Whatever had her so terrified, he didn't thinnk it had been the mention of a children's tale, but she obviously had no intention of telling him what it really had been. "Anything that causes that much fear isn't silly at all."

"Why, Gregory," she gave him a coy smile as she deliberately pressed her soft body against his and slowly ran her finger along his bottom lip, sparking fire in his belly. "How do you know I wasn't just looking for an excuse to be in your arms?"

Gregory hadn't seen this coy, flirty side of her since their wedding night. He held still as she kissed him. But she didn't just kiss him on the mouth. She kissed his nose, and his eyes, and trailed kisses across his cheeks and down his jaw, coming back every once in awhile to his lips as if drawn by an irresistible force. Her hands wove through his hair and rubbed the back of his neck seductively as she pressed even closer.

Closing his eyes, he took a deep breath even as his arms unconsciously tightened around her, and he kissed her back. She had never been this bold before, and it would be so easy to succumb to the intense desire she awakened within him.

But it was all fake.

She acted like this out of fear, maybe, or to cover up what she really felt. Maybe to keep him from pursuing the subject of what had frightened her. Maybe even because she thought he wanted and expected it of her. Whatever the reason, though, to act on his desire right now wouldn't be in her best interest. The conversation had started out with her seeking a closer walk with Jesus, and that's what she really needed.

She might even think that he could fill the void inside her heart. That he could banish the fear, and maybe the loneliness, that held her captive, but he couldn't. Only Jesus could do that completely. No matter how close they grew physically and emotionally there would always be that deepest part inside of her heart that only Jesus could fill. She needed that so much more than she needed him right now.

It took all of his willpower, and a lot of extra help from the Holy Spirit, for Gregory to unwrap his arms from around her and gently set her away from him. Victoria murmured in protest, her lips clinging to his as long as possible, but eventually, she held still. Head bent, he took several deep breaths, trying to bring his rampaging emotions back under control. When he finally felt he could look at her without hauling her back into his arms, he lifted his head.

Victoria stared at him with unshed tears sparkling in her deep blue eyes. Her lower lip quivered slightly. "D…do I displease you?"

Gregory's heart squeezed painfully at her small, hurt tone. "Displease me?" He cupped her sweet cheek in his hand and wiped away the lone tear that had escaped. "Don't you know that you please me more than I ever dreamed possible?"

Her brow furrowed slightly. "Then why…"

"You said that you wanted to know more about Jesus and our faith."

"I do."

"I don't understand what happened earlier. What made you so afraid." Victoria opened her mouth, but Gregory placed his finger over it to shush her.

She kissed it.

He pulled his hand away and tried desperately to bring his thoughts back onto the subject at hand. "I won't press you because I know you don't wish to speak of it. But I know that you weren't so frightened just because I mentioned Little Red Riding Hood."

He scrubbed a hand through his hair. How could he phrase it so she would understand? He finally sighed. "I'm just a man, Victoria. A very sinful man who stumbles and falls more times than I can count. You don't need me right now. You don't need to be seeking me; you need to be seeking Jesus. Even if I knew what was wrong, what causes you fear, I couldn't help you, but I can introduce you to the One who can."

He picked up his forgotten Bible and handed it to her. She clutched it in her lap as she stared at him with wide, frightened eyes. "You're going to leave me alone."

"No, darling," Gregory smoothed her hair back and placed his arm around her shoulders before once again tucking her up against his side. "I'm not going anywhere. I just want you to read the devotions tonight, but first, let's pray. Alright?"

She nodded and bowed her head. Gregory followed suit. "Dear Jesus, we come to You right now for Your precious daughter, Victoria. I am so blessed to have her as my wife, but something is troubling her, Lord. I don't know what it is, but You do. I can't help her, but You can. Jesus, pour Your love into her right now. Give her Your peace and joy. Heal the broken places inside her heart just as You continually heal mine. Teach her of

You, Jesus. She wants to know You more. You have given her this desire, and I know You will fulfill it, for You say in Your Word that any who come to You, You will in no wise cast out. Thank You for that promise. In Jesus Name, Amen."

Tears fell down Victoria's face. She sniffed and wiped them away. "Thank you, Gregory."

He wiped away a tear she had missed. "I think we should start by reading Psalm 27."

He helped her find the right page, squinting towards the Bible she held since he didn't know where his spectacles had ended up. She began reading in a slightly shaky voice. "The Lord is my light and my salvation; whom shall I fear? The Lord is the strength of my life; of whom shall I be afraid?…"

Chapter 9

Victoria drifted towards consciousness. She automatically reached for Gregory. Her hand landed on nothing but a cold pillow. She let it lay there as she struggled to open her heavy eyes. They finally opened a slit as she groggily took in the full sunshine streaming in the room from the large glass windows.

It must be late.

Closing her eyes again, she yawned. After last night, she had been physically and emotionally exhausted, yet her sleep hadn't been restful. Voices and memories had followed to haunt her in her dreams...

The Psalm she had read earlier filled her mind. "The Lord is my light and my salvation; whom shall I fear?"

"Don't you know you please me more than I ever dreamed possible?"

Utter delight shot through her at the memory of those words just as it had when Gregory had first said them.

The delight faded as visions of Rolfe beating her when she had been twelve and had accidentally broken his favorite pen filled her mind. Slowly, Rolfe changed until it became Gregory beating her. She couldn't stop the moans and tears that escaped her at the sheer agony he inflicted. Suddenly, they both would be there, landing unrelenting blows on her body as she sobbed.

Then only Gregory would be there, holding her and comforting her tears away while whispering the words of the Psalm.

"The Lord is my light and my salvation; whom shall I fear?"

The soft rustling of paper pulled her away from the nightmare that continually swirled around and around in her brain.

She turned her head on the pillow and once again forced her gritty eyes to open though they still didn't open very far. Gregory bent over the drawing table working. The sight cleared a bit of the fog from her brain.

Surely it couldn't be late afternoon already?

The bed groaned as she sat up, but the sudden pounding of her head nearly forced her back down. Gregory immediately turned around. When he saw her awake, he came over and sat on the edge of the bed. He tenderly brushed her tangled hair back out of her face. "W…what time is it?" she croaked out in a raspy voice.

"It's almost noon. Let me get you some cold water. It might make you feel better." He went into the washroom but soon returned with a cup of water and a wet washcloth. She accepted the water and drank it. Raw pain scraped up her throat with every swallow, but the water soothed it as it went down.

When she finished, he took back the empty glass and handed her the damp cloth. She stared at it a minute. "What's this for?"

"It's for your eyes. They're pretty swollen from all the crying you did last night."

Crying?

She had been sobbing in her dreams, but she hadn't realized she had actually been crying or that the comforting feel of Gregory holding her had been real. She glanced up at him noticing for the first time that he looked a bit tired himself. "I'm sorry if I kept you awake."

"Don't worry about it." Gregory raised her hand and pushed the cloth against her eyes.

The cold wetness did feel good on her burning skin. If she looked as bad as she felt… "I must look a sight."

"A very pretty sight."

Victoria actually laughed. "For some reason, I don't believe you."

"Well, your face is pale in some places, and a little blotchy, red and swollen in others. But I still think you're pretty."

"You are not helping my pride any." She scooted back until she could lean against the headboard and adjusted the cloth so a new, colder spot touched her eyes.

Wait a second. Had Gregory said it was before noon? But he never worked in the bedroom in the mornings. He always waited until the afternoon. "Why aren't you in the garden this morning?"

He stayed silent so long that she pulled the cloth away from her eyes and looked at him. The swelling must have gone down some because she could open her eyes a little bit wider than before. Gregory looked contemplative, and just the tiniest bit hurt, as he watched her. "Do you really think I would just continue my normal routine and leave you here alone after the rough night you had?"

Put like that, it sounded extremely selfish, but she had never known anyone who would change their plans for her. "I'm glad you stayed. Thank you."

"You're welcome. Do you feel up to eating anything?"

She was starving, but she didn't want to move yet so she put the cloth back on her eyes. "I think I'm going to stay in bed for awhile."

Gregory stood up, probably to return to his work, but a few moments later, he sat down on the edge of the bed again. Pulling the cloth away again, she looked at him in confusion. He gave her a gentle smile. "I rang for Gladys. I think you deserve a breakfast in bed."

Once again, his kindness stunned her, and hot tears pricked her eyes. She quickly replaced the cloth as she blinked them away. She had done enough crying last night to last her for the rest of her life.

She really didn't know what had happened. Since their marriage, she had been fairly comfortable and secure yet still remaining careful not to anger Gregory. It would happen one day, but she had become an expert at not thinking about it. The beatings would come when they came, and she had determined years ago to enjoy the time she had in-between them. That's how she had always managed. But last night, all the fear and insecurity she felt during one of Rolfe's enraged beatings had come rushing upon her, gripping her in a strangling vise, and refusing to let go.

She didn't even know why.

Victoria hadn't realized until last night just exactly how complacent she had become. Since their wedding night, she hadn't once flirted with Gregory. She teased him occasionally, but not with the brazen coquettishness that had been her trademark in London. That outrageous behavior had always stemmed from the terror that had been her constant companion, and it took a strong dose of it to give her the courage to act that way. Last night had been the first time since their marriage that she had felt terrified enough to act.

It frightened her to realize how her fear had faded.

Without it, she had no protection. It gave her the courage to do the things that went so against her nature but appeased men's wrath.

That's what she had been trying to do last night. Appease Gregory's wrath. She couldn't deny that she enjoyed kissing him, but her main motivation had been fear. She hadn't been able to make the vision of Gregory beating her leave her mind. So, she had decided to please him so much that it would pacify any anger he felt thus prolonging her punishment for as long as possible.

But he would have none of it.

It had hurt when he had first pushed her away from him; hurt more than anything else she had ever experienced. To think that he had denied her out of displeasure and disgust had been like a knife straight to her heart.

Don't you know you please me more than I ever dreamed possible?

Gregory's words, and the truth shining in his eyes, the stark, undisguised desire for *her*, had thrilled her beyond words. Even now, giddy happiness swelled within her at the memory of it. Yet, he had pushed aside his own desire to help her because, somehow, he had known the truth about everything.

The Lord is my light and my salvation; whom shall I fear?

The verse made little sense to Victoria for she could think of hundreds of people to fear. Rolfe, Paxton, John, Harriet, Broderick.

Gregory.

In truth, she didn't want to fear Gregory. If only things could be different! She would give anything to know that he would never hurt her.

But he was a man. And that's what men did when they grew angry. It was a simple fact of life.

A soft knock on the door pulled her away from her depressing thoughts.

The bed groaned as Gregory stood up. "Come in."

She pulled away the now warm cloth as Gladys slipped into the room. She gave a small curtsy. "You rang, sir?"

"Yes, we would like some breakfast brought up." He turned to Victoria. "What would you like, sweetheart?"

Sweetheart.

A warm, bubbly feeling rose in her chest. She loved the endearments that Gregory had taken to calling her the last few days.

"I think I'd like some scones and strawberry jam, a soft-boiled egg with toast and some bacon. Oh, and a large pot of tea with honey would be lovely." Maybe the tea would help her feel more human.

"That sounds good. Bring enough for two, please, Gladys."

"Yes, sir." Gladys curtsied again and left the room.

Gregory bent down and took the cloth from her hand. "Let me wet it with some fresh water. It's become rather warm."

"Thank you."

He disappeared back into the washroom. When he came out, he didn't sit down on the edge of the bed again. Instead he propped his pillow against the headboard and crawled in beside her. Wrapping his arm around her shoulders, he pulled her close to him and placed the cool cloth against her eyes.

Letting her head rest on his strong shoulder, she held the cloth in place. After keeping Gregory up all night with her crying, she would have expected him to interrogate her about it, trying to find out what had caused it and to make sure it would never happen again. Not that she would ever tell him the complete truth. She could confess to having a nightmare, but she would never admit what the nightmare had been about.

Somehow, Gregory knew *that*, too, so he just held her and offered silent comfort.

Victoria sighed as she nestled a tiny bit closer.

He was the strangest man she had ever met.

But she liked it. She liked it a lot.

Mrs. Culpepper's voice screamed across the lawn audible even before the cabriolet came to a complete stop in front of the little stone church. Gregory jumped out and grabbed the tether weight. He set it on the ground and clipped the other end onto the horse's bridle before coming around and helping her down. Now that they had arrived butterflies attacked her stomach.

She had never before seen such a small, unadorned church. A single-story stone building with a small spire, weathered, wooden doors and a few plain glass windows. Nothing like the towering cathedral she had always attended in London. An odd mixture of people scattered across the lawn. Most were common laborers wearing coarse, frayed clothing or house servants in slightly nicer dress. But sprinkled throughout the gathering were a handful of the landed gentry bedecked out in all their finery.

Like her.

Feeling a bit conspicuous, she accepted Gregory's arm and allowed him to lead her towards the church. Gregory wore a suit coat but had still dressed more casually than would have been accepted in her church in London.

She had carefully dressed in one of her finest gowns.

Gregory covered the hand that rested on his arm with his own, bent his head and whispered, "Don't worry. They'll like you."

Jumping, she glanced up at him before looking back down at her hand. She had been gripping his arm so tightly that wrinkles creased his sleeve. Giving him a smile, she forced her hand to relax. He was already concerned about her enough. After what had happened Friday night, he had been unsure if she felt well enough to attend church. However, by the time she had finished her breakfast in bed on Saturday, her emotions were firmly back under control, and for the first time in her life she actually wanted to attend church.

Now that they had arrived, terror strangled her.

The first cluster of people they passed consisted of five men, common laborers of varying ages. They all doffed their worn caps when Victoria drew near, and one of them greeted Gregory by his Christian name. He stopped and introduced her to them also calling them all by their first names. She forced herself to smile when they mumbled their "Howdy, do, mum"'s. One man, obviously a hostler, had a distinct odor wafting from him. Dirt and grime encrusted his fingernails and around the edges of his face where the bathwater had apparently missed that morning.

Gregory continued to converse with them even asking the hostler about his ailing mother. After finding out that the doctor had restricted her to bed rest, he promised to keep her in his prayers.

She didn't know what to do as she struggled to keep a pleasant smile on her face. None of her training prepared her for a situation such as this. In London, she would have never dreamed of conversing with rough, uncouth men like these. Yet, they and Gregory seemed completely at ease with each other, speaking as old friends.

Finally, Gregory moved on. He greeted several more people, introducing her to them all, servant and aristocrat alike, before an unnatural quiet suddenly descended. She glanced around. Mrs. Culpepper had stopped talking and headed up the steps into the small church. It seemed an unspoken signal for everyone began moving in that direction. Gregory followed as he led her inside. He took a seat about midway up on the right hand side, scooting down the pew to leave room on the aisle. She sat down beside him, glad to be off her watery legs.

She was completely out of her element.

A middle-aged woman softly played the slightly-out-of tune piano up front. No one stood in the wooden pulpit so Victoria discreetly glanced around the plainly decorated building. They were still one of only a handful of people that belonged to the *ton*. Gregory had mentioned that his parents went to a different, larger church. Probably more like the one she had attended in London, but it would be interesting to see how a church like this operated. Facing forward, she sat prim and straight with her hands folded in her lap as she had been taught. Gregory, however, leaned back and stretched his arm across the pew behind her to get more comfortable.

A few seconds later, a slight scuffling sound in the aisle brought her attention back around. Broderick and his parents slid into their pew. Margaret bent down and gave Victoria a hug before sitting down beside her. "Gregory, Victoria, I'm so glad you're here. We've missed you the past few weeks."

"Thank you. I've missed you as well," Gregory responded.

"Yes, nothing can compare to worshiping with other believers, but I know how important it was for you two to spend the first few weeks of your marriage alone while you became acquainted." She patted Victoria's hands before leaning back in the pew and accepting a Bible from Clarence. Gregory greeted Broderick and Clarence just before a man stepped into the pulpit. Short and stout, wispy brownish gray hair barely covered his balding head.

"Vicar Edmund Mosley," Gregory whispered in her ear.

She nodded.

The talking ceased as everyone who still stood hurried to find seats. "Friends, let's pray," Vicar Mosley invited once the rustling died down. Bowing his head, he led the congregation in a heartfelt prayer. Not memorized like Rector Pitt's, but spontaneous and easy like Gregory did, as if conversing with an old friend.

After the "amen", Edmund beamed out at the congregation, his round cheeks shining red and looking remarkably like an apple. "Before I start the sermon today, I would like to welcome the newest addition to our small congregation. As you know, Gregory was married five weeks ago, and this is the first time his wife has been able to join us. Mrs. Thornton, would you please stand so we may greet you."

Victoria's heart stopped then began racing. Heat flooded her face. Oh, if only the floor could open up and swallow her whole! People turned to face her, but she couldn't move as her stomach writhed in agony.

Placing his Bible on the pew beside him, Gregory stood up and offered his hand to her. It gave her the courage she needed to grab it and be pulled onto shaking legs that could barely hold her upright. She clung to Gregory for support as the congregation applauded, and several voices called out a welcome. Others congratulated her and Gregory on their marriage. She couldn't look anyone in the eye so she stared over their heads as she nodded in acknowledgment of their greetings.

Finally, the applause subsided, and Gregory helped her back into the pew before taking his own seat beside her. "Thank you, Mrs. Thornton, Gregory," Edmund nodded to them before once again scanning the congregation. "As you know, we've been studying the events of the week leading up to the crucifixion of Jesus. Today, we are going to concentrate on the crucifixion itself. Would you please turn with me to Mark 15:15."

Gregory found the appropriate spot in his Bible then held it so they could both see it as Mosley read. "And so Pilate, willing to content the people, released Barabbas unto them, and delivered Jesus, when he had scourged Him, to be crucified…"

What followed was the most unusual and attention-gripping sermon she had ever heard. Rector Pitt used to stand behind the elaborately carved pulpit and read his sermons in a monotone that had everyone's attention straying from the first sentence. Animated and lively, Edmund Mosley paced up and down, even moving in front of the pulpit at times, and spoke in a way that demanded attention. He didn't seem to have any notes but the worn Bible he held in his hand.

Edmund told about the suffering Jesus endured before and on the cross in such detail that tears welled in her eyes. She wasn't the only one affected for quiet sniffs could be heard throughout the congregation. Discreetly, she pulled out her handkerchief and dabbed under her eyes. He went on to explain that Jesus had remained fully in command of the situation as He hung there.

"In John 10:17–18 Jesus says, 'Therefore doth My Father love Me, because I lay down My life, that I might take it again. No man taketh it from Me, but I lay it down of Myself. I have power to lay it down, and I have power to take it again.'

"Listen to that last part. 'I have *power* to lay it down, and I have *power* to take it again.' Jesus had a choice. At any moment He could have chosen to come down from the cross and spare Himself the tortuous agony. With just one word, one *thought,* legions of angels would have come to His rescue. Instead, each second He stayed on the cross was *His* choice; a choice made out of love for you and me."

Edmund's eyes were blazing, intent, as he looked at each person. "When the pain and agony became too much to endure, He thought of *you!*" His finger pointed at everyone in the congregation. Victoria sat stiff and frozen in her place, hanging on his every word. "He saw *your* face, and it gave Him the strength He needed to endure one more second. One more minute. One more hour. Because He loved you that much."

A pregnant pause ensued as he allowed them to ponder that. "Then when it was finally finished, when the price for *your* sin and *my* sin was finally paid, He gave up the ghost. Notice, Mark 15:37 says He 'gave up the ghost.' It was still His choice. No one came and took His life from Him. He gave it. Freely. For *you.*"

He wound down his sermon not long after that, ending with how they laid Jesus in a borrowed tomb. Standing, the congregation sang a final hymn. She followed along by rote, but her thoughts were far away centered on that cross 1800 years ago.

After the song, rustling and voices filled the church as people gathered up their things to leave. She made sure she still had her reticule then waited quietly for Gregory to replace the hymn book in the back of the pew in front of them. He picked up his Bible and smiled at her.

"GREGORY!"

The loud blast nearly jolted Victoria off her feet.

Mrs. Culpepper bore down on them and pulled Gregory down for a kiss on the cheek. "So glad you could make it today!" she roared as he pulled back. She pinched his cheek and gave it two soft slaps before turning to Victoria. "Victoria!" she screamed before pulling her into a hug. "It's good to have a new face in the congregation."

Before she could respond, Mrs. Culpepper moved to Margaret and then on down the pew. She bellowed everyone's name before pulling them into a hug, and she gave both Broderick and Clarence the same pinch, tap, tap routine on their cheeks as she had done to Gregory leaving them all with one reddened cheek.

They all seemed highly amused but indulgent as she continued to scream, telling them everything she had done the week before. She didn't stop to give them time to respond beyond an occasional "yes, ma'am" in answer to a question. Right in the midst of her story about her disgracefully long two hour nap on Thursday, she suddenly yelled that she had to leave and rushed towards another young woman in the congregation who wore the simple blue dress of a servant girl. "Mary!" Mrs. Culpepper shrieked right in her face as she pulled her into a warm hug. "How's your sister?"

Ears still ringing, Victoria felt more than heard Gregory chuckling beside her.

"You have to love her," Broderick said with a huge smile on his face.

Still smiling, Margaret turned back to Gregory. "Would you and Victoria like to join us for dinner today?"

Gregory looked at Victoria, clearly awaiting her response. In truth, she wanted nothing more than to have some time alone to think about the sermon, but she smiled and nodded as expected of her. "That would be lovely. Thank you."

"Oh, I'm so glad." She jumped when Margaret gave her another quick, spontaneous hug. "We've been wanting to have you over, to get to know you, but also because we've been missing our boy so much."

What?

How could they be missing Broderick if he lived at home with them? And what did that have to do with her and Gregory coming to dinner?

She barely heard their goodbye's as Gregory helped her into the cabriolet and drove away from the church. Margaret couldn't have been talking about Broderick. So she must have been talking about Gregory. But why had she called Gregory "our boy"?

Obviously, they were closer than she had realized.

Just then, Gregory turned the horse down a small, unfamiliar road, jolting her from her thoughts. Broderick had told her at the party that they only lived a few miles down the main road from Thornton Hall. "Umm, weren't we going to the Holmes Estate?"

"I have a quick stop I'd like to make first. It shouldn't take long."

"That will be fine." She smiled at him before turning her attention to the passing scenery. Before long, he turned off onto a deeply rutted lane. The cabriolet bounced and jostled her around like a boneless rag doll.

She slammed against Gregory's shoulder. He gave her an apologetic smile. "I'm sorry. The unusual amount of rain this year must have affected the road. We'll be there in a minute."

Victoria nodded and gripped the seat tighter. Her other hand held her elegantly feathered bonnet in place on her head. They finally broke through the trees and approached the tiniest stone cottage she had ever seen. The wail of a baby rent the peaceful afternoon.

Pulling to a stop in front of the door, Gregory jumped down and tethered the horse to the tether weight before walking around the cabriolet to her side. Reaching up, he carefully lifted her down and held her steady as she gingerly placed her feet on the muddy driveway. The heel of her white boots sank into the soft ground, and she nearly groaned. These were one of her favorite pairs, but they would be ruined after this little adventure.

Pasting on a smile, she waited while Gregory lifted a large wicker hamper out of the cabriolet and knocked on the door. So that's what the mysterious hamper was for. She had seen it when they had first left for church but hadn't dared ask about it.

The door inched open a moment later. A harried young man poked his head out. His coarse clothes had faded to a dingy gray color from many washings. When he saw them, however, his plain features transformed into a wide smile. "Gregory! Come in." He held the door open wider before calling over his shoulder, "Ailene, Gregory's here."

Gregory allowed Victoria to precede him into the dimly lit room not much bigger than their changing room. The only furniture consisted of a cupboard, a table with two chairs and a bed. Even those overcrowded the tiny space. A very young woman sat at the table, trying to hush a squalling baby. Though she smiled at them, her skin looked sallow and her cheeks gaunt. Dark circles rimmed her eyes.

Unobtrusively, Gregory set the hamper down by the door and came to stand beside her. "Clinton, Ailene, this is my wife, Victoria."

"Nice to meet you, mum. Please, have a seat." Clinton pulled out the only other chair in the room.

Once again, she pressed on a smile and gracefully sat down on the rough wood. Tiny splinters snagged at the delicate fabric of her silk dress. She held completely still, hoping the material wouldn't be completely ruined the way her boots were. Gregory rested a hand on the back of her chair. Her heart warmed, and she bit back a smile at the slightly possessive gesture. "I had heard that Ailene and the baby were ill and that you had been let go from the Stuart-Hornsworth Manor. You have all been in my prayers."

"Thank you. It's been rough, but the doctor said Ailene and little Clint are both out of danger now. That's the most important thing." Clinton smiled at his wife. "They just need lots of rest and quiet."

"Well, we won't tarry. I just wanted to let you know that we're in need of a new stablehand. Horace will be interviewing candidates tomorrow morning if you'd be interested in applying for the position."

Both Clinton's and Ailene's faces brightened as they looked at each other in silent communication. Victoria sat stiffly at the rough table, feeling like an outsider. Ailene gave Gregory a grateful smile. "Thank you. We've been praying that God would send Clinton work."

"Horace and Father do the hiring, but you're a good hostler. If you arrive early, I think you'll be hired."

Clinton beamed.

A few seconds later, Gregory and Victoria left amid a profusion of thanks. Once they had turned back onto the main road, she spoke. "What was in the hamper?"

"Just some food and a little money."

"Why didn't you tell them?"

Gregory looked pensive for a moment. "I guess I just didn't want to embarrass them. Clinton's a good man, but he's had trouble finding employment since he's had to take care of Ailene and the baby. I really hope Father hires him."

They fell silent after that, and fifteen minutes later, Gregory turned into a winding, landscaped driveway that led to a stone manor. A large estate, but only about a fourth the size of Thornton Hall. More what she had expected country manors to be. He pulled the carriage to a stop by the front door. "Gregory, is the Holmes Estate small?"

"No. Thornton Hall is just very ostentatious." Jumping down, he handed the reins to a stableboy then walked around to her side. He gently lifted her from the cabriolet and set her on her feet. "The Holmes family don't find it necessary to flaunt their wealth or to have enough space to get away from each other."

He said the last with a wry smile as he led her inside. He didn't ring the doorbell or wait for someone to announce them. Instead, he just walked inside and led her straight back to a private dining area. Smaller and obviously intended just for family, the table had already been set for five.

"I see you managed to make it, old chap." Despite his dry remark, Broderick respectfully stood when Victoria entered the room.

"It wasn't easy since we had to step over so many of your *toys* along the way." He seated her next to the head of the table on the left. "Broderick never lets me forget that I'm a decrepit old man, since I happen to be a few months older than he is."

"And to hear *you* talk you'd think I was still in swaddling clothes."

Victoria glanced back and forth between them unsure of an appropriate response.

"Just ignore them, dear," Margaret spoke as she came in. "Truth is, they are both still little boys who don't know when to quit clowning around."

"Aw, Mother," Broderick complained though he stood once again since a lady had entered the room. "You don't have to give away all our secrets."

"Just trying to give Victoria fair warning. Take nothing seriously when these two are together." Her eyes twinkled as Clarence seated her across the table from Victoria.

The men retook their seats. Clarence bowed his head and prayed. Afterwards, Margaret picked up a small silver bell and rang it. Immediately, servants brought in steaming platters of pork chops, carrots, peas and rolls. "How did you like the service this morning, Victoria?"

She accepted a full plate from Clarence before answering Margaret's question. "It was very nice."

"I thought he did a splendid job depicting the agony our Savior went through for us. I knew He had chosen to bear the cross for us, but I had never really considered how each second was another choice as He resisted the temptation to call for help. Had you, Gregory?"

"No, ma'am."

With that, the conversation took off. She could barely keep up as they discussed the sermon, even bringing up Scriptures Vicar Mosley hadn't mentioned. Questions filled her, but she didn't dare voice them. Instead, she smiled and nodded when appropriate while listening intently, hoping not to forget anything.

The conversation eventually drifted to other topics. Margaret told them about a letter she had received from Lucille, an older, married daughter who lived in Liverpool, she explained to Victoria. She, her husband and her three children were doing well and hoping to be able to visit for Christmas.

After dinner, they moved to the back lawn to play a game of pall mall. Victoria leaned against a tree, awaiting her turn and watching Gregory. He, Broderick and Clarence had ganged up and were teasing Margaret mercilessly as she prepared to take her shot. He seemed completely relaxed and open and had spoken more in this one afternoon with the Holmeses than he had for a whole week at home.

She turned her attention to Margaret. Her cheeks were pink and her eyes sparkled as she enjoyed the day with all her "boys" as she called them. She and Clarence seemed to be so happy. Margaret had said things to him Victoria wouldn't dare say to Gregory in a million years. Yet obvious affection underlined every teasing comment and look. They had the type of relationship that she had longed for her whole life.

Yet, who really knew what went on behind closed doors? Could they really be as happy as they seemed?

Impossible.

Margaret hit the ball. Her mallet glanced off of it only sending it a few feet at a rightward angle. She groaned as the men laughed.

Gregory turned to her and held out his hand with a wide smile. "Come on, Victoria. It's your turn, and I know you can do better than that poor shot Margaret made." Before he could move, she lifted her mallet and whacked it across his backside. "Hey!" he yelped.

Primly, Margaret rested her mallet against the ground and folded her hands on top. "That, young man, is to remind you to speak more respectfully about your elders. The only reason why I missed that shot was because you three had me laughing so hard I couldn't see."

They all burst out laughing again. Victoria smiled hesitantly as she approached her ball. "Come on, you can do it," Gregory encouraged. "Put us ahead, honey."

As she lined up her shot, she had to admit that, despite her initial reluctance, she was really glad they had come.

Chapter 10

"Victoria," Gregory's head popped around the doorway of the blue salon. "Do you want to see the hybrid?"

She looked up from her tapestry puzzled. Only an hour since breakfast but this made the fourth time Gregory had come in trying to cajole her into joining him in the garden. She longed to go, but experience warned her not to.

Instead, she gave him a carefree smile. "I'll see it after our ride this afternoon."

Disappointment crossed his face. "Okay, honey."

He disappeared again.

She bent back over her work but had to take her last two stitches out. She finished a blue flower then started changing her thread to white.

Gregory suddenly popped around the door again. "Victoria."

She jumped, and the needle pricked her finger. "Ouch!"

He hurried over. "Are you alright?"

Victoria resisted the urge to stick the offending finger in her mouth like a child. Instead she pulled her handkerchief out of her sleeve only to have Gregory take it from her. Kneeling down next to her chair, he held her hand and carefully wiped off the tiny speck of blood. "I'm so sorry. I didn't mean to startle you like that." He sighed and gave her a rueful grin. "I'm being pretty annoying, huh? Popping in and out like a jack-in-the-box."

"N…no." She couldn't think straight with him holding her hand and kneeling so close she could smell his faint, earthy aroma from working in the garden.

"Is this the tapestry you've been working on?"

She nodded dumbly. Without asking, he sat down on the divan beside her. Her cheeks flamed as he studied it. She'd never expected Gregory to see it, and the picture of her and her horse, Daisy, playing in a field of wildflowers suddenly seemed childish.

"Is that Daisy?" he pointed to the snow white horse rearing in the foreground.

"Yes."

"And that's you." He pointed towards the girl in a blue dress in the mid-ground. Her long brown hair hung down to her waist and blew in the wind. "This is magnificent, Victoria. I didn't realize you were so talented."

Her blush deepened. "Thank you."

"We'll have to hang it above the fireplace in our room when you're done."

Her entire body flushed with pleasure and embarrassment. "It's not necessary. Really. It isn't that good."

"Yes, it is. It's wonderful." He pointed to a conspicuously blank spot in the far background. "What's going there?"

"I…" She hadn't thought she could become any redder, but she did. She couldn't look at Gregory. "I…it's going to be y…you and Liberty. Watching us."

Long seconds of silence ticked by. Agony writhed in her as she waited for him to say something.

Anything.

His fingers suddenly touched her chin, gently urging her to look up at him. She finally glanced at him but couldn't tell what he thought behind the glint of his spectacles until one side of his mouth curled up. "Now I know it's going above the fireplace," he whispered before giving her a kiss. His fingers slid down to her throat before he cupped her nape and urged her towards him. Several minutes passed before he finally pulled back leaving her head spinning from his touch. "Won't you please join me in the garden?"

She studied his face. Why was he so insistent today? "Why?"

"Well, it's just not the same…alone."

Could he really miss her? She wanted to believe him, but experience cautioned her against it. Thinking back, however, she did recall that Rolfe had sometimes required her mother's presence while he worked. These moods were short and infrequent, but apparently Gregory had developed one of those. She would have to play it by ear. At the first sign of annoyance, she would come back inside

"Or we could stay in here," he continued when she hesitated. "You could work on your tapestry, and I could watch or read or something."

"No." A man who liked physical activity as much as Gregory did would quickly become irritated at being stuck indoors. Besides, she really had enjoyed her time in the garden and longed to do it again. "I could come outside for awhile."

"Are you sure? I don't want to pressure you into doing something you don't want to. I would be just as happy in here."

"No, I think some fresh air would be nice." She put her needle up and stood. Smiling, Gregory held out his hand. She slipped hers into his larger one and allowed him to lead her out the back door.

"I was working on the daylilies."

Kneeling down, he showed her how to divide them to keep them vigorous. She only half listened as she studied Gregory. He seemed so happy that she had joined him, so eager to share his love of flowers. Maybe that was it. He'd never had anyone to teach before, and he had enjoyed it.

As long as he continued to be in this mood, she could probably accompany him to the garden. It would be an improvement to being cooped up inside all day. Not that she didn't enjoy embroidering. She did, but doing it all day every day quickly became monotonous.

Turning her attention back to the daylilies, she accepted the garden fork Gregory offered her and attempted dividing them for herself. She quickly became lost in her enjoyment of the garden and her recently discovered fascination of botany. She soaked up everything Gregory taught her like a thirsty sponge. Amazing how much work went into maintaining a beautiful garden like this one.

The morning passed in a haze of happiness. At least until Gregory wanted to prune a few rose bushes after lunch. Panic welled within her as she stood. Heart pounding, she grasped at the first excuse that came to mind. "Gregory, I'm feeling a bit fatigued. I think I'll rest for awhile. If you'll excuse me?"

His eyebrows shot up before he nodded. "Of course."

She gave him a small smile and clasped her hands in front of her. "Thank you for teaching me everything today. I really enjoyed it."

"So did I. Maybe later this afternoon, after our ride, you'll feel like cataloging those specimens we picked."

"I'm sure I'll feel better by then." Just as long as he didn't bring any roses. The mere thought of them made her stomach churn.

Giving him another smile, she turned and made her way back to the house leaving Gregory to go into his rose garden.

Alone.

Victoria hummed as she patted mulch down around the Jacob's Ladder flower beds. A stinky, dirty job, yet she couldn't remember a time when she had been happier. She'd been out here with Gregory for a part of every day the last two weeks, except for Sundays and the two dinner parties they had been forced to attend at neighboring estates. Even the days when she thought he might need some space and stayed inside, he quickly came and cajoled her back into the warm sunshine. Or the drizzling mist as frequently seemed to be the case. She'd begun to realize that he really did enjoy sharing his garden with someone.

Only one dark spot marred her happiness. The large rose section looming ominously in the northeast corner. Every time he worked there, she managed to find some excuse to flee. Gregory's bewilderment about it kept growing, but he hadn't pressed her.

Yet.

She didn't know what she would tell him when he did, but, like always, she decided not to think about it until the time came. Her tapestry had come along quite nicely. She had everything finished except for Gregory and Liberty. She had found time to work on it when Gregory worked in the rose garden or during the frequent visits when Broderick came over to play.

It seemed strange to think of two grown men playing, but they did. They'd fence or hunt and generally become dirty and disheveled having the time of their lives.

If that wasn't playing, she didn't know what was.

Over the weeks, much of her apprehension about Broderick had disappeared as she came to realize that he wouldn't make any passes at her. He seemed to respect her status as a married woman and viewed her as off limits. Not that it let up on his friendly teasing. In fact, it seemed to make it worse since he treated her like a little sister. He had even come with them a few times when they went riding, and it had been a surprisingly enjoyable time. She had also spied that man they'd visited after church, Clinton, working around the stables. Gregory seemed pleased he had been hired, greeting him warmly whenever they crossed paths and asking after Ailene and baby Clint, both of who were improving rapidly by his reports.

But her favorite time had become Sunday dinner at the Holmes Estate. Everyone would sit down and discuss the Bible or the sermon just as they had that first day. She hadn't yet gathered up the courage to ask any questions, but she listened quietly, soaking up what they shared even as their knowledge amazed her. Would she ever know her Savior so intimately?

Jesus, I do want to know You. She lifted her face to the sky and spoke from her heart the way Gregory always did. *But I don't know how. I've been reading Gregory's Bible, but I find a lot of it confusing. Do You think it would be alright if I asked Gregory? I want to, but I'm afraid he'll grow angry at me for my stupid questions.*

That was the crux of the matter.

Her fear. Not just of Gregory, but of God. What if she did the wrong thing, and He punished her? What if she made Him angry? She'd never be good enough. She knew that. So how could she reconcile her faults and failings with God? How could she truly come to know Him when her fear kept her from letting anyone, even God, too close?

The sight of Gregory wheeling another load of mulch towards her brought her out of her troublesome thoughts. Like she did with everything else, she dismissed them to think about another day. "How goes it?" Gregory asked with a smile as he drew closer.

"Fine." She pointed, quite proudly, at the neat row of flowers and the mulch gently packed around them.

He inspected the work for a moment before smiling at her again. "Very good. Soon you won't need me at all."

She blushed even as her entire body tingled with pleasure. A sensation she had begun to grow accustomed to. It seemed wrong to take so much pleasure in his praise, but no one had ever done so before. Growing up, no matter how hard she worked, she had never been complimented just criticized for not being perfect. Yet, as the days went by, Gregory seemed to find more and more ways to compliment her and to lift her up. To make her feel as if she could actually do something right for a change.

Even if it was as simple as laying dirty, smelly mulch around a flower bed.

"I had a good teacher."

"Thanks." He seemed slightly embarrassed as he went down the rows, shoveling the mulch from the wheelbarrow into neat piles for her to smooth down. She had nearly finished her row when it suddenly hit her. Jagged pain bit into her stomach like a ferocious wolf. Gasping, she dropped the trowel as she doubled over in agony.

Gregory rushed back towards her from three rows away. "Victoria! Are you alright?"

Victoria held up her hand to stop him. Experience had taught her that being touched would only make it worse. "I'm alright," she managed to grit out as he came to an uncertain halt beside her. "I just need to return inside and lie down."

"Here. Let me help you." She took his proffered hand and pulled herself to her feet before letting go. She'd only taken two steps when the pain in her stomach latched its fangs into her with renewed force, and she started falling.

Gregory caught her before she hit the ground. Sweeping her into his arms, he ran back to the house. Knowing she'd never make it to their room on her own, she allowed him to even as the pain increased at the gentle pressure of his arms holding her. "I'm sending for the doctor."

"No." She took a deep breath and kept her hands protectively laid over her stomach as he took the stairs two at a time. "The doctor can't help. I just need Gladys and some laudanum."

"Are you sure?"

"Yes. It's alright, Gregory." Or it would be once the laudanum took effect. She usually carried some with her but had forgotten about it with her unexpected marriage and move to a strange house. She didn't even know the location of the infirmary in this colossal place.

Gregory gently laid her on the bed before dashing away to retrieve the medicine. He quickly came back and supported her head as she shakily took a spoonful. Lying back down, she rolled onto her side and curled into a ball, her eyes tightly shut. Sweat plastered her hair to her face from the intense pain.

She could feel Gregory still kneeling beside the bed. She knew he prayed for her, even though he respected her pain and didn't touch her, causing gratitude to fill her heart.

Nearly thirty minutes passed as the laudanum slowly worked into her system. Finally, with one last cresting wave, the agony subsided to a dull ache. Victoria's muscles slowly relaxed, and she opened her eyes. Gregory still knelt there looking more worried than she had ever seen him. "Victoria?"

"I'm sorry."

"No, no you don't have anything to be sorry for." He reached out and hesitantly touched her hand as if still not sure whether his touch would be welcome. She laced her fingers through his and held on tightly, drawing comfort from his strength. Holding his hand was about the only thing she could handle at the moment. "What happened?"

"Nothing. It's just my time of month."

His eyebrows rose. "Is it always this bad?"

"Yes." Normally, she would be about to expire from embarrassment at the personal topic, but the laudanum still worked its soothing tonic. She felt too tired and too languid to care as she stifled a yawn.

"Can anything be done?"

"No. The doctor's think it's because I'm highly irregular. The pain always hits without warning, and laudanum's the only thing that helps. I usually spend three to four days in bed before it subsides." He still looked worried. She gave his hand a reassuring squeeze even as she struggled to keep her eyes open. "I'm fine. Truly I am, but could you ring for Gladys to help me into my nightshift before I fall asleep?"

"Of course." Gregory kissed the back of the hand he still held before getting up. Victoria wasn't really conscious of what happened after that as the drug pulled her deeper into slumber. Gentle hands lifted her, helping her change, before laying her back on the soft pillow. Then everything faded as she drifted away.

Four days later, Victoria awoke to predawn grayness. Her pain had eased sometime during the night. It still hurt a little but remained manageable. Grime seemed to coat her body, and her hair had turned into a greasy rat's nest. Taking a bath would be first priority this morning. Hunger gnawed at her hollow stomach, a sure sign that she had started to mend.

She could feel Gregory's warmth beside her, even though he had been very careful not to touch her in anyway except for the hand which he held cradled in his own. By his deep, measured breathing, he still slept.

Carefully rolling onto her side, she laid there and studied him in the gray light. He had been so wonderful to her the past few days that awe filled her just thinking about it. He'd spent nearly every waking moment by her side, waiting on her hand and foot. Once he found out the laudanum wore off after four hours, he timed the doses, making sure that one never completely wore off before the next one took effect. Doing that had managed to keep the roaring pain at bay most of the time.

Whatever she had needed, he'd been there retrieving it for her. When she slept, which had been most of the time because of the medicine, he spent the time alternately praying for her and working on his book. The few times he'd gone down to the garden were when Victoria had insisted that he needed some fresh air. Even then, he hadn't stayed away long. At night, he'd made no move to hold her as he usual did; instead, he'd just gently held her hand. He'd been so sweet, she wanted to cry.

She had never had anyone care for her so lovingly. Betsy used to sit with her but only because she had to as part of her job. She had been an efficient nurse but cold and distant.

Would Gregory ever stop surprising her?

He suddenly shifted a little in his sleep. Muttering something unintelligible, he groggily blinked open his eyes. They widened when he saw her awake and staring at him. He immediately sat partway up. "How are you? Do you need more medicine?"

Victoria couldn't help but laugh. Still half asleep and his first thoughts had been of her and easing her pain. "I'm doing fine, and no, I don't need any medicine."

"Are you sure?"

"Yes, I'm sure."

Gregory rubbed some of the sleep from his eyes before studying her. "You do look better," he finally said with relief and relaxed back against his pillow. "Are you hungry?"

"Starved."

At her dry tone, he laughed and moved to embrace her. He paused with his arm still raised. "Will it…Is it…I mean…Can I hug you?"

She smiled at him. "Yes, just not too hard yet."

With aching gentleness, he wrapped his arms around her and cradled her against his chest. He brushed a kiss across her temple. "I missed holding you."

Closing her eyes, she snuggled closer. "I missed being held."

They stayed that way for a long while until Gregory finally stirred himself and stood up. "I'd better see about breakfast. You've hardly had anything to eat in days."

After sharing breakfast in bed, he went to check on the garden while Gladys helped Victoria bathe. By the time she emerged from the washroom, worn out and wearing a clean nightshift, Gregory had come back to the room and sat at the drawing table working on his book. She took comfort in his presence even as she drifted back to sleep.

Seated at his drawing table, Gregory watched Victoria sleep. Even on the laudanum, her face had been pale and drawn as she moaned in pain. Now, though, for the first time in days she looked relaxed and peaceful. *Thank You, Jesus.*

He hadn't realized until the last few days just how much he had come to love her. It seemed unbelievable that his love had grown so much in such a short time until it seemed too big for his body to contain. But why had he doubted? He had prayed even before he had met her that God would give him love for his wife. He should have been expecting Him to answer that prayer, instead of being amazed when it actually happened.

Watching her in so much pain these last few days had ripped him in half, especially since he could do nothing to help her except pray. He couldn't imagine that she went through such torture on a regular basis. *Jesus, please touch her with Your healing Hand. Lift this pain from her and make her time easier...*

Chapter 11

"Victoria, dear, would you care to join me in the white parlour?"

At Margaret's gentle question, Victoria looked up and gave her a polite smile. "That would be lovely," she agreed as they finished their Sunday meal. Rain poured down outside, precluding the usual pall mall tournament.

"I have a new sword," Broderick said as they stood. "It's Italian made with detailed scrollwork. A very fine blade."

"You really must see it, Gregory," Clarence added. "I don't think I've ever seen a more decorated rapier."

"Alright." Gregory caught her eye and gave her a smile before the men left the room.

"Maybe we could try it out together…" Broderick's voice drifted back as she followed Margaret to a small, private salon decorated mainly in varying shades of white. Her stomach twisted as nervousness suddenly attacked her. What would she find to say to this kind woman?

"I've wanted to have a private chat, woman to woman, ever since we met," Margaret began as they settled onto the settee. "But I've held off because I didn't want you to think I was being pushy."

"I don't think you could ever be pushy, Margaret."

"Thank you, though you may think differently later. How are things going with you and Gregory?"

"Fine," she answered automatically.

Margaret smiled at her. "You may not know this, but my marriage was also arranged. Clarence and I scarcely knew each other before the ceremony. Goodness knows Gregory has been like a second son to us and I love him dearly, but I do understand how difficult it is for you. I want you to know that you can talk to me anytime about anything that is on your heart. Now, how are things really going?"

For a moment, Victoria just stared at her. But the longing to talk with someone, really talk, finally overcame her fear. "Gregory is… wonderful."

And he was. In the weeks since Victoria had been bedridden, he had become even more loving and gentle, something she would have thought impossible.

Margaret raised her eyebrow. "But…"

"I think he's falling in love with me," she blurted out despite the blush that singed her cheeks.

"And you don't love him?"

Miserably, she shook her head. "I've been so afraid…" Unable to sit still any longer, she stood up and started pacing. "What if he expects something, wants something, from me that I can't give him? These past few weeks, I've tried to force myself to fall in love. I really have, but it's just not there."

Every time she tried to force the emotion her heart became paralyzed, frozen in fear.

"Victoria." Margaret stood up and stopped her pacing by pulling her into a warm hug. "Gregory wouldn't want you to force an emotion that wasn't there. And he wouldn't want you to be so worried and upset." She pulled out her handkerchief and dabbed at Victoria's wet cheeks. She hadn't even realized that she'd been crying. "Tell me, has he told you that he loves you?"

"No."

But when he did profess his love, he would expect her to retaliate. He would surely grow angry when she couldn't. She had been living in dread of that day for weeks.

Margaret pursed her lips. "Knowing Gregory, he probably won't. Speaking of his feelings really isn't his strong suit. Come here, dear."

She led Victoria back to the settee, and they sat down again. "Now, I know Gregory. He's not going to have unreasonable expectations of you. You've only been married close to three months. Give yourself time. Personally, I don't think you can live with a man as nice as Gregory and not fall in love. That's what happened with Clarence and I. He was so kind to me, and I couldn't help but respond to that. You know, though, it took me over four years to realize that I loved that man? Lucille was already a toddler by that time. One morning, I woke up, and I just knew. I think that will happen to you, as well. You will come to love Gregory in time."

"But what if I never do?"

"Do you want to love him?"

"Yes. He deserves a wife who loves him. I'm just not sure I'm the right person."

"Of course you are, or God wouldn't have brought you two together. Why don't we pray and ask God to give you love for your husband?"

Stunned, Victoria could only stare at her. All the time she had spent fretting and worrying about it and she had never thought to pray! "I would like that," she finally said as she took Margaret's outstretched hands. Bowing her head, she listened as the older lady lifted her and Gregory up to the Lord.

Three days later, Victoria sat at the table as the servants picked up the dessert dishes. "I can't believe it's already September. Summer will be gone before we know it and so will the garden."

"That's where you're wrong." Gregory smiled at her as he stood up and held out her chair. "There's still plenty to do in the garden even in winter. We just won't see the fruits of our labor until next spring."

"Really?"

"Really."

"Will you still have time to teach me?"

He looked surprised at her question. "Of course."

"But, what about your work?"

He tilted his head as his eyebrows furrowed. "My work?"

"Doesn't Mr. Thornton expect you to return to the shipping office soon? I mean, it's been really nice that he allowed you all this time off for our honeymoon, but I just thought..." Her voice trailed off when Gregory stopped walking in the middle of the hall.

"I thought you knew."

"Knew what?"

He sighed and ran a hand through his hair as he stared at a picture on the wall. A dour-faced matron frowned back at him. He finally looked back at her. "I'm sure you've noticed that my parents and I aren't very close." She gave a small nod. It had become apparent over the last few weeks that the Holmeses were more like family to Gregory than his own parents were. "They pretty much ignored me growing up. But when I was fifteen, Father decided it was time I learned the family business. He took me to work in the office, but we...clashed. Many of his business tactics are unethical, and I couldn't, in good conscience, carry them out. Off and on for the next three years, he would drag me down there, hoping I would 'grow up' as he put it. But after what happened in London, he stopped trying to teach me."

"You mean...when you refused to duel Silas Newton?"

"Yes. I couldn't fight him, Victoria. The man was insufferably rude, but how could I kill him for that? How could I take a life just because he insulted me?"

But what about your honor?

Immediate shame washed over her. She had been taught that a man must defend his honor, but it went against what she had read yesterday in the Bible where Jesus told His followers to turn the other cheek. "You were right. Jesus wouldn't have liked for you to duel him."

"No," he agreed as he started walking again. "He wouldn't have."

"I imagine Jesus wasn't very happy with the business arrangement our fathers made to see us married," she said out loud as she continued to think along these completely new lines. "Capturing people in Africa to sell as slaves in America doesn't seem like something He would do."

Gregory stopped walking again and turned towards her. "What did you say?"

At his incredulous voice, fear crawled up her spine as her whole body turned cold. "T…the contract. Between Mr. Thornton and F…Father."

"They're planning on capturing and selling *slaves?*"

She barely refrained from taking a step back at his furious roar. "Y…yes."

"How could he…" His angry voice trailed off as his right hand flew up.

Instinctively, she cowered back towards the wall.

Gregory froze with his hand still in his hair, and too late, she realized her mistake. He hadn't planned on hitting her only to run a hand through his hair as he often did. She immediately straightened and gave him a confident smile despite the way her insides quaked.

It always made Rolfe angrier when his daughters showed their fear.

His hand slowly lowered as shocked dismay covered his face. "You thought I was going to strike you."

"Of course not." She automatically gave the response Rolfe had always wanted to hear.

"Yes, you did. You really thought I was going to strike you." He took a step towards her.

Victoria shrank back half a step as her tenuous hold on control slipped. A small whimper escaped. "Please. I know I deserve it, but I didn't mean to make you angry. Honest. I'll do anything you want. Anything. Just don't punish me. Please. I just…" She finally found her backbone again and clamped her mouth shut on her useless babblings.

She should know better by now. Pleading for mercy always led to a harsher punishment.

"Victoria." Such pain vibrated in Gregory's voice that she chanced a glance at his face. He looked utterly devastated.

She jumped when he reached for her, but all he did was pull her into his comforting arms. He cradled her against his chest as if he wanted to block out all the pain the world had to offer. Unable to trust his seeming caring, she held herself tense, her muscles strung tight as a bowstring. Her heart hammered against her rib cage. "Honey, I would never strike you. Never. No matter how angry I became." His voice sounded strangely hoarse. "I would never do such a thing."

Something wet splashed onto the top of her head. She slowly glanced up, shocked to see a few tears rolling down his face. The sight loosened the stranglehold that fear had on her. With a small cry, she buried her face against his chest, clinging to him as if by sheer force she could climb into his skin where she could be safe. Gregory held her closer as he rubbed her back in soothing, rhythmic strokes.

Slowly her muscles unwound, and she relaxed into the comfort of his embrace. She began weeping. Great gulping sobs that had been held in for too many years.

Gregory didn't know how long he stood in the hall with Victoria and held her as she cried. Held her and cried with her because her reaction could only stem from years of abuse.

By her father?

Suddenly, everything made perfect sense, and he nearly groaned. How could he have been so blind? He should have realized what had been wrong by the hints she dropped, but in truth, Victoria couldn't have surprised him more if she had suddenly picked up a shovel and started hitting him with it.

That pain would have been a lot easier to bear than the heartrending agony tearing him apart right now. She felt so small and delicate in his arms. So helpless.

How could anyone have dared to raise a hand to her in anger?

Eventually, her sobs slowed until they became only an occasional hiccup. Gregory led her into the nearest salon and to a settee. A bit dusty from rare use, but he didn't care. They had to talk.

Victoria sniffed and pulled out her handkerchief. "I'm sorry."

"You don't have anything to be sorry for. Did your father…did he beat you?"

She wouldn't look at him. Instead, she seemed intent on studying her fingers as she ran them along the grain of the settee. She finally answered his question with a small nod. "I'm sorry. I didn't mean to fall apart. I've tried so hard to please you. To do what you wanted me to do…"

Gregory slid off the settee and knelt in front of her, cutting off her words. He waited. Nearly three minutes passed until she finally looked at him. "Victoria, what do you think I want you to do?"

"I don't know," she whispered miserably.

He stayed silent a moment as he prayed for guidance. "Do you know what I want?"

Wide-eyed, she shook her head "no."

He gave her a small smile even as the fear in her puffy blue eyes shredded him. "I want you to be safe and happy so you can feel free to just be *you*. That's all I've ever wanted."

If anything, her impossibly wide eyes grew larger.

"It breaks my heart to think of what you've been through, and to think that you're afraid of me is unbearable. I would never hurt you, Victoria, never. No matter what you did or how angry I became, I would never strike you. You may not believe me now, but with God's help, I'll prove it to you. No matter how long it takes."

Victoria looked like she wanted to cry again. He sat down next to her on the divan and opened his arms. She flew into them like a homing pigeon. Her hot tears fell upon his already soaked shirt. *Jesus, it's up to You. No matter what I do healing Victoria's heart is Your department. Help me to fit into my place. Speak through me, and use me, please, because right now I'm at a total loss as to what to do next.*

Chapter 12

At loose ends the next morning, Victoria wandered around the manor. Gregory had excused himself after breakfast, explaining that he wished to speak with his father. They had arranged to meet in the garden in an hour, but the time weighed heavy on her hands. She tried to work on her tapestry, but after making what had to be a hundred mistakes, she finally gave up and decided to go for a walk outside.

Heavy clouds threatened more rain, but she prayed that the storm would hold off until they had time to do some gardening. She would have felt awkward after the incident yesterday, except for Gregory. After their talk, he had continued teaching her in the garden as if nothing had happened.

A stone path wound around the manor. It might be enjoyable to walk the perimeter of her new home. It would take awhile, but she had never seen it from all angles before. Smiling, she set off at a brisk pace.

By the time she reached the first corner nearly twenty minutes later, she huffed and puffed completely out of breath. Sweat trickled down her back, plastering her camisole to her skin. No way could she make it completely around the estate. She would just walk to the next corner instead. That would put her in the garden, and she could wait for Gregory there.

Her legs burned as Victoria continued walking. Why had she thought this might be a good idea? The palatial house seemed to extend on for miles. Needing to rest, she slowed down just as raised voices caught her attention.

"…dare you question my business tactics!"

"How can I be silent when people's lives are at stake? Can you honestly stand there and tell me God condones such activities?"

She stopped and looked up when Gregory answered his father. Their voices floated down from an open second story window in a part of the manor she had never been in. After only a moment's hesitation, she leaned against the wall to shamelessly eavesdrop.

"God has nothing to do with my business decisions. Leave Him out of this for once in your life!"

"I can't leave God out of it, sir. He *is* my life." A heavy pause ensued. "Don't you even care that you are breaking families apart and ruining lives? Men, women and children are torn from their loved ones only to be treated like chattel. Sold with no hope of ever having freedom again."

"Slaving is a perfectly legitimate business in America. It is only here in England that it isn't. Besides, it's your own fault, anyways."

"*My* fault? How can it be my fault? I didn't even know about it until Victoria mentioned it to me yesterday."

"If you hadn't let your fanatical religion make you so *weak,* I would've never had to resort to buying you a bride."

"Buying me a bride?" Gregory's voice sounded strangled.

"Of course! Buying Victoria from Rolfe was the only way he would agree to your marriage. But it worked out well enough in the end. I'm earning a tidy profit in our joint venture, plus Victoria brought a large dowry and many social and business connections that I can exploit in the future. When Rolfe dies, we'll also inherit the bulk of the Bolton wealth. And with that figure of hers, she's beautiful enough to arouse even *your* cold nature, ensuring that the Thornton name will continue. All in all, I don't think I could have made a better match in a hundred years."

The silence stretched so long Victoria decided Gregory had probably left the room. She pushed away from the wall to leave but stopped when he spoke again. His voice sounded unusually quiet and controlled after such a heated debate. "I *am* blessed that Victoria is my wife, but not for the reasons you believe. There's no denying that she is beautiful and wealthy, but her true beauty and wealth lie within."

"For once in your life, can't you speak sensibly?"

"I'm sorry that you don't understand." Gregory sounded sad.

"Understand? What's there to understand but that I sired a lunatic for a son?"

Anger burned in her chest at his callousness. She forced herself to walk away. Her conscious smote her for eavesdropping as long as she had.

Her true beauty and wealth lie within.

Victoria didn't know exactly what Gregory had meant by that, either, but his words made her feel special. As if she had some worth in herself not just for the dowry she brought to the marriage and the future heir she would bear.

Finally making it into the garden, she found a stone bench and sat down to rest. She couldn't stop her mind from replaying the conversation over and over. John hadn't been the first one to accuse Gregory of being cold-natured. She supposed his almost painful shyness, as he had confessed to her one night, coupled with his gentle, unassuming demeanor could leave someone with that impression. However, their marriage had proved him to be warm and…quite passionate.

Her cheeks heated just thinking about it even as longing rose.

No, Gregory was anything but cold-natured. It was just another instance of the upside down standard kept by the *ton*. A standard contrary to what Jesus taught. Gregory showed respect to women so they considered him to be a cold fish. Paxton's lewd looks and comments were the exact opposite, and they considered him passionate and sought after. In truth, Paxton had the cold, uncaring nature for he took what he wanted without any thought for the other person.

Her pulse thundered in her ears, but it was true. Paxton was not a man to be sought after. And with that revelation, she knew she had to reach out to Claudia once again. She had to try to reason with her sister. She and Regina had sent several letters back and forth, but Claudia had remained conspicuously silent. Tonight Victoria would break the silence and write her a letter. Maybe without the emotions a face-to-face encounter provoked, she would heed her warning about Paxton.

Lord, let it be so.

The sudden slamming of a door made her jump. Gregory strode out of the house and into the garden. He stood for a moment with his hands on his hips, taking several deep breaths. Finally, his shoulders relaxed, and he dropped to his knees in the dirt. As unobtrusively as possible, Victoria walked over and knelt down beside him. She didn't know what to pray so she just kept her head bowed and eyes closed, hoping God would understand that she wanted to support her husband.

After several minutes, Gregory raised his head and smiled at her. "Thank you. The conversation with Father was…difficult."

"I know." His eyebrows rose causing her cheeks to flush. "I was walking around the house and overheard part of it through the window."

"I don't know what you heard. Some of it wasn't very…well…" he floundered for words.

"I knew he'd bought me to be your wife. Father told me that when he told me about our engagement."

"I'm sorry, Victoria. I never once thought of it as that."

"I know." She gave him a smile. "So what part of the garden are we going to do today?"

"Well, at the risk of sending you flying back into the house, I really need to work on the roses. I've neglected them too much these past few weeks." At his words, her heart froze, and her blood roared in her ears. Gregory sighed. "I suppose you're going to work on your tapestry."

She closed her eyes and breathed deeply. He sounded so hurt and disappointed. She had to tell him the truth. She had to even if it meant he punished her.

Opening her eyes again, she looked at him. "I have another confession to make. Something that happened not long before we were engaged." Gregory turned to face her more fully but remained quiet. "I had always been afraid of…of men so I never wanted to…to kiss any of my escorts." Victoria paused. Telling him would be harder than she thought.

He touched her hand. "You don't have to tell me."

"I want to. To explain." She took a deep breath. "I learned how to flirt, to cover it up, but that night a rumor started that I'd never been kissed. You know how the *ton* views such things."

He nodded.

"I couldn't let Father find out so I decided to kiss my escort that night. It was Paxton."

"The blond-haired man who was so jealous?"

Gulping, she closed her eyes and nodded. "He took me out into the rose garden, and he...he..." She started shaking.

Gregory pulled her into his arms and rubbed her back. "It's okay, honey. You don't have to say anymore."

Somehow, his touch gave her the strength to continue "He was very harsh. Demanding. He wanted more than a few kisses and planned to take it. But somehow, I managed to talk him into waiting until later. I don't know why it worked. He should have known I would never go back out with him."

"God protected you."

At the quiet words, shock exploded through her, tingling all the way to her toes. "He did! I remember praying for God to help me. I had never prayed outside of church, and I didn't expect Divine intervention. But He did!"

Gregory smiled softly. "Yes, He did."

The elation at knowing God had cared for and protected her faded as she looked back at Gregory. "But if I'd trusted Him from the beginning, I would've never gone into the garden with Paxton no matter what I thought Father might do. I didn't know, but he and Mr. Thornton were already in talks about our engagement. He probably wouldn't have had time to act, but now, every time I see roses, or smell them, all I can remember is Paxton. It makes me physically ill." She took a deep, shuddering breath as she pushed the memories away. "I want to share everything with you, Gregory. Truly, I do, but now...now there's this memory between us that's keeping me from enjoying all of your garden."

Tears stung her eyes. She wanted to be able to share the roses with her husband, but how could she when it made her so nauseous?

He stayed quiet for several minutes. "You said it was the memory of Paxton that makes you ill, so…what if we made a new memory?"

Have Gregory kiss her in the roses? Victoria's heart sped up, and her palms grew damp. Really, she should have better control. Did she really think that he would suddenly turn into a monster like Paxton just because they were surrounded by roses? "I…it might work."

He smiled at her. "All we can do is try." Standing up, he offered his hand. She reluctantly took it. Her heart pounded harder as he led her towards the far side of the garden. At the sweet, heady smell perfuming the air, her stomach churned and black dots danced in front of her eyes. She could not be sick. She couldn't!

Her feet slowed.

Gregory stopped just before the arched entrance and looked at her. "Do you trust me?"

She tried to see him past the fear clawing at her throat and urging her to run away as fast as she could. This was Gregory. Her Gregory who had been nothing but kind to her. Did she trust him?

"Y…yes. I trust you."

She would trust him. She had no choice.

Gregory gave her another gentle smile before leading her under the arbor and into the rose garden. Immediately, they were engulfed in the fragrant blooms. Victoria tried to mentally prepare herself for what was coming, but all too soon he stopped walking.

Panic threatened to overtake her. She wasn't ready for this!

She braced herself, but he didn't take her in his arms. Instead, he knelt down and urged her to join him.

Confused, she knelt down beside him and bowed her head when he did. "Father, thank You for being here with us. You know the scars Victoria has endured, but You are the healer of our hearts. Only You can take every memory and wipe it clean. Only You can take away her fear. We ask, Jesus, that You meet us here. Touch Your daughter, Victoria, with Your healing hand. In Jesus' Name we pray, Amen."

Opening his eyes, Gregory pointed towards…

Shea frowned and leaned closer.

It looked like a pile of dead sticks. Dead sticks with a few dead leaves still clinging to them planted in a large open space between two huge, flowering bushes. "I found that on the roadside a few days ago when Broderick and I were hunting. It's a Mutabilis, a rose of Chinese origin, very rare in England but very precious. The flowers bloom yellow and slowly change to pink and then crimson. Obviously, someone tried to transplant it but threw it out when it withered. I don't know if it can be saved, but I wanted to try. Will you help me?"

She glanced back at Gregory. Was he trying to tell her something? Could this little pile of sticks represent her? Could God take the dead things in her life and bring about something new and…precious?

"Is that the memory you wanted to make?"

"Yes."

She couldn't stop her small bubble of shocked laughter. Gregory looked confused, but at that moment she wanted to hug the stuffing out of him. It had to be the sweetest gesture anyone had ever done for her. "I would love to."

He smiled again. "Well, here's what we need to do…"

For over an hour, they worked on the tiny plant, pampering it well beyond what it needed. Only sheer force of will kept nausea from taking over completely, but Victoria managed to last the entire time without being ill. A giant step in the right direction. Surely tomorrow would be better.

That night, she gazed at Gregory as he worked on his book. His forehead scrunched up as he focused on penciling just the right shading on a Maltese Cross. She smiled at his little boy look of intense concentration. Somehow, their time spent amongst the roses had endeared him to her even more than before. She couldn't think of another man who wouldn't have tried to kiss her. Looking at him now something soft and achingly sweet twanged in the region of her heart.

Could it be love?

She didn't know. The emotion was too new to examine closely so she shied away from it. However, she had one task that could not be put off any longer. She had to write Claudia.

Sitting down at the small correspondence desk, Victoria pulled out a piece of stationary. For a moment, she just traced her finger along the name typed with a flourish in the top right hand corner.

Mrs. Gregory Thornton.

How she loved her title!

Turning her attention back to the letter, she sent up a prayer for guidance and dipped her quill pen in the inkwell. *To my dear sister, Claudia...*

Claudia stood in front of her dressing table critically analyzing the hair style Mary had just completed. Most of her hair had been piled on top of her head in a careful arrangement of haphazard curls. A dark blue ribbon artistically wove in and out along with a white blossom from the arrangement Paxton had sent earlier. The rest of her hair fell in long, tantalizing ringlets around her face and neck. She smiled, satisfied at the results. "That will do, Mary."

Mary curtsied and left the room. Straightening her ballgown, Claudia smiled again at her reflection in the mirror this time making sure her dimple appeared in a flirtatious way. "Claudia, my dear, you are simply irresistible."

Reaching for her bottle of *Aqua Mirabilis,* her eyes landed on the letter that had arrived in that morning's post. Victoria had written to warn her away from Paxton again. She'd described an incident that had happened in their garden where, supposedly, God had intervened to save her virtue from Paxton's insistent demands then went on to extol Gregory's virtues.

Claudia dabbed the perfume on her wrists and behind her ears before picking up the parchment. She quickly scanned it and found the part she sought...

After nearly three months of marriage, I can honestly say that Gregory's touch has never hurt. He has always been gentle and kind. After the incident with Paxton, however, I was sore and bruised for nearly two weeks...

She scoffed and threw the letter back onto the dressing table.

Never hurt? A barefaced lie if she'd ever heard one. A man's touch always hurt a little. She'd certainly kissed enough men to know that!

But two weeks is an awfully long time...

A knock sounded at the door, bringing her out of her musings. "Yes?"

"Miss Claudia, Mr. Paxton Burke is here to pick you up."

For a brief second, her eyes flitted to the letter, lying on her dressing table. With a huff, she dismissed it. "Tell him I'll be right down."

Picking up her reticule, Claudia once again checked her image in the mirror. She had spent three months trying to capture Paxton's attention. Now that she finally had it, she wouldn't throw away the chance of a lifetime just because of a silly little letter. It had probably been written out of jealousy anyway. Besides, since she had just celebrated her sixteenth birthday, she was certainly old enough, and beautiful enough, to handle him.

Satisfied that her every feature had been shown off to the best advantage, Claudia pasted on a welcoming smile and started down the stairs.

Chapter 13

When the elder Thorntons appeared for dinner a few days later, Victoria's spirits took a nosedive. Except Harriet smiled at them as she took her seat.

Beamed, actually.

"Good evening, dear," she said to Victoria as she picked up the small silver bell and rang it. "It's been so long since I've seen you. We really must schedule a girl's day sometime soon. We could visit Brighton for an afternoon. Or perhaps drive down to Lewes for an entire day of shopping."

Who was this woman, and what had she done to Harriet Thornton?

Unable to think of a suitable reply, she nodded dumbly as the servants brought in dinner.

"You know, Gregory, I've been thinking about what you said the other day." Harriet sampled the mutton and patted her mouth with a white napkin before stopping Sarah, one of the servant girls. Sarah seemed to brace herself, but Harriet didn't notice. "You may tell Cook she did a wonderful job with the mutton. It is simply superb."

Sarah's mouth gaped slightly as she executed a small curtsy. "Yes, mum." She looked sideways at Harriet before returning to the kitchen.

"What was I saying?" Harriet looked back at Gregory and brightened. "Oh, yes. I've been thinking about poor Victoria not having a mother all these years, and then being torn away from all that was familiar just to come live in near complete isolation. It must be terribly hard, dear," she told Victoria with apparent sincerity.

Once again, she shocked Victoria speechless. That conversation had taken place over two months before! Harriet continued on without waiting for a reply. "So, I asked myself, what would I want if I were in Victoria's place? And then I knew the perfect answer. Can you guess, Gregory?"

"Well…" He glanced at Victoria as if that would give him a clue. A futile effort since she had no idea what the older woman meant either. Despite Harriet's obvious excitement, a faint sense of foreboding crept up her spine. What on earth could she have planned? "Maybe a…uh…"

Harriet laughed at Gregory's stammering. "Men are so clueless. A party! With all of her old friends from London." Victoria's foreboding turned into full blown dread. "So, I sent out invitations and arranged it. About twenty young people from your set are coming for a week's getaway in the country, beginning next Monday. Aren't you thrilled?"

Thrilled?

She wanted to run and hide until it was all over. She didn't want to be thrust back into that superficial lifestyle. Looking at Harriet, though, she tried to muster up a pleased smile. For the first time since she'd met her, she actually seemed to be doing something nice for someone else. Why, she looked positively giddy at her surprise. "That was very… thoughtful, Mrs. Thornton." The best she could do at the moment even if her smile felt more like a grimace, and her voice sounded flat.

Harriet laughed. "I knew you would love it. And you must stop calling me 'Mrs. Thornton'; it sounds so formal. Like Gregory pointed out, I'm your only mother now, so you may call me Mother Harriet."

"T…thank you, Mother Harriet," she repeated, dumbfounded at her sudden pleasantness. She exchanged a glance with Gregory, but he looked as mystified as she felt.

John continued eating, seemingly oblivious to anyone else at the table. At least *he* behaved in a normal manner.

Harriet tilted her head and studied Victoria. "You know, dear, you really are such a pretty little thing. You and Gregory ought to have beautiful children, but you'd better hope most of them are girls. Oh, I know a boy is necessary to carry on the family name, but they're such dirty creatures. When Gregory was little, he used to run up to me all the time, completely grubby from the garden, and try to give me hugs." Harriet gave a delicate shudder. "He finally learned better. Girls, on the other hand, they're neat and tidy. I always wanted a little girl to dress up in pretty clothes and show off to my friends. Instead, I was stuck with just Gregory."

Anger boiled in Victoria's veins so hard she felt like a teapot about to explode. How could she speak so harshly about her own son?

"But enough about that." Harriet pulled several pieces of paper from her pocket and handed them to Victoria. "Here's the guest list and a schedule of activities for next week. Madame Blanchet is coming tomorrow to discuss new dresses for you. Now, Victoria, order anything you think you need. Money is no object. And Gregory, the tailor is coming over tomorrow as well to fit you with the new suits I ordered."

She quickly scanned the guest list, unutterably relieved when Paxton's name did not appear. However, she saw another name almost as bad.

Miriam Williams.

"I know you've put a lot of time and effort into this surprise for Victoria," Gregory finally spoke. "Thank you, Mother."

"Oh, pish. I enjoyed it."

Victoria forced another smile. "Yes, thank you Mrs…Mother Harriet."

Harriet beamed at them both. "Oh, this next week's going to be such fun!"

Fun? It sounded more like a nightmare come to life.

Early Monday afternoon, Victoria hurried from the back of the house with a sigh of relief.

Her escape had been a success.

What was supposed to have been a fifteen minute final fitting with the modiste had turned into four hours of torture when Harriet had shown up and insisted on making a few "necessary changes". She was supposed to meet Gregory before the guests arrived to check on their rose bush, but carriages had been clattering up the driveway for the last couple of hours. Thankfully, she didn't have to officially greet her guests until the formal dinner party that evening. She had a sneaking suspicion, however, that Gregory had lost track of time and still worked and waited for her in the garden.

Several guests strolled along the meandering walkways, but she steered clear of them as she searched for her husband. It took her nearly fifteen minutes before she saw him in the distance. Kneeling, he carefully pruned a columbine plant.

She hurried in that direction before coming to a sudden stop behind a large hedge. Miriam Williams also walked among the columbine's, but her admiring eyes were fastened upon Gregory, not the fragrant blossoms. Fully immersed in his work, Gregory seemed oblivious to everything else.

As she watched, Miriam drifted a few steps closer to him and delicately cleared her throat. "Excuse me." Gregory looked up, and she gave him her prettiest smile. Respectfully, he stood to his feet. "I must say, you are a wonderful gardener. These flowers are truly magnificent. I don't think I've ever seen any more beautiful." She paused for a moment as she smiled again and took another step closer. "I would really enjoy having an arrangement displayed in my room. If you could help me pick the flowers?"

Unexpected jealousy, white and hot, shot through Victoria from the top of her head all the way down to her toes. Miriam obviously didn't recognize Gregory and merely thought him to be the gardener, but that didn't matter. A man-hunter, she pursued any male she thought attractive whether wealthy or a common servant. She believed that men should fall at her feet, and if they resisted her advances, she merely considered it a personal challenge to bend him to her will.

Gregory gave her a polite smile, oblivious to the danger. "You may pick all the flowers you want, miss, but I'm afraid I won't be able to help you. I'm waiting for someone."

Miriam arched an eyebrow. "Really? And how would your employers feel if they knew you denied a request by one of their guests? I'm sure it would result in an immediate dismissal."

Her words were meant to bring him to heel, and from the satisfied look on her face, she obviously thought fear for his job would make him her personal slave for the next week. Well, Miriam had better understand right now that he was off-limits!

"Gregory! There you are!" She marched down the pathway and slipped her arm through his, squeezing so close to his side she practically crawled in his shirt with him. She affected a surprised look when she saw Miriam before flashing the young woman a wide smile. "Miriam, I didn't realize you were here."

"Yes, darling. I was so pleased to receive your invitation," Miriam replied with false sweetness. Her eyes were shrewd, appraising, as she took in the possessive way Victoria clung to Gregory.

"Oh, you remember my husband, Gregory Thornton? Gregory, this is Miriam Williams."

"How do you do?" Gregory greeted politely.

"Well," Miriam looked at Gregory with new admiration and gave him a flirtatious smile as she sidled a little closer. "I'm afraid I didn't recognize you, Gregory. May I call you Gregory? Victoria and I are such old friends that it would seem insufferably formal to call you Mr. Thornton."

"Ah…of course."

"And you must call me Miriam." She giggled and batted her eyelashes at him as she moved so close they were almost touching. She placed a proprietary hand on his arm.

Gregory took a step back, causing her to drop her hand. A good thing, or he would've had a full blown cat fight on his hands. But Victoria's fingernails still dug into his arm as she tried to control her temper and not actually slap Miriam the way she wanted. She finally pasted on another smile. "Miriam, Gregory and I have a million things to do before tonight so, if you will excuse us?"

"I really must dress for dinner anyway," Miriam flashed Gregory another inviting smile. "But I will request that we be seated together so we can become better acquainted. Until then…" she held out her hand.

Gregory had no choice but to take it as he gave her a formal bow. Relief filled her when he didn't kiss it. Miriam giggled again as if she hadn't noticed. "See you later!" With one last bright smile, she turned and sashayed off.

"Ooohh." As soon as she passed out of sight, Victoria stomped her foot. "Now she's going to spend the whole week trying to capture your attention. I can't stand it!" She stomped her foot again. It probably looked childish, but it sure felt satisfying.

"Victoria…"

"Bad enough when she thought you were just a handsome gardener, but now that she knows you're my husband, she'll do anything to seduce you just to hurt me."

A smile crept across Gregory's face. "You think I'm handsome?"

She frowned at him. "You know you are and don't change the subject. I don't want that woman anywhere near you, do you understand?"

He hugged her. "Victoria, don't you know that you're the only woman for me? I'm afraid you're stuck with me for life so you don't have a thing to worry about."

"Well, you don't know what she's like."

"I don't care what she's like. I only care about you. Do you really think I'm handsome?"

"Gregory!"

"Well, do you?"

Victoria sighed loudly. "You know I do. I think you're one of the handsomest men I've ever met. There. Are you satisfied now?"

Gregory smiled at her, looking almost giddy. "You really do." Before she could respond, he pulled her closer and gave her a kiss that sent her senses reeling. Everything else faded as she clung to him.

When he finally pulled back, she couldn't remember her own name, much less what they had been talking about. Her knees had turned to jelly, and she would have fallen into a puddle on the walkway if he hadn't been holding her up.

She finally grasped the first coherent thought that crossed her mind. "We…ah…we'd better check on our rose bush."

"Hmmm." Looking none to steady himself, Gregory took a step back. "I guess we'd better before Mother sends out the cavalry looking for us."

Feeling slightly disappointed that he'd agreed, she took his hand and followed him into the roses. Desperately, she struggled not to breath too deeply of the perfumed air as her stomach churned. The bush still looked like a pile of dead sticks. They had carefully arranged mulch around it, and now, Gregory checked to make sure the ground had enough moisture.

As she dressed in their bedchamber later, it suddenly dawned on Victoria what she'd done. She'd been so angry at Miriam that she had actually yelled at Gregory and told him what to do!

Trembling overtook her as belated fear tied her stomach into a knot. How could she have lost control so completely? Thankfully, Gregory had been too distracted by her handsome remark to notice so she had escaped unscathed. But she must be more careful. He would surely be furious if it happened again.

Why couldn't he just say it?

Gregory paced in the hall outside their bedroom. They were only a few simple words. Why couldn't he just say them? He'd had the perfect opportunity in the garden. Instead, he'd lost his chance.

Oh, he'd teasingly called her cute when she'd been covered in mud, or even pretty when her face was red and swollen from crying. But to seriously sit down and bare his heart… He just couldn't do it. Why couldn't he just say, *Victoria, I think you're the most beautiful woman I've ever met?*

Or how about something even simpler.

I love you.

Only three little words, but every time he opened his mouth to speak, his tongue froze and terror paralyzed his throat preventing any sound from escaping.

Just three little words.

Three little words that he hadn't said in over eighteen years…

Five-year-old Gregory rarely saw his parents, and when he did, Harriet tolerated his hugs and professions of love, even though she always extricated herself as soon as possible.

This particular day, his parents were arriving home after a month long stay in London. A few of their friends had come with them. Gregory hadn't known this at the time. He'd just been overcome with happiness when he saw his mother alight from the carriage.

"Mother!" He jumped up and ran towards her before his governess had time to react. When he reached the driveway, he threw his arms around her waist and said the only words that seemed to express his joy. "I love you!"

The next thing he knew, Harriet pushed him away so hard and swift that he fell backwards and cracked his head on the stone driveway. Amused chuckles floated through the haze of pain. His parents weren't alone.

Harriet smiled at her friends. "I'm afraid Gregory has never learned to control his exuberance. Why don't you go inside for a cool drink? I'll be there momentarily."

As soon as the door had closed behind them, she turned the full force of her fury onto him. "How dare you embarrass me?" she screeched. Tears welled in Gregory's eyes and streamed down his face."Yelling out that you 'love me' like that. I'm going to be the laughingstock of the ton. And my dress! You've ruined it with your muddy hands." She straightened to her full height and glared down at him. "Well, I won't have any more of it; do you understand? I've let it go on too long, but you're old enough now to know how to behave yourself. Nurse, he's to have no supper tonight and no play time for the next three days. If it ever happens again, I'll make it a month!"

Harriet had swept into the house, leaving Gregory lying on the driveway, hurt and crying.

And ashamed. Mortifying shame that seemed to sink into his innermost being.

He hadn't wanted to displease his mother, but as he had sat in his room doing nothing for three days, he'd finally realized that his love embarrassed her. That it would always embarrass her and be rejected because, somehow, he wasn't good enough. So, he'd buried it deep down and had never said it again.

To anyone.

Meeting the Holmes family a year later had been a surreal experience. They shared love so freely among each other, and they'd included him in it with open arms. Margaret always gave him a hug and said she loved him before he left, but it was not until Clarence had led him to Jesus at the age of twelve that he had finally realized feeling ashamed and embarrassed of his emotions was wrong.

After that, Gregory had tried to say "I love you" back to Margaret, but he never could. The shame and the fear of rejection were so ingrained that the words always became stuck in his throat. He'd even tried practicing in front of a mirror once, but he'd felt so foolish he'd never done it again. Instead, he prayed for God to loosen the vise that always strangled him when he tried to say anything close to his heart.

So far, it hadn't happened.

Gregory ran a hand through his hair. *Jesus, why can't I just say it? Victoria is my wife! We've managed to talk about so many things; why can't I tell her what's on my heart? She deserves to know that she's beautiful. I mean, look how happy it made me when she said I was handsome.*

And it had. His whole life he'd been told that he was ugly, especially with his spectacles on, and he'd been so sure that a woman as beautiful as Victoria would find his appearance repulsive just as Harriet always said. But she thought him handsome, and she had actually been jealous when that Miriam woman had flirted with him!

It made Gregory so happy he almost felt like he could fly.

Not that he wanted any woman's attention but Victoria's. It just proved that she cared. When they came in from the garden, Gregory had pulled Martin aside and asked him to make sure Miriam would be seated well away from them. Faithful friend that he was, the butler had discreetly switched the seating cards when no one watched. Instead of being on his left side, Miriam now sat at the far end of the long table.

The bedroom door opened, and Victoria stepped out wearing a frothy gown in a deep rose color. Once again, her beauty took his breath away. When she saw him, she gave him a shy smile and cast her gaze to the floor. Gregory went to her and took her hand. "Victoria…I…you…" The familiar vise tightened around his throat, blocking the words he wanted to say, and after a few minutes Gregory gave up.

At his stuttering, she looked up at him. Her nervous expression finally softened into a real, albeit amused, smile. "Gregory, your hair is a mess."

"Is it?" He reached up to feel it, and sure enough, it stood on end from nervously running his hands through it. If he came down to dinner like that, his mother would likely have a stroke. "I'll just be a minute."

It didn't take long for Gregory to comb his hair so it looked presentable. Offering his arm to Victoria, he led her down the stairs, all the while trying to gather up enough courage to give her a serious, heartfelt compliment.

It never came.

Soon, they were making their entrance, and he knew that, once again, he had lost his chance. As he shook hands and greeted their guests, he couldn't stop praying.

Please, Jesus, please open my mouth!

Chapter 14

Three days later, Victoria wondered why she'd ever been concerned about Miriam stealing Gregory away. He stayed so attentive to her that she couldn't even turn around without tripping over him.

It was so wonderful she had actually been enjoying her surprise party.

Miriam hadn't quite her flirting, but she could only do so much with Gregory sticking to Victoria like fly paper. For Gregory's part, he remained polite with Miriam as courtesy demanded but cool. The only time he left Victoria's side had been yesterday when he went hunting with a group of men.

At her insistence.

Today, some of the party had taken advantage of the sunshine and gone riding while the rest opted to stay at the manor and play pall mall. Later, they planned to go to the beach for some sea bathing. Gregory followed Victoria around the lawn, carrying her mallet and making sure she had lemonade and plenty of the hors d'oeuvres. More than one of the debutantes eyed her with undisguised jealousy at her husband's obvious devotion. Even Miriam looked put out as she realized her blatant flirtation had no effect.

Victoria's former neighbor, Phyllis, had just taken her shot when hoofbeats pounded up the yard. "Gregory! Hey, Gregory!" Jackson, one of the young men who had gone riding, pulled his heaving horse to a halt just inches from them. "Something's wrong with Lord Thornton. You'd better come."

"John!" Harriet gasped and rushed forward from her lawn chair where she'd been presiding over the proceedings. "What's wrong? Tell me!"

"I'm not sure. He just fell off his horse unconscious. We have attempted to rouse him, but to no avail."

"Victoria, send for the doctor." Gregory's voice came out low, urgent. "And see that his room is prepared." Turning, he ran towards the stables.

"John! John!" Harriet wailed hysterically as some girls led her back to her lawn chair. She would obviously be of no help.

Victoria hurried towards the house but met Martin on the walkway. "Something has happened to Lord Thornton. Please send for a doctor and prepare his room."

"Yes, mum." Martin bowed and hurried away. She paused in the doorway when Gregory galloped Liberty away from the barn. Once he disappeared from sight, she ran inside the house searching for the housekeeper. She found Maggie in the kitchen.

"Maggie, is there anyone here skilled in nursing?"

"I am, mum."

"Lord Thornton is ill. I'm not sure of the particulars, but he fell off his horse and is unconscious. We've sent for a doctor, but it may be awhile before he arrives."

"I'll do my best, mum." Maggie turned to the serving girls. "Leah, make sure Lord Thornton's room is ready for him. Jane, gather up all the extra lamps you can find and take them to his room."

As Maggie continued barking out orders like a general, Victoria sagged against the doorjamb. She knew nothing about tending someone who had fallen ill. Having Maggie take charge was a relief. Within moments, the entire room had emptied except for two young girls left to tend the stove as they all scurried to do their assigned tasks.

Not knowing what else to do, she ventured back outside and sat down on a bench near the door to wait. Occasional bursts of laughter reached her as the guests continued their pall mall game. It seemed irreverent, somehow, as they waited for news of John.

What could have happened? How sick was he? Was there anything else she could do?

You can pray.

The soft whisper humbled her. Prayer. Of course. Why hadn't she thought to pray? *That should have been your first reaction.* It surely must have been Gregory's. She tried to gather her thoughts, but they were so scattered, they made little sense. "God, help us," she finally whispered. Not the most eloquent prayer but definitely heartfelt.

She suddenly straightened. Harriet! The last time she'd seen the older woman, she had been sobbing hysterically in a lawn chair. Surely she could use some comfort. Going back into the house, she stopped the first servant she saw. "Where's Mrs. Thornton?"

"I believe she's resting in the gold salon, mum."

"Thank you."

Victoria slowly climbed the stairs and stopped outside the door of the gold salon. What could she say to Harriet? Would her presence even be welcomed?

Taking a deep breath, she opened the door and stepped inside. Flung over the arm of the settee, Harriet still sobbed. Her coiffure fell in disarray around her red, mottled face. Strands of hair wet from tears plastered to her cheeks in long strings. Victoria hesitated in the doorway. "Mother Harriet?"

Harriet sat up and wiped her nose with a handkerchief. "Victoria. I thought you'd be with the guests."

"No, I wanted to make sure you were alright."

Harriet's red face crumpled. "How can I be alright? Something terrible has happened to my husband. I just know it!" Covering her face with the handkerchief, she wailed loudly.

Sitting down on the settee, Victoria pulled her into a hug and let her cry on her shoulder. "We don't know that, yet. He could be just fine, though maybe…maybe we should pray."

Harriet pulled back and gave her a dour look. The effect was lost when she sniffed. "You are just like Gregory. Pray if you want to, but do it silently. The last thing I can handle right now is some overly pious, fanatical ramblings."

Hurt speared her heart at the rejection of her tenuous offering. Harriet, however, had retreated from her. Tears still ran down her cheeks, but she refused to look at Victoria. For a long time, she sat on the settee, wondering what to do. When it became clear that Harriet wasn't going to soften her stance, she stood up and went to the window.

She still stood looking down into the yard when Gregory rode up, carefully supporting John's slumped figure on the saddle in front of him. "They're here!"

Moving faster than she had ever seen her, Harriet jumped up and rushed downstairs to the foyer. She followed, and they reached the door just as it opened. Gregory held the door as Horace carried John in. John moaned pitifully at every movement, his abnormally gray face a mask of pain.

"John, darling." Harriet took one of his limp hands and followed along as they made their way to his parent's large suite. Horace carefully laid John in the canopied bed before leaving.

John grasped his chest with his right hand as he moaned again. Maggie flitted around the bed, making him as comfortable as possible while checking his pulse and temperature. After several minutes she looked up, silently shook her head and left the room. Harriet sat on the edge of the bed and ran a cold cloth over John's sweaty face. Victoria slipped her hand into Gregory's. "We sent for the doctor," she whispered. "He should be here soon."

John opened his eyes. "It won't be…soon enough," he rasped in a weak, nearly inaudible voice. His eyes fastened on Gregory. "Boy, I need to talk with you."

"Yes, sir." Gregory squeezed her hand before letting go and kneeling beside the bed.

"The shipping business is going to be yours now."

"Father…"

"Now, don't tell me I'm going to be alright. I know it's not true, and so do you."

Harriet looked devastated at his words. Gregory's face paled, but he spoke in a calm, quiet voice. "Father, have you made your peace with Jesus?"

John snorted weakly. "I believe in God and Jesus. I always have. I just never took it to the extremes you did." A grimace crossed his face, and he groaned again.

"John!" Harriet clutched at his hands.

Feebly, John patted her as he continued to look at Gregory. His dull eyes filled with disappointment. "If only I could have had a man for a son."

Victoria held her hands together so tightly that she cut off the circulation, but she couldn't jump to Gregory's defense. John clearly faded away with every second that passed.

A tear fell down Gregory's cheek. "I'm sorry I couldn't be what you wanted."

"I've spent years building up Thornton Shipping Lines to be one of the biggest in the world. You'll probably ruin it within a year with all of your religious beliefs and charitable tendencies." He paused to cough and catch his breath. "Whatever happens…make sure you take care…of your mother."

"I will, sir."

Harriet threw herself across John's chest and sobbed. With what seemed to be supreme effort, he looked at Victoria. "W…when you have… a son…p…please name him…after me…"

John's voice came out so weak, beseeching. Victoria couldn't deny him this last request. "We will, sir."

He closed his eyes again with a sigh.

And went completely still.

Harriet screamed. "Nooo! Nooo!" She started shaking John's lifeless body. "You come back! Do you hear me, John Thornton! You come back! Don't you dare leave me here!"

"Mother." Gregory stood up and tried to help her from the bed. She beat his chest with her fists, going completely wild as she fought his touch.

"Leave me alone! John, come back!" Gregory picked her up and carried her out of the room, dodging her fists as she continued to fight him. "Come back! Come back! John! Don't leave me here!"

Victoria followed them into the hall, closing the bedroom door behind them. Harriet suddenly went completely limp and silent.

Gregory took her to a guest room and laid her on the bed. She rolled over on her side and curled into a ball. Her body convulsed as she sobbed, yet despite the tears streaming down her cheeks, she didn't utter a sound. Her eyes stared vacantly at nothing.

It was more eerie than when she had been wailing.

Gregory turned to Victoria, devastation lining his face. Without a word, she walked into his arms. He held her so tightly she could scarcely breathe, but she didn't care.

Her husband needed her.

The party broke up, and the guests quietly left the next morning. They held the funeral service that afternoon though John's father, the reclusive Duke of Lincolnshire, did not attend. Gregory had quietly explained to her that they weren't close, and the Duke never left his estate. Gregory had actually never even met his grandfather. John left him behind the couple of times he'd visited in his youth, but they had exchanged a few letters of correspondence over the years.

For the first time, Victoria saw Gregory's parents' church, a large, stone cathedral adorned with beautiful stained glass windows. The elaborately robed rector intoned a lengthy memorial address, extolling John Thornton's social status, wealth and his financial backing of the church.

The message left Victoria feeling cold. *What about giving your life to Jesus? Repenting of your sins and asking Jesus to forgive you? Wealth and social status didn't allow you entrance into Heaven as he seemed to imply.*

She wept at the emptiness of it all. It began to rain just as they left the graveyard. The dismal day seemed appropriate somehow. When they arrived home, Harriet immediately took to her bed. Gregory went out to the garden despite the drizzling shower. When she went to find him nearly an hour later, he knelt on his knees in the middle of one of the muddy pathways, sobbing.

Kneeling down beside him, Victoria wrapped her arms around him. He turned to her, burying his face into her shoulder. Rain and tears dampened her shirt as he clung to her. *Jesus, please help us.*

Chapter 15

Over the next few days, Victoria suddenly found herself thrust into the role of mistress of the manor. Harriet lay in bed only allowing her maid, Rhoda, to come in periodically to bring her food. A week after the funeral, Andrew Stokes, John's solicitor, showed up at the house to read his will.

Harriet refused to even come down for that.

Despite the confusing legal terms, the will remained simple. Gregory inherited everything upon his father's death. Folding the papers back up, Mr. Stokes cleared his throat. "Gregory, about the shipping business. Albert Walpole is a competent manager who has been with the line for years. As you probably know, John only spent one day a week going over the most important business contracts. I'm sure you can continue the same policy. However, a few issues have arisen that Albert needs to discuss with you."

"Thank you for letting me know," Gregory sighed. "I'll go to Lewes first thing in the morning."

Mr. Stokes nodded and stood up. "Once again, let me offer my condolences for your loss." He gave them a formal bow. "Good day."

"Mr. Thornton, I'm sure you don't want to tour the cloth factory. There's really nothing there for you to see."

Gregory gritted his teeth against Albert's constant attempts to dissuade him from his indepth tour of the company.

He'd been doing it for the last seven hours.

"As I explained this morning, I intend to inspect everything that belongs to Thornton Shipping Lines."

Albert sighed and checked his pocket watch before giving directions to the carriage driver. He had been unhappy at Gregory's request and made no attempts to hide his displeasure at having his valuable time taken up this way. Gregory didn't care. He knew nothing about the business he'd inherited, but he intended to learn. Part of Thornton Shipping Lines included a cloth factory that produced nothing but sailing cloth. It outfitted not only the Thornton ships, but sold to other shipping lines, including the Royal Navy. It was the last stop on his list. They had already seen the offices, docks, warehouses, shipyards, iron foundry and the vessels that were currently in harbor. The lumber mill, which milled wood for the shipyard, was located several hours away and would require a special trip to visit.

The carriage finally rocked to a stop outside of a gray, soot-covered building. Gregory toured every room of the dismal place asking questions as he went, not only of Albert but the workers as well. He found the same thing here as in every other part of Thornton Shipping Lines. Long hours. Poverty level wages. A blatant disregard for safety. Multitudes of young children working backbreaking, dangerous jobs right alongside the adults. The entire operation focused on making the most profit no matter how unethical the means.

"Well, now you've seen the business, Mr. Thornton," Albert gave him a fake smile as they exited the building. "You can relax on your estate and leave everything to me, just as your father did. I used to come over every Friday with the most important contracts for his consideration. I'll be happy to do the same thing for you."

Getting back into the carriage, Gregory sent up a prayer for guidance. "One thing you will discover, Albert, I am not my father. I intend to learn my business from the ground up and to have an active part in overseeing it."

Albert frowned.

If he didn't like that, he would surely object to Gregory's next statement. "Furthermore, there are certain changes that must be implemented immediately…"

Victoria glanced at the clock on her nightstand.

Eleven-twenty.

Only five minutes later than the last time she had checked. What could possibly be keeping Gregory out so late? She had wanted to stay up until he returned, but she could barely keep her eyes open. If it grew much later…

Stifling a yawn, she looked back at Gregory's Bible in her lap. She had almost finished reading Ephesians 4. She would finish the chapter and then sleep. Locating where she had left off in verse 30, she settled in to read.

"And grieve not the Holy Spirit of God, whereby ye are sealed unto the day of redemption. Let all bitterness, and wrath, and anger, and clamour, and evil speaking, be put away from you, with all malice: And be ye kind one to another, tenderhearted, forgiving one another, even as God for Christ's sake hath forgiven you."

She paused for a moment and read the verses again. For the past few months, every unkind word and look Harriet had given Gregory had caused her bitterness towards her mother-in-law to grow. Now, she could hardly look at the woman without growing angry, but according to these verses, that anger was wrong.

Or would it only be wrong if the anger was uncalled for?

She didn't know. But she did not want to do anything against God's Will. She decided then and there to do a study on what the Bible had to say about anger. Starting tomorrow. Yawning, she placed the Bible back on Gregory's nightstand.

Blowing out her lamp, Victoria snuggled under the covers, but despite her fatigue, she couldn't sleep. She tossed and turned and found herself reaching for Gregory more times than she could count. Finally, she lay on her back and stared up at the darkened ceiling. Doubts and fears assailed her as she recalled all the times Rolfe had stayed out late at night visiting the brothels when her mother had been alive. After she died, he had just brought the women home with him.

"No! Gregory wouldn't do that!"

She jumped at her own loud voice. With a sigh, she curled onto her side and stared at his empty spot in the bed.

He wouldn't do that, would he?

But, why not? He was a man, and she'd never known any man who'd remained faithful to his wife past the honeymoon stage. They had all started off well, but later…

And Gregory *had* been at the docks all day, supposedly an even worse place than the streets of London. *Those* women would be there, flirting with him. Blatantly flaunting their assets.

Tempting him to their beds.

Tears filled Victoria's eyes as her mind conjured up scenario after scenario of Gregory succumbing to another woman, until, suddenly, her eyes fell on his Bible. Just the sight of it cleared some of the confusion from her brain and brought peace to her aching heart. It would be wrong to automatically assume he did something immoral just because she didn't know his whereabouts.

Victoria sighed. If she couldn't sleep, she could at least spend the time doing something productive. Sitting up, she grabbed the Bible and held it in her lap. "Jesus, I don't know where Gregory is. Please keep him safe…"

Half an hour later, she replaced the Bible and closed her eyes to try sleeping one more time.

It proved as futile as the first time.

Well after midnight, a slight swish pierced the quiet. She immediately sat up. "Gregory?"

"Victoria? What are you doing awake?"

A faint fumbling sounded and then a flare of light as he struck a match.

"I couldn't sleep. I was…worried."

"I'm sorry." Gregory lit a candle on the dresser. Picking it up, he carried it over to her nightstand before sitting on the edge of the bed. "I had no idea I would be this late."

In the flickering light, his face looked tired and drawn, and his clothing had become disheveled. But then, he usually looked disheveled. She studied him closely without appearing to. No rogue or powder smeared his clothes. Discreetly, she took a deep breath of air, but she didn't smell any cheap perfume or alcohol. Only the tangy smell of salt and smoke. Perfectly normal for a man who had been working in an office on the coast all day.

Relief filled her so strong she nearly cried. She wanted to touch him, to hold him and have him hold her, but she held still. "How did everything go today?"

"Not very well. There are so many things…" He sighed and shook his head. "I've already made the upper management angry at me. I know nothing about the business, but certain changes couldn't be held off."

"A…are you sure you're doing the right thing?"

"Yes. I'm responsible to God for how I run the line, and common or not, certain business practices are not ethical. That's one reason I have to learn every aspect of the business. I need to have a working knowledge if I'm to know what's going on. I feel so lost. I'm not even sure where to begin."

"I'm sure you'll do the right thing." She hesitated a moment. "You look exhausted, why don't you come to bed? Things might look better in the morning."

"I hope so." Reaching down, he picked up a brown bag that she hadn't even realized he'd carried in. "I brought you something."

Victoria accepted the bag but couldn't speak for a moment, overwhelmed that he had thought of her. She opened the bag and pulled out a Bible with her name engraved on the front of it. Tears pricked her eyes. It had been months since Gregory had mentioned buying her a Bible, yet the first time he had gone into town, he'd remembered. "Thank you," she finally forced from her tight throat.

Gregory smiled and stood up. He lit another candle and made his way to the washroom. She ran her hand over the new leather before flipping the Bible open. Her eye caught on a handwritten inscription.

To my beloved wife, Victoria,

As you read this Bible, may you continue to grow in God's Grace and Love.

Gregory

Victoria smiled tremulously before lovingly placing the Bible on her nightstand. She looked at it a moment before adjusting it to a better angle. Finally, she laid back down to wait for Gregory.

A few minutes later, he came out of the washroom, blew out the light and crawled under the covers. Once he wrapped his arm around her, she finally relaxed. She snuggled a little closer, but his deep, even breathing told her he had already fallen asleep.

Stifling another yawn, Victoria closed her eyes and soon found herself joining him.

Chapter 16

$\mathcal{S}$omehow, the gardens seemed so empty without Gregory tending them. Still, Victoria mustered a smile to give to Perry, the newly hired, gray-haired gardener, as she passed. Making her way to the roses, she knelt down in front of their bush.

It still looked like a pile of dead sticks.

Chuckling, she reached out and smoothed some of the earth around it, still moist from the rain last night. Sitting back on her heels, she took a deep breath of the heavy, gray air and mourned the dying garden. Only a few flowers tenaciously clung to their stems. In a day or two, even those would be gone.

Surprising how much she missed Gregory. Missed the idyllic days spent here with him. Missed learning from him as they helped new life grow.

With Harriet still refusing to leave her bed, the running of the manor took up most of Victoria's days. She only had time for her daily check on their rose bush. And Gregory…he didn't even have time to come out to the garden at all. In fact, in the last three weeks she had only seen him four times. The three Sundays he took off work, and one Thursday when he managed to return home in time for dinner. After eating, he'd disappeared into John's study to do more work.

Not that she blamed him. He had decided that to learn the business, he had to spend time working at every job no matter how menial. So now, Gregory worked ten hour days loading and unloading ships at the docks and spending the nights learning how to manage the business. He left before she woke in the morning and didn't return home until long after she fell asleep. If not for the indention in the bed, she'd never have known he'd been there. She didn't know how he still functioned on so little rest. The last three Sundays, he'd fallen asleep sitting straight up on the Holmes's settee after dinner. Victoria had slipped off his shoes, laid him down and covered him with a blanket Margaret provided. He didn't stir again until time to leave, and only then because Clarence woke him.

With a sigh, Victoria pushed herself to her feet. She had a million things to do. She had to talk with Cook about winter provisions, oversee the remodeling Harriet had started in the north wing of the house and order more carpet for the green salon since it had ripped. That meant she'd have to go into Lewes soon to shop for the carpet not to mention drapes for the green parlour, new pillows for some of the guest rooms…

The list was over two pages long and still growing as she inspected every inch of her new home. But, maybe, when she went into town she could stop by the office and visit Gregory.

No. No, she couldn't interrupt him while he worked. She'd just have to be patient. After all, these long working hours wouldn't last forever.

She hoped.

Opening the side door to the manor, Victoria stopped abruptly as a thought hit her.

She couldn't go shopping.

She didn't have access to any money.

Even before Victoria opened her eyes the next morning, she knew Gregory had already left.

Again.

She'd been trying to wake up before he left but hadn't managed it yet. She had always been a sound sleeper, and Gregory could move so quietly when trying not to disturb her. She'd also tried staying up until he came home, but so far, she'd always fallen asleep before then.

She stretched then sat up before glancing over at Gregory's empty spot. She blinked. A folded piece of parchment laid on his pillow with her name on it. Recognizing Gregory's handwriting, she quickly picked it up. What could he have to say that would precipitate him leaving a note? For a moment, she just stared at her name written in his familiar script as a wave of longing swept over her. Finally, she scrunched her pillow behind her and scooted back against the headboard to be more comfortable and opened the letter.

Dearest Victoria,

Why is it so hard to articulate our deepest feelings? I can't count the times I have attempted to tell you what is on my heart, but the words would never come. It wasn't until I was dictating a letter today that I thought about writing to you.

The truth, Victoria, is that I love you.

I love you more than I ever thought possible. You fill my heart near to bursting with one look, one smile. My life before I met you was like a winter garden, dark and dismal, but with you, Victoria, it's like spring. It's light and warm with new life bursting forth on every plant. I thank God every day that He brought you into my life, for in truth, I cannot imagine life without you.

I love you with all my heart,

Gregory

Tears filled her eyes even as she gave a watery chuckle. Only Gregory would come up with a garden metaphor. The sweet letter touched her deeply, but it also left her in a quandary.

Did Gregory expect a letter back?

But she didn't love Gregory. She liked him. Respected him. Wanted to be with him, but she didn't love him.

With a moan, Victoria buried her face in her hands. What was wrong with her? Gregory was the most wonderful, Godly man she had ever met. Why couldn't she fall in love with him?

Remembering Margaret's advice, she turned her self-recriminating thoughts into prayers. *Jesus, I want to love Gregory because he deserves to be loved by his wife. Please, please give me love for my husband.*

Holding her breath, she waited, but no new feelings suddenly burst upon her.

She sighed. Gregory had told her God always answered prayer, but on His timetable not theirs.

Well, I just won't write a note. Fear quivered in her stomach. *I can't write and lie about my feelings so I won't write at all. But, please Lord, please don't let Gregory grow angry.*

That night, Victoria lay awake in bed, tensed in anticipation of Gregory's return. She tried to sleep, but fear and dread kept her awake. Her day had been horrible as her mind kept conjuring up worse and worse scenarios of when Gregory failed to find a response. Several times she'd sat down at her desk to just write him a letter saying what he wanted to hear. Only the memory of the ninth commandment kept her from completing it.

No matter how she looked at it, writing the letter was a lie so all her attempts ended up being thrown into the fireplace and burned. Now, for the first time, she wanted to be asleep when Gregory returned, but she remained wide awake.

After two in the morning, the soft swish of the door alerted Victoria to his presence. She immediately closed her eyes and feigned sleep. Her heart lodged in her throat at the strike of a match. She carefully regulated her breathing.

Faint light flickered behind her eyelids as Gregory lit a candle. Soft footsteps and the fading light told her that he went into the washroom. Soon, he came out and headed towards the bed.

Victoria's heart pounded harder as sweat broke out on her hands. She laid on her side curled into a ball with her back to Gregory, yet it took all her willpower not to cringe away when he set the candle on the nightstand.

A mere second later, he blew out the light and crawled into bed. Putting his arm around her as he always did, he immediately fell asleep.

For several long minutes, she lay still, tensed under his arm despite his deep, even breathing. Finally realizing that he didn't plan to harm her, she slowly forced her muscles to unclench. Confusion filled her. He hadn't even looked for a note before falling into bed.

Had he not been expecting one?

Or had he been so tired that he'd forgotten?

Uncurling from her protective ball, Victoria rolled over to face him. The movement caused him to mumble incoherently and pull her closer in his sleep.

Lingering fear kept her from relaxing completely. Instead, she rested her head on his chest and listened to the reassuring beat of his heart. Eventually, the steady rhythm lulled her enough that she fell into a fitful sleep.

Nine days later, Victoria found the second note. She hesitated before picking it up. The week before had been a nightmare. She remained constantly on edge, expecting Gregory to remember that he had written her and demand a response. Yet, the week passed without incident, and on Sunday, Gregory had been the same as always. He had even fallen asleep on the Holmes's settee again. She finally relaxed completely but still felt utterly miserable.

With trembling hands, she opened the paper to find only three words. *I miss you.*

A startled laugh escaped even as tears once again welled up in her eyes. Gregory didn't hold it against her that she'd been unable to answer his first letter, but this one she could.

Getting up and going immediately to her correspondence desk, Victoria placed his note in the drawer with the first one then wrote her response. *I miss you, too.* She folded it and put his name on the front.

Carefully, she placed it on his pillow.

Standing back, she smiled at it before making her way to the washroom feeling lighter and happier than she had in days.

Two mornings later, she found another note. *How is our rose bush doing?*

How had he known that she still checked on it?

Getting out another sheet of paper, she wrote. *It looks exactly the same...a pile of dead sticks!*

Ha. Ha. Very funny. Victoria smiled as she read his response the next day. *Actually, on Sunday I would like to cover it before the cold weather hits. Please remind me...and make sure I wake up in time to return home before dark.* He'd added a silly smiley face at the end.

But on Sunday, she found herself hesitant to wake him. Each week, the dark circles under his eyes were more pronounced, and he'd begun to lose weight. Today he looked positively terrible. How much longer could he keep up this pace? Even the Holmes family were worried about him.

Margaret found her standing uncertainly in the doorway of the parlour. "What's the matter, dear?" she asked in a whisper.

"Gregory asked me to wake him in time to arrive home before dark, but look at him. He's exhausted. I think he even slept through the sermon this morning."

Margaret gave her a hug. "I know, but this can't go on much longer. Surely Gregory sees that. If he asked you to, I think you should wake him. He can sleep at home as well as he can here."

Victoria hesitated another moment before nodding. Going to the settee, she knelt down. "Gregory." He didn't even stir at her soft voice. "Gregory, it's time to wake up." She reached out and gently shook his shoulder. "Come on, Gregory. Wake up."

He groaned but slowly blinked open his eyes. When he saw her, a sleepy smile crossed his face. "Hey."

"Hey, yourself. It's time to leave if we're to arrive home before dark."

Covering a yawn, he sat up. He rubbed sleep from his eyes before taking his shoes from Victoria. "Thank you."

As they said their goodbye's to the Holmes family, Margaret stopped them before they stepped into the carriage. "Gregory, how long do you think you can keep on like this?"

"I don't know. I'm hoping I'll be able to slow down in a couple of weeks."

"Weeks? I don't know if you can last that long." She pulled him into a long hug. "I'm worried about you."

Gregory hugged her back. "Just keep praying for me."

"You know we always do."

"Try to schedule me in sometime, too," Broderick put in as Gregory helped Victoria into the buggy. "I've discovered it's no fun going hunting alone."

Gregory clapped him on the back before getting in the drivers seat. "I'll try."

The buggy had barely started rolling when Victoria spoke. "Do you really think things will be better in a couple of weeks?"

"Yes. I should be finished working on the docks by then and move on to clerk. I'll spend my mornings clerking and continue going over management decisions with Albert in the afternoons. That way I will be home in time for dinner every day."

"Why don't you do that now?"

"Some things happening at the docks have troubled me." He hesitated a moment. "Actually, I've caught several of our employees smuggling." Victoria gasped. "I alerted the police, but they're waiting for the next shipment to arrive so they can catch everyone at once, including the buyers. From what I overheard, it's on a ship coming sometime in the next two weeks."

"So you're staying on the docks to let the police know when the ship comes in. But why don't the police send one of their men down to do that?"

"The smugglers would be leery of a newcomer and possibly remove the evidence. They don't trust me, but they accept my presence. I can come and go as I please without arousing anyone's suspicions."

"It sounds dangerous."

"Not really," Gregory gave her a smile. "All I'm doing is loading and unloading a million pounds of goods a day and keeping my ears open."

Despite his reassurance, Victoria didn't feel any better. "Be careful."

"I will be."

When they arrived home, he turned the buggy over to Horace before taking Victoria's hand. "Come on, we have to make sure our little rose bush is ready for winter.

She laughed as she followed him to a shed. "And how do we do that?"

"We shall cover it to keep it warm." Gregory dug around in the shed before emerging with a ratty old blanket and a tarp. "Here we go."

Still smiling, she followed him to the rose bush and helped him carefully wrap the sticks. Stepping back, they observed their mummified bush. "It looks ridiculous."

"Maybe," Gregory casually put his arm around her waist and pulled her against his side. "But it should protect it in case of a bad freeze."

She didn't answer as she looked at him. His move had been unconscious. As natural as breathing. He didn't even realize he held her as he continued to study the bush. He had always been careful not to embrace her in the roses, but to Victoria's shock, she felt no fear. Thinking back, she realized that it had been a long time since the sight and smell of roses had reminded her of Paxton. Now, when she came to the rose bush, she remembered Gregory. Something he said or the way he looked while puttering in the garden. The change had been so gradual that she hadn't even noticed.

Tears pricked her eyes. Gregory had been right. *Thank You, Jesus, for giving me such a wonderful husband.*

Smiling, Gregory looked down at her. At the sight of the tears in her eyes, his smile turned to a look of horror. He jumped back as if scalded. "I'm sorry, Victoria. I didn't think…I mean…I didn't mean… I…"

His stuttering apology came to a halt when she walked up to him and slipped off his spectacles. She put them in his pocket before sliding her arms around his waist. The sight of his eyes, staring down at her in confusion, took her breath away. She had forgotten how beautiful they were. "Kiss me."

His eyes widened. "What?"

Victoria smiled up at him. "I just realized something. I'm not afraid."

"You're not?"

"You were right. The memories of working on our bush have superseded the old ones, and now, I want to make another one. Please kiss me, Gregory."

Slowly, Gregory put his arms around her. As he lowered his head, she tilted hers up to receive his kiss, but he stopped just shy of her mouth. "Are you sure?"

She couldn't stop another smile from spreading across her face. "Yes."

He touched his lips to hers. Soft, gentle and achingly sweet.

Tears slid down her face as she absorbed the solid feel of him. His strong arms around her. His tender touch. The clean smell uniquely Gregory. How she had missed this the last few weeks!

When he started to pull back, she whimpered a protest and tugged him down for more. With a groan, Gregory pulled her closer as he rained fervent kisses over her face. "I've missed you so much." His words came out broken between the kisses.

Victoria didn't try to answer with words. Instead she kissed him back with all the longing filling her heart.

The next morning, she found another letter on Gregory's pillow and eagerly picked it up.

Dearest Victoria,

For the longest time after I awoke this morning, I could not bring myself to leave you. Instead, I prayed and watched you sleep.

You are so beautiful.

I know that is something else I've never told you though I must think it a hundred times a day. You are more beautiful than I could have ever imagined, inside and out. God blessed me more than I deserved when He gave you to be my wife. I want to spend the rest of my life treasuring you.

With all my love,

Gregory

Tears once again rolled unchecked down her cheeks. Sniffing, she wiped them away. "Ever since I married you, I've turned into a crybaby," she told the letter accusingly. "But how can I not cry when you continue to surprise me with your sweetness?

Standing up, Victoria walked over to her desk and opened the middle drawer. She placed a kiss on his name before putting the paper inside with his other letters.

Chapter 17

Gregory bent down coiling up a rope. The sound of furtive whispers reached his ears. "The Merriweather's just pulling into dock.

"That's the third ship today."

"Yeah." Satisfaction filled the tone. "We've got to unload the shipment first. We can smuggle it to the buyer easy. Everyone will be so busy no one will take notice of us. Now, I need you to..."

The voices trailed off as the two men walked past the spot where Gregory crouched. His heart pounded. He finally had the information the police waited for. If everything went well all the smugglers would be rounded up, and he could go back to seeing Victoria every day.

Gregory forced himself to finish coiling the rope then saunter off the docks to his waiting carriage. He gave directions to Brad then settled back in the seat happier than he had been in weeks.

Victoria sat at her desk composing a note to Regina when sudden agony ripped into her stomach. She gasped at the intensity of it, but this time she was in her room and prepared. Pulling a small bottle out of a pocket in her dress, she took a sip before standing unsteadily to her feet. She staggered towards the bell cord but fell before she could reach it.

Moaning, Victoria crawled the rest of the way. Using the dresser for support, she managed to stand to her feet and pull the cord. Taking deep breaths, she leaned against the dresser and gathered strength. A few seconds later, she pushed herself off the dresser and stumbled to the bed.

With a groan of relief, she collapsed onto it and curled into the fetal position. How many times had she done this? Crawled to her room when she could or just collapsed where she stood and waited for the medicine to take effect?

Rolfe had always been furious with her, especially the few times it had happened at a social event. Gregory had never been angry though, and lying there, her heart ached for missing him. She wanted to feel his presence kneeling beside the bed as he prayed for her. Even if he couldn't touch her.

She could at least hold his hand.

A soft knock sounded on the door, but Victoria couldn't answer. A few seconds later, Gladys opened the door and poked her head in. "Miss Victoria?" Seeing her curled on the bed, she hurried over and took in the situation at a glance. "Did you take the laudanum, mum?"

Victoria could barely nod her head yes. Hurrying away, Gladys readied her nightshift. When the pain finally eased, she helped her change and tucked her into bed as gently as if she were a newborn babe. Pulling up Gregory's desk chair, she sat down in it. "Don't worry, mum. I'm going to stay right here in case you need me. And I'm going to watch the clock to make sure you get the doses on time."

Victoria felt too tired to even say thank you as the drug swirled her away into sleep. She was only vaguely aware of Gladys waking her up to give her more medicine and wiping her face with a cool cloth, but try as she might, she couldn't wake up. Then Gregory sat there doing the same thing. She wanted to ask him why he had come home so early, but the words wouldn't come out as she drifted away again.

By the time she could force her heavy eyes to open, morning sunlight streamed into the room. To her surprise, she felt Gregory in the bed beside her. She rolled her head on the pillow to look at him. That slight movement woke him, and he sat up. "Victoria, are you in pain?"

It still felt eased. However, the ferocious agony seemed to be hovering just above her, waiting to pounce. "I'm okay," she rasped before licking her dry lips. Gregory immediately grabbed a glass of water off the nightstand. He carefully supported her head as she drank it. "Thank you."

"You're welcome." He set the glass down and put on his spectacles before looking at the clock. "You still have fifteen minutes until you need to take the laudanum again. Do you want to take it now or wait?"

"Wait." Definitely wait. "I don't like the drugged sleep." Gregory leaned back against the headboard and watched her. He kept his hands carefully folded in his lap. Victoria tried to think past the medicine's fogging effects. "Was it my imagination or did you arrive home early yesterday? For that matter, why aren't you at work now?"

He smiled at her. "I did arrive home right after dinner. The ship came in, and the police arrested the smugglers so I took the rest of the day off. I actually decided to take a few days off."

"Because of me?"

"That, and to catch up on my sleep."

"Are you planning on taking off every time this happens?"

"Why not? It's one of the benefits of owning my own company. I can take vacations whenever I want."

"I wouldn't call this a vacation."

Gregory's brow furrowed. "No, it's not. I can't stand to see you in pain like this."

She reached out and took one of his hands. "I'm alright. At least God's provided something to ease it even if it does make me sleep, right?"

"Right." He gave her hand a squeeze and looked at the clock. "Speaking of, it's time to take your medicine again." Victoria groaned as Gregory pulled out the bottle. Once again supporting her, he gave her a spoonful. "Are you hungry?"

"No."

"It's no wonder you're so tiny. You never eat enough."

"Just because I don't have a hollow leg like you…"

"Hey," Gregory gave her an offended look before smiling. "I'm still a growing boy."

Victoria laughed. Still smiling, Gregory put his eyeglasses back on the nightstand and laid back down. He carefully took her hand and linked his fingers with hers. Victoria relished the warmth of his hand even as the laudanum pulled her back into darkness.

Four days later, Victoria felt like a new woman. She woke early and quietly slipped on a simple house dress without bothering to ring for Gladys. Gregory still slept, and she didn't want to disturb him. Actually, he'd slept almost as much as she had the past few days, but he had needed it. The deep bags that had developed under his eyes were finally disappearing. Braiding her hair, Victoria left it hanging down her back and went to find something to eat.

She was ravenous.

Making her way to the kitchen, she found Cook seated at the table drinking a cup of tea with Maggie. Both looked surprised to see her. "Good morning, mum," Cook stood up and headed for the stove. "I wasn't expecting anyone to be awake this early."

"I know, but I just woke up hungry."

"What would you like to eat, mum?"

Victoria smiled. "Whatever is the quickest. I'm starved."

"How about some porridge with currants?"

"That sounds wonderful." She took a seat at the wooden table. Maggie pulled another teacup out of the cabinet and poured her a cup from the teapot on the table. "Thank you."

Sipping her tea and looking around the spacious room, she realized that she had woken up even before the scullery maids. The kitchen seemed so large and empty without the trio of chattering girls bustling back and forth. Out of the corner of her eye, she noticed Cook making hand motions at Maggie. Maggie frowned and shook her head. They both stopped when Victoria looked at them. "Is something the matter?" she finally asked.

"Well…" Maggie glanced back at Cook who gave her an encouraging nod. "I know it's been rough, losing Lord Thornton, and I haven't wanted to say anything, but…" She took a deep breath and looked straight at her. "The truth is, Miss Victoria, the servants haven't been paid since

Lord Thornton's death. And some of them are really hurting for the money."

Mortification writhed through Victoria. "I'm so sorry. I never even thought…"

"I know, miss. It was always Lady Thornton's job, but since she's…" Maggie's voice trailed off, and she shrugged. She didn't want to speak disrespectfully, but the truth was that Harriet still hadn't left her bed.

And Victoria still didn't have access to any money. Somehow, she had to find out about the household accounts even if Harriet refused to speak to anyone. Victoria took a deep breath. "Thank you for telling me. I will speak with Mr. Thornton about it today."

"Thank you, mum." Cook set a steaming bowl in front of her. Trying to overcome her embarrassment, she bowed her head for a silent blessing before taking a bite of the cinnamon flavored goodness.

She tried not to fret about the matter, but the hours until Gregory woke stretched long before her. Victoria found herself unable to concentrate on work so she went into the bedroom to sort through her correspondence.

It ended up being a disaster as well. Both the *Magazine of Domestic Economy and the Gardener's Magazine* had arrived in the post, but she had been unable to concentrate enough to read either one. Nor had she been able to respond to the personal missives she'd received. After throwing a dozen half-started letters into the trash, she just sat there watching Gregory sleep, willing him to wake up.

When he finally blinked open his eyes, she nearly collapsed with relief. Standing up, she hurried over to him. "Gregory, I have a problem."

"Huh?" His raspy voice still sounded half asleep as he rolled over and squinted up at her.

Victoria picked up his eyeglasses and put them on his face before sitting down on the edge of the bed. "I have a problem."

"A problem?" he asked around a yawn. "Can it wait until after breakfast?"

"No." Victoria wrung her hands. "It's terrible, but we haven't paid the servants in nearly two months."

"Wait just a second." Gregory scrubbed a hand through his hair as he pulled himself up. He sat there for a moment as if waiting for her words to make sense in his sleep fogged brain. He finally looked at her. "We haven't paid the servants?"

"No. Your mother always did it so I didn't even think of it. I have no idea where the household account is, what the budget is, how much we owe, what the wages are, how to access the money…"

"Whoa…" Gregory held up his hand. "I guess Mother hasn't been any help?"

Victoria shook her head. "She hasn't spoken to anyone but her maid since the funeral."

Gregory sighed. "And I haven't been much help, either. I never meant for the business to consume all my time; there was just so much to learn and changes that couldn't wait even for a few weeks. Like ordering all the slave ships to cease operations and then making sure they actually did."

"No one's blaming you. You've had so much to do."

"That's no excuse. I should have been here for you and Mother. Managing the business was overwhelming, and it was easier to throw myself into that then facing my own grief. Instead, I let everything fall onto your shoulders and neglected Mother in her sorrow. I was wrong, Victoria. That's one thing I've come to realize in the past couple of days. Do you know how long it's been since we've had devotions together? I've asked God to forgive me, but I need to ask your forgiveness as well."

Victoria didn't know quite what to say. "You've had so much to do," she finally repeated a bit lamely. "There's really nothing to forgive, but we do need to pay the servants."

"Yes, we do. I don't know anything about it either, but we'll find out today. I'll go through everything in Mother's desk. If it's not there, we'll move on to Father's study. But first, I'm going to have some breakfast."

Nearly an hour later, after she joined Gregory for her second breakfast of the day and their devotions, he knocked softly on the door to Harriet's bedroom. No one answered, but he opened the door anyway. "Mother?"

The drapes were open, allowing sunlight into the room. Harriet looked at Gregory then rolled over and faced the wall. He sighed and sat down on the edge of the bed as Victoria stood uncertainly in the doorway. "Mother, I'm sorry. I didn't mean to neglect you, but I did. I'll do better."

He put a hand on her shoulder. She shrugged it off. Other than that, she made no move to show that she heard or even knew he was there.

Gregory put his hand back on his knee. "Mother, we've run into a bit of a snag. The servants need to be paid, and Victoria needs access to the household account. Where do you keep the records?"

She didn't even flicker an eyelash. Gregory sighed again. "We're going to go through your desk, alright?"

No response.

Standing up, Gregory motioned Victoria to follow him as he went across the room to a small, elegant desk. Victoria felt like an intruder as they went through the drawers, but Harriet never moved. At first, all they found were personal correspondences, ideas for a new ball gown, a list of measurements for the drapes in the south wing…

In the bottom right hand drawer, Gregory finally pulled out the household ledger. He also found boxes of old receipts and a stack of bills that were still to be paid. Gathering everything up, they headed back to the hall. In the doorway, he stopped and turned back to Harriet. "We're going now, Mother, but I'll be back to visit with you tonight," he promised.

No movement from the bed.

After a few seconds, he softly closed the door. "Let's go to Father's study. It has a large desk where we can sort through all this."

"Alright."

He led her down the hall and through parts of the house she'd never seen before. He finally opened the door to a large, book-lined study. A massive walnut desk dominated one side, and they spread everything they had found onto it. It took hours to figure out Harriet's system, bring everything up-to-date and calculate the servant's wages. Several large bills, mainly for Victoria's party, were past due.

Gregory pocketed them. "I'll pay these tomorrow when I'm in town."

Victoria leaned back in her chair and sighed. "Well, now I know what we owe, but that still doesn't give me any money."

Giving her a smile, Gregory stood up and swung back one of the floor-to-ceiling bookcases. Victoria gaped at the iron door that stood behind it. "I don't know if Mother has a personal stash somewhere else or not, but Father always kept a substantial amount of cash in here. Come here, and I'll teach you the combination."

Hesitantly, she approached, eyeing the padlock warily. "Are you sure you want me to know it? I mean, Father just gave Mother an allowance every month. She never had access to his money."

For a moment, Gregory just looked at her before reaching out and gently touching her cheek. "Everything that's mine is yours, remember? I trust you, Victoria, and I want you to have access to the money in case you ever need it. Now, turn the left dial until you reach 8."

He walked Victoria through opening the padlock then made her repeat the combination until she had it memorized. Inside the room, the walls, floor and ceiling were all made of iron. She had never seen anything like it. A hidden room made completely of iron!

Gregory showed her the ledger. "If you take money out just put the amount in this column and what it's for. If you put money in, it goes in this column. Periodically, we'll add it all up and make sure that what's in the room matches the book."

Victoria nodded. A simple system, but she couldn't keep her wide-eyes off the piles of banknotes and bags of gold coins stacked on the shelves. She didn't think there could be any more money locked up in the Tower of London!

Pulling down several stacks of banknotes, Gregory had Victoria carefully record it in the ledger before handing it to her. "I would like to give the servants a bonus," he said as he shut the door and locked it. Stepping back, he swung the bookcase closed. "They've been so patient and loyal, working without pay these last few weeks. I think they've earned it."

Victoria agreed. Gregory stayed and helped her sort the money into envelopes with the servant's names on them. Several thousand pounds were left over, but he insisted she keep it. "I always keep a little money in my desk. It's just too hard to come open the safe every time I need a few pounds."

To Victoria, nearly five thousand pounds was more than just a "little" money, but Gregory refused to be dissuaded. He also dug around in the desk and came up with a brand new ledger for Victoria to start her book-keeping fresh in. "Now, Mrs. Thornton," he smiled at her as she carefully recorded the final amounts from Harriet's book onto her first page. "All that's left is to put you on the bank accounts and acquire you some checks. Oh, and I want you to go over Mother's monthly budget, checking it against our actual expenditures. If you need more money than what's been allotted let me know, and we'll work out a new budget together."

The amounts looked generous enough to Victoria, but it made sense to check it first. "Alright."

"I'm returning to work tomorrow so why don't you come into town with me? We can go to the bank first thing then you can have the day to shop. Maybe we could even meet at Lindy's for lunch."

Victoria thought about her ever growing list. "That would be wonderful, Gregory. There's actually quite a few things that we need."

"Well, be sure to buy something nice just for you," he leaned down and kissed her. "You deserve to be spoiled a little."

Victoria blushed as she gathered up the envelopes. "I'd better give these to Maggie so she can hand them out." Gregory just grinned at her as she made her escape out the door.

Victoria dressed carefully for her first foray into Lewes, wanting Gregory to be proud of her. Standing back, she scrutinized her appearance carefully. She had chosen a green silk brocade day dress with a matching pelerine. Gladys had coiffed her hair into the newest pompadour currently popular in London. She carefully placed the flower-trimmed bonnet on her head over her lace day cap before picking up her green reticule and white gloves.

She was ready.

"You look beautiful, mum. You'll do Mr. Gregory proud."

Victoria smiled at her faithful maid trying to hide the nervnous fluttering of her stomach. "Thank you, Gladys."

She made her way downstairs. Gregory already waited for her in the foyer. He smiled when he saw her though he didn't speak. Instead, with an elegant, formal bow, he offered her his arm and led her to the waiting carriage.

During the hour long ride into Lewes, Victoria nearly mangled her reticule, she clutched it so tightly. She finally forced her fingers to unclench and smoothed the material. Looking up, she found Gregory watching her with a smile. "Nervous?"

At his question, her mind flashed back to their wedding night.

He'd asked her the same question then, and she had hidden her true feelings from him, fearing they would make him angry. They had come a long way since then, she realized in surprise, for she didn't even think about hiding it from him now.

"I'm terrified," she admitted. "I don't want to disappoint you."

"You won't," Gregory assured her. "You could never disappoint me."

The tender expression on his face more than his words calmed her. She smiled at him as she relaxed.

It would be a glorious day.

After their business at the bank, Brad dropped Gregory off at the office and then drove Victoria to the shopping district. George, one of their footmen, dutifully followed her around as she shopped to her heart's content, finding nearly everything on her list. She felt a little guilty at spending so much in one day, but she really had just bought the necessities. Not wanting to take advantage of Gregory's generous nature, she very carefully compared the goods in different stores, buying quality goods at the least expensive price. It disconcerted her how each shopkeeper's manner changed as soon as they heard her name. They practically stayed glued to her elbow, saccharine helpfulness personified, while they let those with less money fend for themselves.

She found it terribly annoying.

As promised, Gregory met her at Lindy's tea room at noon. They ate a leisurely lunch before she hit the shops again. She arranged for everything to be delivered except for a few small packages that George placed in the boot of the carriage. Just before six, Brad pulled up in front of the Thornton Shipping Line Offices. Victoria timidly entered the huge building. It fairly hummed with activity as people scurried about their tasks. Straight back chairs lined one wall and served as a waiting room. The many potted plants and flowers that were strategically arranged throughout the entire office in a profusion of color alleviated the stark utilitarian feel somewhat.

Victoria smiled sure they were Gregory's idea. A young woman sat at a desk just to the right of the door. She quickly scanned Victoria before offering her a polite smile even though she still managed to look bored. "May I help you?"

"I'm Mrs. Thornton. I'm here to see my husband."

At the name, she immediately straightened. Jumping out of her chair, she came around the desk to Victoria's side. "I'm Lorraine Huxley," she purred. "It is *so* nice to meet you. Let me show you to Mr. Thornton's office."

She ushered Victoria up the steps to the third floor, practically gushing with helpfulness. Victoria nearly sighed.

Stepping onto the third floor landing seemed like stepping into a palace. Victoria's feet sank into the rich wine colored carpet of the large, lavishly decorated waiting room. Gilded mirrors and expensive paintings hung on the walls and comfortable chairs and settees were clustered in pleasing arrays. Here, too, the potted plants and flowers abounded.

Several doors led off the waiting area, but Lorraine led her to the one directly across from the stairs that had Gregory's name emblazoned on it with the title *President* underneath. Inside sat another secretary, an older woman with her gray hair drawn back into a bun. She looked at them sternly over a pair of spectacles perched on the end of her nose. "It's Mrs. Thornton," Lorraine gushed as she came in.

"Well, we've been expecting her." Her brusque manner didn't change as she stood up and came around the desk. She frowned disapprovingly at Lorraine. "You may go back to your desk."

Lorraine pouted a moment before finally flouncing out. The older woman held out her hand. "I'm Mrs. Sheridan. Mr. Thornton's been expecting you and said for you to come right on in when you arrived."

The fact that she didn't fawn or scrape over her felt refreshing, and Victoria gave her a warm smile. "Thank you."

She opened the door indicated and stepped into a large airy office. Gregory sat behind a huge mahogany desk, his black hair standing on end. His suit coat and tie had been carelessly tossed on a settee along the wall. The top buttons on his shirt were undone, and his sleeves were rolled up as he searched through his desk drawers, muttering to himself.

He looked up with an irritated frown. "Mrs. Sheridan, I need…"

His voice trailed off when he saw her, and he smiled. "Are you done shopping already?"

"Yes, and I found nearly everything on my list."

"Wonderful. Do you mind waiting a few minutes? I really need to dictate a letter before we leave."

"Of course not. I'll just wait outside."

"No need for that. You can stay here."

A soft knock sounded on the door before Mrs. Sheridan opened it. "Sir, I have the Carthage file."

"Excellent." Gregory accepted the thick file and leafed through it. Mrs. Sheridan sat down in a chair facing the desk, pad and pencil in hand. Feeling like a fifth wheel, Victoria hesitantly sat down on the settee next to Gregory's clothes. Picking up the jacket and tie, she held them in her lap and absently tried to smooth out the wrinkles.

After a few minutes, Gregory pulled out a few sheets of paper and studied them intently before speaking.

"Dear Sirs: In response to your letter of the twenty-ninth, the terms specified therein are acceptable. Upon receipt of the signed contract in this office, two ships will be sent…"

A few minutes later, he finished the letter, and Mrs. Sheridan stood up. "I will have these finished and ready for your signature first thing in the morning, sir."

"That will be fine. Thank you." She picked up the Carthage file and left. Gregory straightened a few things on his desk before standing up and rolling down his sleeves. Victoria also stood and held his coat out to help him into it. He smiled and slid his arms into the sleeves before turning around. "Thanks, honey." Giving her a quick kiss, he ushered her out the door.

Downstairs, Lorraine called out a syrupy goodbye. Gregory helped Victoria into the buggy, and she sat down with a sigh. Though the day had been fun, it had worn her out. After giving instructions to Brad, Gregory sat down next to her. "Did you have a nice day?"

She smiled at him. "Yes."

"That's good." He linked his hand with hers and studied their clasped hands pensively. "Victoria, do you have any more large purchases you need to make?"

"No, just a few small things."

"That's good," he repeated before finally looking up at her. "I'm afraid money might be a little tight for awhile. I discovered today that Father has been cheating the workers, setting the clocks and bells so that they worked longer hours without realizing it. I've adjusted them to ring true, but I'm going to recompense our people for the time they worked without pay and give them a bonus. It's going to take most of our ready cash."

Victoria gasped, thinking about all the money she had spent that day. "I'm so sorry…"

"No," Gregory interrupted her. "I'm glad you were able to shop today, and we are certainly not destitute. The bulk of our wealth is in London invested in securities that can easily be turned into cash if necessary. Though if we're careful I think we can weather this without touching them. I just wanted you to know. But if something large comes up that you need or want that's fine. Just let me know a few days in advance so I can arrange to have the funds delivered. Now," he smiled at her. "Did you buy you something for yourself?"

Victoria blushed, thinking about her purchase. She'd gone into Madame Blanchet's shop to browse, and the older woman had been delighted to see her. She'd just finished sewing a new nightshift, from a Paris pattern, and it looked nothing like the simple flannel ones Victoria had always worn. Instead, it had been made of ivory silk and elegantly adorned with ribbons and lace. Madame Blanchet had insisted that she try it on. The cool, sleek material had skimmed her figure flatteringly, and the color set off her dark hair and eyes to perfection. The price had been outrageous, but Victoria had fallen in love instantly. Thinking of the way Gregory's eyes would surely lighten when he saw her in it, she had signed for it and had it packaged. It rode in the boot right now, waiting for tonight.

She blushed again, but she met his gaze. "I bought something for us."

One of his eyebrows rose. "Us? What is it?"

Her cheeks grew hotter. "I'll show it to you tonight. It's a surprise."

He looked slightly confused, but he didn't press. Instead, he smiled at her as he settled back against the seat for the ride home. Victoria did the same, but she couldn't stop a small smile from curving her mouth as she thought about her surprise.

Chapter 18

Shivering, Victoria pulled her shawl closer around her shoulders. She had pulled her chair near the fireplace so she could be warm while working on her tapestry though a chill still hung in the air. But what could she expect with December only two days away? She only hoped that the ratty blanket and tarp would be enough to keep their rose bush warm.

Over the last ten days, Victoria had finally arranged her household duties into a workable routine. Gregory, also, had arranged his schedule so that he arrived home in time for dinner every night though he sometimes still had to work in his study afterwards. Every day after dinner, he faithfully visited Harriet, but she never once acknowledged his presence. Victoria had begun to despair that she would ever speak to anyone besides her maid Rhoda again.

Victoria hadn't had time to work on her tapestry since the middle of summer so she had decided to take an hour off before dinner and embroider. After all, it *was* her eighteenth birthday. This time to relax was her gift to herself.

Gregory and Liberty were the only things left to stitch. At the moment, they were nothing more than a vague outline looming in the background. Picking up her needle, she carefully threaded it with a dark glossy brown silk thread. The rich color would do well for Liberty's mane and tail.

As she worked, Victoria's thoughts wandered to the dark green velvet ball gown that had arrived that morning from Madame Blanchet's shop. She thought it exquisite and wanted to surprise Gregory when she wore it to the first Christmas ball of the season, two days hence. It had been carefully styled to flatter her figure, and she secretly hoped it would elicit a compliment from him. She knew now that Gregory thought her beautiful, and when doubts occasionally assailed her at his continued silence, she would reread his letters. Perhaps the stunning party dress would finally free the words from his mouth. Her new nightshift hadn't two weeks ago though the look in his eyes had almost been just as good. Still, she longed to hear him say it.

Jesus, is it wrong to want his affirmation so much?

Victoria honestly didn't know. She only knew that she did want it.

The past few weeks, they had been inundated with Christmas invitations. Balls, masquerades, plays, recitals, military reviews…the list went on and on. At first, Victoria had thought they would have to attend the entire, dizzying lot, but Gregory had explained that no one would expect them to put in an appearance at more than a handful of the gatherings. They were still in mourning, but enough time had passed that it would be considered rude not to send the invitations. One night, he had helped her sort through them and choose the ones that they felt the most comfortable with.

But the most surprising invitation had arrived only that morning. On blue paper, an invitation to the Earl of Holland admitting him to the Chapel, St. James Palace, on the fourth of February, 1840. For the royal wedding of Queen Victoria to Prince Albert of Saxe-Coburg and Gotha. Though the match had been expected, Queen Victoria had resisted all attempts to rush her into marriage the last few years making the sudden announcement a surprise.

At least to Victoria who hadn't been privy to any gossip since her own marriage five months previous.

Changing her thread to a lighter brown, Victoria went to work on Liberty's face. A few moments later, Maggie appeared in the doorway, wringing her hands. "Miss Victoria? I'm afraid something's come up that needs your attention in the blue salon."

Victoria quickly put her needle away. The blue salon had become her favorite because of the expansive windows that overlooked the garden. "What is it, Maggie?"

"Well…" Maggie's slight hesitation caused her alarm to escalate. "It's hard to explain, mum. I think you'll just need to see it."

Wondering what on earth it could be, Victoria hastened to the blue salon. She came to a sudden halt in the doorway. The room had been rearranged, and instead of the fainting settee, a small, intimate table for two had been set up in front of the windows, covered with a lace tablecloth and set with their finest china and silver. Gregory, dressed in a fashionable evening suit, stood by the table holding a single white Christmas Rose.

He walked towards her and held out the flower. "Happy birthday, Victoria."

Speechless, she automatically accepted the flower as she stared at him. He smiled at her. "I wanted to surprise you."

Surprise her? He had flummoxed her! They'd never talked about it, so she naturally assumed that he didn't know the date of her birth. After all, she didn't know when he had been born, either. "H…how did you know it was my birthday?"

"I asked Regina before we left London."

Tears pricked her eyes, but she tried to hide them by looking down at her ordinary brown wool day dress. "Look at me. I'm a mess."

"Well, when Maggie helped me arrange this she insisted that you'd want to have time to dress so Gladys has one of your evening gowns ready. Dinner won't be for another hour…" His voice trailed off.

Victoria smiled at him. "Thank you, Gregory." Standing on tiptoe, she gave his cheek a quick kiss. "I'll be down as soon as I can."

Before she could leave, Gregory pulled her close and gave her a real, knee-melting kiss. "I'll be waiting," he murmured huskily when he finally pulled back.

Mind still whirling, Victoria somehow made it back to their bedroom. Gladys waited for her with one of her favorite dark blue evening gowns ready. She hesitated a moment before making a quick decision. "I think I will wear my new green gown."

Gladys smiled. "Yes, mum."

Forty-five minutes later, she dabbed on some perfume as Gladys hooked her mother's pearls around her neck. Her hair had been artistically swept up into curls and adorned with carefully placed pearl combs. Gladys pinned the flower Gregory had given her above her left ear as a finishing touch.

"You look beautiful, mum."

Victoria smiled at Gladys in the mirror. "Thank you."

Now, if only Gregory thought so.

She made her way back to the blue salon. Gregory immediately stood up when he saw her in the doorway. "Victoria…."

Walking towards her, he lifted her hand for a kiss as he gave her a formal bow. Tingles radiated up her arm at the brush of his lips, reminding her of the first time she had met him. Straightening back up, he pulled her arm though his and led her to the table. Candles had been lit and strategically placed to give the room a dim, romantic air. Outside the expansive windows, darkness settled over the land as stars began to appear in the sky.

Gregory held Victoria's chair as she settled into it. Taking his own seat, he bowed his head and prayed, not only for the food but for her, that she would be especially blessed this day. Victoria could have told him that she already had been. His thoughtfulness in seeking out the day of her birth even before they knew each other and then arranging this surprise dinner for the two of them was far more special than any of the grand parties Rolfe had thrown in an effort to impress his peers.

After he said amen, the servants brought in steaming plates of food. When her plate was set before her, Victoria nearly gasped at seeing the roasted duck with apple sauce and asparagus soup. How had he known her favorite meal?

She looked up at him and gave him a tremulous smile. "Thank you," she whispered.

Gregory watched her with such a soft expression, her heart nearly melted. "I'm just glad that you're pleased. I didn't know if you would want a large party or…"

She stopped him by placing her hand on his. "This is perfect, Gregory. Spending this time with you is much more special than having to entertain people who are still practically strangers." She squeezed his hand before taking a bite of the succulent duck. "This is wonderful."

"I think Cook outdid herself. She wanted it to be special for you."

For her?

Victoria thought it was more for Gregory. All the servants loved and respected him so much that it naturally flowed over to her because she was his wife.

"Gregory, when is your birthday?" She sent him a sheepish smile. "It sounds horrible, but I don't know."

"April fourteenth."

She sighed in relief. At least she hadn't missed it. "And you'll be twenty-four?"

"Yes."

"Hmmm." Victoria's thoughts raced as she ate. What could she possibly do for his birthday that would be as nice as this?

"Victoria."

"Yes?" She glanced up to see an amused smile on Gregory's face.

"You don't have to plan my party tonight." Victoria's blush tinged her cheeks with fire. How easily he'd read her thoughts! "Besides, I don't need anything special."

She disagreed but chose not to argue about it today. Later, she'd have to get together with Margaret to find out what he might like. Glancing out the window, she gasped in delight. "Gregory, look!"

A third-quarter moon slowly rose, huge and silvery white in the night sky, like a jewel on a bed of black velvet. They continued to watch the moon as they ate the rich plum cake and molded royal ice cream cook had prepared. As the servants cleared away the dishes, Gregory rose and pulled several packages out of a drawer in the sideboard. He set them in front of her with a shy smile. "I hope you like them."

It overwhelmed Victoria. Not only had he arranged this beautiful, romantic dinner, but he'd thought to buy her presents as well. "Oh Gregory, it's wonderful."

He laughed as he sat back down. "You haven't opened them, yet."

She gave him a sheepish grin. "I don't care. It's still wonderful." Picking up the first package, she carefully untied the ribbon and folded back the material to reveal a thin black box. She lifted the lid and gasped in delight.

Inside, carefully nestled against a bed of white velvet, lay a complete set of the most beautiful jewels Victoria had ever seen. Dark blue briolette cut sapphires were carefully mounted in delicate braided gold and accented with small diamonds. The set contained a necklace, bracelet, ring, earrings, and even matching combs and pins for her hair.

Several moments passed before Victoria could even speak. "Gregory… these are beautiful…but surely they're too much…"

"I wanted to give you something special. I picked the sapphire because…" Gregory paused and cleared his throat. "The dark blue color…and the way they sparkle reminded me…reminded me of your eyes," he finished his words in a rush even as faint red blotches crept up his neck.

Victoria nearly melted at his compliment. She didn't know why it was so hard for him to say it, but the fact that he kept trying touched her deeply. Getting up, she walked around the table and only hesitated a second before sitting down in his lap. She slipped his spectacles off so she could see his eyes before speaking. "Gregory, that's the nicest compliment anyone has ever given me. Thank you."

"Oh, Victoria," Gregory pulled her closer. She wrapped her arms around his neck and leaned her cheek against his soft hair. "You deserve someone so much better than I. Someone who can tell you what they feel without stuttering and stammering through it."

She pulled back so she could see his face. "Don't you ever say that. Don't you even think it. There isn't anyone better than you."

A slight smile crossed his face before fading again. "If only I could articulate what's in my heart. How…how full you make it, but it's so hard." He gave a rueful chuckle. "I even know *why* it's so hard, but I can't seem to overcome it."

Victoria tilted her head. "Why is it so hard?"

"Do you really want to know?"

"Yes. If you don't mind telling me. If you don't want to, I understand," she added hastily in case she had overstepped her place.

"I don't mind telling you," Gregory assured her before taking a deep breath. Slowly, haltingly, he told her about that day when Harriet had rejected him. She nearly cried to think of five-year-old Gregory hurt and crying on the driveway feeling ashamed of his honest love. The anger she felt towards Harriet rose hot and almost uncontrollable. *Jesus, help me with this anger.*

"Ever since then when I try to tell someone how…how I feel about them…the words always stick in my throat. I know it's wrong, and I've prayed for God to loosen my tongue, but so far it hasn't happened."

Once again, Victoria wrapped her arms around him, cradling his head against her as if she could comfort and wipe away the tears that he had shed so many years ago. "Thank you for telling me," she finally whispered. It had been hard for him, she could tell, but she felt so proud that he tried. That he remained open and willing for God to change him thrilled her. Suddenly, she remembered all the times Gregory would start to say something then stop just as he had when she'd first arrived in the salon earlier. Dawning realization hit her. All those times, he'd been trying to tell her what he felt, but the words just wouldn't come! She sighed in contentment.

"I didn't mean to turn you birthday dinner so morbid," he said breaking into her thoughts.

"You didn't," she assured him as she pulled back again.

"Do you want to finish opening your presents?"

Victoria nearly laughed at the hopeful expression in his beautiful hazel eyes. "Alright." She started to stand up, but Gregory held her fast in his lap.

"You could open them sitting right here," he suggested with a roguish grin.

This time, Victoria did laugh before giving him a flirtatious smile. "If it pleases you, sir," she said coyly, surprising even herself. For the first time in her life, she had flirted with a man out of fun not out of terror.

"Oh, it does," Gregory's eyes twinkled in merriment as he held her a little closer.

Pulling the rest of the packages towards her, Victoria decided not to think just yet about why she had flirted with him. To her delight, she found a beautiful, leather bound sketch pad, charcoals,and two different packets of seeds for fuchsia flowers. "You mentioned one day that you liked fuchsia's the best so I thought you might enjoy trying to make a hybrid of it. You can document it with the pad and charcoals," he explained.

"It's wonderful." Impulsively, she kissed him. "Thank you, Gregory. You've made this the best birthday of my life."

Gregory didn't say anything as he pulled her back for another kiss.

Christmas day dawned gray and dreary with cold rain slashing at the windows. Victoria didn't mind the weather for the agonizing pain ripping through her stomach had finally become manageable. She had been afraid that she would sleep through Christmas because of the laudanum's drugging effects. She'd felt bad enough missing the Christmas Eve service. Especially since, for the first time in her life, she had wanted to celebrate the real reason for Christmas.

Already awake, Gregory leaned against the headboard reading his Bible when Victoria opened her eyes. He immediately put his Bible on the nightstand. "Do you need something?"

"Yes. Would you have Gladys prepare me some chamomile-ginger tea and then draw me a hot bath?"

"We don't have to visit the Holmes Estate today. We can just send them a note explaining that you've been ill. They'll understand."

"I know, but I am feeling better. If it becomes too much, you can always bring me back home." He didn't look convinced. "Please, Gregory. I really do want to go."

"I just don't want you to be in pain. You'll let me know the minute you begin feeling poorly?"

Victoria smiled. She would never get used to his caring concern. "I will, and I'll take some of the laudanum and tea with me just in case."

"Alright," he finally smiled back at her. "You do look a little better, and I should know by now that I can't deny you anything anyway."

The tea helped, but Victoria still moved slowly as Gladys helped her prepare for the day. She always felt a little weak and shaky for a day or so after the pain subsided. After lunch, Gregory insisted on carrying her to Harriet's room where they had decided to exchange gifts. Harriet still hadn't spoken to them or acknowledged their presence in all this time, but Gregory thought they should include her for Christmas day.

Victoria had been forced to agree.

Like every other time they entered her room, Harriet rolled onto her side and faced the wall. At first, Victoria had thought it part of a dramatic act she carried out, but over the months, she had slowly come to realize that Harriet really had loved John.

Deeply.

Her staying in bed and not speaking to anyone might partly stem from her dramatic side, but also from her heavy grief. Knowing that had somewhat softened Victoria's heart towards her mother-in-law, but it had still been a struggle to let go of her anger at her treatment of Gregory. She had finally managed it only after studying what the Bible had to say and asking God to help her each and every time she had an angry thought.

And He did.

It still awed her. That the God Who created the universe had listened to her feeble petitions and cared enough to help her with her personal problems seemed almost too much to take in.

Now, as Gregory carried her in and sat her down in a chair and Victoria looked at the still figure in the bed, she felt compassion instead of anger. Gregory approached the bed though he didn't touch his mother. Harriet always shrugged his hand away. "Merry Christmas, Mother. Victoria and I thought we'd exchange gifts in here with you."

They had learned to talk as if she heard them but not to expect an answer. "Merry Christmas, Mother Harriet," Victoria also greeted as Martin carried in the presents. Gregory did the honors of sorting the packages and handing them out. He laid Harriet's on the bed beside her though she made no move to touch it.

Gregory took the seat beside Victoria. "Open yours first."

He'd given her a small but heavy package wrapped in red silk. Victoria carefully pulled away the material and opened the box beneath. She had to pull away some packing before lifting out a beautiful inkstand. Small and elegantly made, obviously intended for a woman's use, it looked to be solid silver. Delicate, trailing flower vines were etched on the surface for decoration. "It's beautiful," Victoria breathed as she traced one of the flowers. "And it reminds me of our garden. Thank you."

Gregory gave her one of his shy, bashful smiles that showed he really felt pleased that she liked it before turning to the gift in his lap. Victoria held her breath as he pulled on the ribbon. She had agonized over what to give him and prayed he would like it. Pulling away the material, he picked up the cloth underneath and unfolded it.

For a moment, he stared at it before a delighted smile crossed his face. "It's your tapestry."

She nodded. "I hope you like it."

"I do." Gregory pulled it closer and studied it carefully. Victoria had finally finished Gregory and Liberty the week before. She had waffled back and forth on her decision to give it to him but decided to just do it. "You are so talented," he murmured before turning to her. "Thank you, Victoria. It's perfect, and I'm going to make sure it's hung over the mantle immediately."

This time, Victoria's smile came out both pleased and embarrassed. Gregory carefully refolded the tapestry before turning to the bed. "Mother, would you like to open your present now?" After a few moments of silence, he stood up. "Maybe you will feel up to it later. Victoria and I are visiting the Holmes family for the afternoon, but we'll see you again later tonight."

Victoria held the tapestry and inkstand as Gregory picked her up again. "I really can walk," she told him when they were in the hall.

"I know, but you should save your strength. Besides, I like carrying you." Victoria gave him a playful swat on the arm.

Back in their room, he insisted on hanging the tapestry before they left. Victoria sat on the settee and directed him until he had it straight and centered above the fireplace mantle. Stepping off the ladder James steadied for him, Gregory sat on the settee with her and studied it again. "Thank you for including me," he said as he turned to her and smiled.

Victoria didn't know what to say so she just smiled back before glancing at the clock on the mantle. "We should probably go."

"It is getting late," Gregory agreed. Standing back up, he retrieved their coats as James carried the ladder from the room.

He helped Victoria into hers before slipping into his own. She pulled on her hat, gloves and scarf then reached up to adjust Gregory's scarf to fit more securely around his neck. "It's cold out there," she explained.

"Oh?" Gregory raised an eyebrow as a slow smile crossed his face. "Are you volunteering to keep me warm, Mrs. Thornton?"

Victoria giggled. "I guess I am, Mr. Thornton." Gregory gave a playful growl before sweeping her up into his arms again. She laughed as he strode to the door. They were in the hall before she suddenly remembered. "Oh, I forgot my reticule."

Gregory did an abrupt about-face and the suddenness of it elicited another laugh from Victoria. For some reason, she felt almost giddy today. She reached down and grabbed her reticule from the dressing table before Gregory carried her outside. Martin held an umbrella over them as they walked to the carriage, and Gregory gently placed her inside. Still, a few icy drops of water managed to find their way onto Victoria's face. He stepped in after her, and Martin closed the door. Their presents for the Holmes family were already nestled on the opposite bench. Bricks had been heated, wrapped in a blanket and placed on the floor to warm their feet. Gregory carefully arranged the fur lap robe around them before pulling Victoria into his arms. "Are you warm enough?"

She nodded just as the carriage started down the driveway. The rain thrummed on the roof sounding unusually loud in the confines of the coach. "I feel sorry for Brad having to drive in this weather."

"He always insists that with his slicker and hat it doesn't bother him."

Victoria couldn't imagine such a thing. "It would still bother me."

"Me, too."

The sound of the rain and the relaxing warmth of Gregory's arms almost had Victoria asleep by the time they pulled up in front of the

Holmes's Estate. She blinked her eyes groggily and sat up when the carriage came to a stop. "Remember, you tell me the minute you feel any pain or tiredness, and we'll return home," Gregory admonished.

"I will."

The Holmes's butler, Walter, opened the door and held the umbrella as Gregory stepped out of the carriage and carried Victoria into the cheerfully decorated house. He went all the way back to a large private parlour that seemed to explode with Christmas cheer. A massive, heavily adorned tree stood in the corner with brightly wrapped packages mounding underneath it. A wooden nativity stood prominently on a sideboard. Ribbons, pine boughs and candles swathed every available space. Inside were not only the Holmes family, but a couple Victoria had never seen before and three children chasing each other around one of the settees while squealing with laughter.

Seeing them in the doorway, Margaret immediately came over. "Gregory, Victoria. I was afraid you wouldn't be able to come after you missed the service last night." She somehow managed to give them both a hug even though Gregory still held Victoria.

Anywhere else, Victoria would have been embarrassed to be carried into a room, especially with strangers present, but the welcome bursting within wouldn't let her. "I insisted we come," she told Margaret with a smile.

"Though we may have to leave early if Victoria begins to feel poorly." Gregory finally set her on her feet by one of the settees and helped her off with her coat.

"Are you ill? We have a large infirmary if you need anything."

"No, I'm not ill. It's nothing to worry about. Truly."

Margaret studied her for a moment before understanding filled her eyes. "I'll have one of the maids brew you some chamomile-ginger tea, just in case."

Victoria smiled at her as she sat down on the comfortable sofa. "Thank you. The room looks lovely, Margaret, though I've never seen a Christmas tree before. It's a German tradition, isn't it?"

"Yes. My great-grandparents are from Germany, and we've always had a tree."

Gregory handed their wraps to the butler who stood in the doorway as Margaret gave instructions to a passing servant girl. That done, she grabbed the other couple and pulled them over to where Victoria sat. "Lucille, William, this is Gregory's wife, Victoria."

A tall, stately woman, Lucille had a shining mass of red hair carefully swept up. Her husband was also tall though a little portly. Already, his brown hair thinned on top though he looked to only be in his thirties. "Pleased to meet you," Victoria said sincerely.

To her surprise, Lucille sat down on the settee and clasped her hands. "Oh, you don't know how glad I am to finally meet you. Mother's written me all about you, and I just know we're going to be the best of friends. I have so many things I want to talk about, but first, I want you to meet my children."

Dumbly, Victoria nodded.

"Children, come meet Mrs. Thornton," William called in a surprisingly deep voice. The three small children who had been chasing each other about came to a screeching halt beside their father. After a tiny bit of pushing and shoving they fell into line by age. They had obviously been dressed in their Christmas finest that morning, but now their clothes were hopelessly wrinkled. Both boys had lost their cravats, and their shirts were partially untucked. Victoria thought she spied some cookie crumbs spilling out of one boy's coat pocket. The youngest child, a brown-haired girl, had a rip in her stocking across the knee and her large hair ribbon hung drunkenly on the side of her head.

Lucille smiled at them before introducing them to Victoria. Despite their rather wrinkled appearance, each child respectfully bowed or curtsied when Lucille said their names. The oldest was a nine-year-old brown-haired boy named Richard. Next, his eight-year-old brother, Henry, and then the six-year-old little girl, Elizabeth. Victoria smiled at them slightly fascinated. Rolfe would have never tolerated her or her sisters to be seen in such a state.

"If you're married to Uncle Gregory does that make you our aunt?" Henry, red-headed like his mother with a persistent cowlick standing up in the back, asked with a gap-toothed smile.

Startled, Victoria glanced at Lucille who laughed. "They have always called Gregory 'uncle', but they can call you Mrs. Thornton if you're more comfortable with it."

Before she could think of a suitable response, Gregory walked up behind Elizabeth and swung her up in the air. She squealed in delight as he settled her onto his shoulder. "How's my favorite niece?"

"I'm your only niece," Elizabeth protested.

"Really?" Gregory asked in apparent surprise. "I thought for sure I saw another one running around here somewhere."

"That was my doll," she informed him seriously.

The adults all burst out laughing. As Victoria watched Gregory talking to the boys with Elizabeth still perched on his shoulder, she made a sudden decision. "I don't mind if they call me Aunt Victoria," she told Lucille.

Lucille smiled at her as Gregory swung Elizabeth back down. "I knew I was going to like you."

Margaret sat down on Victoria's other side as all the men and the children cleared a large space in the middle of the floor then knelt down and proceeded to arm wrestle each other. "That's why I always have the Christmas party in here. The furniture is old and comfortable, and it's a place where the children can run around and just be children. And I do mean *all* the children," she added with a laugh and a knowing look at her husband as Clarence pretended to be beaten by Richard. Richard's thin chest puffed out with pride as Clarence praised him for his strong grip.

"It's wonderful," Victoria assured her although she still felt slightly dazed. No one seemed to mind the children laughing and playing. They were still respectful and obedient to their elders even as they enjoyed themselves. The complete opposite of her experience growing up.

For as long as she could remember, she'd been told children should be seen not heard. Her clothes and hair had to be spotless, and she always had to sit straight and still. The slightest fidgeting on her part would bring either a sharp rebuke, or more often, the back of Rolfe's hand. Christmas dinners had been long, formal and mostly silent affairs.

Victoria liked this cheerful and slightly rowdy atmosphere much better. This is what she wanted for her children. A happy place where they could romp and play like the children they were.

Just then, Gregory looked at her over the top of Henry's head as they took their turn at arm wrestling and gave her a warm smile. A few seconds later, Henry jumped up in victory, blocking Gregory from sight. A maid walked in and placed Victoria's tea on the table in front of the settee.

"I can see that Mother was right." Lucille's voice broke into Victoria's thoughts. "You have been good for Gregory. I don't know when I've seen him so happy."

Happy?

Victoria turned back to the chaos in front of her as she absently picked up her teacup. She really wanted Gregory to be happy, more than anything, and the thought that she might be the cause of his happiness filled her with a warm glow.

After awhile, Margaret gathered the family around the piano. She played while they all sang Christmas carols declaring and celebrating the birth of their Savior. As she sang, Victoria looked around at the family gathered. William had draped his arms around Lucille as she leaned back against his chest. Broderick held Elizabeth in his arms with the two boys standing on either side. Clarence stood behind Margaret resting his hands on her shoulders. They all looked so happy and content.

For a second, Victoria's voice faltered as an aching loneliness filled her. Though part of this happy scene, she still stood apart. Everyone here belonged to a family, loving and being loved. Sharing it freely among each other. Victoria had no one…except maybe Gregory.

Shyly, she glanced up at him as he stood beside her. His hands were clasped behind his back as he sang.

It wasn't the same.

As much as she liked him there was no love. No trust. Not like she saw on the faces of the people around her. Would she ever have someone she felt so free with? Or would she always be standing alone and apart?

You have Me.

The soft whisper across her heart caused Victoria to stop singing all together. Goosebumps raced across her skin. Could it actually be God speaking to her?

I am here, My child. I love you, and I will never leave you or forsake you. I am all you will ever need.

It took all of Victoria's willpower to keep from crying. God was here with her. She could feel Him almost like a tangible Presence all around. Surrounding her with love. After a few moments, Victoria got her tears under control and started singing again. A huge smile bloomed on her face as she turned to look at Gregory.

Had he ever experienced something like this?

As if sensing her question, he turned to her and smiled. Putting his arm around her shoulder, he pulled her close against his side. Victoria put her arm around his waist as she leaned against him. She could feel the Presence of God growing bigger until they were both wrapped in His arms of love.

Chapter 19

December faded into a wet, foggy January. After quietly celebrating the New Year at home, Gregory returned to work at the Shipping Office. Victoria found herself missing him more than ever, and the heavy, gray skies and frequent freezing rains didn't improve her mood. She became irritable and some afternoons found herself so tired it took all her willpower not to take a nap. She had begun to wonder if something were wrong with her.

She also worried about their rose bush and the hard overnight frosts. Several times a day, she made the trek out to check on it, but it always looked the same.

A pile of dead sticks wrapped up in a blanket.

Finally, near the end of January, the sun decided to make an appearance. Sunday morning dawned bright but remained bitterly cold. Ecstatic to see the sun, they all bundled up after dinner and went outside despite the freezing temperature. Broderick brought out his swords and engaged Gregory in a fencing match while Clarence looked on. Margaret asked if she would like to take a turn around the lawn.

Victoria accepted gladly. She had some questions that needed answers, and Margaret was the closest thing she had to a mother. But asking proved harder than Victoria thought, the delicate subject not considered appropriate conversation between friends. Their breaths puffed out white on the cold air as she tried to work up her courage. "Is anything wrong, dear?" Margaret finally asked as they reached the boundary between their lawn and the beginning of the apple orchard.

"No, nothing's wrong," Victoria hastened to assure her. "It's just… may I ask you a personal question?"

"Of course."

"How do you know if you are expecting?"

"You miss your time of month."

"Is that the only way to know for sure?"

"Yes."

Victoria frowned. "That doesn't really help."

"It doesn't?"

"I'm irregular," she explained. "It's only been a month, and I've gone up to four months inbetween times before."

"I see." Margaret stopped by one of the apple trees and looked at her with a mischievous smile. "Do you think you're pregnant, Victoria?"

"That's just it. I don't know."

"What makes you think you might be?"

"Well," she shrugged suddenly feeling foolish. "I don't know. I just… feel different. But it's probably because we've been shut in the house so long."

"Hmmm." Margaret didn't look convinced as they started walking again. "Have you had any morning sickness?"

"No."

"Feeling overly tired lately?"

"Y…yes."

"Irritable?"

"Yes," Victoria agreed with a laugh.

Margaret smiled and put her arm around Victoria's shoulders "You know your own body better than anyone. If you think you're with child then you probably are. Have you told Gregory of your suspicions?"

Victoria gasped. "No, I wanted to wait until I was sure. You won't tell anyone about this, will you?" Victoria hoped she didn't sound as panicked as she felt.

"Of course not. This conversation is strictly between you and I until you feel confident enough to tell everyone yourself. But I wouldn't wait too long to tell Gregory. He deserves to know even if it does turn out to be a false alarm."

Victoria fell silent as they neared the courtyard where the men fenced. Tell Gregory? The very thought filled her with terror. What if she proved to be wrong? They had never talked about children, but men wanted an heir as soon as possible. She and Gregory had been married for over seven months now with no heir in sight. He hadn't mentioned it, and she had no intention of drawing his attention to her failure. It would surely bring his wrath. No, she would wait until she knew without a doubt that she carried a child, but even that might not be enough to spare her.

Broderick won the fencing match. Everyone moved to congratulate him, but Victoria stood frozen in place, her thoughts far away. What if she carried a child but gave birth to a girl? Rolfe had been furious that all his children were born girls. After Regina's birth, he had gone on a rampage.

Suddenly, Victoria was nine again, huddling in the dark hallway listening as Rolfe screamed obscenities at her mother. The midwife had hurried out of the room carrying the bawling newborn infant. Victoria had stayed up all night hiding in the hallway, wanting to see her new sibling, but now she felt too terrified to move. The sound of flesh hitting flesh filled the air as Rolfe cursed her mother and her inability to conceive a male heir. She had covered her ears, but she couldn't block out the sounds of the beating or her mother's agonized cries. Shudders racked her body as it went on...and on...and on...

"Victoria, you must be freezing."

The sound of Gregory's voice beside her startled her back to the present. She wasn't a nine-year-old child anymore but a grown woman. A grown, married woman who might be expecting her own child. Yet, even as she turned and looked up at him, she couldn't stop her trembling. A second later, Gregory finished unbuttoning his great overcoat, pulled it off and wrapped it around her shoulders. "You're shaking like a leaf. We need to get you into the house where it's warm. A cup of hot tea should help."

Yet, as he put his arm around her and guided her to the house, Victoria knew that no amount of hot tea would warm her frozen heart.

Nervously, Claudia glanced out the hired cabby's windows. The drizzling rain that had been falling steadily all day had finally begun to slack off. According to her calculations, she should arrive at Thornton Hall in about twenty minutes. Hopefully she would have a chance to speak to Victoria before Gregory threw her out. Surely her sister could use her influence and convince him to let her stay.

Clasping her hands together, Claudia tried to stop their shaking. She really had no reason to believe Victoria would welcome her; they had never been close, but desperation drove her.

She had nowhere else to turn.

At the Almack's ball last night, someone had noticed the small bulge her stomach had become and spread the rumor that she carried a child. Rolfe had become livid and barely waited until they reached home to try to beat the truth out of her. Claudia could no longer deny the obvious fact that she carried a child, but she had refused to divulge the identity of the child's father.

If she had, Rolfe would have forced them to marry.

The very thought caused Claudia to shudder violently. How could she marry the man who had forced himself on her? The man who had laughed at her terrified screams and ineffectual efforts to escape? The man who had delighted in the pain he caused, and purposely, deliberately, hurt her worse?

No, even if Rolfe beat her to death, it would have been preferable to being married to *him*.

When Rolfe had finally realized that she wouldn't bend, he'd ordered her to be out of the house by morning. Claudia had just been glad that it gave her time to pack her things. It had taken her an hour to find a cabby willing to drive her all the way to Thornton Hall. She had to promise him double payment when they arrived, and she could only hope that Gregory would be willing to pay the exorbitant sum.

Of course, that really was the least of her worries. Her main concern being if she'd be allowed to stay. Gregory had no reason to open his house to her, especially after the way she had treated him in London, but Claudia was desperate enough to do anything. Beg with him. Plead. Throw herself on his mercy. Work for him without pay just so long as he offered her and her child a place to live, clothes to wear and food in their stomach's. That was all she required.

Suddenly, a towering stone edifice began to rise out of the foggy mist. The driver turned into the circular driveway, and Claudia knew she looked at the imposing, palatial Thornton Hall.

Clutching her reticule in one hand, she tried to still the hammering of her heart and gather her courage. This was it. Her life, and the life of her child, hung on what transpired in the next few minutes.

Taking a deep breath for courage, she stepped out of the buggy and onto the wet flagstone.

Victoria hummed as she made her way to the kitchen with the pay envelopes to give Maggie. A week had passed since her talk with Margaret, and she had decided to do what she did best. She pushed her predicament to the far corners of her mind and refused to think about it. After all, she couldn't do anything about it. She couldn't force herself to be with child or not to be, and if she were expecting, she couldn't force the child to be a male. So, there was no use worrying about how to appease Gregory's anger until she had to.

Maggie wasn't in the kitchen, but Cook directed her to the solarium. Victoria found her there, inspecting a newly hired maid's work. "Here is the pay for this month, Maggie," she said as she handed over the envelopes with a smile.

"Thank you, mum," Maggie took the envelopes and put them into her apron pocket. "I'll pass them out tonight before everyone leaves."

Victoria left Maggie and started upstairs. She had noticed that some of Gregory's suits were looking a little worn. She wanted to go over his clothing carefully and order new ones from the tailor if necessary. Martin intercepted her just before she reached the bedroom door. "There's a Miss Claudia Bolton here to see you, mum."

Claudia? Here?

She tried not to show her shock. "Thank you, Martin."

"And, mum, the cabby driver who brought her is demanding a hundred pounds payment for driving her out."

What on earth?

"Thank you, Martin. I'll take care of it."

Going on into the bedroom, Victoria went to her desk. She still had most of the money Gregory had given her weeks earlier. Pulling open her bottom right drawer, she pulled out a hundred pounds and placed them in her dress pocket. She didn't know what sort of game Claudia might be playing, but she wanted to be prepared.

Slowly, Victoria made her way back downstairs. She had never received an answer to the one missive she'd sent her sister, making it almost seven months since they'd spoken. What on earth could have driven her to show up on her doorstep so unexpectedly?

Claudia stood in the entryway next to an impressive pile of trunks and valises. She looked nervous as her light blue eyes caught Victoria's darker ones.

Victoria's heart squeezed. Despite the liberal use of powder, the puffy discolorations on her delicate face could not be hid. "Hello, Victoria." Her voice sounded stiff.

"Claudia." On impulse, she moved over and pulled her sister into a hug. To her surprise, after a moment, Claudia relaxed and returned the embrace. "It is good to see you," she said when they pulled back.

Tears sparkled in Claudia's eyes as she nodded. "I don't have any money for the cabby."

"And she promised me double payment when I got here," the middle-aged cabby driver interjected. "That's one hundred pounds."

An exorbitant amount to pay for a cab, but after seeing the bruises on Claudia's face, Victoria didn't care. She pulled the money out of her dress and handed it to the cabby. "Here's your money."

"Thank ya, mum," he doffed his hat before turning around and leaving.

"Come with me," Victoria turned and led the way upstairs to the blue salon. Inside, she pulled the bell. Claudia, who still wore her heavy winter coat, hesitantly sat down on the edge of the settee. She lacked the haughty, commanding air that had always surrounded her. Instead, she seemed almost lost. "I'll order some tea then we can talk."

"Alright."

"Aren't you hot? I can take your coat."

"No." Almost protectively, Claudia clutched her coat tighter around her. "I'm fine."

Sally appeared a moment later. "You rang, mum?"

"Yes, some tea and scones, please."

"Yes, mum." She curtsied and left again.

Victoria's curiosity and uneasiness were growing, but she waited in silence until Sally brought the tea. She fixed them both a cup, noticing how in all that time, Claudia had looked everywhere but at her. Handing her sister her tea, Victoria picked up her own and settled back more comfortably against the settee. "Alright, Claudia, I'm ready to know why you're here."

Claudia looked down at her tea as she listlessly stirred it. "I had nowhere else to go," she whispered.

"I don't understand."

She sat the untouched cup on the tea table and sighed, still not looking at her sister. "Father disowned me."

"What? Why?" Victoria's mind whirled.

"Because I am with child, and I refused to tell him who the father is."

Her words stunned Victoria. It took her several moments to collect herself enough to set the teacup down. "How did it happen?" Her voice came out surprisingly calm.

Claudia fiddled with one of her gloves as a lone tear slipped down her pale cheek. "You were right," she finally whispered after several long minutes of silence. "Paxton was too insistent in his demands."

No! Please, God, no!

Victoria's mind denied her statement even as her stomach churned in dread. Burying her face in her hands, Claudia began sobbing uncontrollably.

Shudders racked her slender frame and jolted Victoria out of her shock. "Oh, honey." She pulled Claudia into a hug. She clung to her as she cried. Slowly, broken words and phrases began to pour out of her. Horrified, Victoria listened to the unspeakable brutality Paxton had perpetrated on her sister. On the way back from the ball, his driver had taken them to a secluded park where Paxton had kept her for hours, forcing himself on her several times before finally taking her home just before dawn. Victoria closed her eyes and could barely hold back her own moans. *Jesus, help us! I don't know what to say to comfort her!*

After a few minutes, Claudia pulled back and tried to wipe the moisture off her red face. "I'm sorry. I didn't mean to break down. I just…" She took a deep breath and visibly straightened her spine. "I just need a place to stay. Do you think that Gregory would let me stay here?"

Victoria hesitated a moment as doubts assailed her. "I think so, especially after I tell him what happened."

Claudia looked at her in horror. "You're not going to tell frog face!" Victoria gasped at the same time Claudia did. "I'm sorry. I'm so sorry. I don't know why I called him that; it just became a habit. I didn't mean it." Her face crumpled. "I don't know why I'm so horrible. How can you stand me? I don't even like myself!"

Victoria pulled her back into a hug as she silently prayed for the words to say. "You're my sister, and I love you. More importantly, Jesus loves you." Claudia made a scoffing sound, but it lacked conviction. "Jesus loves you enough that He came down to this earth He created and bore the punishment for your sin by dying on the cross. He's waiting for you to accept His gift of salvation. It's the only way to truly change…by allowing Him to change you. We can't do it on our own."

"Do you really believe that?"

"Yes, I do."

She stayed quiet a moment. "I want to change, Victoria."

"Do you believe in Jesus?"

"Yes."

Victoria smiled. "Then tell Him."

"I…I don't know how."

"Just talk to Him the same way you're talking to me right now." She clasped Claudia's hands in hers as she stumbled her way through her first prayer. The words, and the lack of eloquence, didn't matter, just the faith behind them. Victoria's heart felt as if it would burst with joy as Claudia committed her life to Jesus.

After she said "amen", Claudia looked up and smiled. "I feel different. Cleaner, somehow."

She hugged her sister again, and before she knew it, they were both laughing and crying together. Now, she was not only her sister by birth, but her sister in the Lord as well. As they rejoiced together, Victoria sent up another silent prayer. *Please, Jesus, please let Gregory give her permission to stay.*

Nervously, Victoria pulled back the sheer curtain and looked at the driveway.

Still no sign of Gregory.

Sighing, she dropped the curtain and paced around the parlour. After their tea, she had given Claudia a guest room. Exhausted from her travels, she now took a nap. Victoria had spent the time since then in the front parlour, waiting in ambush for Gregory to return home from work. He didn't usually arrive until five, but some days he surprised her by coming in early. She wanted to be sure to speak with him before the servants mentioned Claudia's arrival.

Peering out the curtain again, she looked out on the misty, foggy land. No buggy clattered up the drive. The clock suddenly chimed, making Victoria jump. She glanced at the mantel.

Four-thirty.

It wouldn't be long now.

Once again, she started pacing as her mind spun. How could she convince Gregory to let Claudia stay? After the way she had treated him in London, he had every right to order her out of his home. Every argument she came up with sounded so weak and childish. *Lord, please give me the words to convince him.*

Before she felt ready, she heard the clattering of the carriage. Victoria ran to the window and looked out just as Brad pulled the horses to a stop. A few seconds later, Gregory stepped down. Victoria pulled back from the window so he wouldn't see her and took several deep breaths. It was now or never.

Hurrying into the foyer, she arrived just as Martin opened the door. "Good to have you home, sir."

"Thank you, Martin."

Martin took his coat as Victoria rushed up to him. "Gregory."

Gregory smiled. "Well, this is a surprise." Ignoring their audience, he pulled her close and landed a quick kiss on her surprised mouth. "Did you miss me?"

Victoria blushed. She had never rushed to the foyer to greet him before, and he had obviously mistaken her eagerness to see him. "Y…yes," she finally stammered, reminding her conscience that it was the truth. She always missed Gregory when he worked in the office. She waited until Martin shut the door and discreetly left. "Gregory, I need to speak with you."

Gregory smiled again. "Alright."

Taking his hand, she led him into the parlour and sat him on the settee. Now that he had arrived, she found that the words stuck in her throat. Unconsciously, she paced as she tried to gather her courage.

The smile faded from Gregory's face as he watched her. "What's wrong, honey?"

Victoria paused and looked at him. The candlelight glinted off his spectacles. No way would she be able to tell him without being able to see his eyes. Walking over, she pulled the spectacles off his face and tucked them in his pocket. Gregory looked slightly confused, but he didn't say anything.

Staring deeply into his beautiful, kind eyes, Victoria finally gathered a few tattered remnants of courage together. "Claudia's here," she told him in a rush. "But I want you to listen to what I have to say before you throw her out."

Gregory frowned. "Victoria…"

"Please, just listen. You can always make her leave afterwards if I don't change your mind."

"Victoria." Gregory grasped the hands she wrung in front of her and gently tugged on them until she sat down on the settee beside him, though she held herself slightly away.

Tense.

"Gregory…"

He put his finger on her mouth shushing her. Tears pricked her eyes as she studied the settee underneath her. She had failed to change his mind. Failed Claudia, and now what would her sister do?

"Victoria, look at me."

For the first time, she didn't want to. She kept her head down, hiding the tears. "Come on, honey." Even the endearment failed to stir her as he put his fingers under her chin and urged her face up. His eyes weren't hard or angry as she expected, but soft and gentle as he studied her. "I will listen to everything you have to say, but first, I have one question. Why do you think I would throw her out?"

She blinked. Wasn't that obvious? "In London…she…" Her whispered words trailed off when Gregory shook his head slightly.

"She's your sister. Of course she can visit you any time."

Victoria licked her dry lips as she studied the apparent sincerity in his face. "W…what if it isn't just a visit? What if…if she needs a place to stay indefinitely?"

His brow furrowed slightly. "If she needs a place to stay then she can stay here. When I married you, your family became mine just as mine became yours. Family takes care of each other."

For a long moment, Victoria just stared at him. As the import of his words sunk in the tension suddenly drained from her. With a small cry, she launched herself into his arms. The tears that she had been trying so hard to hold back trickled down her face. "Thank you, Gregory. Thank you. Thank you. Thank you."

"Hey," Gregory pulled her away just enough so he could wipe the wetness from her cheeks. "There's nothing to thank me for, sweetheart. Now, why don't you tell me what happened?"

Her mind spun as she wondered where to start. How could her heart be so full of unspeakable joy and fury at the same time? Joy that Claudia had come to know the Lord, joy that Gregory would let her stay, and fury at Paxton for what he had done to her; fury at Rolfe for his reaction to it. She decided to just begin at the beginning. "I haven't heard from Claudia since we were married, until she showed up today…"

As she told him what Paxton had done, Gregory went rigid. His teeth clamped together so tightly a muscle jumped in his jaw. She went on to tell him about Rolfe trying to beat the truth out of her and then disowning her. Anger and disgust warred in his eyes. "How dare that man even call himself a father!" He pulled Victoria a bit closer, as if protecting her from Rolfe. "Doesn't he even care that he might have hurt the baby, his own grandchild? He could have killed them both! And Paxton! It's a good thing they're not here right now or I'd…" his voice trailed off, but for some reason, his almost palpable fury at them comforted her.

Victoria nestled a little closer against him. "Rolfe has never cared for anyone but himself and his position. In truth, he treated Mother very much like P…Paxton did Claudia." Horrified, Gregory stared at her. Tears once again sprang to her eyes as she thought about her beautiful, sweet mother who had become frail and old years before her time. She had never fully recovered from the beating Rolfe had given her when Regina had been born. "T…that's why I was always afraid of men. She told me about the…the tortures a woman had to endure to please her husband. She wanted to prepare me, and I thought that's the way it was." She looked at Gregory and gently touched his cheek. "Until I met you."

"Oh, Victoria," Gregory moaned as he pulled her close and buried his face in her hair. Victoria wondered why she bared her heart to him, but she couldn't seem to stop herself. Hearing what Paxton had done had brought up all the old memories.

"That first night, I was terrified," her voice came out muffled against his neck. "All I could remember was what Mother told me. I expected you to be like that."

"I didn't know," Gregory whispered in a voice filled with pain. "I'm so sorry, honey. I never would have…"

"No," Victoria pulled back and covered his mouth with her fingers. "Don't ever apologize. You were so gentle with me, so tender that I was amazed. I hadn't realized before how much I craved a kind touch, but I couldn't get enough of it." She gave him a watery smile. "I still can't."

Reaching up, Gregory caught the lone tear that escaped with the pad of his thumb. It stunned her to see that he had tears in his own eyes as well. "I don't blame Mother," she continued in a whisper. "She thought she was doing the right thing telling me. It was all she had ever known, and she wanted to make it as easy as possible for me because she loved me. I just wish that once, at least once, she could have known the kindness of a man like you."

Gregory pulled her close, and they clung to each other, offering and receiving comfort. "Thank you for telling me," he finally murmured in a thick voice. "I am so, so sorry that you had to go through that, but I'm honored that you trusted me enough to share it." He took a shuddering breath. "You are the most precious gift God has ever given me, and with His help, I will spend the rest of my life treasuring you, showering you with the kindness and gentleness that you deserve."

Her heart too full to speak, Victoria kissed him even as she silently praised God. Rolfe could have married her off to a man like Paxton, and she would have never known of the sweetness that could exist between a husband and wife. Even worse, she might never have come to know Jesus and the fullness of His love nor would she have been able to lead Claudia to the Lord.

At the thought, she suddenly realized that she had forgotten to tell Gregory the most important part, but already completely caught up in enjoying his ardent caresses, she decided to wait until later. She didn't even notice when they slowly fell back against the settee cushions.

The sound of a gasp penetrated through Gregory's brain. Pulling back from Victoria's sweet, tempting lips, it shocked him to discover that they were lying on the settee instead of sitting on it. How had he lost his head so completely?

He sat up and squinted towards the door. A blurry figure with blond hair whirled around to leave. It had to be Claudia. "Claudia, wait!" Gregory stood up as the indistinct form froze. Reaching down he helped Victoria, who still looked dazed, to a sitting position before patting his rumpled coat looking for his spectacles.

"I'm sorry," Claudia's voice trembled. "I was just looking for Victoria. I didn't know you were home or mean to interrupt you."

Finally finding his spectacles in his top pocket, Gregory slipped them on and tried to think past the lingering passion that fogged his brain. But all he could think about was Victoria. He wondered if she knew what she did to him when she kissed him like that. She was so sweet, so innocent, that she ignited a desire in him that would surely frighten her if she knew the full force of it.

"It's alright," he finally managed to say. He ran a hand through his hair but stopped, startled, when he realized that it was already disheveled from Victoria's caresses. Victoria sat on the settee trying to straighten out her own rumpled clothing and hair, but she didn't look embarrassed. Instead she sent him a warm smile. Relieved, Gregory smiled back before turning to Claudia.

She had been staring at him wide-eyed but averted her gaze as soon as he looked at her. Even from this distance Gregory could see the swelling and bruising on her delicate face. The sight brought him back to earth with a jarring thud, and his face burned at the impression she had surely received from walking in on them in such a position. Why, she probably thought he was no better than Paxton!

He cleared his throat and walked towards her. Seeing how she shrank slightly back, he stopped and cleared his throat again. The loose dress she wore couldn't hide the slight mound in her stomach, and his heart ached. She looked little more than a child herself.

"Claudia," he tried to keep his voice soft, non-threatening. "I'm truly sorry to hear about…what happened. But I want you to know that you and your child are welcome to stay here as long as you wish."

"Thank you," Claudia murmured in a barely audible voice. She didn't glance up from the rug under her feet.

Victoria walked up beside him and slipped an arm around his waist. "I forgot the best part," she told him before reaching out and grasping one of Claudia's hands. Claudia gave her a tiny smile. "Claudia received Jesus as her Savior today."

For a moment, Gregory stared at her before joy bloomed in his heart. "Praise God! Claudia, I am so happy for you."

"Thank you," Claudia murmured again though she still wouldn't look at him.

Just then the clock chimed the hour. Victoria glanced at it. "Cook should have dinner ready. Why don't we go see? We can talk more while we eat."

"It sounds good to me. Claudia?"

Still not looking at him, she nodded and followed them into the dining room. He respectfully held out her chair. She hesitated before slipping into it. He helped Victoria into her seat before taking his own. "We always pray before meals," he explained to Claudia before bowing his head. "Jesus, thank You for this day, that our sister Claudia is here. Like the angels in Heaven, we rejoice in her salvation and pray that You heal the wounds she carries. We love You Jesus, Amen."

Victoria turned to him as the servants carried in the platters. "How do you know the angels rejoice?"

Surprised, Gregory looked at her. She never asked questions about the Bible. "Jesus says it in Luke 15, if I'm not mistaken. Would you like to study that for our devotions tonight?"

"If you don't mind."

"Not at all," Gregory glanced at Claudia. "Perhaps we could hold our devotions in the blue salon so Claudia can join us. If she would like to."

Victoria beamed at him. "That's a wonderful idea. Now that she's given her life to Jesus, she needs to know more about Him. You will join us, won't you?"

"If you want me to," Claudia's answer seemed to be directed at her plate.

"It's settled then." Gregory took a bite of his venison roast even as he wondered what he'd gotten himself into.

That night, he read Luke 15 out loud then they all knelt for prayer. The entire time, Claudia made sure to stay as far away from him as she could. Out loud, Gregory once again thanked God for Claudia and for His blessings to be poured out upon her and her child. Silently, he pleaded with Him for help in dealing with another wounded, scarred spirit. He had made so many mistakes with Victoria, and he didn't want to repeat them with her sister. He felt nearly overwhelmed to realize that his shoulders now carried the responsibility for a younger sister with a baby on the way.

After he finished, he paused as he always did in case Victoria wanted to pray though she never had in all the time they were married. He opened his mouth to say amen, but a slight tightening of Victoria's hand on his stopped him. "God," she began in a small voice that trembled slightly. Gregory found himself staring at her instead of keeping his head bowed. Her face scrunched up as if she searched for the right words.

Or perhaps courage.

"T…thank You for Claudia. For leading her to You today."

Several moments passed before she opened her eyes and looked at him as if for help. Gregory gave her hand a reassuring squeeze even as his heart nearly burst with joy. "In Jesus Name, Amen."

Chapter 20

To Victoria, a month never flew by so fast. Claudia's arrival started a flurry of activity, and for the first time, she began to become acquainted with and know the younger sister she had always loved. At Victoria's insistence, they made several shopping trips into Lewes once the bruises on Claudia's face faded. Claudia agreed only because a loose cloak hid evidence of her condition.

On the first trip, she bought Claudia her very own Bible to have during their devotions. Every morning and evening the three of them gathered in the blue salon as Gregory read the Bible and prayed. Yet Claudia continued to be wary in his presence.

For Gregory's part, he had been more than generous when Victoria hesitantly approached him about all the things Claudia would need. Now, Claudia not only had her own ladies maid, but a suite in the same wing as theirs. It was in the process of being remodeled to include a nursery. Madame Blanchet had come and made her a whole new wardrobe to fit her expanding waistline. Victoria had bought yards of soft cloth and yarn to make baby clothes. Still, Claudia refused to attend church or to socialize in any way. She wouldn't even join them at the Holmes's even though Victoria had pleaded with her to do so. She felt too embarrassed and afraid not wanting to face the whispers or judgmental looks when people found out she carried a child out of wedlock. Victoria had spoken with Gregory about it one night, but he had said they shouldn't press her yet.

"She's been through so much," he had told her in a compassion laden voice as he had held her close in the darkness of their room. "Maybe she needs this time with just her and the Lord so she can heal."

Victoria had been forced to agree. She didn't think Claudia could hide out forever, and though not everyone at church would accept her, there were people, like the Holmes family, who would. Having real friends would be a new experience for her just as it had been for Victoria, and she ached with the desire to share it with her sister. She had told Margaret about her, and she knew Gregory had confided in Clarence and Broderick, as well. The family had committed to praying for her daily, and Broderick had even stopped dropping by Thornton Hall in an effort to give Claudia time to adjust and to feel safe before being forced to entertain new people.

Claudia had refused to travel with them to London when they attended the Queen's wedding. Worried at leaving her sister alone, she had asked Gregory if they could keep the trip short. He'd agreed, and they left Thornton hall early on the ninth. The wedding the next afternoon at St. James Palace proved to be a lavish affair despite the dismal, drizzling rain. The Queen wore a gorgeous white dress of silk satin trimmed with Honiton lace and carried a wreath of orange blossoms. Twelve young bridesmaids carried her train. The wedding reception was held at Buckingham Palace and included the largest cake Victoria had ever seen. At least three yards in diameter, she heard some speculation that it weighed up to 300 pounds!

Rolfe once again escorted Julia Hastings, and they came over to exchange perfunctory greetings before excusing themselves to the dance floor. Seeing her father left a sour feeling in Victoria's stomach. But she completely forgot about the incident and nearly fainted when the newlyweds approached her and Gregory several minutes later. She had never before spoken with the Queen and did her best to remember all the etiquette required while her shaky legs threatened to give out on her at any moment. Gregory seemed to have no such difficulties, but then, he had apparently been classmates with Prince Albert at the University of Bonn when he had attended a semester there in 1837 at

John's insistence and had continued a correspondence with him ever since.

Something he had neglected to mention to her before Albert recognized him and came over to renew their acquaintance, bringing the Queen with him!

She really needed to have a talk with her unassuming husband and remind him that, as his wife, she needed to be kept informed of certain things. Like the fact that he was apparently good friends with the new royal consort!

Despite the excitement of the wedding, Victoria only felt relief as she climbed into the carriage early on the eleventh. After the vast openness of Thornton Estate, London felt dirty and stifling. Coupled with her worry for Claudia, it had made the short stay in the city nearly unbearable.

The servants had taken excellent care of Claudia in their absence, and her sister seemed well-rested and refreshed when they arrived home. She had even begun piecing together a baby blanket. Each day thereafter, she and Claudia spent a few hours sewing up tiny baby clothes and making little hats and booties.

Victoria secretly wondered if she would soon have to do the same things for her own child. She still had nothing definite to go on other than the fact that she felt slightly different, and when Claudia took a nap in the afternoons, Victoria had been unable to keep herself from retiring as well. She had also started becoming a little hungry between meals.

They were sewing in the blue salon one afternoon when Claudia brought up the subject of Harriet. "I haven't seen Mrs. Thornton since I arrived. Does she disapprove of my being here?"

Victoria sighed. "Mother Harriet hasn't been out of bed or spoken since Mr. Thornton died five months ago. Gregory and I visit her every evening, and we've told her about you. As to what she thinks about it…" Victoria shrugged before holding up the finished garment. A tiny nightgown in pale yellow that included booted feet. Victoria had embroidered colorful flowers on it and adorned it with a darker yellow ribbon around the neck. "How's that?"

Claudia smiled at her even as she rested a hand on her slowly expanding stomach. "If it's a girl, she'll love it. If it's a boy…" she shrugged and then laughed. "I guess he won't know the difference until he grows up."

Victoria laughed with her. "Well, it will keep my little niece or nephew warm."

"Yes." Claudia's smile grew pensive. "It's kind of strange. The night that Paxton…" She stopped and shook her head. "I was terrified that I would be with child. I was sure it was the worst thing that could happen. That I would hate the baby because of it's father and the way it had been conceived." She stayed silent a moment. "I did feel that way until the first time I felt it move. Just the smallest flutter, as soft and helpless as a butterfly's wings, but I knew it was my baby." She gave Victoria a smile. "I fell in love in that moment."

Victoria smiled back despite the tears in her eyes before reaching out and pulling Claudia into a hug. She could feel her small stomach, hard and round, pressing against her. "You're going to make a wonderful mother," she whispered.

"I hope so, Victoria. I truly hope so."

February slowly changed to March. Ecstasy filled Victoria as the first signs of spring poked through the frozen earth. The air still held a raw edge, but the days were starting to become sunny again. Soon, the garden would begin growing. Victoria longed to go out in the sunshine and dig her hands into the warm soil. She wanted Gregory beside her as he taught her how to do her hybrid fuchsia's that he had given her for her birthday.

Beginning to feel more comfortable running the business and confident that the management would continue with the changes he made, Gregory planned on cutting back his hours and only going in three days a week. Victoria thrilled at the thought of having him home more often.

A few days into the new month, she woke up to sunlight streaming in through the windows. Tuesday, the first day Gregory planned to spend at home. Opening her eyes, she saw her husband already dressed in his gardening clothes and working at his drawing table. A sight she hadn't seen in over five months.

She had missed it dreadfully. *Thank You,* she prayed silently before sitting up.

Gregory glanced over his shoulder and smiled at her. "Good morning."

"Good morning." Victoria stood and walked over to give him a hug. "Are you ready to work in the garden today?"

"Yes. I think we can even uncover our bush." He gave her a quick kiss before pointing at the paper he worked on.

Victoria leaned over his shoulder. A halfway finished page in his book for a foxglove. "It's beautiful. Do you think you'll be able to finish the book now?"

"I hope so."

Gregory leaned back over the table as Victoria went to ring for Gladys. Halfway to the bell cord, sudden nausea attacked her stomach. She put a hand over her mouth, but it refused to be quelled. Dashing for the washroom, she barely made it in time.

She was still bent over the basin when Gregory poked his head in a few seconds later. "Honey, are you alright?"

She couldn't answer him as her stomach heaved again. He came in, holding her long hair back and supporting her as she continued retching. Several long minutes later she finally felt well enough to lean against the wall though she still felt shaky and weak. Gregory wet a cloth and handed it to her. She held it against her head for a moment relishing the coolness before she wiped her mouth off. "Thank you."

"Do you feel sick? Do you need the doctor?"

Victoria shook her head. "No. It's probably just something I ate. I'll have Gladys prepare some tea and crackers, and I should be fine."

As he helped her back to bed, Victoria couldn't stop her mind from whirling. Was it something she ate? Or could it be morning sickness?

She didn't know, but within an hour she felt perfectly fine. Gladys helped her dress, and she and Gregory joined Claudia for morning devotions. Later that day, Gregory held her hand as he led the way through the garden to their rose bush. They unwrapped it being careful not to break off any of the fragile branches.

Sitting back on her heels, Victoria reluctantly admitted to herself that it looked exactly the same as before. "Do you think it's even alive?" she asked a bit mournfully.

"I don't know." Gregory poked around, checking the ground for moisture. "All we can do is wait and see. If it is alive, it should start putting forth leaves soon."

Victoria stared at the small pile of sticks. If sheer willpower could make it live, it would surely be the healthiest bush in England. It had become such a special plant to her, and she didn't want to have to uproot it and throw it away. "Well, we've done all we can," Gregory finally said as he stood back up. He held out his hand. Victoria took it and allowed him to pull her to her feet. Still holding hands, they walked through the barren garden. Gregory stopped every once in awhile to check on certain plants, but he seemed pleased at the way Perry had kept the garden up in his absence.

They finished their tour just before lunchtime. Gregory slipped his arm around her waist, and she leaned against him with a sigh. "I miss it," she admitted. "I miss the days we spent together working in the garden. If I had known how short they were going to be..."

"I know." Gregory pulled her a little closer. "It's hard leaving you to work in the office. I would much rather stay here with you the way we did before."

"Me, too." Victoria sighed again before smiling up at him. "At least now you can spend a few days at home. I'm glad for that."

"So am I." Gregory placed a soft kiss on her mouth before leading the way into the house. Claudia already waited for them in the small, private dining room. As they ate, Gregory and Victoria started making plans for the garden. He explained some of the processes they would have to undertake to make her hybrid work. Claudia stayed silent but seemed to be listening.

They were just finishing dessert when Martin appeared in the doorway. He wore a frown. "Sir, there's a gentleman here to see you. He said his name is..."

"I'll introduce myself to the old man."

Paxton strode into the room looking as suave and confident as ever.

Victoria gasped. Claudia dropped her fork. It clattered loudly on her dinner plate in the sudden silence. Gregory stood up, but Paxton paid him no attention as, unasked, he plopped down into the chair beside Claudia. He put his arm around her shoulders even as she shrank from his touch. "Hello, darling."

With a cry, Claudia jumped from her chair and ran around behind Gregory who had started towards them. Victoria jumped up and put her arm around her sister. "You are not welcome here," Gregory told the intruder in a low, biting tone Victoria had never heard him use before.

Paxton just leaned back in his chair with a smirk. "Now, you don't know that, old man. I'm here to discuss business. Personal business that involves you, Claudia and that brat she's carrying." Paxton lazily scanned Victoria's figure with his cold eyes. Victoria shivered and wondered how she could have ever considered him to be handsome.

He was a viper.

"It's been too long, Victoria," he practically purred.

Gregory took a half-step forward before stopping. "Victoria, you and Claudia wait for me in the blue salon while I deal with this."

Gregory never took his eyes off Paxton as Victoria ushered a shaking Claudia out into the hall. Claudia stopped as soon as the door swung shut behind them. "I have to know what's going on," she whispered.

Victoria hesitated a moment before nodding. They crept over to the door and pressed their ears against the wood.

"Aren't you even going to ask me to eat, old man?" Paxton sneered.

"What's on your mind?"

Paxton laughed. "What's on everybody's mind? Money. I need money and lots of it. Fifty thousand pounds ought to do."

Victoria gasped before placing a hand over her mouth, praying they hadn't heard her inside.

"Why do you think I would give you any money?" Gregory asked in a hard voice.

"You will, old man, if you want to keep what you have here. Two sisters for the price of one isn't such a bad setup." The lewdness in

Paxton's voice made Victoria want to march back in there and throttle him.

"And if I don't give you the money?"

"Simple. I tell old man Bolton whose child Claudia is carrying. He'll force her to marry me, and I'll have her dowry."

This time Claudia gasped. Her fingers dug into Victoria's arm in a vise-like grip. "I can't marry him. I can't!" she whispered desperately.

"Shhh." Victoria's heart pounded as she tried to listen.

"I came to you first because I don't really want a snotty nosed brat...for a wife or for a kid," Paxton continued. His voice turned cold. "But I need the money. I have some gambling debts and the creditors are pressing me. If I have to marry Claudia to get them off my back, I will."

"I see." Silence reigned for a moment. Victoria held her breath. *Please, Jesus, please let Gregory pay him so he'll go away!* "That's a lot of money, Paxton," Gregory finally said. "I would have to think about it."

"Don't take too long, old man. I expect my money by tonight."

"I'm afraid that would be impossible. If I do decide to pay you, I would have to go to London to retrieve the funds."

"I don't mind waiting here while you're gone. Thornton Hall is just to my tastes."

"I would expect you to return to London with me," Gregory told him with a slight edge in his voice.

"Impossible." Paxton sounded smug. "If I show my face in London before I receive the money, the creditors might kill me. I'll expect your answer by tonight. Right now, I want something to eat."

A few seconds of silence followed before Gregory spoke. "Martin, see that Paxton is fed."

"Yes, sir."

The door suddenly swung open and almost hit them. Gregory looked surprised before shutting the door with a cautious glance behind him. He put a finger over his mouth and led them to a private parlour. "Why didn't you go to the blue salon?"

"Claudia wanted to know what was going on," Victoria explained.

Claudia's fingers still dug into her arm. "Please, please pay him the money. I'll do anything you want. Anything! As long as I don't have to marry him!"

Gregory sighed as he looked down at her. "I would pay him the money in a heartbeat if I thought he would leave you alone, but he won't. He'll keep coming back expecting more."

"I can't marry him. I won't!" Claudia sounded almost hysterical. Tears running down her face, she turned towards the door.

"Listen to me!" Gregory grabbed her shoulders to keep her from running from the room. "Listen," he said a bit softer when she calmed down a little. "I won't let Paxton near you. If we have to, I'll sneak you out of the country on one of my ships, but I want that to be our last resort." He let her go when she gave a small nod. "Right now we need to pray that God will show us another way." Claudia gave him another jerky nod. Gregory turned to look at Victoria. "I want the two of you to go into the blue salon and stay there. I have a lot to do, but I'll send one of the servants up to stay with you."

"Alright," Victoria whispered.

Gregory gave them both an encouraging smile before letting them out of the room. Victoria hurried Claudia to the blue salon. She began pacing and praying. Claudia sat on the settee, weeping. *God, please give Gregory wisdom! Show him what to do.*

A few minutes later, a knock sounded at the door just before a footman entered. He gave her a nod and stood guard by the door. Victoria couldn't keep her eyes from the pistol tucked into his belt.

Could he overpower Paxton if the need arose?

Hurrying to the study, a crazy plan began to form in Gregory's mind that might actually work. He just didn't like leaving Paxton here while he went to London. He didn't trust that man near Victoria or Claudia. Or any of the serving girls for that matter. Unfortunately, if he ordered him to leave and stay at an inn, Paxton might be prideful enough to go straight to Rolfe. Then he'd have to sneak Claudia out of the country, and he really didn't want her to be alone in a strange land. Especially with a newborn babe.

Sitting down at the desk, he scribbled a quick note to Broderick. He found one of the footmen to deliver it for him and then had Maggie call all the servants together in the kitchen. All except Martin who kept a watch on Paxton while he ate. It looked like so few to keep watch over his precious family. He prayed Broderick would be able to bring more men.

"I'm going to leave for London, and I'll be gone overnight," he began without preamble. "Paxton will be staying here. I don't trust him, and I don't want him around any of the women not even our serving girls."

Gregory looked each of the men in the eye. They all knew what Paxton had done from overhearing conversations, and their faces were grave. "That means all of you are going to have to work in the house." The stable hands nodded in agreement. Gregory wished that Horace were here, but he had gone on several errands and wouldn't be back until late that night. "I want a man with Paxton at all times, and one of you must be with my wife and her sister at all times. Even so, they are not to leave each others company." Gregory took a deep breath. "The girls can do their normal duties as long as Paxton's not in the room. If they see him, they are to go immediately where someone else is even if it puts off their chores. I've asked Broderick to come. He'll be in charge until I return. Clinton, I need Liberty saddled for me."

"Yes, sir."

"The rest of you men, come with me."

Spinning around, Gregory made his way to the bedroom. He quickly explained what he wanted done, and as they rearranged the room, he packed a small valise. It would have to do because he planned to ride horseback to London. It would cut several hours off the trip, and if everything went smoothly, he could be back in time for lunch tomorrow. He checked his pistol before tucking it in his pocket.

Now, he could leave as soon as Broderick arrived.

Victoria stopped pacing when Gregory appeared in the doorway. "Gregory!" She rushed across the room but stopped when she noticed his bag and coat. "You're going to pay him."

Gregory set down his valise and pulled her into his arms. "Yes. I have a plan, Victoria. Keep praying that God will work out the details."

She nodded. "I will." *Please, God!*

Guiding her to the settee, he sat Victoria down before kneeling in front of Claudia. Her face had become red and splotchy from crying, and her eyes still held wariness as she looked at him. "I meant what I said," he told her softly. "Paxton will not touch you. I will sneak you out of the country before I let him marry you, but if my plan works, you'll be able to stay here. Just keep praying and trusting God."

Once again, Claudia just nodded.

"Hey! Where's the fire?"

Victoria turned when she heard Broderick. He stood in the doorway tugging off his gloves. He still wore his overcoat with a white scarf carelessly flung around his neck. His gaze flicked to Claudia and stayed. Something flashed across his face but left before Victoria could discern what it meant.

Claudia gasped and shrank back even as Gregory stood. "Thank you for coming so quickly. This is Claudia. Claudia, Broderick Holmes," he introduced in a rush. "I need to speak with you."

"Sure." Broderick followed Gregory back into the hall.

"Victoria…he's…" Claudia's voice sounded strangled.

Victoria winced. Broderick's unfortunate resemblance to Paxton would not ease her sister's mind. "I've known Broderick since I've been here, and he is an honorable man," Victoria tried to reassure her.

Claudia did not look reassured.

When they came back in, Broderick looked gravely serious for the first time since Victoria had known him. Gregory shrugged into his coat and picked up his valise. He stopped and looked at her. "I'll be back as fast as I can. Hopefully by lunchtime tomorrow."

"God be with you," she whispered.

He nodded and left. Standing up, Victoria went to the window and waited. Several minutes later she saw Gregory galloping Liberty down the driveway. He disappeared from sight just as a cloud covered the sun. She shivered and turned back to the room. "Now, what?"

"Gregory wants you and Claudia to stay hidden, either here or in your bedroom. If you need anything send a maid to fetch it. I'll keep Paxton occupied today, and tonight we'll all stay in your room."

Victoria blinked at him. "*All* of us?"

"Yes." A slight red hue crept up Broderick's cheeks. "You and Claudia will share the bed, and I'll sleep on the settee. The servants are rearranging it to give you privacy." He glanced back at the door. "I'll see you tonight."

Victoria stared after him as he left until she noticed Claudia trembling violently in her chair. She hurried over and put her arms around her. "It's alright. You don't have to be afraid," she soothed. "No one here will hurt you." Casting about desperately in her mind for something comforting to say, she finally recalled the Bible verses Gregory had quoted when she'd been so terrified after her introduction ball. "The Lord is my light and my salvation; whom shall I fear? The Lord is the strength of my life; of whom shall I be afraid?…"

Chapter 21

Hours later, Victoria stood in awe as she stared at her bedroom. The bed had been pushed over in front of the changing room, and the settee, covered in blankets and pillows, stood where the bed used to be. A large, heavy curtain had been strung between the two for privacy. More men scurried about the house than she had ever seen before. Gregory had surrounded them by a veritable army.

Claudia hadn't relaxed even though they had not seen Paxton or Broderick again. Now, exhaustion visibly clung to her, and Victoria insisted that she retire. Gladys came up to help her get Claudia settled. Once in her nightshift, Victoria tucked the covers around her as if she were a little child again. She looked so small and helpless in the huge bed.

"Victoria, I'm scared," she whispered. "Please don't leave me."

Victoria's heart clenched. "I'm not," she assured her. "Just let me change." She didn't really feel tired, but she couldn't leave her.

Once in her own nightshift, Victoria crawled into bed with Claudia and wrapped her arms around her. Gladys blew out the candles and drew the curtain. The only light came from the banked fire. "The Lord is my light and my salvation; whom shall I fear? The Lord is the strength of my life; of whom shall I be afraid?…" Victoria once again quoted Psalm 27 from memory. Soon, Claudia's body relaxed, and by her deep breathing, she had fallen asleep.

Sometime later, she heard a soft knock on the door. She stiffened as Claudia jerked awake. The door swished open. "Victoria?"

Victoria relaxed when she recognized Broderick's voice though Claudia remained tensed. "We're here."

The door closed. "I just wanted to let you know that I was here." She could hear movements as he climbed into his bed on the settee. Then all became silent again.

"It's okay," she whispered to Claudia who nodded but remained tense. Time slowly passed. Claudia eventually fell asleep again. Victoria's own eyes grew heavy as she drifted off.

Some hours later, she startled awake. Her heart pounded though Claudia remained sleeping beside her. Complete blackness blanketed the room.

What had awoken her?

Suddenly, she heard the noise again. The soft sound of someone shuffling along on the rug.

"Vic-tor-ia," Paxton's voice called softly, alluringly.

Claudia jerked awake with a gasp. Victoria immediately clapped her hand over her mouth, but Paxton heard it. He chuckled softly. "Light a candle, darling. We have some unfinished business to attend to."

Silence.

She heard the shuffling noise again as Paxton tried to walk in the dark. He bumped into something and uttered a soft curse. She held Claudia close as her sister trembled violently.

Or was it her?

Where on earth was Broderick?

"Victoria, where are you?" Paxton singsonged. "I don't want to hurt you, honey, but you owe me, remember? Come on, darling. Light the candle." He paused a moment before calling her name again.

"Victori-AHHH!"

His sudden scream made Victoria jump nearly a foot straight into the air.

"Who are you, and what do you want?" Broderick growled in a low voice.

"B…Broderick? I…is that y…you?" Paxton's voice came out high-pitched and squeaky.

"Yes."

Paxton regained some of his usual bluster. "Remove your sword off my throat, man, before you kill me."

"Not until you tell me what you're doing in my room."

"Your room? I thought it was Vic…I thought it was my room," he corrected himself.

"Oh?" Broderick didn't sound convinced. "Well, you're not only in the wrong wing you're on the wrong floor."

"It's not my fault. This place is colossal; it's easy to become lost."

"Then why were you calling for Victoria?"

A second of silence passed by. When Paxton spoke again, he sounded a little nervous. "I…I was just calling for a valet. Now, remove your sword off my throat. You're drawing blood."

"A valet?" Broderick questioned.

"You rang, sir?"

Victoria nearly went limp when she heard James's voice.

"Yes, James I did. It's good to see you back, Horace."

"I just arrived, sir," Horace's deep voice rumbled through the room. "Can I be of assistance?"

"Yes, actually. It seems Paxton is in need of a good valet to show him to his room…and to make sure he stays there. I think you should do nicely."

If Victoria hadn't been so scared, she would have giggled. The hulking hostler would be able to handle anyone.

"With pleasure, sir."

She heard a strangled gasp then the door shut. "How did he get in here?" Broderick demanded.

"I don't know, sir," James answered. "A man was stationed outside of his door."

Pacing sounded. "Well, station two outside of his door and two more outside of this one. I don't want him near the women again."

"Yes, sir."

The door opened and shut; the pacing stopped near the curtain. "Victoria, are you both alright?" Broderick asked in a noticeably softer voice.

"Y…yes." She couldn't quite keep the tremble out of her own.

"Don't worry. I think we've seen the last of him."

Victoria could only pray it was so.

Gregory reached London at almost midnight, but he went directly to the Bolton home. He had learned on his last visit that Rolfe stayed up at all hours of the night. The lights shining from the upper windows proved that he had been right. Dismounting, he tied Liberty to a hitching ring and knocked on the door.

A few seconds later the butler, Claude, opened it. "I need to see Rolfe. I'm his son-in-law, Gregory Thornton."

Claude hesitated a moment before taking his hat and coat. "Wait a moment, sir, and I'll see if he's available."

He waited impatiently until Claude returned. "Right this way, sir." He led him down the hallway and pointed towards a partially opened door. "He's in his study."

"Thank you."

Gregory pushed open the door and walked in but stopped when he saw Rolfe practically lying on the settee.

A feminine giggle filled the air.

"Rolfe?"

At his voice, Rolfe sat back, revealing a woman underneath him. A dirty, tattered silk dress left scant to the imagination. Gregory's cheeks heated up as he took a step back.

"Come on in, boy. Don't be bashful." Rolfe waved him in even as he reached for another glass of port from the nearly empty bottle on the table. "What brings you here?"

Gregory glanced back at the woman, uncomfortable discussing his business in front of her. She lazily stretched and put her arm on the pillow above her head as she sent him a flirtatious wink. Cheeks burning even hotter, Gregory turned back to Rolfe. Maybe he would send her out. "Business. Personal business concerning your daughter, Claudia."

Rolfe drank his full glass before pouring another one. "She's not my daughter anymore."

"Still, I need to speak with you about her."

He waved his hand dismissively. "Tomorrow's soon enough to talk business, boy. I'll have Claude fix you up a room."

"That's not necessary. I'll stay at an inn."

"Nonsense. You're my son-in-law, and I insist you stay here. I'll have Victoria's old room fixed up."

Only the mention of Victoria kept Gregory from leaving. He already missed her so much. The thought of staying in the room where she grew up teased at his tired mind. "Alright," he finally agreed. "I'll see you tomorrow."

"Tomorrow?" Rolfe looked surprised. "Why don't you stay and join the fun? I'm sure that…that…" he waved his hand vaguely towards the woman a moment before he turned to her. "What's your name, honey?"

"Hester," she reminded him with an inviting smile.

Rolfe gave her a lecherous grin in return as he stroked her arm. "I'm sure Hester has a friend she could find for you."

Aghast, Gregory stared at him. It took a moment before he found his voice past his shock. "No," his tone came out curt. "I'm tired and just want to sleep."

Rolfe merely shrugged his attention already back on Hester.

"Too bad, handsome." Hester sent him another wink over Rolfe's shoulder. "We could've had fun together."

Practically shaking in anger, Gregory rushed out of the room. He wanted to grab that despicable man and pound him into a pulp at his feet. His fists clenched as he remembered what he'd done to Claudia. To Victoria. Gregory had never before in his life wanted to hit someone, but he wanted to now. Praying furiously for control, he strode back outside and pulled his bag off Liberty's saddle.

His anger didn't abate, but he felt God's peace slowly twine around his heart. Going back inside, he found Claude standing in the foyer with a lit candlestick in his hands. "This way, sir."

Gregory followed him up the stairs. "I need someone to see to my horse."

"Yes, sir."

He went down several halls before stopping in front of a closed door. "This is the room, sir."

Gregory took the candlestick from him. "Thank you."

Claude hurried back down the hall. With a sigh, Gregory opened the door. He heard a soft thud then the sound of running feet. "Who's there?"

No answer. He set the candlestick and his bag on a dressing table and pulled his pistol from his pocket. He gazed slowly around the dimly lit room. The bedcovers were rumpled as if someone had been sleeping in them.

There. The curtains on the window moved slightly. He stealthily moved closer with his gun drawn but stopped a few feet away when he saw a pair of small, bare feet sticking out of the bottom. It looked like a child.

Regina?

"Regina, is that you?"

A small gasp sounded. "W…who are you?" Regina asked in a frightened little voice.

Gregory put his gun up. "It's Gregory Thornton. Victoria's husband."

The curtains opened a crack, and he saw an eye peeking out at him. Slowly, she stepped out from behind the curtains though she kept her face down. Her hands wrung the front of her nightshift.

Tiredly, Gregory rubbed his eyes. "What are you doing here?" he asked as he took a step towards her.

She shrank back. It reminded him so much of Victoria that he stopped as all tiredness left him. "I'm not going to hurt you," he told her softly.

Slowly, he walked over and knelt down in front of her. She kept her head so low that he couldn't see her face. He gently forced her to look at him. Even in the dim light of the candles, he could see the fear in her eyes and the dark bruise along her chin. He gently touched it. "What happened?"

Regina looked back down and shrugged. "He grew angry when he couldn't take Julia riding this afternoon. I happened to be there."

She said it so simply as if it made perfect sense. Gregory closed his eyes as he once again struggled to control the visceral urge he had to pound Rolfe to within an inch of his life. "Shouldn't you be in bed?" he finally asked when he could speak again.

"I was." Regina looked past him to the rumpled bed. "I came to sleep in here after Father brought that woman in."

Why would she sleep in Victoria's old room, unless…

"You miss Victoria a lot, don't you?" Gregory guessed.

Tears filled her big brown eyes as she nodded. His heart squeezed painfully. "Well, young lady. I think it's time you were asleep." Standing up, Gregory held out his hand and waited. She wiped her nose and sniffed before taking it. Her hand felt so small and fragile in his. He led her over to the bed and waited as she clambered back into it.

Pulling the covers up, he tucked them around her before turning to leave. "Can I come live with you and Victoria?"

Regina's question stopped him in his tracks. He sat down on the bed and sighed. "I would love for you to live with us, but it's not that simple. Rolfe is your father. Legally, you have to live where he says."

Her eyes welled with tears again.

"I have an idea, though," Gregory continued. "I'll ask Rolfe if you can come visit us for a few weeks."

Regina's face lit as she sat up. "Would you?"

"Yes," he pushed her back down onto the pillow. "Now, the decision is up to him, but I'll ask him tomorrow."

"Thank you, Mr. Thornton."

"You're welcome." He pushed some of the tangled brown hair off her forehead before standing up. Taking the extra pillow and the blanket folded at the foot of the bed, he made himself a pallet on the floor. Tired as he felt, he couldn't sleep for the aching in his heart. He'd prayed to love his wife, but he hadn't known how much he would come to love her sisters as well. Claudia and Regina felt like his own sisters and to see them in such pain…

Gregory rolled over and stared up at the dark ceiling. *Jesus, I want to help them both. Show me what to do. How can I help Regina?*

It was afternoon before Claude told Gregory that Rolfe would see him. He had been playing a card game with Regina in Victoria's old room. Regina jumped up when he stood. "Don't forget to ask him…please?"

Gregory smiled down at her. "I won't."

Going downstairs, he found Rolfe standing by the door in his hat and coat. "Come on, boy," he said gruffly. "I'm on my way to White's."

Taking his own hat and coat from Claude, he followed Rolfe out to the carriage. Gregory had never been to White's, a notorious gentleman's club famous for its gambling. Still, gentlemen often met there to discuss business. If Rolfe agreed to his plan, it would be the perfect place to procure a couple of witnesses.

In White's, Rolfe commandeered a table near the famous bowed window and ordered some food. "Now," he said as he leaned back in the chair. "What is it you want to discuss?"

A waiter came over and offered them brandy. He poured Rolfe a large glass, but Gregory declined. "It's about Claudia," he began when the waiter left. "She's been staying in my home the past few weeks."

"I'd heard that you'd taken her in," Rolfe took a sip of his drink.

Gregory took a deep breath. "If she is to continue to live at my house, I need to have legal guardianship."

Rolfe's eyes narrowed. "You want to be her legal guardian? Why?"

"I heard that you disowned her."

"That's right." The waiter brought over two steaming plates of food. Rolfe dug right in, but Gregory's stomach had knotted up too much to eat.

"All I want is that you make it legal. Since she has been in my home, certain…issues have arisen. I must have legal guardianship to resolve them."

Rolfe studied him before a smirk crossed his face. "I see what you mean. As her legal guardian, she would have to do what you say. Kind of like your own personal slave." He laughed. "Not bad thinking, boy."

Shocked, Gregory just stared at him. Rolfe took another drink before nodding. "Alright. Your marriage netted me over a hundred thousand pounds. I can do you a favor and help you pay Claudia back for how she treated you. She deserves it anyway after what she did to me. I could have made a lot of money off her marriage, as well, if she hadn't become pregnant."

Angry words burned on Gregory's tongue, but he bit them back. Antagonizing Rolfe would only hurt Claudia. He pulled out the paper Andrew Stokes had prepared before he left Lewes and handed it to Rolfe. "This was drawn up by my solicitor. All we need is your signature and that of two witnesses."

"There's Baron Alvanley and the Earl of Strafford. Will they do?"

"Yes." Rolfe called them over. The waiter brought a quill and ink, and the paper was quickly signed.

Gregory sighed in relief as he put the paper back into his pocket. Claudia's future had been secured. Now he had to secure the future of her child. That couldn't be done until he reached Lewes again. He finally took a bite of the food as he thought again about Regina. "Actually, I wanted to talk with you about Regina as well."

Rolfe scoffed. "That girl is more trouble than she's worth. Fat and freckled. I'll probably have to pay money to get her married off."

Once again, Gregory found himself biting his tongue to keep from spewing out his angry thoughts. Regina happened to be an adorable child. The freckles sprinkled across her nose were cute, and while she wasn't skinny, she certainly wasn't fat, either

"When a man gets to be my age, he shouldn't have girls to worry about," Rolfe continued. "I've done my duty as a father, and now, I should be able to relax, marry that pretty Julia Hastings and finally get a male heir. Unfortunately, Julia doesn't want to be saddled with a nine-year-old stepchild."

"I'll take her." The words popped out before Gregory could stop them.

Rolfe glanced at him in surprise. "What did you say?"

"I said I'd take Regina off your hands."

Sitting back in his chair, Rolfe studied him through narrowed eyes. "Are you expecting me to pay for her upkeep?" he asked gruffly.

"No. All I would require would be legal guardianship. Just like with Claudia." Gregory held his breath as Rolfe started eating again.

"I don't know..." he finally muttered. "I'll have to think on it."

Disappointment filled Gregory. "Well, I had planned to ask that she be allowed to visit us this summer. I know Victoria has been missing her."

"I'll think about it," Rolfe repeated.

"Just let me know." Gathering up his hat and coat, he stood.

"Where are you going?"

"I must return home as quickly as possible," Gregory explained as he slipped into his coat. "Good day."

Rolfe raised his eyebrows as he hurried away. "Odd duck," Gregory heard him mutter under his breath.

As he wound through the tables, Gregory could only pray that Rolfe would think about his suggestion and send Regina to live at Thornton Hall. Right now, though, he had to concentrate on keeping Claudia safe from the more immediate danger. *Jesus, the plan has worked so far. Thank You that the second part will go as smoothly as the first.*

Stepping out into the street, Gregory hailed a cab.

Chapter 22

Victoria paced in the blue salon like a caged tiger. She was about to go out of her mind! Nearly suppertime, and Gregory had yet to return. Being confined to just two rooms all day scratched along her already frazzled nerves. She wanted to be out in the sunshine, but here she and Claudia sat, prisoners in her own home because of Paxton. Last night, Horace had found Clinton knocked unconscious outside his door which explained how he had snuck into their room.

Because of that, Broderick had stayed with them all day long, leaving Horace and the other servants to deal with Paxton. Victoria had been sick again this morning, but just like yesterday, it had passed within an hour. Thankfully, Claudia had still been asleep. She didn't feel like answering any questions until she was sure. Gladys had a speculative gleam in her eye as she fed her tea and crackers for the second morning in a row.

Victoria knew Gregory had hoped to be home soon after lunch, but the hours dragged by with no sign of him. Claudia sat stiffly in her chair staring out the window. Broderick sat nearer to the door, but he kept glancing over at Claudia who steadfastly ignored him.

Victoria paced around the room again. "Relax," Broderick advised for the umpteenth time. "He'll be here when he gets here. Wearing a hole in the rug certainly isn't going to help matters." She glanced at him but kept pacing.

He sighed.

Several minutes later, Claudia suddenly jumped up. "I think I see him."

Victoria hurried to the window and peered out. On the driveway, Gregory dismounted from Liberty as a carriage rattled to a stop behind him. Her heart leapt with joy. "Gregory," she whispered. Turning, she ran towards the hall.

"Victoria, wait!" She ignored Broderick's call as she dashed down the stairs.

Gregory had already stepped into the foyer when she arrived. "Gregory!" Her mad dash slowed as she took in his obvious fatigue. He gave her a tired smile and opened his arms. She practically leapt into them. "I was worried," she murmured against the thick material of his overcoat.

Broderick arrived in the foyer, dragging Claudia behind him. He stopped and dropped her arm when he saw her with Gregory. "You scared me."

"I'm sorry," Victoria smiled apologetically at him over her shoulder.

"What a touching scene." Paxton's mocking voice broke in like a bucket of ice. Victoria stiffened. He leaned against the doorway of the formal parlour with Horace looming behind him, his massive arms crossed over his chest. "Would you kindly order this human watchdog to stop following me everywhere I go?" he asked angrily. "I ought to double the amount after the way I've been treated."

"I'm sorry if you don't like our hospitality," Gregory told him formally. "Let's all return to the parlour, and we can conclude this business as quickly as possible."

"That's more like it." Paxton straightened with an avarice gleam in his eye.

"This way, gentlemen." Gregory gestured with his arm for the others to go first. For the first time, Victoria noticed that he had Andrew Stokes, Earl Thomas Browne and Baron Ernest FitzClarence with him.

Victoria put her arm around Claudia as they followed everyone into the parlour. She stopped near Gregory as Andrew pulled bundles of banknotes out of his satchel and set them on the tea table. "Count it if you wish," he told Paxton. "You'll find it all there."

Paxton reached for the first stack, but Andrew's voice stopped him. "However, you must sign this paper before receiving a shilling."

Anger darkened his face, and he jumped up. "What kind of game are you playing, Thornton? I didn't agree to sign any paper!"

"It's very simple and straightforward. I want some assurance that you will keep your end of the bargain. By signing this paper, you give up all legal claim to the child."

Victoria held her breath as Paxton glared at Gregory. A calculating look suddenly entered his eyes, and he smiled. "Alright. I'm willing to do that." Taking the paper, he gave it a cursory glance before taking the quill and ink Andrew offered him and signing it with a flourish.

"Gentlemen?" Andrew held out the pen.

Thomas and Ernest both signed the paper before Gregory picked it up, folded it and placed it into his pocket. "Thank you."

"Glad we could help," Thomas told him as they left.

Paxton busily counted his money and stuffed it in his pockets. "Looks like it's all here, old man," he finally said a bit mockingly. Standing up, he shoved the last pile into his coat. He gave Gregory a smirking smile. "I'll be back when I need more."

"I don't think so." Gregory's voice sounded like ice.

Paxton laughed. "Because I signed that stupid document? You know it's not worth the parchment it's written on. All I have to do is tell Rolfe about the child. He's her legal guardian, and he'll force her to marry me." His voice took on a threatening tone. "That is, unless you continue pay."

Claudia gasped. Victoria held her close even as Broderick took a threatening step forward. Gregory stopped him. "Why don't you tell him, Andrew?"

"With pleasure." Andrew turned back to Paxton. "While in London retrieving the money, Gregory also obtained something else just as important. Legal guardianship of one Claudia Bolton. If you want to marry Claudia, you'll have to present your case to Gregory."

Red anger suffused Paxton's face. "You tricked me!" he yelled before taking a swinging punch at Gregory. Victoria and Claudia instinctively ducked back, but Gregory caught Paxton's arm midswing and twisted it up behind his back.

"You're leaving right now. And if you ever step foot on my property again, I'll see you jailed for trespassing."

At a nod from Gregory, Horace grabbed Paxton by the scruff of his neck and hauled him out the door. Gregory and a grinning Broderick followed him. Andrew picked up his satchel and gave Victoria and Claudia a smile. "It looks like I'm not needed here anymore. Ladies." He tipped his hat and walked out the door.

Dazedly, she looked around the empty room. The tension and fear of the last day slowly drained away.

It was over.

Relief filled her, and she laughed. "He did it, Claudia. God did it! You're safe!" Claudia stared at her with a stricken expression. She instantly sobered. "What's wrong?"

"Can't you see what he's doing?"

Confused, she stared at her. "What are you talking about?"

"Gregory! He's arranged all of this so he owns me! He's going to exact revenge for what I did to him, how I treated him. Can't you see his plan?"

Victoria shook her head. "You're wrong, Claudia. He's only trying to protect you and the baby."

"How can you be so blind?"

"You do not understand. Gregory's not that way. He wouldn't do anything like that. He couldn't!"

Victoria stopped in shock as the truth of her own words slammed into her. Gregory wouldn't do that. Gregory would never deliberately hurt her in anyway. Her mind whirled as she stumbled back.

"Victoria?" She barely heard Claudia's confused voice.

Gregory. Dear, sweet, precious Gregory. All this time she had been afraid of him...for nothing! The truth shot through her like a blinding light piercing through her heart, wiping away every fear. Victoria felt light, buoyant. She didn't have to fear Gregory.

With that thought came another one just as staggering.

She loved him.

Victoria gasped at the intensity of the love that filled her. It seemed too big for her frail, human body to contain. Looking back, she realized that she had loved Gregory for a long time, but her fear blocked it from growing. With the fear gone, the love blossomed until it filled every corner and crevice.

Gregory.

She had to tell Gregory.

Turning, she started towards the foyer. "Where are you going?" Claudia asked in alarm.

"I have to find Gregory," she hollered over her shoulder.

Rushing outside, Victoria looked around the front lawn.

Empty.

Where had he gone?

Frantically, she spun in a circle, trying to find him. She finally spied Gregory and Broderick walking back from the driveway. Gregory suddenly stopped and knelt down to examine the bed of azalea's just beginning to grow. Lifting her skirt, Victoria ran that way even as she drank in the precious sight of him. "Gregory!"

Gregory looked up just as she launched herself into his arms. Off-balance, he toppled into the flower bed as Victoria landed on top of him. She didn't care as she wrapped her arms around him and kissed him for all she was worth.

"I love you, Gregory," she finally whispered between kisses. "I love you. I love you. I love you."

She kissed him again not even aware when Broderick quietly excused himself and left.

Gregory lay stunned in the azalea bed as Victoria continued kissing him. His spectacles had been knocked off, and they were squishing the fragile, new stems just poking through the soil, but he didn't care.

Victoria loved him!

"Vic…mmm."

Victoria kissed him.

"I…mmm."

She kissed him again.

"Lo…mmm."

Gregory couldn't get the words out, but for the first time it wasn't out of fear or shame. He felt like shouting it from the rooftops, but Victoria wouldn't stop kissing him long enough for him to say it. She finally pulled back slightly for a breath. "I love you, Gregory."

"I lo…mmm."

A long time later, she came up for air again. "Do you know how much I love you?" she asked as she rained kisses all over his face.

"I'm getting an idea," he murmured. "Victoria, I…mmmm."

After awhile, she pulled back and stared down at him with stars shining in her eyes. Gregory smiled at her. Finally, he would be able to say it. "Victoria, I…"

She suddenly started laughing. A free, joyous sound he'd never heard before. "Oh, Gregory. Your poor eyeglasses. They're broken." She reached above his head and picked up the wire frame. Both lenses were cracked. With abandon, she tossed them into the air and laughed again. "I broke your eyeglasses!"

Who cared about his spectacles? "I lo…mmm."

Giving up, Gregory just held on for dear life and kissed her back.

Claudia sat in the foyer nervously pleating her skirt with her fingers. Victoria had run outside looking for Gregory like a woman possessed. She'd seemed so sure that he wouldn't try to exact revenge, but fear still crawled through Claudia's stomach.

She jumped when the door suddenly opened, and Broderick walked in. He smiled at her before holding out his hand. "Dinner should be ready, and I'm starved. What about you?"

"W…where's Gregory and Victoria?"

He looked back at the door and laughed. "They're a bit busy right now. I'm sure they won't mind if we eat without them. Come on, I know you're hungry," Broderick cajoled when she hesitated.

Still, Claudia couldn't seem to move from her chair. All signs of teasing faded as he knelt down in front of her. "Look, I know men have treated you shamefully, and you're afraid." Claudia's face burned at his direct words. "But you don't have to be afraid of me. I would never hurt you." His eyes were gentle as he held out his hand again.

Claudia ignored his hand, but she did stand up. Instead of being angry, Broderick smiled as he stood. "That's a step in the right direction. Now, let's go eat."

He let Claudia proceed him into the dining room before holding out her chair. Bowing her head, Claudia listened as he said a short prayer then servants brought in the food. As they ate, Broderick kept up a light banter that had her relaxing in spite of herself.

Opening Gregory's desk drawer, Victoria pulled out his extra set of spectacles. "Here you are, darling."

Gregory held out his hand, but instead of giving them to him, Victoria stood on tiptoe and slipped them on herself. He thanked her by stealing another kiss. "I love you, Victoria," he murmured against her lips.

"And I love you." Victoria kissed him again before pulling back slightly. "Did I thank you for what you did for Claudia?

He gave her a slow, heart-stopping smile. "I believe you did."

Victoria laughed and blushed at the same time. She could hardly believe that she had thrown herself on him like that, especially on the front lawn where anyone could see! And laughing when she broke his spectacles! Disgraceful behavior. She hadn't laughed because of the eyeglasses, though. It had been the complete lack of fear she had felt when she saw them.

Gregory grew pensive. "It was…difficult in London. Rolfe thought I wanted legal guardianship in order to exact revenge. It was why he consented."

Victoria sobered. "Actually, that's what Claudia thinks, too. I tried to tell her that you weren't like that, but I do not think she believed me."

"It will take time for her to learn to trust others. Just as it did you."

Victoria smiled at him. "But I'm not afraid anymore."

Gregory kissed her again. "I have another confession to make. Something I want you to pray with me about."

"Oh?"

"I saw Regina while I was in London."

"How was she?"

"Quiet. Subdued."

Victoria frowned. "That doesn't sound like Regina."

"I know." Gregory sighed and pulled her a bit closer. "She had a bruise on her jaw. It was the hardest thing I ever had to do, leaving her there."

"Oh, Gregory." Tears gathered in Victoria's eyes.

"But what I want you to pray about is this. I offered to take her off Rolfe's hands. To become her legal guardian like with Claudia. He said he'd think about it."

"Do you think he would agree?" Victoria could barely dare to hope.

"He seemed interested. We just have to keep praying."

"I will."

Gregory gave her another smile. "Right now, I should probably talk to Claudia. Try to assuage her fears."

"I suppose so," Victoria agreed reluctantly. The discovery of her feelings still felt so new, and she found that she didn't want to share him just yet. "But first, we should clean you up a bit," she added with a smile.

Finding the dust brush in the changing room, Victoria took her time getting the dirt and grass off the back of his coat and out of his hair. Eventually, they were both presentable and made their way down to the dining room.

Broderick and Claudia were just finishing their dessert. "I see you didn't wait dinner on us," Gregory said as he held out Victoria's chair.

"I wasn't sure how long you'd be," Broderick remarked dryly.

Victoria's face flushed until she knew she had to be beet red. Claudia stared at her in confusion. "Well, we're here now," she said quickly. "Gregory, would you like to pray?"

He gave her an amused smile that had her blushing again before holding out his hand. She took it, relishing even that simple touch. Oh, how she loved this man!

She bowed her head as Gregory prayed. He thanked God for Victoria, for the gift of having her as his wife. He thanked Him that Claudia and her child were safe. He thanked Him for the gift of friendship he had in Broderick and the Holmes family. In the servants who had been willing to put themselves in danger to protect his family. He prayed for Rolfe's heart to be softened and that Regina would be allowed to come live with them. He even prayed for their rose bush that it would live. Victoria had begun to think he'd forgotten all about eating when he said… "And bless the food. In Jesus' Name, Amen."

Giving her a secret smile, Gregory squeezed her hand before letting go. Victoria smiled back knowing she would never get used to this love.

Epilogue

A week later Victoria waited in ambush in the front parlour for Gregory to return home. She hopped from one foot to the other in excitement as she looked out the window. Nearly five o'clock. Why didn't he come?

"I don't know why you are so excited," Claudia remarked from the chair where she sat. She had an open book in her lap, but she hadn't read a word. Victoria glanced over at her saddened by the confused expression on her face. She couldn't understand how Victoria could want Gregory to be home.

"I love him," Victoria explained to her for the umpteenth time. "I miss him when he's gone. Besides that, I have some news to share." Just the thought caused her to bounce again.

Claudia shook her head but didn't say anything more. Victoria glanced back out the window and gasped. The carriage had just pulled into the drive. "He's here!"

Whirling around, Victoria rushed into the foyer and out the door. Gregory had just stepped down from the carriage when she reached him. "Come on," she grabbed his hand and started tugging him back into the house.

Gregory laughed. "What is it?"

"I have something to show you."

He laughed again but willingly followed her as she led him through the house and out into the garden. Going to the roses, she dropped his hand and pointed to their bush. Gregory smiled as he bent closer. Victoria could barely keep from hopping again in excitement.

Clinging to the barren sticks were a few hard green nubs. So tiny, they were barely discernible, but they were there. "It's starting to put forth leaves," he pronounced as he stood back up.

"I know. Isn't it exciting?"

"Yes."

They stood in companionable silence staring at their bush. Victoria scooted a tiny bit closer to him. Gregory didn't seem to notice. She scooted a little closer, but he still didn't get the hint. She smiled before grabbing his hands and wrapping them around her as she leaned back against his chest. He chuckled. "Miss me?"

"MmmHmm." Victoria cradled the hand that pressed against her still flat stomach, positive now that she carried their child. She had been sick every morning that week though she had hid that fact from Gregory. She pressed his hand a bit firmer against her stomach, wanting their baby to know his gentle touch from the earliest possible moments.

"Have I told you lately how much I love you?" he whispered against her ear.

She felt another smile curving her lips. Ever since she had declared her love, a floodgate had opened. Gregory couldn't seem to say it enough, and she couldn't hear it enough. "Not since this morning."

Gregory chuckled again before pulling her a bit closer as he placed a kiss behind her ear. "I do love you, Victoria. I love you more than I could ever say." He trailed kisses down her neck. She arched her head slightly to the side to give him better access even as she shivered in pleasure. "You are so beautiful," he murmured.

At his words, Victoria turned around in his arms until she faced him. "Will you still think I'm beautiful when I'm old and gray?"

"You'll still be the most beautiful woman on earth." he assured her.

"What if I grow fat?"

"Fat?" Gregory laughed. "You could never be fat."

Smiling, Victoria pulled his spectacles off and tucked them in her pocket before wrapping her arms around him. "But what if I do?"

"You'll still be the most beautiful woman in the world to me."

"That's good because I think I might gain weight over the next few months." Victoria smiled impishly up at him. Gregory arched an eyebrow clearly confused. "Of course," she continued still smiling hugely. "It won't be for long. Maybe seven months or so, if my calculations are correct."

"Victoria, what are you talking…" His voice trailed off as realization dawned on his face. "Do you mean…? Are you…? Are we…?"

She laughed and nodded. Gregory pulled back and stared at her flat stomach before hesitantly reaching out and touching it with his fingertips. "Are you sure?" he whispered.

"Almost positive."

A smile slowly inched across his face until he grinned from ear to ear. "A baby. Victoria, we're going to have a baby!" Picking her up, he started swinging her around as she laughed. "A baby!"

As suddenly as he'd picked her up, he put her down again. "Are you alright? Do you need anything?" he asked worriedly.

Victoria laughed again and gently touched his cheek. "I'm fine, darling."

He started grinning again. "A baby!" Pulling her close, he kissed her until her knees went weak. She clung to him for support as she kissed him back.

"Victoria!"

The faint cry barely penetrated her fogged brain. Gregory started to pull back, but she murmured a protest as she tugged him back down again.

"Victoria!"

The voice came louder. This time, Gregory did pull back as she tried to think. It almost sounded like…

"Victoria!"

A second later, a small body barreled against her as small arms clung around her waist. Victoria would have fallen if not for Gregory still holding her up. She glanced down in shock at Regina who smiled joyously up at her. She gave an excited bounce. "Father says I get to live here with you!"

Victoria gasped. "What?"

"It's true! He said I get to live here forever." Regina suddenly let go of Victoria and gave Gregory a small curtsy. "Mr. Thornton, our driver is waiting in the foyer with a letter from Father."

For a moment, Victoria stared up at Gregory, knowing that she couldn't hide the wild hope shining in her eyes. He smiled at her before reaching out and touching Regina's head. "Why don't we see what he has to say?"

"Yes, sir!" Regina bounced again before grabbing Victoria's hand and swinging it as they walked back to the house. She jabbered on about the long trip and how exciting it had been. They were nearly to the foyer before Victoria remembered Gregory's spectacles. She sheepishly pulled them out of her pocket and handed them to him as Regina kept talking. Gregory gave her another smile as he slipped them on.

One of the Bolton footmen waited in the foyer next to Regina's trunks. "Mr. Thornton, sir, Lord Bolton asked me to deliver this to you."

"Thank you." Gregory accepted the fat envelope and broke the wax seal. She noticed a frown mar his brow as he read, but Regina kept talking, distracting her.

When Claudia walked into the foyer a few minutes later and Regina ran to give her a hug, it gave Victoria the opportunity to step up beside Gregory and put her arm around his waist. "What's wrong, dear?"

Gregory looked down at her and attempted to smile. "Rolfe's given me legal guardianship just like we prayed; it's just…" he shook the letter in frustration. "He makes me so angry."

Leaning against him, Victoria read the letter he held out for her.

Gregory,

I have thought over your suggestion about giving you legal guardianship of Regina. I have decided that you are right. I have more than fulfilled my duties as a father. The benefits I might gain from Regina's marriage are not worth the expense of feeding and clothing her for the next eight years. Unlike her sisters, she is too homely to be profitable to me therefore I am giving you legal guardianship. I am sure, however, that you will be able to profit from the arrangement. With a little training, she would make an excellent servant or even a nurse for your children more than paying you back for the little it would cost to feed her and provide her with a uniform. The legal papers are enclosed and have been duly signed and witnessed.

Sincerely,

Rolfe Bolton, Marquess of Hartshorn

Victoria had to consciously force her hands to relax when she finished reading the letter. Putting his arms around her, Gregory cradled her against his chest. "A man like that has no right being a father," he muttered against her hair.

"No," she agreed then smiled when she heard Regina laugh at something Claudia said. "But at least Regina's safe, and she's here!"

"Yes, and though she's not going to be a nurse, she will be an aunt." Gregory pulled away and looked at her. "Are we really going to have a baby?"

Victoria laughed. "Yes, we're really going to have a baby."

Hearing simultaneous gasps behind her, Victoria turned to see both her sisters staring at her with mouths open. Claudia looked almost horrified, but Regina's squeal quickly brought Victoria's attention to her excited face. "I'm going to be an aunt. Twice!"

Running over, she threw her arms around Victoria. She laughed again as she and Gregory included the excited girl into their hug. "Congratulations," Claudia told them quietly.

Reaching out, Victoria pulled her into the hug before glancing back up at Gregory with her eyes shining. "Thank you."

The words were not only in answer to Claudia's felicitations but a prayer straight from her overflowing heart. Thanks to God for giving her this man for her husband. A man who not only had taught her about God and how to love and trust again but who had willingly taken on the responsibility of caring for her sisters. Leaning her head against Gregory's chest, Victoria relished the strength of him. *Thank You,* her heart whispered again as she clung just a bit tighter to Gregory and to her family.

She had never been so happy in her life.

Acknowledgments

All Praise and Honor and Glory go to our Lord Jesus Christ, Who died on the cross and rose again three days later so we could live forever with Him. Hallelujah! I thank You, Jesus, for not only putting the dream in my heart of becoming an author but being with me every day as You brought it forth to completion. I love You, Lord! May this book be used mightily for Your Kingdom!

To my family who has stood with me and supported me in my dream of being an author. My Mom in Heaven and my adopted Mom still here, my Sister, my Dad, and my Grandparents. I thank God everyday for you!

To Janny Grein, Psalmist of the Lord, whose ministry, music and friendship has sown so much into my life.

To Anjelica and Ben Childs for their friendship and for modeling and photographing my book cover. Thank you!

To everyone who has encouraged me in my writing and prayed for me through the years. I love you guys!

About the Author

Jessica Hallmark is a talented author, actress and opera singer; her passions are books, plays and movies that glorify God. She has been reading Christian Fiction since kindergarten, however, it was not until eleventh grade that she felt God calling her to write. After graduating college in May 2008, she state-hopped before finally settling in the beautiful Blue Ridge Mountains. A neck injury in 2010 has prevented her from working outside the home. Praise God, He healed her, and Jessica is now able to turn her attention to the mission God laid on her heart back in 11th grade: pursuing a full-time writing career to share with others, through captivating fiction, God's great Love and Mercy!

You can connect with her at www.jessicahallmark.com.

Coming Soon!